W9-ADQ-728

SEALS EAGLE FORCE
EAGLE STRIKE

O R R   K E L L Y

AVON BOOKS ◆ NEW YORK

This is a work of fiction. Names, characters, places, and incidents either are the product of the author's imagination or are used fictitiously. Any resemblance to actual events, locales, organizations, or persons, living or dead, is entirely coincidental and beyond the intent of either the author or the publisher.

AVON BOOKS, INC.
1350 Avenue of the Americas
New York, New York 10019

Copyright © 1999 by Orr Kelly
Published by arrangement with the author
Library of Congress Catalog Card Number: 99-94796
ISBN: 0-380-79115-3
www.avonbooks.com

All rights reserved, which includes the right to reproduce this book or portions thereof in any form whatsoever except as provided by the U.S. Copyright Law. For information address Avon Books, Inc.

First Avon Books Printing: September 1999

AVON TRADEMARK REG. U.S. PAT. OFF. AND IN OTHER COUNTRIES, MARCA REGISTRADA, HECHO EN U.S.A.

Printed in the U.S.A.

WCD   10 9 8 7 6 5 4 3 2 1

If you purchased this book without a cover, you should be aware that this book is stolen property. It was reported as ''unsold and destroyed'' to the publisher, and neither the author nor the publisher has received any payment for this ''stripped book.''

To the brave men and women who go in harm's way
so the rest of us can live in peace.

CHARACTERS IN BRIEF

Ben Bernard, 38, known as Big Dog, former SEAL, foe of Nelson's, leader of mercenary commando team.

Chief Jack Berryman, SEAL, expert with .50-caliber sniper rifle.

Command Master Chief Jeff Bonior, 40, senior SEAL, only black member of Eagle Force.

Vice Admiral John "Bull" Bridges, 50, commander in chief, Pacific

Cindy Carson, Secret Service agent assigned to protect the First Lady and her son.

Patricia Collins, 27, team's intelligence expert, widow of Jim Collins, close friend of Chuck Nelson, mother of two children.

Rear Admiral Jerry Harmony, task force commander aboard USS *Kitty Hawk*.

Dick Hoffman, 24, former member of Bernard's mercenaries, now SEAL member of Eagle Force.

Master Sgt. Tim Hutchins, 36, Air Force Special Tactics combat controller.

Major Jack Laffer, Pave Low co-pilot.

Wiremu Kingi, Maori leader, descendent of one of the last Maoris to resist white colonists in New Zealand.

Dr. James D. Malcolm, 67, Eagle Force's science advisor.

Rex Marker, 23, youngest member of Eagle Force, in charge of communications.

Adm. Norris McKay, 54, a submariner and chairman of the Joint Chiefs of Staff.

Lucia McKenzie, 56, secretary of defense.

Chief Jeremy Merrifield, SEAL, explosives expert.

Lazslo "Luke" Nash, one-time Hungarian freedom fighter and CIA pilot, now operating behind the scenes to gather wealth and power.

Cdr. Charles "Chuck" Nelson, 37, SEAL, leader of Eagle Force.

Abdul "Abe" Rahman, president's national security adviser.

Lt. Col. Mark Rattner, 38, Pave Low pilot, second in command of Eagle Force.

Lt. Sam Simmons, young navy intelligence officer with contact in Chinese embassy in Washington.

Henry Trover, 66, secretary of state.

David Walker, 9, son of the president and Mrs. Walker.

Maynard Walker, 53, president of the United States.

Marcia Carter Walker, 47, wife of the president.

Wang Dongfang, young Chinese intelligence officer in Washington.

A NOTE ON TIMEKEEPING

Early in the American involvement in the conflict in Vietnam, officials in Washington made several serious miscalculations because they didn't realize that there was a difference of one hour between the local times in Hanoi and Saigon.

Similarly, the characters in this book—and the reader—have to deal constantly with differences of time in the three major scenes of action: Washington, Hawaii and New Zealand (or Aotearoa).

As a rough guide, remember that when it's noon Monday in Washington, it's 6 A.M. the same day in Honolulu but already 5 A.M. on Tuesday in Auckland.

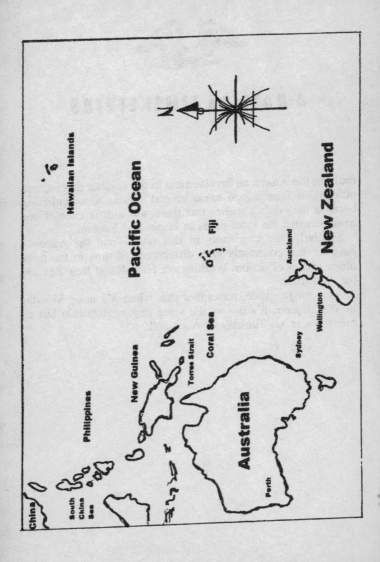

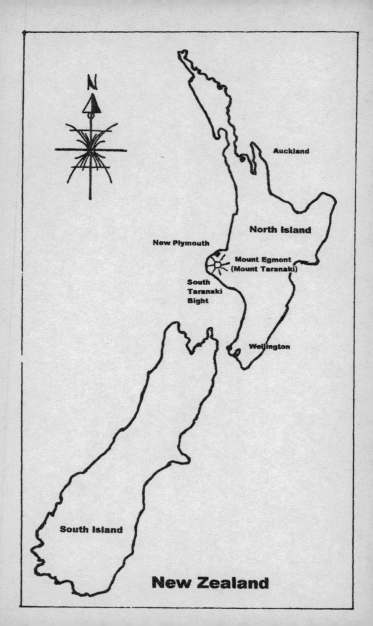

PROLOGUE

A SLIVER OF THE MOON IN ITS LAST QUARTER CAST A SILVER glow across the four-foot swells coursing toward the shore, two miles away. It was late October—spring Down Under—and an unusual soft wind from the east carried the fresh smell of earth out across the waters.

Silently, the USS *Kamehameha* broke the surface of the water in the South Taranaki Bight, off the west coast of New Zealand's north island. As soon as the submarine came to a stop, gently rocking with the movement of the water, the door of the large dry deck shelter bulging from the aft deck swung open. Crew members quickly slid two SEAL delivery vehicles out onto the deck.

Commander Charles Nelson stepped out of the shelter and touched the arm of the submarine crewman in charge of preparing the SDVs.

"Chief, let's make sure we get the ballast right." Nelson recalled an incident during the Vietnam War when an improperly ballasted SDV sank to the bottom and was damaged when the submarine rolled against it.

The submariner turned and flashed him an "I know my business" look, but all he said was "Aye, aye, sir."

Standing behind Nelson were eleven members of the elite Eagle Force, his combined SEAL-Air Commando unit, each man clad in a wet suit and a Draeger underwater breathing apparatus. One man carried a heavy .50-caliber sniper rifle,

1

and another shouldered an M-60 machine gun. The others carried their own favorite weapons. Several preferred the light H & K MP-5 submachine gun, so smooth-operating that a man could spray out its thirty-round magazine while holding the weapon in one hand. Others favored the navy-issue M-16 rifle, coated with Teflon and fitted with drain holes to operate after long immersion in salt water. Each of the men carried an automatic pistol strapped to his waist. Several of them carried the standard-issue K-bar knife, but others had their own special knives. Two were encumbered by heavy coils of rope, carried over one shoulder and across the chest.

At a signal from the chief, the men quickly took their places in the SDVs and connected their masks to the crafts' air supplies. Two men—a driver and a navigator—took the front seats of each SDV.

At a signal from Nelson, the two SDVs were slipped over the side, one after the other, and quickly submerged.

Moments later, the submarine disappeared. It had been on the surface no more than fifteen minutes. No hint remained that just below the waves there lurked a powerful nuclear-powered warship and two tiny, battery-powered submersibles carrying a dozen of the world's deadliest commandos.

Master Chief Jeff Bonior was at the controls of the lead SDV, with Nelson beside him acting as navigator. Bonior and Nelson concentrated on the instruments before them, glowing eerily in the darkness. Behind them, the other members of the team sat in total darkness, with nothing to do except shiver in the fifty-eight-degree water that surrounded them. As they moved slowly toward shore, their fingers and lips turned blue with cold. Their bodies drew blood toward their hearts and then, sensing the accumulation of fluids, signalled their kidneys to expel some of the liquid. A flow of urine down a leg provided a pleasant but fleeting sensation of warmth.

When the two craft reached a point a hundred yards from the rocky shore, Bonior gently parked on the bottom. The other boat pulled in behind him. Nelson set an electronic signal that would permit them to find their way back to the SDVs if necessary. The men released their safety belts, formed up in two-man buddy teams, and swam toward shore.

They surfaced just to the seaward side of the breaker line and watched the waves crashing against the rocks. Then, swimming rapidly to follow a wave in, each of the men grabbed a rock and swung around to put the rock between himself and the following breaker. As the wave receded, they scrambled quickly to the top of the bank and dropped flat on the beach grass. In the lull after each wave hammered the shore, they listened intently and scanned the area in front of them for any sign of light or movement.

After lying motionless for nearly five minutes, Nelson gave an arm signal, and the men moved foward by twos to a stand of tall eucalyptus trees. In their shelter, they quickly stripped off their breathing rigs and wet suits, buried them in a hole they dug in the sand, checked their weapons and radio equipment, smeared camouflage paint on their faces and the backs of their hands, and then sat down to wait. Smoking was not permitted, lest the flare of a match or the smell of smoke give away their position. Several of the men quietly chewed tobacco, occasionally turning to spit into the sand.

In the dim light, they could make out the figure of their leader, standing a short distance away. Like many SEALs, Nelson, who was thirty-seven years old, was not tall but had a chunky build—five feet, eight inches, and 155 pounds. He had an open, friendly face that caused his men—and even new acquaintances—to like and trust him. His face was set off by warm brown eyes and a shock of unruly black hair with only a touch of gray at the sideburns.

Nelson stood looking north at the almost perfectly symmetrical volcano rising more than eight thousand feet above him. In the faint light of the moon, he could see the mantle of deep snow that capped the mountain and reached far down its south side in sheltered crevasses.

Captain James Cook, sailing past in 1770, had named the mountain Mount Egmont for John Perceval, second earl of Egmont and Britain's First Lord of the Admiralty in the years preceding Cook's voyage. But the Maori, who had colonized the islands of New Zealand centuries before the coming of the white man, had long known it as a sacred mountain. With their name, they honored a god who took the form of a mountain.

"So this is Taranaki," Nelson murmured to himself.

But Nelson lost no time admiring the mountain's name or its spectacular beauty, which rivaled that of Japan's Mount Fuji. Instead, he concentrated on the job ahead—the most difficult and demanding he had ever faced in the more than a decade and a half that he had served as a navy SEAL.

The words of Admiral Norris McKay, chairman of the Joint Chiefs of Staff, remained vividly in his mind:

"I don't have to tell you how important this mission is, Chuck. Your job is to rescue the hostages and bring them home safely. Failure, or even partial success, is not among your options. You must succeed!"

Nelson and McKay had had a long and friendly relationship. The older officer had served as a kind of "sea daddy" to the younger man, making sure at each step of the way that his career remained on the fast track. And it was McKay who had tapped Nelson to head the Eagle Force, to be available for just such demanding missions as this.

In the years that he had been associated with the admiral, Nelson had never heard him speak in almost formal terms of the urgency of success on an assignment. Previously, the importance of the mission had gone without saying. They both understood that the Eagle Force was called on only when the stakes were high, as were the odds against success.

But this mission, of course, was different. No military unit had ever been given an assignment quite like this one, which involved both national security and the strongest personal emotions.

Staring at the mountain, Nelson knew the hostages were up there somewhere. He could only hope that they were still alive and in good health and that, by this time tomorrow, he and his men would be celebrating a successful operation.

Nelson turned back to his men, who were quietly moving amongst the trees, finishing their preparations.

Dick Hoffman, a SEAL chief petty officer, and Air Force Master Chief Tim Hutchins were standing off to one side, talking quietly, as Nelson approached.

"Okay, you guys know what you have to do. If you end up in jail, you're on your own."

Hoffman, who had rejoined the SEALs after serving briefly in a mercenary commando outfit, laughed. "Being thrown in jail would probably be a lot better than being caught by some angry New Zealander."

Hutchins and Hoffman quickly moved out, jogging along the side of the road that led to the little town of Opunake, a mile to the west. As they approached the town, they left the pavement and moved over into the shadows beside the road. Hoffman took the lead, moving up the right side of the road from one parked car to another, quietly trying the doors.

He stopped beside a Land Rover, eased open the door, and checked the gauge. It showed a half tank of gas. Hoffman turned and gave Hutchins a thumbs-up signal.

As Hoffman slipped into the Land Rover, Hutchins continued down the street until he came to a van with the doors unlocked. The gas tank was nearly full.

Hutchins slid into the driver's seat on the right side of the van. Pulling a chisel and a hammer from a pocket on the leg of his coveralls, he knocked out the steering wheel lock with one sharp blow. Reaching under the dashboard, he quickly located the ignition wires. Then he looked back toward the Land Rover.

Once he saw Hoffman wave his arm out the window, Hutchins crossed the wires under the van's dash. The engine caught, Hutchins put the vehicle in gear and, after Hoffman passed him in the Land Rover, rolled quietly down the road without lights, following Hoffman out of town. Behind them, a lone dog barked frantically and then, as the two vehicles disappeared in the darkness, lapsed into silence.

Hoffman pressed the button on his radio and spoke a single word into the tiny microphone suspended in front of his lips: "Heist."

"Okay," Nelson said. "They're coming."

The ten men formed up beside the road in two five-man squads, ready to climb quickly into the stolen vehicles as they crept past.

Nelson got into the front seat of the Land Rover next to Hoffman.

"Any problems?"

"No problems at all, sir. Just like when I was a kid."

"One of my men a car thief?"

"No, not really, sir. But we all knew how to do it."

"You're okay on the navigation?"

"Yeah, I've got it memorized. . . ." He paused as he swung to the left onto a road coming in from the north. "We take this road up past Taungatara, and then we turn off on a new road that goes up the mountain alongside the . . . the . . . I forget the name of the river."

"Waiaua, or something like that." Nelson helped him out.

"Right, the Wye-oo-a. We go up that road and stop before we get to the guard post."

"Good." Nelson scrunched down in his seat, crossed his arms over his chest, and shut his eyes. It was going to be a long night.

"Sir."

Nelson felt the vehicle slowing and was instantly awake. "Getting close?"

"Yes, sir, I think so. According to our intel, there should be a guard post and a barricade across the road about a mile from here."

"Okay, Dick. Kill the lights, and let's creep up here just a little farther."

Hutchins, in the following vehicle, switched off his lights and followed Hoffman until he pulled to the side of the road and stopped.

The four men designated during the pre-mission planning to take out the guard station stepped forward.

"This has to be done quietly," Nelson whispered. "We don't want to give them time to set off an alarm, and we don't want them firing their weapons."

The team members nodded and started up the road, keeping in the shadows to the right of the pavement, spaced out in the traditional formation of an infantry patrol.

Jeff Bonior moved ahead as point man. A quarter mile later, he raised his hand to stop the column. Ahead he could see a guard leaning against a bar like that at a railroad crossing, blocking the road. Another man was visible in a lighted guardhouse, apparently absorbed in a paperback book.

Bonior studied the scene. Both men were vulnerable. But the challenge was to take out both of them without giving either the time to alert the other or anyone else.

A plan formed in Bonior's mind. He signaled the SEAL behind him to move forward and then whispered instructions in his ear. The man worked his way up the side of the road toward the guardhouse, keeping well over in the shadows, moving slowly, deliberately, gently.

When he came to within twenty yards of the guard at the roadblock, he edged into the woods and circled behind a tree. Then he threw a handful of gravel into the trees in front of him.

The guard straightened up and turned toward the sound. Holding his automatic rifle at the ready, he walked across the road, peering into the darkness. As he moved into the shadows, the SEAL stepped from his cover, grabbed the sentry from behind, and drew his knife across his throat. The man died without a sound.

Lowering the body to the ground, the SEAL wiped his knife on the dead man's uniform and then turned his attention to the guardhouse. The sentry inside was still busy with his paperback. Moving again with great care, the SEAL worked his way around behind the guardhouse. From the holster at his waist, he pulled out his Sig Sauer P-226 nine-millimeter pistol and attached a silencer to the muzzle. He liked the Sig Sauer because its only safety device was a double-action trigger. When he pulled the trigger, he knew it was going to fire. Holding the pistol at the ready in his right hand, he quietly grasped the door handle with his left. Then, jerking the door open, he pressed the tip of his silencer against the base of the guard's neck and fired a single shot. The movement was so fast that the guard didn't even have time to turn his head, let alone cry out, before he died.

The SEAL leaned over the body and pulled the lever to raise the barrier blocking the road. He spoke a single word into his microphone: "Clear."

Moments later, the two vehicles carrying the commandos rolled past the guardhouse, paused to pick up their man, and continued on up the mountain without lights.

"Let's take it real easy here, Dick," Nelson told his driver. The guardhouse seemed to have been located at the snow line. Almost as soon as they passed that point, they saw piles of recently-fallen snow beside the road. Hoffman felt the thin patches of ice where the snow had melted during the day and then frozen as the temperature dropped after dark.

Nelson shined a light on the dashboard and watched the odometer as they crept up the road.

"I figure it's a mile from the guardhouse to the compound," he said. "Let's allow about a quarter of a mile and then go the rest of the way on foot. . . . Okay now, just a little bit farther . . . here. Let's pull off here."

Hoffman eased the vehicle to the side of the road, careful not to slide on the ice. Hutchins stopped behind him. The men climbed out, stepping cautiously to avoid slipping, and formed up in two six-man squads, one on each side of the road. Nelson stepped out as point man of one squad; Bonior headed the other. Normally the unit commander would not take the point, but Nelson wanted to be where he could assess the situation and direct their action.

Silently, the two squads snaked up the road.

Nelson pressed the little button that illuminated his wristwatch. It was a quarter to one in the morning.

He inched forward around a bend and then signaled to his men to lie down. He pulled a pair of night vision binoculars from a case at his waist and scanned the scene in front of him.

From the satellite photos he had studied, he knew it would be tough getting into the compound where the hostages were held. But seeing the situation they faced in person was a shock.

Rising in front of him was an almost-sheer wall of black lava thirty feet high. Where the road passed through a narrow cut in the rock wall, it was blocked by two tall steel doors. A small guardhouse nestled against the wall to the right of the doors. Nelson could see only two guards in the small building.

Raising his glasses, Nelson scanned the top of the lava wall. As he had feared, it was topped by rolls of razor-sharp concertina wire.

Nelson raised an arm and motioned to the left. Bonior and his men moved off in that direction. Nelson led his men to the right, toward the base of the rock wall.

One man in each squad carried a roll of rope over one shoulder and diagonally across his chest. Nelson signaled his rope-carrier forward. He laid the rope on the ground, pulled out an end to which a grappling hook with four barbs was attached, twirled it around, and threw it high up on the wall. He pulled on the rope to set the hooks, and then he and another man put their full weights on the rope. The hooks held. A short distance away, on the other side of the road, Bonior's squad made the same preparations.

"Okay, get up there and make sure that thing is secure." Nelson tapped the rope-carrier on the shoulder.

The SEAL went up the rope hand over hand, bouncing his feet against the rock as he went. In a few seconds, he had reached the top of the wall and checked the hooks. He pulled the rope up and down as a signal, and the other men quickly clambered up the cliff, spreading out along the ledge.

When they had all reached the top, the man who had been carrying the rope unwrapped a tightly woven mat that he had carried around his body. He spread the mat over the concertina wire and then lay down on it. He lay still as the other men, one after the other, used his body as a stepping stone to vault over the wire.

As the men crossed the wire barrier, they spaced themselves out in a single line. From their position, the lava sloped sharply downward. Ahead of them, about fifty yards away, they could see the outline of a two-story building. The roadway blocked by the large steel doors entered the building at ground level through another set of tall doors. It looked as though the entranceway had been designed so that trucks could move heavy equipment directly into the building.

Nelson studied the scene through his night vision binoculars. He found himself wishing he could turn the clock back and make a different approach to the building. By climbing the wall at two points, his men had successfully gotten inside the first line of defense. But in doing so, they had placed themselves on different sides of the roadway that entered the building.

Nelson spoke into his microphone. "Jeff, can you get your guys over on this side of the road?"

"Yeah, we'll patrol down there and sneak across."

Bonior moved his squad down the lava slope toward the building and then across to the edge of the road. They found themselves atop a ledge eight feet above the road.

The first two men lowered themselves carefully down the wall and dashed across the road. One man boosted the other up the wall on the other side. From the top of the wall, the first man lowered the muzzle of his rifle and used it to pull his buddy to the top.

The second two men quickly followed.

As the last man clambered up the wall after crossing the road, a chunk of lava broke loose and clattered to the roadway.

The men dropped to the ground and lay motionless for more than a minute. Then, just as they were preparing to move out and join up with the other squad, a bank of lights along the top of the building flashed on. As a loud siren sounded, the doors to the building swung open and a guard force platoon ran out onto the roadway, swinging their weapons from side to side, looking for the intruders.

The squads headed by Nelson and Bonior were still separated by about thirty feet, but the two squad leaders acted instinctively at the same moment, shouting, "Lights!"

Within seconds, the commandos had shot out all the lights atop the building. Swiftly they pulled night vision goggles down over their eyes.

The members of the surprised guard force didn't enjoy the benefits of such equipment. When the lights went out, their pupils were still contracted, and they found themselves groping in the dark. They were also hemmed in by the walls of lava on both sides of the roadway.

Nelson and Bonior quickly deployed their commandos along the edge of the wall to begin picking off the men milling about below them. A couple of the guards tried firing back at the muzzle flashes, but then those who were still standing turned and ran back toward the safety of the building.

As suddenly as it had started, the firefight was over. But Nelson knew their advantage was fleeting. A reinforced guard force would soon be coming through the doors looking for them.

"Jack, let's get their power supply," Nelson said, grasping SEAL Chief Jack Berryman by the elbow.

Turning to the other men, he instructed them to remove their goggles.

On a rise to the right side of the building, a large tank sat on a platform. From their intelligence briefing, Nelson knew it contained natural gas, piped in from the gas field at Kapuni, a dozen miles away on the south slope of Mount Taranaki. The gas was used to run a large generator that supplied power for the entire complex.

Berryman fitted a steel-tipped shell into his .50-caliber sniper rifle and fired a single shot at the tank. Then, slipping an incendiary round into the chamber, he drew a bead on the spot where gas was now leaking from the tank.

There was a small flash where the shell struck before the tank erupted in a boiling fireball, streaked with exotic colors. The commandos threw themselves to the ground and buried their heads in their arms as the initial waves of intense heat swept over them.

"Okay, let's go," Nelson commanded a moment later, rising from the ground and running, in a crouch, toward the building. He could feel the heat burning the exposed skin of his face and hands.

With the butt of his rifle, he smashed a large plate-glass window, knocked loose the glass around the edges, and jumped into a large room filled with laboratory benches covered with beakers and other chemical paraphernalia.

Back in Hawaii, training for the mission, Nelson and his men had carefully memorized the layout—or at least the best description they could put together from a variety of intelligence sources—of the compound where they now found themselves. Nelson only hoped that the blueprint was reasonably accurate.

Nelson slipped his night vision goggles back down over his eyes and crossed the room to a door that swung inward. Slowly, he inched it open until he could peer out into an internal corridor. Another door on the other side of the room, he knew, led into the large central hallway that the guards had emerged from. He didn't want to go that way.

Seeing no one in the corridor, Nelson signaled his men to follow him, moving slowly, cautiously, their backs against the wall and their weapons at the ready.

Nelson led his men along the corridor until it was intersected by another hallway. Turning right, he worked his way down the new corridor. After proceeding twenty yards, he stopped.

If his intelligence was correct, the hostages should be behind the second door on the right. Nelson was surprised to find no guard at the door. If there was a guard, and he was inside, that complicated his task.

Silently Nelson deployed his men on both sides of the door. They had all spent hours practicing this very maneuver over and over until every movement was automatic: Break open the door, enter quickly, identify anyone with a weapon, and kill swiftly with a shot to the head.

Nelson thought of the alternative they had often practiced: break in the door and then toss in a flash-stun grenade that would temporarily blind and disable everyone in the room. It might be the safer way to go, but Nelson wasn't going to do that to *these* hostages.

At a signal from Nelson, Jeff Bonior, the largest member of the team, kicked in the door and went right on through. Three other members of the team were right behind him.

Bonior swept the right side of the room. The man behind him covered the left side, finger on the trigger of his automatic rifle.

Then the two men strode slowly across the floor as other members of the team moved in behind him.

Bonior turned. "Boss, there's no one here."

Scanning the room, Bonior could see scattered items of clothing. On a large table were plates with the leavings of a recent meal.

One of the men dropped to a knee on the other side of the room from the dining table.

"Look at this, Chief." He pushed up his night vision goggles and shined the beam of a flashlight on the floor. Bonior and Nelson joined him, looking down over his shoulder.

On the floor was a large, reddish brown stain.

Nelson reached down, touched the stain with an index finger, and then brought the finger up into the light of his flashlight.

"Blood. And it's still wet."

The direct line to the White House on McKay's desk had not even completed the first ring when the admiral picked up the receiver.

"Any word yet, Mac?" The admiral could sense the tenseness in the voice of President Maynard Walker.

"No, sir. I don't expect any for at least a few more minutes. The force has a total blackout on transmissions until the mission is wrapped up."

McKay heard a long sigh. "Yes, I understand. Please let me know as soon as you hear anything."

The president put the phone back in its cradle and stared into the distance. He was the most powerful man in the world. He had at his fingertips nuclear weapons, billion-dollar attack craft, and small, elite commando units. Yet he felt totally helpless.

It had been more than two weeks now since the president's wife and son had been kidnapped during a state visit to New Zealand, seventeen long days since they'd been spirited away to a mysterious compound on the slopes of Mount Taranaki.

CHAPTER 1

LIEUTENANT COLONEL MARK RATTNER TAPPED ONCE ON THE door of Chuck Nelson's office and entered as Nelson looked up from the stack of paperwork on his desk. Rattner dropped onto the couch across the room and stretched his long legs out in front of him.

"Hot out there?" Nelson's question was a meaningless one in Arizona. Of course it was hot in the desert in early September. It was always hot.

It was also incredibly secluded. Site Y, the World War II training base that had been brought back to life when Nelson's Eagle Force was formed, lay about equidistant from both Phoenix and Tucson, far enough from both major cities to attract as little attention as possible.

Rattner dropped his cap on the couch beside him and ran the back of his hand across his brow. "Hot? I hadn't noticed."

"What's up, Mark?" Nelson had been quick to notice the worried look on the sweaty face of the air force pilot who served as second in command of the task force.

"We've got problems, Chuck. I just got a call from a buddy at the Pentagon. He says they're cutting orders for me and the other air force guys on the team, pulling us out and giving us other assignments. Direct orders from General Torkelson."

Gen. Norvid "Tork" Torkelson was the four-star chief of staff of the air force and a fighter pilot single-mindedly devoted to getting new fighter planes into the air force inventory

14

as fast as possible. Everything else—especially special operations—barely made it onto the bottom of his list of priorities.

Nelson nodded. "Yeah, I've been afraid of that. General Torkelson is not one of your fans."

"To put it mildly. He doesn't have any use for us or any other special operations types. It's the old fighter pilot mentality. He thinks it's a waste of money and manpower to fool with anything that doesn't fly at Mach two."

"If he pulls you guys out, that puts us out of business."

"It sure as hell does, dammit. He'd like to shut down the whole Air Force Special Operations Command, but he can't do it. AFSOC is part of the air force, but it gets its money and its orders from the U.S. Special Operations Command. Torkelson has used his power as chief of staff of the air force to chip away around the edges—assignments, promotions, that sort of thing. But he's stuck with AFSOC. So he's going after us."

"I thought you liked Torkelson."

"That's the frustrating thing about it, Chuck. He was my wing commander when we were flying F-16s during the Gulf War, and he was the best CO I ever had. He backed up his pilots a hundred and ten percent. And he's one of those guys who leads from the front. Whenever we had a tough mission, he was right out there in the lead position. That first night over Baghdad, they were throwing up so much flak it looked like the biggest Fourth of July you've ever seen, and he was right in the middle of it."

"You've got to respect a guy like that."

"I do respect him. They still tell stories about him in 'Nam. He volunteered for Wild Weasel missions. He'd go out alone ahead of the bomber strikes and make himself a target, trying to get them to shoot a missile at him. Then he'd zap the site with a missile that homed in on the signal from their radar. It was the toughest, most dangerous job you could ask for."

"So now he's trying to zap us?"

"That's what it amounts to. Eagle Force is pretty irregular, and that makes us vulnerable. When Admiral McKay set us up, it kind of took us out from under the AFSOC umbrella, where we had some protection. So General Torkelson can quietly reassign us—as individuals. You'll be left with a bunch of SEALs, but without the pilots, the air crews and the Special Tactics guys from the Air Force, you SEALs might as well hitchhike to your missions.''

Nelson toyed with a .50-caliber machine gun shell that he used as a paperweight.

''Well, I guess that puts the ball in Admiral McKay's court. You haven't actually gotten these orders yet, have you?''

''No. I just got a heads-up from a friend. It'll take a few days, maybe a week or a little more, for the paperwork. But once we get the orders, we're going to be out of here in a hurry.''

''I'll give the admiral a call today. The chairman of the Joint Chiefs should be able to handle something like this.''

''I hope so, Chuck. But Torkelson didn't become chief of staff of the air force just because he's a hot fighter pilot. He's a superb politician, not only within the air force but up on the Hill, too. He's very close to the chairman of the House National Security Committee. He and Torkelson are from the same area down south, and the old man thinks of him almost like a son. So I'm not going to bet against Torkelson, even in a showdown with the chairman.''

Critics seemed never to tire of complaining about President Walker's choices for membership in his national security team. Members of the other party complained that politics had dominated the president's thinking. Members of his own party, talking among themselves, had just the opposite complaint—that the president's choices were, at best, politically neutral and, at worst, politically disastrous.

As he sat in the cabinet room with his back to the window, the president studied the two men and a woman seated on the opposite side of the table. He was pleased with what he saw. Whatever the critics said, he had a team with whom he was comfortable—confident they would give him the best, most honest advice of which they were capable, uncolored by their own ambitions or private agendas.

On the left was Henry Trover, aged sixty-six, an investment banker of immense wealth who had served a long succession of presidents of both parties, laying aside his personal business whenever he was called on. As secretary of state, he was an almost perfect example of the white, Anglo-Saxon, Protestant, Eastern Establishment males who had traditionally shaped and carried out American foreign policy.

In the center was the secretary of defense—by far, Walker's most controversial appointee. Lucia McKenzie was a petite, fifty-six-year-old woman whose closely cropped gray hair seemed to fit her head like a helmet. The longtime president of a prestigious New England college for women, she had served on the boards of a number of the nation's major corporations. Walker had first met her when, before he was president, they served together on the board of a major defense contractor. Like most men, he saw her first as a delicate, almost frail, woman. But then he had noticed the steel in her gray eyes. When he named her as the first female defense secretary, he emphasized not only her experience as an administrator and corporate board member but also her early service as a noncommissioned officer in the army.

On the right sat Abdul Rahman. At six feet, five inches, and 230 pounds, he looked as though he might have belonged to the Chicago Bears linebacking corps. Born Henry Jones, Rahman had escaped the poverty of his birth as a member of a southern black family by joining the army. His intelligence helped him move rapidly up through the enlisted ranks and on to officers' candidate school. It was as a young second lieutenant that he had adopted the Muslim religion and legally changed his name. Rahman was a fast-rising forty-two-year-old brigadier general with a doctorate in political science when Walker tapped him to head his national security staff.

Beside the president sat his wife. In another year, Marcia Carter Walker would reach the half-century milestone, and she didn't like to think about it. But the years hadn't treated her badly. If anything, they had made her even more attractive.

Her shoulder-length auburn hair framed a face of almost flawless alabaster skin set off by luminous brown eyes. At nearly six feet tall, she had a commanding presence that drew admiring and respectful glances from women as well as men.

As the first person to continue her own career while also serving as First Lady, Marcia Walker seldom took part in meetings with the president and members of his staff, although he often consulted her in private. But this was a special case: they were debating whether Mrs. Walker and their son, David, should go ahead with a tentatively planned trip to Australia and New Zealand.

As the senior cabinet member, Henry Trover spoke first.

"Mr. President, we consider the proposed visit of the First Lady and your son to Australia and New Zealand as a major foreign policy initiative. I am afraid that we have tended to neglect our friends Down Under. But that is a neglect we can no longer afford. As the Chinese become stronger economically, their influence in that part of the world will increasingly be felt. As that occurs, we will, as they say, need all the friends we can get. By strengthening our ties with Australia and restoring our historic ties with New Zealand, we will help to bolster the will of our other friends—the so-called Tigers of Southeast Asia—in pursuing policies that are independent of those of China and favorable toward us.

"By sending your own wife and son on this goodwill visit, you will be making a visible and very personal gesture of friendship toward those two strategically placed countries. We strongly recommend that this visit go ahead as now tentatively scheduled. Our embassies in both countries assure us that Mrs. Walker and David will receive a warm, perhaps even tumultuous, welcome."

The president nodded. "Thank you, Henry. Lucia?"

"I am very much in agreement with what the secretary of state has said, Mr. President. However, I cannot help but interject several notes of caution."

She held her delicate left hand in front of her and pointed to each finger in turn as she ticked off the points in her argument.

"First, Mr. President, I am concerned about the reaction of the Chinese, especially at this time. Our intelligence indicates that the Chinese plan a major naval operation in the vicinity of the Spratly Islands in the South China Sea in the near future. If Mrs. Walker's visit coincides with those maneuvers, the Chinese might well see the visit as a provocation.

"Second, our military forces in the Pacific are probably weaker than they have been at any time since the period immediately prior to World War II. The reduction in our armed forces since the end of the Cold War has taken its toll. Our forces are more powerful, of course, than those of any other nation. But, with a limited number of ships, planes, and men under arms, we must be very careful how we use our forces. If we concentrate our power at any one place, that could leave us unable to respond to a crisis elsewhere in the Pacific or Southeast Asia.

"Third, as you know, Admiral Bridges, our commander in chief in the Pacific, is a very—how should I put it?—pugnacious officer. He plans a very aggressive effort to monitor the Chinese operations in the South China Sea. Arrangements have even been made to fly surveillance missions out of Hanoi—a remarkable development in our relations with our former adversaries in Vietnam. I don't want to restrain Admiral Bridges unnecessarily, but the combination of his aggressive nature, the assertiveness of the Chinese, and the First Lady's visit all make me a little—no, more than a little—nervous."

"Thank you, Lucia." The president turned toward his national security adviser.

"Mr. President, there is one other issue I think we should consider," the secretary of defense interjected. "Perhaps this is more in the purview of Henry and his diplomats. But our intelligence indicates an increasingly assertive Maori political movement in New Zealand. The First Lady's visit could be seen there as taking sides in a domestic issue." She shrugged. "It may not be as significant as other potential threats, but it is something we should consider."

"Good point." The president turned to Rahman, using the nickname his army colleagues had quickly given to him after his name change. "Abe?"

Rahman had been taking careful notes while Trover and McKenzie spoke. He prided himself on being the president's honest broker, helping to provide him with all the necessary information and then, if asked, guide him toward the correct decision.

"Sir, I think Secretary Trover and Secretary McKenzie have clearly laid out the issues. There would be distinct foreign policy benefits from the visit. But, as Secretary McKenzie has pointed out, the Chinese maneuvers complicate the question. And I think serious attention should be paid to the point she raises about the Maori movement. Relations between the races in New Zealand have traditionally been remarkably harmonious. But I think there is some danger, perhaps minimal, to the First Lady and David during the New Zealand phase of their trip."

"Well," the president said, turning to his wife. "Maybe we should hear from the person who would actually make the trip. What do you think, Marcie?"

The president's wife had also been taking notes, listing pros and cons in two columns on a yellow legal pad.

She looked down at the sheet before her. "My pro column is longer than my con column. That, of course, doesn't give proper weight to the issues on each side. Let me ask Lucia a question.

"Lucia, you in effect played devil's advocate, listing the problems my visit could cause at this time. But I didn't hear you say that you are opposed to the visit—at least with nothing like the strength with which Henry favors the visit. Do you oppose the visit, or does it just make you nervous?"

"Oh, very much the latter, Mrs. Walker. I understand the arguments in favor of the visit. But I think it is my job to think about things that might go wrong and to consider how well prepared the military is to respond if called upon."

Mrs. Walker turned to her husband. "It seems clear to me that the arguments in favor of the visit outweigh those against it. The one personal note I might add is in response to Lucia's mention of possible danger during the visit to New Zealand. I really don't think we should let a hypothetical danger deter us from doing what we think should be done. We should simply prepare a contingency plan, just in case. If you ask for my opinion, I say we should start packing.''

The president grinned and stroked his wife's hand. After a very rocky period in their marriage, occasioned by his dalliance with a beautiful Eurasian woman, Maynard and Marcia Walker seemed more devoted to each other than ever.

''I agree. Marcia, you start packing. And Lucia, you watch to make sure that Bull Bridges doesn't get us into trouble out there.''

CHAPTER 2

CHIEF PETTY OFFICER JASON LIND DID NOT NEED A CUP OF coffee to get himself going in the morning. Just the thought of beginning the day in the same room as Adm. John "Bull" Bridges, commander in chief of the U.S. Pacific Command, was more than enough to get his adrenaline pumping.

It was precisely 7 A.M. when Lind heard the knob turn in the door to Bridges's office at Camp H. M. Smith on Oahu's Halawa Heights, six hundred feet above Pearl Harbor. Lind pushed down the lever on the toaster, which held two slices of whole wheat bread. He reached for a cup and saucer bearing the CINCPAC seal, filled the cup with coffee, and placed it on the circular desk near Bridges's right arm as the admiral slipped into his chair.

" 'Morning, J.J. How's the message traffic this morning?"

"It appears to be fairly light, sir. However, your intel people gave me a heads-up that there are some new developments in the Chinese situation."

"Mm-hmm." Bridges chewed on a piece of dry toast as he flipped through the messages arranged in neat little piles. Bridges loved his job commanding the American military forces in the vast, 100-million-square-mile empire that stretched from the west coast of the United States to the east coast of Africa and from the Arctic to Antarctica. But he always had the feeling that time was out of joint. Even though he got to his office at 7 A.M. after a brisk five-mile run, it was already late afternoon in Washington, and the day's business there was nearly done. But off to the west, it was still the middle of the night for many of the forces he commanded. And then, of course, there were those forces on the other side of the International Date Line for whom it was already tomorrow. Bridges had spent much of his career as a destroyer and cruiser commander in the seemingly endless expanse of the Pacific, but he still found it a chore to keep track of the time.

Bridges forced himself to swallow, then bellowed, "This tastes like shit!" He sent the half-eaten piece of toast skimming across the room like a Frisbee.

Lind silently took away the remaining toast and refilled the admiral's coffee cup. The rejected piece was exactly the same as the toast Lind made every morning and Bridges seemed to enjoy, but he didn't mention this. For the admiral's little tantrum, Lind understood, was a sign that something was weighing on the officer's mind. Bridges was a man of action. Except for the dreary months on staff duty and in the obligatory service schools, he had spent his entire career on the deck of a ship. Sitting at a desk, Bridges had no release for the adrenaline that surged through his veins when he faced a challenge. Toast-tossing was probably the least objectionable way he had to work off nervous energy.

With the admiral again buried in his reports, Lind went to one side of the room and set up two easels for use by the officers who would arrive in a few minutes to give Bridges his usual morning briefing on the status of his forces, the activities of potential foes, and the world situation.

At precisely 7:30 A.M., there was one quick knock on the door and the briefing officers trooped into the room, carrying charts in large folders under their arms.

" 'Morning, gentlemen and Lieutenant Schroeder. Let's do intel first. Vickie?"

Lt. Victoria Schroeder placed her charts on an easel and opened the folder to a large map of the South China Sea, with the southern coast of China to the north and the eastern shore of Vietnam to the west. The Philippine Islands lay to the east

and the big island of Borneo to the south. It was an area
Bridges had sailed many times, since his first assignment more
than thirty years before, during the Vietnam War, as an ensign
fresh out of Annapolis. He had been a gunnery officer on an
old World War II—era destroyer and still considered it the best
job he'd ever had.

Bridges rose, paced around his desk to get closer to the map,
and stood, feet apart, arms folded across his chest.

"Sir, this is developing as a major exercise for the Chinese.
We now believe that there will be some fifty ships of all types
involved in the maneuvers and that they are all already in the
South China Sea or are rapidly approaching. It is now clear
that this will be even bigger than the show they put on in 1996
between the mainland and Taiwan."

"We got their attention that time," Bridges growled. The
United States had sent a powerful sixteen-ship task force from
the Seventh Fleet sailing boldly down into the maneuver area.
The move was intended as a signal to the Chinese not to interfere in elections on Taiwan and a gesture of support to the
Taiwanese. "Looks to me like this operation is going to be
centered on the Spratly Islands."

Lt. Schroeder shifted her pointer to the spots in the middle
of the South China Sea that designated the islands, which were
potentially rich sources of oil and whose ownership was bit-
terly contested by China and Vietnam. With their country already an oil importer and with their own oil reserves expected
to run out before 2020, the leaders in Beijing were looking
with increasing concern for new sources of petroleum under
their control.

"Yes, sir. It looks as though almost everything they own is
headed in that direction. We have identified two Han-class
nuclear-powered attack submarines, and we think they have
also sent two of the Kilo-class submarines they recently obtained from Russia. It's hard to track the Kilos because they're
diesel-electric and run very quietly. Most of the surface com-
batants we have seen are quite old, armed with guns and
surface-to-surface missiles. But we have identified two new

destroyers with modern engines, weapons, and radar. And of course there are a number of supply ships.''

''What about air?'' Bridges asked.

''We have seen southward movement of a number of air-craft to fields in this area,'' she replied, pointing to the south of China. ''Their fleet is normally supported by a mixed bag of land-based aircraft, most of them antiquated. But the air units in this area also include a squadron of quite capable SU-27 Flanker fighter-bombers obtained from Russia.''

Bridges stood for a moment, silently studying the material on the easel. ''Where are the Kilos?''

''Sir, as you know, they are relatively slow-moving. They left port ahead of the rest of the fleet, and they are moving to the southeast. We believe—but of course we are not sure—that they will take up station here.'' She pointed to an area northeast of the Spratly Islands and several hundred miles west of the coast of the southern Philippines. ''We believe that, rather than actually taking part in the maneuvers, they will serve as a picket line, in position to screen any approach to the maneuver area by our ships.''

''When does the action start?''

''There have already been several missile firings into this area,'' she said, pointing to the ocean south of the Spratly Islands. ''They have issued a warning to mariners of possible danger here.'' She pointed to an area crosshatched with red stripes.

''Well, bullshit!'' Bridges exclaimed. ''Those are international waters. They better be careful what they do.''

Several of the briefing officers awaiting their turns at the easel exchanged glances. It was common for many countries—including the United States—to designate areas of the open ocean where they intended to engage in the firing of missiles or other weapons. Normally, ships prudently stayed out of the way.

But, they thought, this was typical Bull Bridges. More than a decade earlier, as a one-star, Bridges had established legendary status for himself by leading Cruiser Destroyer Group One into the Sea of Okhotsk and simulating attacks on Petropavlovsk and other Soviet military bases along the Siberian coast—as close to war as the navy could come without actually shooting. The operation was kept secret at the time, but word quickly spread through the navy. COMCRUDESGRU One, it was agreed, had earned the right to its motto: "Fortune Favors Boldness."

"Thanks, Vickie. Okay, ops, what have we got in the area?"

Another officer dimmed the lights, clicked on a projector, and used a tiny flashlight as a pointer.

"Sir, these are the forces we have available." The image projected on the screen listed a carrier, two Ticonderoga-class cruisers, four Spruance-class destroyers, four Burke-class guided-missile destroyers, and two Perry-class frigates. In a separate column were three nuclear-powered Los Angeles-class attack submarines. Another column listed aircraft.

"These are the forces we have at sea." He pointed at the listing of ships and one column of aircraft. "In addition, sir, we have a squadron of air force F-16 Falcons operating out of Noi Bai Airport at Hanoi."

"Our new gook friends," Bridges grunted. Hanoi's airport had remained off-limits to U.S. bombers throughout most of the Vietnam War because it was used by commercial airliners carrying members of an international control commission—even though American pilots could see MiG fighters waiting on the ground for orders to intercept the attackers. Now, in one of those strange flip-flops in international relations, the Vietnamese had not only permitted the United States to use the airfield but had offered an open-armed welcome. Although the Vietamese had fought bitter, decades-long wars with the French and the Americans, they had feared, distrusted—and sometimes fought with—the Chinese for centuries. In the long view of history, it was not surprising that the Vietnamese welcomed the help of a recent foe in keeping an eye on a traditional—and much more proximate—one.

"Good, good. I want those SOBs to know we're there," Bridges said. "Let's get those three subs right up around the Spratlys where they can see what's going on. I want 'em to run noisy, so they'll know we're there, and I want them right in close to those Chink ships.

"And those aircraft. I want those Chinese skippers to feel what it's like to operate when someone else has total control of the air. Get 'em down on the deck and boom those ships day and night. When they move their air down into the maneuver area, I want our guys to intercept them and light 'em up with radar as soon as they cross into international waters.

"And let's keep close track of those submarines—especially those damn Kilos. Stay right on top of them."

The admiral strode back to the other side of his desk and turned to face the assembled briefers.

"Message the fleet: 'Bull Bridges sends: Aggressive. Aggressive. Aggressive.' "

"Anything else?" He looked around the room.

"Yes, sir, one other matter," one of the officers said. "The First Lady and her son are just about to begin their trip through Australia and New Zealand. Their visit will coincide with the Chinese maneuvers. The *Beijing Youth Daily* has an editorial today calling their visit a provocation. The editorial says the whole purpose of the visit is to stir up anti-Chinese sentiment Down Under."

"Marcia Goddamn Carter Walker!" Bridges spat out the words. "Who does she think she is, the secretary of state? Why can't that damn woman stay at home and mind her own business?" He picked up a heavy glass paperweight from his desk and hefted it in his hand. A couple of the officers winced, but no one actually ducked. The one officer, years ago, who *had* ducked when Bridges took up a piece of office equipment in anger, *had* drawn five—then been exiled from Bridges's command. Now Bridges just shrugged, putting the object back on the desk. "Well, that's above my pay grade. If she makes Beijing mad, maybe that's even a plus."

Adm. McKay settled into the chair in the barbershop on the lower level of the Russell Senate Office Building and greeted his favorite barber.

"How's it going, Milt? Still betting on those Redskins?"

"Absolutely, Admiral. Betting—and losing—ever since they moved out to that new Jack Kent Cooke Stadium." He ran a comb through McKay's thinning gray hair. "Same again today, sir?"

"Yeah, Milt, just keep it neat."

McKay didn't really need his hair cut every week and a half, but he had found the Senate barbershop an excellent listening post ever since, earlier in his career, he had spent a tour of duty as a legislative liaison officer, working the Hill for the navy. For many officers, such an assignment not only provided a crash course in Washington politics but helped single out those earmarked for rapid advancement.

As a white-haired man settled into the adjacent chair, McKay said, "Maybe you can work up a bet with Senator Terry, Milt."

"You know I'm not a betting man, Mac," replied Terry. "But if I were, I'd put my money on Atlanta." The senator, who somehow managed to look distinguished even while wrapped in a barber's apron, was the chairman of the Senate Armed Services Committee—one of a succession of Georgians to head the committee—and one of the most powerful men in Washington. Well-known for his fair-mindedness as chairman, he was equally known for his hopeless bias toward the hapless Falcons.

McKay's barber finished his work just a few minutes before Senator Terry's barber held up a mirror to give him a look at the back of his head.

McKay's timing was just right as he retrieved his hat and coat from the rack and pivoted slowly as Milt brushed a few hairs from his navy blue uniform. The admiral had planned it that way.

"Heading back to your office, Senator? Mind if I tag along?"

"Please do, Admiral. You know I always enjoy the company of the distinguished chairman of the Joint Chiefs of Staff." As he stepped from the chair, he turned and gave McKay an elaborate wink. "And I know the Admiral always enjoys my company—especially when he wants something.''

The senator took McKay's arm as they left the shop. ''What's on your mind, Mac?''

''I've got a problem with General Torkelson, sir. He's about to pull his special operations folks out of Eagle Force. If he does that, my guys are out of business.''

''That's that special group of commandos you set up, isn't it?''

''Yes, sir. It's a black outfit—well above top secret. But we've kept your staff briefed on them. They're the guys who saved us from disaster last year when that madman was going to destroy the St. Louis convention.''

''Nothing ever came out about that, did it?''

''No, sir. It was very tightly held. We were afraid of a terrible panic if people knew of the danger. The problem is that, since we can't brag about what we've done, the public doesn't know—and most members of Congress don't know, either. From the outside, General Torkelson's orders to reassign a few helicopter crews and Special Tactics guys doesn't sound like much. But to this outfit, it's life or death.''

The senator chuckled. ''Old Tork, he's a smooth operator. He's real buddy-buddy with my counterpart over in the House. They're always going off shooting ducks.''

The two men had reached the door of the senator's office. Unlike other senators, who had vied for space in the neighboring Dirksen Senate Office Building and the even newer and more modern Hart Building, Terry had clung to his comfortable office with its old-fashioned high ceilings and dark wood paneling in the building named for Senator Richard Russell, his predecessor and role model.

Senator Terry paused with his hand on the doorknob. ''Give me a couple of days, Mac. I'll see what I can do.''

''I'd appreciate it, Senator. I can't tell you how important those few men can be to our national security. We don't need them all the time, but when we do need them, we need them real bad.''

———— ★ ————

"Sir?" The yeoman paused in the doorway until Nelson looked up. "Sir, these orders just came in by fax. I thought you would want to see them right away."

The yeoman handed Nelson the sheets of paper.

"Yes, thanks." Nelson flipped quickly through them. "I've been expecting these."

Each sheet of paper carried orders for an air force member of the team, transferring him to new duties.

Nelson scanned the cryptic orders, with their jumble of abbreviations, looking for the effective dates. He shook his head. Normally, in the peacetime military, service members received orders at least six months in advance so they would have plenty of time to plan their moves. In this case, the orders were effective in just two weeks.

"Man!" Nelson muttered to himself. "Admiral Mac better work his magic quickly."

CHAPTER 3

MARCIA WALKER AND HER SON, DAVID, LEANED CLOSE TO THE windows as the new Boeing 757 with "United States of America" boldly lettered on its side turned above the port city of Fremantle and then descended over Perth, the sparkling but remote city on Australia's western coast.

Down below, they could see the broad expanse of the Swan River, dotted with sailboats. Two ferry boats were making the crossing from the business area to the suburbs. Looking off to the left, they saw the green eminence of Kings Park, with its commanding view of the tall buildings of downtown Perth.

Marcia put an arm over her son's shoulder and drew him close as they watched the view below. "Isn't this exciting, David!"

David was tall for a nine-year-old, and his long, thin legs, encased in knee-high stockings, protruded from his shorts like stalks. He wore a lightweight dress shirt, open at the collar. His normally unruly shock of blond hair was covered by a bush hat the Australians had sent to the White House before their departure.

"Mm-hmm. When do we get to see the dolphins, Mom?"

"I think we're going to do that tomorrow when we go up to Shark Bay."

She could feel an involuntary shiver ripple across her son's shoulders. "Shark Bay?"

"Yes, that's where the dolphins are, at a place called Monkey Mia. We won't see any sharks."

They could feel their ears pop as the plane banked and dropped down for its landing at Perth International Airport. Unlike most long-distance travelers, Marcia and David Walker felt refreshed and ready to go when the plane landed. They had slept peacefully in comfortable berths on the long nonstop flight from Honolulu and had showered and had a leisurely breakfast in preparation for a full day of activities in Perth.

A motorcade with sirens warbling carried them swiftly along the highway leading into the city.

David kept a solemn look on his face as a procession of officials queued up to shake hands and welcome them to the city. Squinting in the bright sunshine, he tried not to look bored as a woman with a too-shrill voice made a long speech about the close ties between the United States and Australia.

David thought she would never stop. After she finally did, Marcia and David led a gaggle of dignitaries as they strolled down Hay Street along the pedestrian mall that cuts through the heart of downtown Perth. Smiling, cheering Australians lined both sides of the street, waving American and Australian flags. It was the most exciting thing to happen in Perth since, several years before, Elle Macpherson, the supermodel, had arrived with her troupe of lingerie models and tied Perth traffic in knots.

Cindy Carson did not like this at all. Recently appointed chief of Mrs. Walker's Secret Service detail, she thought this stroll through such a multitude of strangers, reaching out to touch and shake hands with the First Lady and her son, was foolhardy. She would have been much happier to have the mother and son safely tucked away in a bulletproof limousine. But this was the way the people of Perth wanted it, and Mrs. Walker had enthusiastically agreed to the stroll.

The Secret Service agent walked parallel to Marcia and David Walker, keeping a close eye on the crowd and monitoring the movements of her own Secret Service detail and the Australian plainclothes police helping with security.

Carson let out a sigh of relief when she closed the door on the limousine that was to take the Walkers to a luncheon in their honor.

Late that afternoon, the Walkers boarded an Australian Royal Air Force helicopter that took them skimming along the coast north of Perth. They passed over Kalbarri National Park, at the mouth of the Murchison River, as the sun, dipping into the ocean to the west, brought out the brilliant red tones of the earth. It was shortly after dark when they landed at Monkey Mia and were shown to their accomodations in the unpretentious Shark Bay Hotel, near the beach.

Just after seven o'clock the next morning, even before the sun was up, David and his mother joined a small cluster of visitors along the water's edge, scanning the sea for sign of the dolphins' dorsals.

"I want to remind you," a park ranger told them, "that these are wild animals. I will give them a few fish—not enough to make them dependent on us for food—and they will stay here for a few minutes. Then they will swim back out into the sea. This is the only place in the world that humans come into direct contact with these animals in their natural state. As they swim by, you may stroke them along their sides with the back of your hand. But avoid touching their fins or their heads. We don't want to take a chance on harming their 'sonar,' which helps them to find their way under the sea."

She slowly waded into the surf, a bucket of fish in her hand. A dolphin surfaced in front of her and hovered there, its mouth open. Two other of the sleek mammals swam back and forth, parallel to the beach.

Letting go of his mother's hand, David waded boldly into the water toward the ranger. A dolphin swam slowly by, brushing against his legs. He reached down and petted it on the side as it passed by and then turned to catch his mother's eye, a broad grin of pleasure on his face.

After a few minutes, the dolphins swam back out to sea, leaving as quietly as they had come.

"I touched one of them! Did you see me? I petted one of them! Did you pet one, too?" David exclaimed as he stood watching the dorsal fins of the dolphins as they moved away.

His mother had a similar look of pleasure on her face. "Yes, I petted one, too. They feel so smooth! Don't you wish you could swim like that?"

On an impulse, David turned and dived into the water, swimming a few quick strokes. Cindy Carson, wearing a black maillot, had been standing quietly on the shore while her charges played with the dolphins. Two of her agents, dressed in casual clothes with loose jackets to hide their weapons, stood a short way back on the beach. As David began his swim, Cindy ran forward, dived into the water, and surfaced beside the boy, swimming with a strong sidestroke.

David rolled over onto his back and floated, paddling lazily. "This is fun, Cindy. Did you pet a dolphin?"

She swam easily by his side. "I saw you. You were actually touching the dolphin. I think he liked you."

"How do you know it was a 'he'?"

Cindy laughed and splashed him playfully. "Who knows? Maybe it was a girl. David has a girlfriend!"

"Cindy, why do they call this Shark Bay?"

The agent looked over her shoulder out to sea.

"I don't know, David, but I can guess. Maybe it's time we got out of the water."

The two of them swam toward shore. As they emerged, two attendants were waiting with towels and cups of hot tea.

That afternoon, they flew directly back to the airport at Perth. The air force pilot was waiting to greet them at the top of the stairs leading to the plane's cabin.

"Are we going to fly over Australia? Can I see some kangaroos?"

The pilot took David's hand. "No, we're not going to fly over much of Australia. Come on up here to the cockpit, and I'll show you why."

Pointing to a chart laid out on the navigation table, the pilot explained. "We're going to fly from Perth, here, to Canberra, the capital, over here. But we won't fly straight across as it appears on this flat map. Instead, we'll fly what we call a great circle route—actually the shortest route between two points on a globe. That means we'll swing down here to the south so most of our route will be over the water, over the Indian Ocean. You won't see much today but ocean, but you'll see plenty of kangaroos before this trip is over.''

The next week would seem to David like a blur of activity. He would be fascinated by the visit to Australia's new Parliament House in Canberra—built partially underground, so unlike the Capitol building in Washington—and, as usual, he'd be bored by the speeches.

From Canberra, they would fly south for a brief visit to Melbourne and then north to Sydney, for the obligatory visit to the opera house and a tour of Sydney Harbour. After a weekend in the peaceful atmosphere of the Blue Mountains, west of Sydney, they would fly far to the north, to Cairns, for a few days at a resort featuring sailboat rides and scuba diving.

Their rapid swing through Australia would end with a stop in Brisbane, on the east coast, a few miles inland from the Coral Sea.

But even before it began, Cindy Carlson had begun worrying about her charges' security. She now took advantage of the flight to Canberra, asking the plane's crew to patch her through on a secure line to her boss, Derek Shepherd, in Washington. It took only a few minutes to make the connection.

"Good to hear from you, Cindy. How are things going out there—or, rather, down there?"

"Very smoothly, sir. Almost too smoothly. It makes me nervous."

"That comes with the job. What's worrying you?"

"Nothing specific, sir. It's just that my counterparts here seem to be much more casual about security than we are. That walk down the pedestrian mall in Perth sure didn't help my blood pressure. And the New Zealanders . . . I've had some telephone contact with them, and they seem even more relaxed than the Aussies. And Mrs. Walker herself, she has this urge to get out and press the flesh with the local folks. I guess I can't blame her, but it doesn't make things any easier."

"I know how you feel, Cindy. We've all been through that same kind of conflict. None of our intelligence indicates any specific threat. So I guess all I can say is, just hang in there and do the best you can."

"Thank you, sir. I'll be in touch."

Carson hung up the phone and sat for a long time trying to calm herself and chase away the many threats she'd been trained to recognize and which now plagued her imagination. A week of letter-perfect events would do little to assuage her.

CHAPTER 4

REAR ADMIRAL JERRY HARMONY SWIVELED SLOWLY BACK and forth, savoring the warmth of the afternoon sun as he watched the planes, far below, move slowly up into position and then go rocketing off the bow of the USS *Kitty Hawk*.

This was what Harmony liked best: watching the planes being catapulted, two at a time, out over the sea and then following them until they disappeared among the towering thunderheads growing off to the west. Tonight, when they came groping their way back through the dark to the blacked-out carrier, would be the time for that nervous knot in the stomach and hands clenched on the railing that circled his aerie above the flight deck.

"Sir, a message from the combat control center." The yeoman handed him a flimsy piece of paper.

Harmony studied it for a moment and then turned to an aide.

"That damned Kilo is cutting across our path. Get him the hell out of there!"

During launch operations, the one thing a carrier demanded was a long, narrow piece of the ocean, stretching straight into the wind toward the horizon. If the Chinese submarine did not get out of the way, the carrier would have to slow or turn, or both, throwing off the tight launch schedule that was designed to clear the deck in time for the return of a squadron that had been launched earlier in the day.

Far astern, an American destroyer followed the carrier, ready to carry out a rescue operation if any of the planes went into the sea. Off to the ship's port side, a small Chinese frigate struggled to keep up. Harmony knew the Chinese ship was back there—and, in fact, he wanted it there. He wanted the Chinese to be aware of the powerful American presence near their maneuver area. But for a ship—especially a submarine— to put itself out in front of the carrier during launch operations was just asking for trouble.

Aboard a Spruance-class destroyer, Cdr. Craig Butterfield received the message from the carrier moments after Harmony had issued his order. All morning, Butterfield had had his helicopter patrolling the area far in front of the carrier task force, dropping sonobuoys and trying to keep track of the quiet little Chinese submarine. He was the one who had sent the warning to the carrier that the sub was moving over into its path.

At a brief order from Butterfield, the ship's four gas turbines—each as big as the engine on a DC-10 airliner—spun up to full power, putting out 80,000 horsepower so quickly that crew members who were not holding on were sent staggering.

"Let's go quiet," Butterfield ordered. As the ship surged forward at thirty-three knots, thousands of bubbles of air were expelled from tiny holes along the hull. The ship had been carefully designed to run quietly. The bubbles masked what few sounds remained.

Aboard the submarine, a sonarman who had been keeping track of the American destroyer all morning suddenly lost contact. The only noise coming through his earphones didn't sound like a ship. If anything, it sounded like a passing rain squall, the drops pattering on the ocean's surface.

At full power, Butterfield cut in front of the sub, switching on his powerful active sonar to hammer the submarine with nerve-shattering torrents of sound. The message was clear: Turn aside.

The American destroyer turned off its active sonar, slowed and made a leisurely turn, listening to see whether the Chinese skipper had changed course. The helicopter made a pass over the area and dropped two more buoys. The sounds they picked up indicated the Chinese sub was still moving into the path of the carrier.

Butterfield turned for another pass, moving so that he would come up from the rear, pass alongside the submarine, and then cut in front of it, hitting it again with the active sonar as he passed by. He thought his signal would be clear: Turn to starboard and move away from the carrier's path.

Aboard the sub, Lieutenant Commander Jiang Wei leaned over the shoulder of his sonarman, studying the lines and dots on the screen. Sweat ran off his forehead and down into his eyes. Jiang blinked rapidly, trying more to clear his mind than to relieve himself from the sweat. His training had never involved this kind of close contact with a hostile ship. The four-dimensional situation was taxing his mind in a way he'd never known.

"Where was the carrier?"

"What was the destroyer doing?"

"How did his course relate to what the destroyer was now doing?"

A more experienced submarine commander would simply have descended to a layer of the sea where he was unlikely to be detected and remained there, silently listening until the danger passed. But Jiang had never before confronted a destroyer as technologically sophisticated with a skipper as aggressive as the American up above. Jiang blinked again and ordered a sharp turn to the right. At the same moment, he succumbed to the great temptation felt by every submarine commander: the overwhelming compulsion to see what was going on. He ran up the periscope for a quick look at what was happening on the surface. In actual combat, he knew, such an action was like waving a red flag and shouting "Here I am!"

He wiped his brow with his hand and leaned into the eyepiece. Far in the distance he thought he could make out the superstructure of the carrier, just peeking over the horizon. Swiveling around, he saw open ocean and then, suddenly filling his field of vision, the bow of the American destroyer.

Jiang opened his mouth, but, for an instant, nothing came out. Then he managed to shout, "Dive! Dive! Dive!"

Aboard the destroyer, the sonarman saw the submarine's abrupt turn into the path of the American ship. He shouted, "He's turning into us!"

"Reverse all engines!" Butterfield ordered. But, as the ship slowed and prepared to back up, its momentum still carried it forward, slashing a jagged hole in the conning tower of the submarine.

The periscope struck Jiang like a blow from a giant baseball bat. His second in command picked himself up off the deck, noted that the captain was dazed, and began issuing orders to surface and prepare to abandon ship.

The destroyer commander studied the surfaced submarine through powerful glasses and saw crew members scrambling out onto the deck. The sub was listing heavily to port and seemed, even as he watched, to be sinking lower into the sea. Crew members of the destroyer were already lowering lifeboats into the water as the American ship stood to, fifty yards from the sub.

Butterfield's most immediate concern was for the safety of his own vessel. Reports from crew members throughout the ship came flooding into the bridge. It took only a few minutes before Butterfield's engineering officer was able to assure him that the hull of the destroyer had not been breached and that the ship was not in danger. Both men assumed that the big dome housing the sonar, jutting out from the bow below the surface, had been battered. Only later, when there was time to send divers down, would they know the full extent of the damage.

The skipper turned to his executive officer. "We've got a Chinese speaker aboard, don't we?"

"Yes, sir. One of the deck crew grew up in California, but he was born in China."

"Get him over there with a bullhorn and comm so I can talk to him."

By the time a lifeboat approached the submarine, the deck was crowded with men, and water was already beginning to slosh across the deck. In the bow of the lifeboat, a crew member balanced himself with a line coiled in his hand.

As he prepared to toss the line, Lt. Cdr. Jiang appeared at the top of the conning tower, waving a pistol. He fired a single shot into the air to get their attention and then began shouting orders to the crew members down below. Blood streaked his face where the periscope had struck him during the collison.

Crew members looked up at Jiang and began to shout back at him. The coxswain of the U.S. boat swerved sharply away from the sub and circled.

Moments later, another boat pulled up alongside, carrying the Chinese-speaking seaman holding a bullhorn. He listened to the exchange between Jiang and his crew members and then turned to an officer standing at his elbow.

"That guy up there is apparently the skipper. He's ordering the crew to get back inside and save the sub. They're saying, 'Bullshit. It's sinking!' He says he's going to start shooting if they don't obey him."

As he spoke, the officer relayed the information back to the bridge of the destroyer. Butterfield had an intelligence report on the submarine spread out before him.

"Tell our man the skipper's name is Jiang—Juliette, India, Alpha, November, Golf. Try to talk some sense into him. I don't want to have to take him out, but we don't have much time before that boat goes down."

The message was relayed back, and the translator sailor put the bullhorn before his mouth. "Commander Jiang!" The Chinese words boomed across the water. "Commander Jiang! Your ship is about to sink, sir. You must abandon ship now, sir."

Jiang and the men on the deck stopped their furious exchange and turned to stare openmouthed at the source of the words. Here was an American addressing them in Mandarin, and he even knew their captain's name.

"Commander Jiang! Please put down your gun and order your crew to abandon ship. Your boat is sinking now, sir."

Jiang looked around in bewilderment and gradually lowered the pistol.

"You and your crew will be treated humanely. You will be honored guests of the United States Navy until you can be returned to your homes and loved ones."

As the sailor's words were relayed back to Butterfield, he shook his head. "That's really laying it on pretty thick. Hope it works."

The men on the deck of the submarine looked up at Jiang, waiting silently for his reaction. After a full minute, he spoke, giving the order to abandon ship.

"We will now approach your ship and begin the rescue operation. If that is acceptable, please climb down to the deck."

Jiang tucked the pistol in the waistband of his trousers and climbed, hand over hand, down to the deck as the American lifeboats pulled alongside and began to take the Chinese sailors aboard.

As the rescue operation got underway, Butterfield turned to his next big problem: making a report back to the task force commander aboard the carrier, describing the circumstances of the accident and the rescue. It was not a task he relished. He had followed orders precisely: "Aggressive! Aggressive! Aggressive!" And it was the Chinese skipper who had suddenly turned in front of him. Still, a collision at sea would take a good deal of explaining and, in the end, would probably not turn out to be career-enhancing. He read over his account of the incident and ended with a suggestion that the Chinese be transferred to the roomier carrier as soon as possible.

By the time his message was ready to be transmitted, Butterfield could see the carrier itself rapidly approaching the scene of the accident. His decks were now crowded with Chinese, many of them barefoot and shivering. His crew members moved among them, passing out blankets and plastic cups of tea. The destroyer's helicopter hovered over the submarine, lifting Jiang and the last few men left on the deck to safety just before their boat slowly disappeared below the ocean's surface.

The carrier stopped alongside the destroyer, and boats from the two ships immediately began transferring the Chinese to the bigger ship. Butterfield watched the process from the bridge. This had not been one of his better days. He became aware that a sailor was standing silently at his elbow.

"Yes, what is it? Oh, it's you." He glanced down at the seaman's nameplate. "Seaman Chang? Good work out there. We could have had a disaster on our hands."

The crewman who had talked the submarine commander into abandoning ship stood at attention.

"Thank you, sir. Sir? I've been listening to those men we rescued. I don't know what's going on, but some of them aren't sailors. It's not clear to me what they're doing on the sub, but these passengers, they're apparently some kind of scientists."

CHAPTER 5

TO A CASUAL VISITOR, THE LITTLE STAND ON THE DESK OF THE
secretary of defense seemed strangely out of place. It consisted
of a base from which rose a curved, clear plastic support arm.
At the tip of the arm hung three small brass balls like those
traditionally used to mark a pawnbroker's shop.

Word of the significance of the object quickly spread
through the Pentagon. It was a subtle reminder that the first
woman to head the nation's military not only had balls of
brass—but she had one more than the men who reported to
her.

As Lucia McKenzie scanned through the message one more
time, she pressed a button on her intercom that connected her
directly to the office of her assistant secretary for public affairs
on the second floor of the Pentagon. Her voice was soft but
clearly audible: "I need your advice, dear. Would you please
come on up? Thank you."

Claudia Bishop picked up the pad and pen that always lay
ready on her desk, quickly climbed the stairs to the third floor
and strode halfway down the long corridor of the E-ring to
the secretary's office. She was the first woman and the first
person with a strong background in television to hold the post
as the chief spokesperson for the Pentagon. It was a tribute to
Lucia McKenzie's powers of persuasion that she had con-

vinced Claudia Bishop that it was her duty to her country to lay aside her career as a co-anchorperson on a major television network, with a salary of more than a million dollars a year, to take the Pentagon post at barely a tenth of her former income.

Since childhood, Claudia Bishop had been known as "Cookie." When she moved into her Pentagon office and assumed a civilian title equivalent in rank to that of a four-star general, she realized it was far too late in life to ask people to call her by a more dignified name.

When the press secretary arrived in the antechamber of Lucia McKenzie's office, a secretary peeked through a tiny peephole in the door to confirm that her boss was on the phone, signaled Bishop to a chair, and handed her a copy of the message that had just come in from the commander of American forces in the Pacific.

"Admiral Bridges." McKenzie's voice had lost any trace of gentleness. "Are you trying to start a war with the Chinese?"

"Not at all, Madam Secretary, not at all." Bull Bridges had been prepared for this call, but the tone in his boss's voice left him slightly unnerved. If he had had time to think about it, he might have realized that he was experiencing the same sense of apprehension he had felt as a child being reprimanded by his third-grade teacher.

"This is going to cause us all sorts of problems, Admiral. As you, of all people, must be aware, our relations with the Chinese are very delicate right now. As soon as I hang up this phone, I am going to have to inform the president, the secretary of state and key leaders on the Hill about this deplorable incident. None of them is going to be pleased."

Bull Bridges had not been reluctant to talk back in the third grade, and he wasn't afraid now.

"Madam Secretary, I share your dismay about this incident. But, as I explained in my message, this occurred in international waters, where we have a perfect right to be. It happened because an inexperienced Chinese submarine commander—a man who would be chipping paint if he were in our navy—did an incredibly stupid and totally unexpected thing. He turned abruptly, directly into the path of our ship. A collision was inescapable. And it was all his fault. I personally issued orders to our forces to operate aggressively in those waters, and our destroyer commander was doing exactly what I had ordered him to do.''

McKenzie knew she was listening to vintage Bull Bridges. Still, the boldness with which he took responsibility and defended the actions of his subordinates while other men would be shifting the blame and rushing for cover left her almost speechless.

''What is the status of the Chinese crew?''

''The entire submarine crew was rescued by Commander Butterfield and taken aboard his destroyer. I must say that it was an impressive display of seamanship that our people were able to save that crew before their boat sank. The submarine skipper and a couple of his men had to be snatched off the deck by helicopter just before the boat went under.

''The Chinese have now been transferred to the *Kitty Hawk*, and we are making them as comfortable as possible. I have a team of Chinese-speaking intelligence officers, and they are now en route to the *Kitty Hawk* to interrogate the men from the submarine.''

''Admiral, I'm not sure I like the word 'interrogate.' After all, these men are not prisoners of war.''

''No, no, Madam Secretary, we are treating them as victims of an accident at sea. But, while they are our 'guests,' I think it would be unfortunate if we didn't listen politely to anything they would like to tell us about themselves and their navy.''

''Admiral, are the Chinese aware yet of the loss of their submarine?''

''No, I doubt it very much. It would not be unusual for a submarine to operate for hours, even days, without radio contact with its home base or other elements of the fleet. Unless they have managed to read some of our message traffic—which I doubt—they would not be aware that anything had happened to the sub until it failed to make a scheduled report or arrive for a rendezvous.''

''All right, Admiral. We'll leave it at that for now; I have my press secretary here with me. I assume the State Department will notify the Chinese through diplomatic channels. Meanwhile, we will prepare a news release.''

As she hung up the phone, the secretary in the outer office saw the light go out on her phone console and motioned Claudia Bishop to go on into the ballroom-sized office.

She took up her usual position on the couch nearest the door and rested her pumps on the edge of the heavy wooden coffee table.

McKenzie swiveled around to face her. ''Cookie, you've seen the message from Admiral Bridges. He reports directly to me on operational matters like this. But I'm sure the folks in the fleet are creating their own message traffic about this incident. It's going to start leaking out very soon. I want you to get on top of it and put out an accurate version of the incident as soon as possible.

''I'm going to alert the president and Henry Trover at State as soon as we're through. I want you ready with an announcement, probably within the hour.''

The press secretary crossed one leg over the other and braced her pad against a knee as she made notes.

''Do you think we've got the straight story here? As you know, I'm a strong believer in getting the bad news out fast, but we also want to make sure we've got our facts straight.''

Too often, she knew, officers far from the Pentagon were tempted to cover up, withhold facts, and shift blame when something bad happened. When the truth eventually came out, it was the defense secretary and his or her press secretary who bore the blame and lost credibility.

''Do the best you can, Cookie. That's why our taxpayers pay you so lavishly.'' McKenzie picked up the phone, indicating that the meeting was over. ''Please get me the president. Tell them it's urgent.''

———— ★ ————

As soon as Claudia Bishop had moved into her office in the Pentagon, she had deliberately set to work creating the same kind of personal network that had served her so well as a reporter. She knew that, if many people in the Pentagon had their way, the press secretary would always be the last to know—if she was told anything at all. Her network served her well every day, keeping her informed of what was really going on behind the constant blizzard of top secret papers that swept across her desk and helping her to avoid the more dangerous bureaucratic minefields that seemed to stretch out in every direction. It was on days like this that the network really paid off.

Her first move upon arriving back in her office was to dispatch her military aide, Terry Glenn, down the hall to the Pentagon's command center to glance through the most recent message traffic and gossip with friends over a casual cup of coffee. Glenn, a tall, handsome black navy captain, had the kind of warm, engaging personality, coupled with a self-deprecating sense of humor, that had gained him a host of friends and admirers during his navy career.

Then she placed a call to a navy commander whose office adjoined that of the secretary of the navy on the fourth floor. Although his first loyalty was to his boss, Claudia had found him to be a straight shooter, a valuable source of accurate information passed along without any service "spin."

Down the hall in the Directorate for Defense Information, officers set about calling the "regulars" in the Pentagon press corps, alerting them that a press briefing would be held within the hour. When, as expected, each reporter asked, "What's it about?" the officers could honestly answer that they didn't know because they hadn't been told.

Claudia Bishop was relieved as her network of contacts in the Pentagon reported in; the initial report from Admiral Bridges was pretty much on the mark.

She ordered the preparation of a bare-bones news release telling what had happened and prepared to do the briefing herself when reporters gathered in the small auditorium across the hall from her office.

Lucia McKenzie spent almost a solid hour on the telephone, filling in the president, the secretary of state, and key members of Congress on the incident.

Maynard Walker, whose temper was legendary, was not pleased.

"Can't those people do anything right? They've got a whole ocean to play in, and they have to go and sink a Chinese sub. What were they thinking of?"

The defense secretary listened patiently, waiting for the storm to pass.

"Mr. President, I have talked with Admiral Bridges myself. From what he tells me, the fault for this incident clearly falls on the inexperienced Chinese skipper, who was operating in the path of our carrier during flight operations and who turned directly and unexpectedly into the path of our ship. I think we can be very grateful that our destroyer wasn't also sunk and that its crew was able to save the Chinese crew before the sub went down."

"Where are the Chinese now?"

"They're aboard the *Kitty Hawk*."

"What are we going to do with them?"

"I want to talk to Henry Trover about that. I'll call him as soon as we hang up. The disposition of the crew is clearly something the State Department will want to have some input on."

"You're going to announce this?"

"Yes, sir. We're alerting the press corps now." McKenzie was simply following the standard procedure: Good news is announced by the White House; bad news comes from the Pentagon.

As Henry Trover listened to Lucia McKenzie, he drew a line down the center of a page in a pad of yellow legal paper. In the left-hand column, he made brief notes of the details of the incident. In the right-hand column, he jotted down thoughts, as they came to him, on how the sinking should be handled.

"I assume you'll want to inform the Chinese through our ambassador, won't you, Henry?"

It was a moment before Trover replied. "No, I think not, Lucia. I think our first consideration here is to handle this in such a way that the Chinese are not put in a position where they will feel that they have lost face. Perhaps we can let them know what has happened without a formal confrontation at the ambassadorial level. Perhaps a military-to-military contact can be arranged. Does the navy have someone with a personal contact at their embassy just off Connecticut Avenue?"

"Yes, I suppose so. But isn't that a kind of devious way to do business?"

"It is indeed. The Chinese love deviousness and intrigue. All we have to do is let them know in this unofficial way what has happened. Then, when we announce it publicly, they will be prepared to respond. We can follow up later by going through the procedures provided in our new incidents-at-sea agreement with the Chinese.

"I'm sure we will hear some very angry words from Beijing. But what we don't want are imprudent actions. We don't want them shooting at one of our ships or trying to sink one of our submarines. A subsequent incident at sea could ruin everyone's day."

"That makes sense, Henry. I'll get our people working on that immediately. I think we have to move fast before one of the networks gets hold of this and broadcasts it before we have made an announcement."

"I agree, Lucia. We do have to move fast. In the meantime, I'll begin alerting our allies so we'll get some expressions of support when this comes out publicly. The Brits and the Germans will be supportive. The French? Who knows how they'll be feeling today? I'll personally talk to the Russian ambassador. We have a long experience with the old Soviet Union of handling many serious incidents, including some collisions at sea, in a way that they didn't blow up into international crises.

The Russians might be willing to say, in effect, 'Cool it. These things happen.' "

Wang Dongfang hung up the phone, picked up his hat, and headed out the door of the Chinese embassy and then down Connecticut Avenue. If he walked at a moderate pace, he should arrive at the Italian restaurant above Dupont Circle about the same time Lt. Sam Simmons reached their meeting place by taking the metro from the Pentagon.

The two young intelligence officers had known each other for two years and had grown to like and trust one another. Wang could tell from the sense of urgency in Simmons's brief phone call that they were about to become involved in something that would normally be far above their respective pay grades.

Simmons had just taken a seat when Wang stepped into the coolness of the restaurant and spotted his friend.

"What's doing, Sam?"

Simmons had purposely taken a table near the window that would be beyond earshot of the nearest neighboring diners if they kept their voices down.

"Sit down, Bud." At their first meeting, Simmons had ruled out calling his new friend by his family name, Wang. Instead, in typical American fashion, he had taken to calling him "Bud." Wang, far from being offended, had quickly adopted the nickname and even used it on his business cards.

Holding his menu so that it shielded his face from the side, Simmons leaned forward. "We're the designated messengers, Bud. One of our destroyers banged into one of your subs in the South China Sea and sank it. Your people in Beijing don't know about it yet. My bosses want me to pass the word along—back channel—through you. In effect, we want to give your people a heads-up before this becomes public."

"Do you have any details, Sam?"

Simmons handed him an envelope. "Yeah, here's a summary of what happened—time, location, ships involved, that sort of thing. Do you think you can handle it?"

Wang extracted a sheet of paper from the envelope and glanced through it.

"The crew okay?"

"Yeah. I assume arrangements will be made right away to get them home."

Wang folded the paper, put it back into the envelope, and slipped it into his pocket. "I'll take care of it, Sam. I'd better get on back to the embassy."

Simmons rose and shook hands with the Chinese. "Sorry to make you rush off. I owe you a lunch."

By the time Admiral Bridges's staff gathered for his usual briefing the following morning, it was already afternoon in Washington, and the collision at sea had gone through a full news cycle. Bridges's press officer led off the briefing.

"Listen to this, sir, from Beijing radio." He read from a piece of wire copy.

"With reckless disregard for human life, the criminal commander of an American destroyer deliberately crashed into and sank a Chinese submarine in international waters. This depraved act will not go unpunished. . . ."

Bridges grunted. "Got their attention, didn't we?"

"Sir, we have received a number of requests from the networks for permission to interview the Chinese crew."

"Negative on that. We're not through 'interviewing' them ourselves.

"And another thing," Bridges said. "I want to send a personal 'attaboy' to Commander Butterfield and get it into his record before anybody takes a notion to mess with his career."

The operations officer broke in. "Sir, will there be any change in orders to the task force as a result of this incident?"

Bridges fixed him with a hard stare. "You mean back off? Not a chance."

CHAPTER 6

AS SOON AS HE LEARNED THAT THE *KITTY HAWK* WOULD PICK up the First Lady and her son and take them from Brisbane to Auckland, Adm. Harmony had checked with a friend in the Australian navy to learn if it would be possible to sail the 80,000-ton vessel up the Brisbane River to the city itself.

"Oh, good Lord, I don't think one of your carriers has been there since World War II—and of course they were much smaller then," his friend said. "I wouldn't dream of going up the river. The best bet for you is to anchor off the Stradbroke Islands at the entrance to Moreton Bay. That way, you'll avoid the local shipping traffic, and you won't even need a harbor pilot. Your guests can fly out to the carrier."

Glancing at the radar screen, which showed not only a number of ships but also a series of islands in Moreton Bay, Harmony was grateful for his friend's advice. No sense looking for trouble. He'd have enough explaining to do about the collision between a Chinese submarine and one of his escort destroyers.

"Sir?"

Harmony became aware of a young Chinese-American officer standing at his side. As soon as he caught the admiral's attention, he snapped off a brisk salute.

"Yes, what is it?"

"Sir, we are just about through our attempt to interrogate the men we rescued from that submarine. They'll be leaving the ship soon to be flown back to China."

"Have you learned anything useful?"

"Not very much, sir. We got a lot of 'name, rank, and serial number' answers. We really don't know whether the Kilo was going somewhere and just happened to be in front of the carrier or whether it was on picket duty as part of their maneuvers. Commander Jiang has proved very uncommunicative."

"I guess I don't blame him. I'd hate to go back to Beijing and explain how I'd lost one of their submarines in a collision at sea. They are not likely to be pleased. What about the other crew members?"

"Most of them, at least, didn't know much about their mission. They were just doing what Jiang told them to do. We did manage to elicit a fair amount of information about the condition of their boat, their training, and their operational practices. But we really didn't learn much about where they were going or why."

"What about those 'scientists' who were aboard?"

"Yes, sir, six of them. Same story there, sir. We got names, but they didn't even have ranks or serial numbers. They were very closemouthed about why they were so far at sea on a warship. You can understand how they might go out for a day or so. But the point where that collision took place is a long way from home for them."

Harmony moved about the bridge, using his binoculars to check the positions of his escort vessels as they came to anchor. The young intelligence officer followed along.

"Sir, we did learn one interesting thing—kind of puzzling. One of the scientists, it turns out, has studied in the U.S. and speaks fairly good English. He asked us how the Dallas Cowboys were doing. We found out that he spent a year studying at the Center for Nanoscale Science and Technology—the CNST—at Rice University in Houston."

"Nanoscale science? You've lost me, son."

"Lost me, too, sir. It has something to do with very small-scale stuff—atoms and molecules. We're trying to find out more about what they do there and what that might have to do with a submarine."

"You don't have much more time. As you said, we're going to have to send them ashore in a few minutes so they can head on home."

Patricia Collins served as Eagle Force's civilian intelligence expert. Twenty-eight years old, she kept herself in top physical condition and had even run a marathon once before convincing herself that the pounding a person's body took in long-distance running would almost certainly take its toll later in life in the form of aching bones and joints. Her face was distinguished by high cheekbones and flashing blue eyes, framed by shoulder-length brown hair. The faint lines etched across her brow and at the edges of her eyes were the only visible signs of the sorrows she carried in her heart.

And her fingers tapping erratically on the arms of the chair across the desk from Chuck Nelson were the only signs of how hard she was resisting getting up, walking around the desk, and taking Nelson in her arms. But, despite their growing love for each other, they had adopted a seldom-violated rule against any show of affection while on the job.

"Dammit, Pat, I'm normally a pretty optimistic guy—you know, the glass-half-full kind of person. But this business really has me feeling blue. I guess it's even worse because there's nothing I can do about it. In a couple of weeks, this task force we've worked so hard to create is just going to be history."

Collins brushed her hair back away from her face with both hands and regarded Nelson with her luminous blue eyes. "I know how you feel. It's not the same, of course, but I feel a sense of loss, something like the way I felt when Jim died. Like a death in the family."

Nelson held her gaze for a moment, then blinked and looked away. He had been with her husband when he was struck by a ship and killed while they were on a routine training mission at the SEAL base in Little Creek, Virginia. There was nothing he could have done to avoid the accident, which left Pat Collins a young widow with a boy and girl to raise alone. But he still carried the loss of his friend like a heavy weight in his heart and felt a sense of guilt that he had lost his "swim buddy."

"What have you heard from Admiral McKay?"

"Not much. He's been trying to apply some pressure from the Hill to get General Torkelson to change his mind and not pull the air force guys out of the team. I don't want to bug the admiral. I figure he'll tell me if there's any good news. In this case, no news is bad news."

They both sat silently, preoccupied with their own thoughts. Finally, Nelson broke the silence. "Want to take a walk? Let's go see how Mark is doing."

The two of them blinked and shaded their eyes as they stepped out into the brilliant autumn sunshine. The sun was already far enough down in the southern sky that it seemed to be aimed directly into a person's eyes. It was hot, but the sun carried only a hint of the blazing heat with which it had seared the desert in midsummer.

When they entered Mark Rattner's office, the air force officer was busy slipping file folders into packing boxes. The room was a mess.

"Hi, Mark. Going somewhere?"

Rattner looked up as they entered.

"Afraid so, Chuck. I guess the admiral hasn't been able to work his magic. Tork is a tough customer when he sets his mind on something."

"He's really going to split you guys up, isn't he?"

"I think it's on purpose. Only a few of us are even going to stay in special ops."

"If your assignment is typical, it isn't as though he's mad at you personally."

"That's one of the frustrating things. He's pulling me out of a job I love—one I think is important for the country's protection. But I'm going into a pilot's dream job."

"The F-22?" Pat Collins asked.

"Right, Pat. I'll be flying the air force's newest fighter and preparing to take the first squadron operational. I couldn't ask for anything better than that—if it didn't mean breaking up our outfit.''

''How much more time do you have—a week?'' Nelson asked.

''Eight days and we're out of here.''

''Well, as long as you're here, we're going to stay right on our regular daily training schedule. There's always the chance that we'll get those orders changed. Morale is already bad enough. I'm not going to let it get any worse by beginning to close down and have these guys just sitting around here.''

''You're right, Chuck. My guys are better off keeping busy, too, even if we are all beginning to think about our new assignments. We'll stay right on schedule, just as though nothing has happened, until the day we say good-bye.''

CHAPTER 7

AS THE 80,000-TON USS *KITTY HAWK* CRUISED SLOWLY INTO the port of Auckland, Marcia and David Walker stood on the glass-enclosed bridge of the ship. Spreading out around the huge vessel were so many white-sailed boats that it was difficult to glimpse the blue surface of the water.

The mother and son studied the scene through binoculars provided by Adm. Harmony. If either of them had shifted their glasses toward the War Memorial Museum on a hill known as "The Domain," rising to the north of the city center, they might have picked out a strange sight.

On the edge of the parking lot, looking down at the scene in the harbor, stood a tall, solitary figure dressed in the style of a chieftain of the Maori, the Polynesian people who had colonized New Zealand centuries before the arrival of the first white man. He leaned slightly to the right, resting his weight on a long spear—a sharp stone head attached at the end of an intricately carved wooden shaft.

A light breeze caused an occasional flutter of the earth-colored cape that hung loosely from his shoulders, but otherwise he was as still as if he had been carved from stone. In contrast to his stoic appearance, Wiremu Kingi's mind raced, filled with thoughts of the last few months and, even more, of the next few days.

It had all begun nearly a year earlier on one of the days when Kingi earned a few dollars escorting visitors—from one of the big tour boats tied up in the harbor—through the Maori exhibits in the War Memorial Museum.

He began with a chanted greeting: *"Haere mai! Nau mai! Haere mai!"* Then, looking over the group, he spoke a more casual greeting: *"Tena koutou katoa. Kei te pehea koe, Pakeha?* Greetings. How are you, strangers?"

A slight, embarrassed murmur rippled through the tour group.

"How many of you are from America?"

Half the group raised their hands.

"Can any of you tell me how long ago your Civil War was?"

A boy in the front row raised his hand and answered quickly: "More than a hundred years ago, sir."

"Right! More than a hundred years. Actually, more than 130 years ago. Your Civil War—or the War between the States—began in April 1861 and lasted just about four years, until the spring of 1865. Now all of you have heard about the American Civil War. But how many of you know that New Zealand also endured a war at almost the same time as the American Civil War, from roughly 1860 to 1865, although there were battles before that period and continued resistance afterward? It was on a far smaller scale than the American war, involving thousands rather than hundreds of thousands of men, but it was also a long, bloody, bitter conflict between the British army and the European settlers on one side and the *tangata whenua*—the native Maori peoples—on the other. The history books call that period the Maori Wars. We Maori refer to it as *te riri pakeha*—the white man's anger.

"I have a very personal interest in that war. You see, I was named for my great-great-grandfather, Wiremu Kingi, who was an important leader of the Maori resistance in the western portion of the North Island, around what we Maori call Mt. Taranaki, although it is shown on the maps by the name Captain Cook gave it: Mt. Egmont.

"The war, like so many conflicts, was over land. We know very little about the first humans who came to New Zealand. We know they arrived many centuries ago and found a kind of Garden of Eden. Since New Zealand is so far from any other land, it had its own unique flora and fauna. The earliest people found several species of large birds. Since there were no cats or other predators, the birds had not bothered to learn to fly. When these early inhabitants arrived here—probably in about the eighth century, or some 1,300 years ago—they found vast flocks of these birds, these *moa,* grazing on the grasslands. We call those early people the moa-hunters.

"They were followed by another wave of Polynesian immigrants—the ancestors of today's Maoris. According to our Maori traditions, these people came in a great fleet several hundred years later. But it now seems likely that, instead of a large fleet, small numbers of people arrived over a long period of time—many, if not most of them, by accident.

"There is no question, of course, that they came by sea, since New Zealand is an island. We Maori call it *Aotearoa,* 'the land of the long white cloud.' "

Kingi moved into the exhibit area.

"Here is a hundred-man canoe of the type we believe the early inhabitants used to reach these islands. You can imagine their voyage across what must have been at least a thousand miles of uncharted ocean. And then they saw, in the distance, a long white cloud where the moist ocean air was pushed upward by the tall mountain ranges of both the north and south islands. They probably saw some shore birds and even sniffed the earth smells as their long voyage neared its end.

"Our ancestors were the greatest of the Polynesian peoples, and they were, I must admit, very warlike. They fought with clubs and spears and knives, and—yes—the losers were sometimes eaten by the winners. It was not until the early nineteenth century that we acquired guns—what we called *pu*— or, even better, the *tupara* or double-barreled musket.

"War was almost constant, and the many little wars almost all involved control of land. We have an old saying: *He wahini, he whenua i mate ai te tangata*—Women and land are the reasons why men die. But the individual Maori did not own land themselves. The land was owned by the group, or tribe, and the individual was permitted the use of a portion of the land. This practice set the stage for the prolonged war between the *tangata whenua* and the *pakeha*. The European settlers were hungry for land, to raise crops and sheep. But our ancestors did not own land individually, so it required the approval of an entire tribe to transfer title to the land.

"Wiremu Kingi, my great-great-grandfather, moved into the Taranaki area with a group of followers in 1848. They had been living near Wellington, but they claimed the Taranaki land as their own. They refused to sell their land despite relentless pressure from the settlers—backed up by the power of British troops. When one meeting broke up, my ancestor declared, 'All I have to say to you, O Governor, is that none of this land will be given to you, never, never, not till I die.'

"At one point, the Maori controlled most of the central portion of the north island. They carried out raids in which they burned settlers' farms and killed their animals. The *pakeha* even feared that the tribes would unite and attack Auckland itself. But I must admit we were not as good at guerrilla warfare as we might have been. Our favorite tactic was to build a *pa*, a fortified position on a hill, and challenge the soldiers to attack us. They would suffer heavy casualties, and then, as they were about to take the position, we would melt away into the forests or swamps.

"The common soldiers grew to admire us. An historian quotes one soldier who said that we were 'on the whole the grandest native enemy that he had ever encountered.' And, oh, did we love to fight. If we ran short of ammunition or water, or if the soldiers ran short of food, we would ask for a truce while both sides stocked up so the fight could go on."

The tourists followed Kingi through the exhibit rooms, clustering closely to catch his every word.

"The wars came to a conclusion of sorts in 1865, when the soldiers surrounded about three hundred Maori at a village called Orakau. For three days, the Maori held off two thousand troops. Finally, they were out of water, and the only ammunition they had consisted of bullets carved of wood. The British general pleaded with them to surrender, or at least to permit the women and children to leave. But they replied, '*Ka wha-*

whai tonu ake! Ake! Ake!'—'We will fight on forever! Forever! Forever!' "

The tourists were startled by the intensity with which Kingi made the exhibit hall ring with the words *Ake! Ake! Ake!* He hammered the floor with the butt of his spear with each word.

"The battle ended when the Maori suddenly poured out of the *pa*, overran a portion of the army line, and disappeared into the swamps. Half of our people died—but half of them got away.

"After that, many of the people lost heart. Vast tracts of land were sold to the settlers. But Wiremu Kingi and his followers retreated into the Taranaki area and continued resistance until 1872—just as a few of the Confederate officers continued to resist long after the surrender at Appomattox."

Kingi paused and looked over the group. "Are there any questions?"

A man in the center of the group raised his hand. "Is there still resistance by the Maori?"

A cloud seemed to pass over Kingi's face, and he glared at the man for a few moments before answering.

"Yes, there are Maori who still feel they are not treated fairly although the white people boast of the good racial relations in New Zealand." He stopped, continuing to glare. "But this is not the place for me to talk politics. If you will proceed through that door over there, your bus will be waiting at the foot of the stairs."

During Kingi's lecture, a tall, broad-shouldered man had taken up a position on the fringe of the tour group. As the tourists moved off toward the exit, he stepped forward.

"Mr. Kingi, my name is Bernard, Ben Bernard. My employer would like to have a word with you. He's waiting outside, if you'll come with me, sir."

Kingi looked him up and down. "What's this all about?"

"It will all become clear in a few minutes, sir. If you will please come with me." He moved his hand as though to take hold of Kingi's arm but thought better of it and let his hand drop back down by his side.

Kingi turned and headed toward the exit with long strides, almost leaving Bernard behind.

At the foot of the stairs, he found a tall, athletic-looking man of about sixty dressed in a trim black suit and wearing sunglasses with lenses so dark that they totally obscured his eyes. His head was totally bald.

The man stepped forward, extending his hand. "My name is Luke Nash, Mr. Kingi." The Maori paused a step above Nash and stood staring down at him. After a few moments, he stepped down, shifted his spear to his left hand, and grasped Nash's outstretched hand.

Kingi greeted him and asked if he spoke Maori: *"Tena koe, Paheka. E Korero Maori ana koe?"*

Nash's lips spread into a thin smile, and he shrugged. *"He iti iti nao iho taku mohio,"* he replied—I understand a little. "But we'd better speak in English."

"Okay with me. What have you got on your mind?"

"Let's take a walk over here where we'll have a little privacy." He led the way across the parking lot to a point where the land began to slope down toward the city below.

"I heard part of your little lecture in there. Did the resistance to the white men really end in 1872?" Kingi stopped and turned a questioning look on Nash. "No, it didn't, did it? It goes on to this day—and you are the leader of that resistance."

"You seem to be well-informed, Mr. Nash. Go on." The two men resumed walking.

"I have done some careful research. My information indicates that you have the base for a significant resistance movement among the relatively few pure-blooded Maoris remaining in New Zealand—in Aotearoa—and even among many of those of mixed parentage."

"Mr. Nash, I wouldn't talk to you, a stranger—a *paheka* in the literal sense of the word—about any so-called resistance even if I were involved. But go ahead. I'm listening."

"You have several thousand men—and women, too—I am told, who are committed to a radical change in the situation in New Zealand—a change that would restore the Maori to the dominant position they held here for many centuries.

"I have studied your chances for success." He stopped and looked Kingi in the eye. "Frankly, they are not very good. You are woefully underfinanced. As a result, your people are very poorly armed. Admittedly, the New Zealand military and police forces are not very formidable—but they are certainly far better financed and armed and much better led than your people.

"Are you following me?"

Kingi nodded slowly. "And what business is this of yours, Mr. Nash?"

"What I propose, Mr. Kingi, is to change the odds dramatically in your favor. I will provide you with superior modern weapons. I will arrange for the training of your people. Most importantly, I will provide you with leadership, guidance, and a sound strategy. With my assistance, what is now a quite unrealistic dream can become a reality."

The two men walked slowly together in silence, the butt of Kingi's spear making a solid thumping sound with each step.

"And, Mr. Nash? And . . . ?"

"What strings are attached? Yes, there are strings. But I don't think you will find them burdensome. Let us say that it will be in my interest to see you successful in establishing Maori control of New Zealand—or, if not the entire country, certainly of the north island. I have one immediate request. The Maori people—and especially the Taranaki tribes with which your family has long been identified—consider Mount Taranaki and the area surrounding it to be sacred.

"I would like your permission—your blessing, if you will—to build a modest-sized complex on the south slope of Mount Taranaki as headquarters for my enterprises. We would follow your guidance in making the complex as unobtrusive as possible.

"In return for your agreement to cooperate, I will begin to channel—through you—a monthly payment for the support of your resistance movement." Nash reached into the deep pocket of his trench coat and extracted a thick envelope. Opening it, he took out a bundle of thousand-dollar bills. He fanned the bundle with his thumb. "Here is one hundred thousand in U.S. dollars. Each month, you will receive another fifty thousand dollars. In addition, I will acquire suitable weapons, communications equipment, and other matériel and provide them to your people, at my expense."

Kingi looked hungrily at the bundle of cash. It was more money than he had ever seen before in his life. His hand seemed to reach instinctively for the money, but he held it back with an effort of will.

"I don't know, Mr. Nash. Mount Taranaki is, as you say, sacred to our people. There might be some real resistance to permitting you to build a structure on the mountain."

Nash fanned the bundle of cash again and held it out toward Kingi. "I am sure you can be very persuasive, Mr. Kingi. We're talking here about the difference between a dream and reality."

Kingi took the money and slipped it into a pocket on the inside of his cape.

Nash turned and looked back toward the museum. At a signal, Ben Bernard, who had been standing some distance away, came toward them.

"Mr. Kingi, you met Ben Bernard briefly inside. He is a former U.S. Navy SEAL and a formidable warrior. He will be working directly with you to whip your people into shape. With his guidance, and with the arms I will supply, they will quickly become a force to be reckoned with."

Thinking back over the time since that first encounter, Kingi was pleased with the way things had worked out. Bernard had augmented his Maori force with a group of professional soldiers who formed a kind of shadow army, backing up his officers and noncommissioned officers. Kingi was surprised when they began showing up. They seemed to have come from all over the world: Serbs from the former Yugoslavia, Gurkhas from Nepal, a few army Green Berets and navy SEALs from the United States, and their Russian counterparts, the Spetznaz. Kingi's force was now superbly trained and equipped with a whole range of weapons, from automatic pistols and rifles to light machine guns, mortars, and rockets.

Nash's complex on Mount Taranaki had been a problem. Many of Kingi's people objected to any construction on their sacred mountain. Some of them even accused Kingi of selling out to the *paheka*. If they had known how much cash came into his hands each month, they would have been sure of it. But Kingi kept his financial relations with Nash a closely guarded secret. As construction work on the complex ended, the opposition and questioning gradually died out.

Now, Kingi thought as he looked down on the *Kitty Hawk* and the harbor full of sailboats, now is the time! The dream is about to come true!

CHAPTER 8

"NO, CINDY. I UNDERSTAND WHAT YOU ARE SAYING. BUT THE answer is still no. We will not sneak in the back door. This is the opportunity for official New Zealand to extend its hospitality, and we are going to do it their way."

Marcia Carter and Cindy Carson sat facing each other in the First Lady's stateroom on the *Kitty Hawk*, which was anchored in Port Nicholson, just off New Zealand's capital of Wellington.

"But, ma'am . . ." The Secret Service agent stopped and flashed a quick, mirthless smile. She shrugged, signaling defeat.

This was Cindy Carson's first trip as head of the Secret Service detail assigned to protect the First Lady and her son, and she had been nervous from the moment they had stepped off the plane in Perth two weeks earlier. Both the Australians and the New Zealanders had given the American visitors a heartwarming welcome, but their security arrangements were, in Carson's view, far too casual and relaxed. She had had some heated arguments with her counterparts in both countries, and they had let her know that they found the big-footed Americans just a trifle too demanding and arrogant for their taste.

Shortly after the *Kitty Hawk* had left Auckland and turned south along the Coromandel Peninsula, Carson had flown ahead to Wellington to meet with New Zealand security officials.

After a quick tour of the city with her own advance people, she had proposed that the Walkers fly by helicopter directly from the carrier deck to a landing pad near the Parliament building and then walk quickly along a secure, roped-off corridor into the building itself. That way, they would avoid direct contact with the large turnout of citizens expected to gather to see the American president's wife and son. More important, they would be isolated from a group of Maoris who planned a noisy antigovernment demonstration.

Crowds of any kind made her nervous. Crowds of angry demonstrators made her even more so.

The senior New Zealander was almost literally looking down his nose at her as he delivered his condescending response.

"I am sorry you are unhappy, but I assure you, Miss Carson, that Mrs. Walker and David will be quite safe traveling through the city in a motorcade and then entering the Parliament building the proper way—through the front door. There will be some demonstrators, but we are all Kiwis and we are a peaceable people. No one will harm your First Lady." He seemed to Cindy to stop just short of concluding, "No one will harm your First Lady, *little girl.*"

His patronizing tone angered her, and she had a hard time not showing it. When she suggested that the ride from the waterfront to the Parliament be made in a closed, bulletproof limousine, he chuckled as though she had told a joke. "Oh, that won't be necessary, not at all. Why, even our prime minister doesn't go about in an armored car."

When the helicopter deposited Cindy back aboard the *Kitty Hawk*, she was still seething. The ship was just turning into Cook Strait, which separates the north island of New Zealand from the south island. She stood on the flight deck for a long time, letting the wind buffet her as the ship maneuvered around Turakirae Head and entered the harbor.

"Aren't you cold out here, Miss Carson?" One of the pilots who had been assigned to act as her host aboard the carrier stood at her side.

"No, I'm okay. Actually, this wind feels good."

"This is a beautiful harbor—actually formed by the crater of an ancient volcano. But I think it makes Admiral Harmony nervous."

"Why's that?"

"Well, as you can see, except for this passage we're sailing through, it is almost completely surrounded by hills. That provides protection in a storm. But it is also possible to get some terrible winds coming down off these hills. In 1968, an almost-new car ferry—a big ship called the *Wahine*—was caught by one of these violent windstorms and thrown up on Barrett's Reef, which we have just passed. Then the winds drove the ship off the reef and into the middle of the harbor, where it sank with considerable loss of life. I think our skipper will rest easier when we're back out on the open ocean again."

"He's not the only one, Lieutenant. I'm not worried about winds or reefs, but I will be very happy when we've finished our little visit here."

Carson stepped through a hatchway out of the wind, pulled her parka hood down onto her shoulders, and ran her fingers through her short hair. It was time to visit Mrs. Walker and see if she could talk some sense into her.

When the captain's gig docked at Queens Wharf the next morning, Cindy Carson was the first one ashore, quickly looking around to size up the situation. At the head of a line of limousines, an open convertible waited for the Walkers. Carson could not help thinking: Dallas, November 22, 1963. At least the New Zealanders had agreed to her demand that a utility vehicle carrying Secret Service agents be inserted in the column directly behind the First Lady's car. Two of her detail were already in position at the rear fenders of the convertible.

Mrs. Walker and David took their places in the back seat of the car. Cindy slid into the left front seat, next to the driver. The New Zealanders had insisted that one of their men be at the wheel.

Attached to a strap over her shoulder, Cindy Carson carried a large handbag containing a small nine-millimeter pistol and a radio, linked to an earpiece by a cord that ran inconspicuously under her jacket.

The motorcade moved slowly along Customhouse Quay and then up to Lambton Quay, curving through the business district toward the Parliament buildings at the northern end of the city. Carson relaxed a little. The crowds were large and loud, but orderly. Many of the people along the way waved American flags while, overhead, the street was decorated with crossed American and New Zealand flags.

As the convertible stopped in front of the Parliament building, Cindy stepped out quickly to place herself between the Walkers and a group of chanting Maoris. Although they were restrained by a band of yellow tape, they were far too close for her comfort.

The governor general and the prime minister strode quickly down a long red carpet to greet the American visitors.

The prime minister, wearing small, crossed American and New Zealand flags on her left lapel, reached out with both hands to grasp the hands of the visitors.

"Oh, Mrs. Walker and David, we are so honored to have you come visit us here in Wellington." She stepped between the two and took each by an arm. The governor general stood awkwardly, a little to one side. "Come, let me show you our new-old Parliament building."

She guided them up the red carpet toward the entrance to the stately brownstone building that looked as though it might have been transported magically from a historic corner in London.

"You are fortunate to come at this time. We have just completely remodeled this building, which was built in 1911. We have used the most modern building techniques to make it virtually earthquake-proof. While the construction was under way, our Parliament met in that building over there—we call it the beehive building, and you can see why.

"I'm glad you've allowed time for a brief tour of Wellington. We're very proud of our city—even though, like Chicago, it can sometimes be a bit windy. People in Wellington like to think of their city as New Zealand's San Francisco, while they think of Auckland, which is bigger and perhaps a little less charming, as our version of Los Angeles.''

Carson, only half-listening as the prime minister chattered on, thought, ''So far, so good,'' as the little procession entered the building. She looked back over her shoulder at the Maoris. They were chanting loudly, and some of them were waving what looked like Stone Age weapons, but they still remained obediently behind the yellow tape.

Inside the Parliament chamber, members of the Labour Party sat on one side, members of the National Party on the other. Between each two members was a telephone. Many members sat on sheepskin seat-covers, a tribute to the extent to which the nation's economy relied on the export of wool and lamb. On both sides, members were chatting quietly among themselves; the day's ceremony had imposed an unusual degree of decorum on the normally raucous house. In the front row sat members of the diplomatic community.

As they moved into the chamber, the prime minister stepped briefly to one side to slip a white wig over her head and don a black robe. Other members of the leadership were already wearing their wigs.

The prime minister moved to the dais.

''It is a great pleasure for me to be able to welcome to New Zealand, and to Wellington, Mrs. Walker and David. We are deeply honored to have them visit us up here, so far from their homes down there.'' Her remark was greeted by a ripple of appreciative laughter, reflecting the way many New Zealanders and Australians had begun to cast off the Down Under terminology, hang their maps with the South Pole at the top, and think of the rest of the world as Down There.

''I have looked forward to this opportunity to visit with Mrs. Walker. I have long admired her from afar, aware of the pioneering way in which she has managed to combine her very successful career as the head of her own executive personnel business with her very demanding role as wife of the president and as First Lady of the United States—to say nothing of her role as mother to her fine young son, David.'' She smiled down at the boy sitting quietly beside his mother. ''And now, without further ado, I give you Marcia Carter Walker.''

Marcia Walker moved to the dais, and Cindy Carson took up a position against the wall where she could observe the entire chamber.

''Thank you, Madam Prime Minister,'' the First Lady said. ''Distinguished members of the government. Representatives of the diplomatic corps. Members of Parliament.'' She paused and looked quietly around the room, reaching up to touch her hair. ''You'll have to excuse me. I forgot and left my wig at home.''

The room erupted with laughter. When it subsided, Mrs. Walker glanced down at her prepared speech and then pushed it to one side. ''My speechwriters prepared some words for me,'' she said, ''but why don't we just talk as friends? I know that relations between our two countries have not always been entirely harmonious. We are friends, but we have also agreed sometimes to disagree. Now, I hope my visit will mark a new era in an even deeper degree of friendship and understanding between our two countries—two countries that, while separated by the vastness of the Pacific Ocean, still have much in common, especially our commitment to representative democracy and to the rule of law.''

She paused and looked toward the door, puzzled by a sharp, staccato sound. Suddenly, the door burst open, and three men holding small machine guns dashed into the chamber. One of the men wore Maori attire. The other two were clad in black jumpsuits.

The heads of everyone in the room swiveled, as one, toward the intruders. For a moment, they all sat, stunned. Then a wild scramble ensued. A woman screamed. Men shouted and swore. Many members of the audience slid down under their seats and huddled on the floor. Others tried to run toward the exits at the side and front of the chamber, stumbling over those crouched on the floor.

The din from the shouting and the clatter of those fighting their way toward the doors was punctuated by the sound of shots.

A security man at the main entrance was the first to die, shot through the head. Three other members of the security force, including two American Secret Service agents, drew their weapons, but all three were cut down as the gunmen moved down the center aisle. More armed men poured through the door.

One Secret Service agent, who was seated directly behind David, rushed forward to position his body between the boy and the intruders. He, too, was shot.

For a moment, Mrs. Walker stood at the podium as though hypnotized, and then she dropped to a crouch and slipped down off the stage trying to reach her son, who was now huddled by his front-row seat with his hands over his ears.

In her position at the side of the hall, Cindy Carson was hidden momentarily from the view of the gunmen. Her first reaction was to pull her own weapon and try to protect Mrs. Walker. But, she thought quickly, if these men intended to kill the First Lady and David, they would have done so already. This was a kidnapping.

Using the line of ambassadors as a shield, she moved toward the center of the room, toward Marcia Walker and David. As she did so, she pulled her radio from her handbag, slipped the earpiece out of her ear, and dropped them both under a seat. She removed the little lapel pin that marked her as a Secret Service agent and slipped the pistol from her purse down her skirt and under her panty hose.

While the first gunmen continued working their way down the center aisle, others spraying random fire in the air to keep fear levels high, dashed along the side aisles, roughly pushing through those scrambling for the exits. One of the gunmen gestured to the prime minister, the governor general, and the other dignitaries to move over against the wall.

"Everyone, freeze!" The voice of a man who had just entered the room rose above the pandemonium. Those scrambling for the exits suddenly stopped and turned toward the voice. An eerie silence filled the chamber, broken only by the gunmen giving terse commands as they established full control over the room. Marcia Walker and Cindy Carson, however, kept moving, until they reached David at the same moment. Cindy shoved the two Walkers to the floor and fell on top of them, shielding them with her body.

Out of the corner of her eye, Cindy saw the gunman clad in Maori garb standing at the lectern where Mrs. Walker had been speaking a few moments before. His machine gun hung from his shoulder by a strap. In his right hand, he held the gold-colored mace that normally stood in the well of the chamber as a symbol of authority.

As he prepared to speak, four gunmen moved up beside the Walkers, pulled them to their feet, and pushed them up the aisle toward the entrance.

Cindy Carson found herself hustled along with them, almost running toward the door. There she heard the Maori begin as she was shoved out: "I am Wiremu Kingi. Today, more than a century and a half of injustice comes to an end. . . ."

Outside the building, they almost tripped over the body of a New Zealand plainclothesman, his blood forming a large puddle on the red carpet where the visitors had walked a few minutes earlier. Cindy Carson swept the area with her eyes, looking for any sign that members of the security force were offering resistance. What she saw made her heart fall. A few yards away, the Secret Service van stood abandoned, its sides riddled with bullet holes. Two of the agents under her command lay dead beside it.

A group of armed men formed a secure perimeter around a helicopter; its blades were already turning. Carson looked them over with a professional eye. These weren't amateurs. Some of those whose faces she could see obviously weren't Maoris.

A tall, broad-shouldered man—the same one who had taken command with his shout of "Freeze!"—stepped forward to take Mrs. Walker's arm and hurry her toward the helicopter. He pushed her up the steps and then turned to lift David bodily into the craft. He turned, fixed Cindy Carson with a glare, and grabbed her arm.

"You, too. Get in!"

The Secret Service agent strapped herself in. Mrs. Walker was already seated with a protective arm around her son. Cindy reached over and took Mrs. Walker's hand, giving it a reassuring squeeze. As the helicopter rose above the Parliament building, she checked the time. It was 10:47 A.M. Looking out the window, she gauged by the shadows on the ground that they were flying roughly to the north.

Traveling a bare fifty feet above the ground, the chopper skimmed up over the brow of the hills rising behind the Parliament and then quickly passed above the shoreline and continued out over the sea.

Aboard the *Kitty Hawk*, Adm. Harmony had welcomed the respite provided by the Walkers' visit to Wellington. A senior officer, along as an aide to the First Lady, had accompanied her into the city, leaving Harmony free to catch up on the never-ending pile of paperwork that came with his job.

He had given up his large cabin suite to Mrs. Walker and her son and sat hunched over a desk in a small cabin down the corridor.

"Harmony here." He answered the phone before it had completed the first ring. He sensed the tension in the young officer's voice as soon as he began to speak.

"Sir, the local radio is reporting that Mrs. Walker and her son have been kidnapped."

"Kidnapped?" Harmony couldn't believe what he had heard. "I'll be there in a minute." He bolted out the door and ran to the combat control center, the ship's brain. He was breathing hard when he entered the room, dimly lit by the glow of red lights.

"What's going on?"

"Sir, we don't have all the facts yet. The local radio had a man at the Parliament. He reports that a group of Maori demonstrators broke into the building during Mrs. Walker's speech. They took her and David away in a helicopter."

"Do we have any people on the scene?"

"We are supposed to be in constant contact with the Secret Service detail, but we have been unable to raise them."

Turning to another officer, Harmony asked, "Do we have anything that can follow that chopper?"

The officer shook his head. "Not really, sir. None of our birds is on alert because we are in harbor. I've ordered one of our helos to go after them, but it will take a good twenty minutes before they're airborne. That's a long lead time."

A yeoman approached and stood silently until Harmony looked in his direction.

"Sir, we're getting a little more from the local television. They have just played a tape of a man who says he is a Maori king, claiming they have taken over the government in a coup. He apparently grabbed the microphone in the chamber after Mrs. Walker was seized."

"Do we know anything about these people?" Harmony turned to his intelligence officer.

"No, sir. We knew there was going to be a demonstration, but there was no indication from our New Zealand contacts that any trouble was expected—certainly nothing like this."

"Then we don't know how big a thing this is. We don't really know what the hell is going on."

"That's right, sir. We're in the dark. . . ."

"I don't like this." Harmony began issuing orders to get the big ship under way and out to the open ocean. "If this is anything more than a half-assed little coup attempt, there could be people with rockets up in these hills around here. If there are, we're a sitting duck."

A slight vibration found its way through the metal of the deck and up through the soles of the shoes of those in the combat control center as the engines, far down below, built up steam and the ship began to move.

Harmony stood in the center of the room, scratching his head and staring unseeing at a control panel as he pondered what to do next. His training had prepared him to deal with almost anything, from a collision at sea to nuclear war. But no one had taught him what to do if the president's wife and son were stolen away and he had no way to go after them.

After a few moments, he reached a decision: "Patch me through to Admiral McKay."

Thirty seconds later, a yeoman handed him a phone. "Sir, I have a duty officer at the Pentagon on the line." Harmony glanced at his watch. It was going on midnight in Washington.

"Sir, the admiral was just about to leave home to come down here. I'm trying to catch him."

Moments later, Harmony heard the gruff voice of the chairman of the Joint Chiefs of Staff on the phone.

"What the hell is going on out there, Jerry?"

"Mrs. Walker and David have been kidnapped."

"Yes, yes, I know that. They've just read me a wire service story out of Wellington, and CNN is beginning to come up with some details. But what do you know?"

"I'm afraid we know very little, sir. We have been unable to raise the Secret Service detail ashore. What little information we have has come from watching the local TV station, which had a team at the Parliament. I'm getting my ship out of the harbor. Someone up in these hills could do us a lot of harm in a hurry. And, at this point, we don't know who's in charge ashore."

There was a pause on the line, longer than the normal delay as one end of a conversation flashes up to a satellite, 23,000 miles out in space, and back down again. Finally, McKay spoke resignedly. "I guess that's the best you can do. Things are bad enough without getting your ship shot up. I'm going down to the Pentagon now, right after I talk to the president. We'll be in touch."

CHAPTER 9

ADM. MCKAY KNEW THAT MEN AGED IN THE PRESIDENCY, BUT he was startled to see how much Maynard Walker seemed to have aged just in the last twenty-four hours since the kidnapping of his wife and son. Perhaps part of it was McKay's imagination, but the president's hair seemed a little grayer, the lines in his face a little deeper, his brow a little more furrowed. The pronounced pouches under his eyes bore witness to a sleepless night.

At the door to the Oval Office, the president greeted McKay with a handshake and led him to a seat facing his desk. Then Walker stepped around the desk and took his own high-backed executive chair.

"Any word at all, Mac?"

"No, I'm afraid not, Mr. President. The perpetrators, whoever they are, have imposed a fairly effective blackout on communications between New Zealand and the rest of the world. Some little information is getting through from folks with satellite communications capability and amateur radio operators, but it doesn't help us much."

The president swiveled around so he could look out over the Rose Garden. He spoke without turning his head. His voice sounded weary. "Why don't you just run through what we know? Let's see if anything makes sense."

"Well, as you know, sir, Mrs. Walker had just begun her speech to the New Zealand Parliament in Wellington when a

78

group of heavily armed men entered the chamber and took her and David captive. We have not been able to account for all the members of Mrs. Walker's Secret Service detail, but we fear that all of them, along with a number of New Zealand security personnel, were killed in the takeover.

"The helicopter in which they were taken away was seen to fly off in a northerly direction. But, by the time we were able to get some aircraft airborne from the *Kitty Hawk*, the helicopter had already disappeared. We can only surmise that they were taken to, and are being held at, some point to the north of Wellington."

The president swiveled back to face McKay. "What do we know about these Maoris?"

"Very little, sir. We have intercepted a broadcast in which a man who calls himself Wiremu Kingi has declared himself the new ruler of New Zealand—or, as he calls it, Aotearoa, which, I am told, means 'the land of the long white cloud' in Maori. He claims to be descended from a Maori leader who was responsible for last-ditch resistance to the white settlers in the latter half of the last century.

"Unfortunately, New Zealand has never been a high priority for our intelligence agencies. We have tended to rely on the New Zealanders and Australians for intel in that part of the world. We knew that there was some unhappiness among the Maori minority, but there was no hint of this kind of violent action."

The president toyed with a silver letter opener.

"How thorough is their takeover?"

"We are trying to find out. We are having difficulty contacting any New Zealand military installations. We suspect that the rebels have taken control of those facilities, along with the telephone and broadcast systems—at least on North Island. We have made contact with New Zealand military units in Christchurch and Dunedin, on South Island, but they are as much in the dark about what is going on on North Island as we are."

"This seems to be a remarkably well-organized coup, doesn't it, Mac? I mean, how could a bunch of Maoris put together the arms and the leadership and the planning for an operation like this? And do it without a lot of people knowing about it and doing something to prevent it. I wouldn't be surprised if there's a lot more here than a spontaneous native uprising.''

''That's what we're thinking, too, sir. The New Zealanders have small military and police forces, but it would obviously require a pretty sophisticated operation to take over the entire island so quickly and, apparently, successfully. But who or what is behind it, we simply don't know.''

''My guess, Mac, is that we will soon know. Whoever took Marcie and David did so for a purpose. I suspect we will be hearing from them with a list of demands very soon.''

McKay nodded affirmatively. ''I'm sure you're right, sir. I'm a little surprised we haven't heard something already. But they are probably waiting until they have consolidated their position.''

''This whole thing seems crazy to me,'' the president responded. ''What could they possibly want, that they would go to these extremes? And, even more perplexing, who could be behind such a thing?''

''There's one mystery here, sir. Before communications were cut off, a television crew on the scene photographed a young woman entering the helicopter. The TV image was taped aboard the *Kitty Hawk*, and we now have a copy of the tape. The photographer was apparently jostled as he took it, so the image is not very good. So far, we haven't identified the woman.''

The president rose and walked around to lean against the desk, his arms folded across his chest. ''What's our course of action now, Mac?''

''Our first priority, of course, is to gather intelligence. But New Zealand is far from the areas on which we normally focus our intelligence, resources. We are reprogramming several satellites to gather communications intelligence, and we hope to get some images from a photographic satellite. We will also begin sending U-2 planes over to photograph the area north of Wellington. But it will be some time—perhaps even several days—before we begin getting anything useful from these sources. Meanwhile, we'll wait for word from the kidnappers.''

"What about a rescue attempt? I don't want to get Marcie and David hurt.''

"I understand, sir. My recommendation is that we prepare for a commando raid once we know where they are being held. I have already alerted the Eagle Force to begin preliminary training for such an effort, but we have one problem, sir.''

"What's the problem?''

"General Torkelson, the chief of staff of the air force, doesn't have much patience with any kind of special forces. He wants to use all his resources to build up his fighters and bombers. He has issued orders reassigning the air force members of the Eagle Force. In fact, they're due to leave in a few days. Without them, we're left with a group of SEALs without the means of getting to where they're needed.''

"That does sound like a problem.''

"More than a problem, sir. If those men are pulled out, the unit will cease to exist as an effective military unit. And I don't need to tell you how valuable such a specialized unit can be when you really need it. I've been talking to some folks on the Hill and thought I'd be able to handle it, but we're out of time.''

"What do you want me to do?''

"Sir, I'd like you to issue a secret presidential order that will prevent the transfer of the air force personnel and keep the unit intact.'' McKay reached into his briefcase and pulled out a piece of paper. "I had such an order drafted and brought it along for your signature, just in case you agreed with my suggestion.''

The president grinned. "Just in case, Mac?''

"Never hurts to be prepared, sir.''

The president laid the paper on the edge of his desk, scribbled his signature, and handed it back. "Make sure my people have a copy.''

"I've got one right here, sir,'' McKay said, pulling another sheet of paper from his briefcase.

The lights illuminating the wall-sized map of the Pacific flickered over the gray head of Adm. Bull Bridges as he paced back and forth before the map.

"It's got to be the Chinese—goddamn Chicoms." Bridges still clung to the old military acronym for the Chinese Communists, which had long gone out of favor in more politically correct circles.

On a large television screen occupying much of another wall, the image of the kidnapping was playing one more time. Bridges and his key aides had spent more than an hour watching the scene over and over, trying to extract from it every bit of intelligence they could, even a hint of who was behind the kidnapping and what they might expect next.

Tiny ship symbols indicated the positions of American and Chinese naval vessels on the map. A cluster of red symbols indicated the Chinese ships still conducting their maneuvers in the South China Sea. A line of black symbols to the east indicated the positions of the U.S. Navy ships observing the maneuvers.

The American force was considerably weaker than it had been two weeks earlier when the *Kitty Hawk* and two escort vessels were sent, on orders from Washington, to pick up the First Lady and carry her from Australia to New Zealand and then from Auckland to Wellington. Bridges had grumbled about the orders—"Goddamn chauffeur service"—but had obeyed them. Now he wished he had the carrier back up where the Chinese force was concentrated.

"Sir, we show several of the Chinese vessels moving to the south and east." Lt. Victoria Schroeder, Bridges' intelligence briefer, pointed to an area of the ocean between the Philippines and Borneo. "They are still quite some distance from New Zealand, but they are moving in that general direction."

Bridges studied the map. He couldn't look at that part of the world without a fleeting sense of regret that he had been born too late to take part in some of the epic sea battles of World War II. The geographical place names automatically took on the names of battles in his mind: the Battle of the Coral Sea, the Battle of the Java Sea, Guadalcanal, the Solomon Islands.

The admiral stood, hands on his hips, staring at the map. "What the hell are they up to?" He paused and then continued, thinking out loud rather than addressing the aides who stood clustered behind him. "Could this be a Chinese operation? While we're worrying about the Spratly Islands and Taiwan, the Chinese take over New Zealand? No way! But still . . ."

He turned to the group of aides, his mind made up. "Okay. If that's their game, we can play, too. I want everything we've got down there. Alert the marines on Okinawa. Tell them they may get a little on-the-job training on amphib operations. What have we got in the way of air?"

"Sir, the *Kitty Hawk* and her escorts are standing off Hawke Bay, on the east side of North Island," his operations officer reported. "That will give us a total of around seventy-five aircraft to support whatever action becomes necessary. I don't think we should count on Vietnamese cooperation in permitting the air force planes based at Noi Bai to carry out attacks on the Chinese vessels if it comes to that. So it will be up to the *Kitty Hawk* to carry the load."

"Yes, you're right," Bridges interjected. "It's always up to the carriers when the tough jobs have to be done."

"Here, let me try, Pat." Jeff Bonior grasped the knob on the door of the old World War II barracks, braced one foot against the jamb, and pulled. Nothing happened for a moment, and then the door suddenly gave way and came off its hinges, sending Bonior stumbling backward.

Chuck Nelson and Pat Collins, the team's intelligence officer, jumped to one side and stood there laughing.

"Good work, Jeff." Collins leaned over to help him to his feet. "We don't really need doors here in Hawaii."

The three of them stepped cautiously through the gaping doorway, brushing away the cobwebs that seemed to fill the cavernous lower bay of the two-story barracks.

"This is like stepping through a time warp," Nelson said. "It's going to be a job for us to get rid of fifty years of dust and cobwebs."

Bonior strode the length of the building, leaving a little cloud of dust behind him. "Is this the same place where the UDT guys trained in World War II?"

"No, I don't think so. We're on the Big Island—Hawaii. As I recall, they did some of their early training on Oahu, but most of their training took place on Maui."

"We're probably better off than those guys," Bonior said. "I bet they lived in tents when they first set up shop in the islands."

"What do you think, Pat?" Nelson turned to her.

"Oh, we can make it liveable. It looks like we're going to have to patch some of these floors so people won't fall through, and I'll bet the plumbing really needs some work. But I've seen worse."

Bonior wiped the dirt from one window with the side of his hand and peered out at the breakers hitting the rocky shore. "At least we've got a lot of ocean to train in. Actually, when we get these barracks fixed up, they'll probably be better than those tar-paper shacks we camped in at San Clemente."

During their training, Bonior and Nelson and other would-be SEALs had spent four weeks at a primitive camp on San Clemente Island, sixty miles off the Southern California coast, firing their weapons, swimming long distances in the open ocean, and practicing nighttime patrols through the brush-covered hillsides.

"Okay, Jeff, first thing, I want you to work out a training syllabus. We're not going to have any outside support, so the guys are going to have to spend part of each day getting this place fixed up. But I still want plenty of training. Let's figure we've got two weeks. We'll start with sharpening up our close-combat skills. Let's do some mountain work. And I'll arrange some time with a submarine. It's deep right offshore here, so we can do that without leaving home. Then, as soon as we know more about where we're going and what we're going to do, we'll focus on specifics.

"Pat, we'll set up your intel shop as soon as we can. I want you to be our outside contact. We've got electricity. Let's get phones in here as fast as we can. Jeff will tell you what construction materials we need—not a lot of fancy stuff, just the essentials—and you order it. Rent us several pickup trucks and half a dozen ATVs."

"Aye, aye, sir." Collins, a grin on her face, gave him a snappy salute—with her left hand.

Brushing dust and cobwebs from their clothes, they stepped outside and stood looking over the small compound.

"Jeff, looks to me like there's room enough over there for a helipad. We won't even have to cut any of those palm trees."

"Yeah, there's plenty of room there, boss. If Pat can get us a dozer in here for a few hours, we can smooth it off and get it in good shape."

Nelson looked at his watch. "We're going to have to work fast. The guys will be arriving at oh-nine-hundred tomorrow. Pat, we'll have to have the vehicles to pick them up by then. And then, Jeff, we'll put them right to work here so that by tomorrow night they'll have a place to sleep. Okay, let's get back into town. I've got some phone calls to make, and you two have a lot of work to do."

As soon as they arrived back at their hotel in Hilo, Nelson placed a call to Adm. McKay. He knew it was late in Washington and he hoped he didn't have to wake the admiral, but things were moving too fast to wait. An aide at the Pentagon patched him through to McKay's home.

"Getting set up out there, Chuck?"

"Yes, sir. We've taken over an old military station, and we'll have it in decent shape in a day or two. But I need your help, sir."

"Name it."

"I think our best bet for an undetected arrival in New Zealand will be to come ashore from a submarine. We're going to have to do some training with a sub. The *Kamehameha* is based at Pearl, and it has a dry deck shelter. Can you set it up for them to drop whatever they're doing and spend some time with us?''

''Yeah, we can do that, Chuck, but it's going to be a little delicate. He's trying to be quiet about it, but I think Bull Bridges is getting ready to invade New Zealand. It's his chance to fight World War II. I want to keep your operation very hush-hush. If Bull gets word that we're thinking of a small-scale commando operation, he'll try to put the kibosh on it.

''So this is what I'll do. I've still got a lot of friends in the submarine community. I'll go back-channel through the Pacific Fleet and get them to cut orders for the *Kamehameha*. Bull doesn't need to know anything about it.''

Nelson couldn't suppress a chuckle. ''Sounds pretty devious, sir.''

''Keep your eyes and ears open, son, and you'll learn how the navy really works. I swear, during the war in 'Nam, everybody was using back channels. It got so bad that the navy even had a spy in the White House to keep track of what was really going on.''

When he had hung up, Nelson sat with his hand on the phone, thinking. Finally, he picked up the receiver and dialed the number of Pat Collins's room. The number was busy. He walked to the balcony and looked out over the hotel grounds sloping down toward the beach before he returned to redial the number. This time it rang.

''Hi. How's it coming along?''

''I think we're in pretty good shape, Chuck. I've got the vehicles lined up, and I've arranged with a hardware-lumberyard to give us expedited deliveries on our orders. Now it's mostly a matter of waiting until the guys come in tomorrow.''

''I was thinking, Pat. Why don't we have a swim and then order up something for dinner in the room? We're not going to have much time together from now on.''

''Sounds good, Chuck. Just give me about half an hour. I want to get some stuff into my computer. I'll meet you down at the beach at—let's see—about five o'clock."

"See you then."

Nelson slipped into his trunks, threw one of the hotel's thick, man-sized white towels over his shoulder, and headed down to the beach. He knew the hotel preferred to pass out towels in the swimming area, but what the hell. . . .

He dropped the towel on the sand, tucked his room key under it, along with his flip-flops, and then entered the water, stroking strongly through the huge breakers. Sometimes he felt like a true amphibian. While most humans have at least a tiny, residual fear of the water, SEALs are trained to think of the water as their best friend. When you are surrounded and all hope is lost, they are taught, head for the water. Most pursuers will wade out waist-deep, fire a few ineffective shots, and then give up.

The tensions of the last few days—first the worry that the team was about to be disbanded and then preparations for their part in the attempt to rescue the First Lady and her son—seemed to wash away in the salty water. He rolled over on his back and floated lazily, watching the white cumulus clouds floating across the azure sky.

"Can a lady use part of your ocean, sir?"

He rolled over and saw Pat at his side, doing a lazy sides-troke. He touched her arm, and for a while they swam silently together, rising and falling on the rollers out beyond the breakers.

Later, in the hotel, as they got off the elevator at their floor, she brushed the damp hair back from her forehead and looked up at him with a smile on her face. "Your place or mine?"

He smiled back. "How about mine?"

He pulled her into his room and took her in his arms, feeling her body close against his as they kissed deeply.

He took her head in both hands and looked into her eyes.

"I love you very much, Mrs. Collins."

Her hands were around his waist, and she pulled him closer against her. "I love you, too, Chuck. I love you very much."

He ruffled her hair with his hands. "You've got salt and sand in your hair. I think you need a shower."

Their towels dropped to the floor as they walked, each with an arm around the waist of the other, toward the bathroom with its large, tiled shower.

Nelson reached in, adjusted the water, and then stepped into the enclosure, drawing her to him under the strong spray from the showerhead. He brought his hands up behind her back and under the straps of her maillot, slipping them off her shoulders. As the suit fell down around her waist, he cupped her breasts in his hands and leaned down to kiss one nipple and then the other.

She found the drawstring on his trunks and pulled it. The wet knot resisted and then pulled free. She ran her hands down along his flanks, sliding the suit downward.

Then she turned her back to him, resting her head against his shoulder.

Slowly, he worked her suit down over her hips and let it fall to the floor. She kicked both suits aside so they wouldn't stop up the drain. She could feel his hands touching her breasts, his fingers playing with her nipples. Then he was running his hands down over her abdomen and feeling through the soft hair between her legs. She arched her back and leaned into him, feeling him strong and erect. She reached back and caressed his thighs, reaching down to feel him with her fingers.

"Chuck?"

"Mm-hmm?"

"How are we going to do this?"

"I think we're doing just fine. Are you ready?"

"I think so. Just about."

"Just lean forward and put your hands on the wall. Spread your legs a little more."

He seemed to come up from somewhere down below, and then he was deep inside of her. At the same time, his fingers were busy doing something very exciting just above where he had entered her.

They both gasped for breath as the shock waves of their lovemaking swept over them.

Slowly, their heartbeats returned somewhere close to normal. She turned and they kissed. Then she reached for a bar of soap and began to rub it over Nelson's body.

He took one of the small containers of shampoo provided by the hotel, poured it over her head, and worked his fingers through her hair, raising a thick lather. Then he helped her rinse it out.

She stepped out of the shower and slipped into a thick terry-cloth robe. He followed her, pulling on his robe.

He led her to the bed and pulled back the covers, then slipped the robe off her shoulders and pushed her gently down onto the crisp white sheet. He stood beside the bed for a moment, looking down at her, letting his eyes feast on her nakedness. The last rays of the setting sun shone on the bed, imparting a radiant glow to her entire flesh.

"You are one very beautiful, very sexy woman."

He let his robe slip from his shoulders. An involuntary shiver ran through her as she looked down his body and let her gaze rest purposely on the visible indication of his excitement.

She raised her arms to him. "Come here, you lover."

Soon the waves of excitement swept over them once more.

"Was it even better than before?" she asked.

He was still panting, leaning over her on his elbows. "Maybe it keeps getting better and better until you just die."

"Chuck? Are we going to keep on this way?"

"No, darling, I think we're going to have to start using the 'M' word."

"Dial 'M' for 'married'?"

"Yes, I think we should. How about right after this op?"

A shadow passed over her face, and she bit her lower lip.

"That scares me, Chuck. After this, it'll be another op and then another. I don't think I could stand it if they told me you weren't coming back." She ran a finger down the scar line where a bullet had torn into his shoulder on an operation in northern Iraq the previous year—a bullet that had almost cost him his life.

He held her close and stroked her hair, still damp from the shower. "I know, I know. I can't kid you. You know what my business is like better than any SEAL wife. It's not just the ops. Every day I go to work is dangerous. But this won't last. In a few years, they'll put me behind a desk, and you'll be complaining about how dull life has become.''

She laughed. ''And I'll still love you when you're like those old SEALs with their beer bellies and their receding hairlines and their dull desk jobs. I guess I'm just being crazy. I'm afraid to marry you because I'm afraid I might lose you. But if I *don't* marry you, I'll lose you. I'm just all mixed up, Chuck.''

When she woke, the sun had set and a golden moon was rising over the water. Chuck, clad in a robe, stood at the window, staring out at the sea. She slipped out of bed, drew a robe over her shoulders, and joined him at the window.

''Worried?''

He turned and put an arm around her waist.

''Mm-hmm. Can't help it. I just keep thinking of all the things that can go wrong on this op.''

CHAPTER 10

THE TALL MAN WHO SEEMED TO BE IN CHARGE AND THE TWO other guards all twisted in their seats to watch the ground as the aircraft descended toward a landing pad marked by a large white *X*.

Cindy Carson checked the time. It was 11:57 A.M.

Four armed men dressed in black jumpsuits were waiting as the helicopter settled to the ground. Four other armed men stood off to the side. As Mrs. Walker, David, and Cindy stepped down, the waiting men moved forward to take each by an arm. They were hustled from the helipad through one building, across a courtyard, and into another two-story building.

Mrs. Walker stopped and turned to take her son's hand. The men holding them by the arms allowed this after a pause and a guarded look, then pushed them forward roughly down a long, brightly lighted corridor.

The tall man had gone ahead. He stopped and opened a door, guiding the two women and the boy into the room.

The tall man stood with his back to the door and indicated with a gesture that the three guards who had accompanied them were dismissed. As they left the room, he spoke, directing his remarks to the First Lady:

"Mrs. Walker, my name is Ben Bernard. You are an intelligent woman. I think you can understand that you are completely in my control. You will do exactly as I tell you. If you cooperate, you will not be harmed.''

Marcia Walker looked him up and down and then fixed him with a glare. ''I don't know what is going on here, Mr. . . . Bernard, is it? But I assure you that you are making a terrible, terrible mistake.''

Bernard returned her glare. ''No, Mrs. Walker, we have not made a mistake. We know precisely what we are doing, and you and your son—and Miss Carson—are going to play your part. Willingly—or unwillingly—you are going to do exactly as we tell you.'' He paused, letting his words sink in. ''Now, there are beds for you here. You will find toothbrushes, toothpaste, shampoo, towels—a regular little Comfort Inn. You will be provided with changes of clothes.''

Bernard looked from one to the other, then turned abruptly and left the room. They heard him speak briefly to a guard posted outside the door as a key was turned in the lock.

The three of them looked around the room. It was a square, windowless room about fifteen feet on a side. Against one wall there were three beds: a cot and a double-deck bunk bed.

David sat on the lower deck, grabbed the railing of the upper deck, and swung himself up onto the upper deck. Lying on his belly and looking down at the two adults, he announced, ''I get the upper bunk.''

His mother laughed. ''I'm sure you're very welcome to the upper bunk, David. That's all right with you, isn't it, Cindy?''

''Oh, yes, Mrs. Walker, quite all right.'' She smiled at David, who had vaulted down and opened a door at the rear of the room.

''At least we've got a bathroom,'' he said. He opened a neighboring door. ''And a big closet. We can keep all our stuff in here.''

In the center of the room was a rectangular metal table with a vinyl top. David and Cindy took seats on each side of the table. Mrs. Walker sat at the head. Someone who didn't know the circumstances might have thought she was presiding at a meeting of the board of directors of her firm.

Before the First Lady could speak, Cindy Carson suddenly held a finger to her lips, then whispered into the First Lady's, then David's ear: "The room is probably bugged. We can talk, but be careful!"

The mother and son nodded.

The First Lady looked around, wondering where a bug might be hidden. She spoke haltingly at first. "Well, let's take stock. Can we figure out where we are? Or why we've been kidnapped?"

"I have a very rough idea of where we are, Mrs. Walker." Cindy Carson made some quick calculations on a pad of paper that was lying on the table. "We were airborne for about an hour and ten minutes. I tried to see the pilot's control panel. As near as I could tell, we were flying at an indicated airspeed of about 100 to 110 knots on a heading of about 345 to 355 degrees—just a little bit west of north. A nautical mile is a little longer than a statute mile. So let's say we're something like 120 to 140 miles north of Wellington.

"In the last fifteen minutes or so, we seemed to be climbing. As we got out of the helicopter, I got a quick look at the instrument panel. The altimeter registered about fifteen hundred feet, so we're probably on the southern side of a mountain near the west coast of North Island."

"That's very good, Cindy. Are you a pilot?"

"Yes, for a couple of years now."

While the adults talked, David had taken a sheet of paper and begun to draw.

"Mom?"

"Yes, what it is it, dear?"

"I know where we are."

The two women leaned over to look at the rough map the boy had drawn.

"Remember, you made me learn all about the Aussies and the Kiwis before our trip? Well, look. This is North Island. Here's Auckland, where we were the other day, up here. And here's Wellington, down here. There's a big bulge over here on the west. See? And there's a big volcano right in the middle of that bulge. I'll bet that's where we are."

Cindy nodded thoughtfully and then looked up. "I'll bet he's right. That fits right in with what I figured out about our flight. Do you remember the name of the mountain, David?"

"Mount Egmont."

"Very good, David." His mother patted his hand. "It really helps to know where we are."

She took her hand off her son's and suddenly reverted to her chairman-of-the-board mode. "That's one bit of the puzzle. Next question: Why are we here?"

There was silence around the table. She glanced from her son to Cindy with a questioning look. "Any thoughts?"

"Well, Mrs. Walker, it seems clear that we are being held as hostages in some kind of very high-stakes game. Someone must want something very badly to take the risk of kidnapping the wife and son of the president of the United States. My guess is that they will soon communicate their demands to your husband—if they haven't done so already."

"One thing I don't understand is why I was not killed. The man who brought us here knew my name, and there are beds for three people, so it's not just an accident that I am here."

"Hopefully they'll let us in on the answer to that question when we find out why David and I are here. For the moment, though, do you think we're in danger?"

Cindy tilted her head slightly to indicate David and then caught Mrs. Walker's eye. "Oh, no. I don't think they—whoever they are—intend to harm us. I think we are quite safe. We are just being held as hostages."

Marcia Walker nodded her understanding and again put her hand over her son's where it lay on the table.

The rattle of a key in the door broke up the conference. The door swung open, and a young woman dressed in a black skirt and freshly starched white shirt entered carrying a tray of sandwiches, potato salad, and soft drinks. She set the tray on the table and left, having said nothing.

"Do you think it's safe to eat, Cindy?" the First Lady asked.

"Probably, but there's only one way to be sure." Cindy took a bite of sandwich and a scoop of potato salad, washing each down with a gulp of soda. The First Lady and David stared at her, clearly anxious, as she casually chewed. "Now we wait," Cindy said.

A moment later, feeling no ill effects, Cindy picked up her sandwich again and proclaimed, "I think we can dig in."

They were just finishing their lunch when the young woman returned carrying an armful of clean clothes.

After she left again, still offering no word or even a nod, Marcia Walker sorted through the clothes. Picking out a pair of lightweight wool slacks, she checked the size in the waistband and then held them up to her waist. "These are exactly my size. Somehow, I don't think this was just a spur-of-the-moment enterprise."

She handed David a shirt, a pair of slacks, and a sweater and looked through the rest of the clothes. "It looks as though they knew you were coming, too, David. And you, too, Cindy. I think this blouse and these slacks might fit you. Why don't you go ahead and get changed?"

Cindy Carson stepped into the bathroom, unsnapped her skirt, and pulled her blouse over her head. Then she reached down into her panty hose and retrieved the small plastic Glock nine-millimeter pistol she had hidden during the initial confusion in the Parliament building. She lifted the lid off the toilet tank. The water came to within about four inches of the top.

She slipped the clean blouse the maid had brought off its hanger and then twisted the hanger back and forth in her hands until it broke. She then broke it in another place so that she had a straight six-inch piece of wire. Bending a hook into each end of the wire, she slipped one hook through the trigger guard of the pistol and hung the other hook over the back lip of the toilet tank. Then she dropped the bent remains of the hanger into the bottom of the tank and slid the lid back into place.

The three of them had just finished changing clothes when they heard a key in the door. Ben Bernard entered, accompanied by the young woman. He looked around the room and turned to her. "Get this stuff cleaned up," he said, indicating the dirty dishes and the clothes lying on the lower deck of the bed.

"Where's your weapon?" Bernard suddenly confronted Cindy Carson.

"I dumped it."

He glared at her for a moment. "You dumped it?"

"I quickly saw that there was no way to resist your people. I also got rid of my radio and my Secret Service pin."

"Search her."

The young woman set aside the clothes she had been gathering up and signaled to Cindy to go into the bathroom. Drawing the door closed, she ran her hands over the agent's body, feeling under her arms, between her legs, and down her legs to her ankles.

"Take off your blouse."

She felt the binding of Cindy's bra and the waistband of her panty hose, making sure she had not hidden a tiny knife or even a long pin that might be used as a weapon.

"She's clean, Mr. Bernard," she said as they emerged from the bathroom.

Bernard looked Cindy up and down as though he were conducting his own search with some kind of X-ray vision. Then he turned to Marcia Walker. "Mrs. Walker, please come with me."

She hesitated, looking him up and down, then straightened her shoulders and moved toward the door. "Very well."

Bernard paused at the doorway and looked back toward David and Cindy. "I'll bring her back in a few minutes."

He guided her down the hall, across the courtyard to the neighboring building, and into a large room. One wall consisted almost entirely of a huge picture window that framed the snow-capped cone of Mount Taranaki. The glass was heavily tinted, however, so the mountain appeared almost as it would on a moonlit night.

A bald-headed man rose from a desk where he sat with his back to the window and advanced to meet the First Lady as she entered the room.

"Mrs. Walker. Welcome to Taranaki Lodge." He strode across the room and extended his hand. "I am Luke Nash, your—how should I put it?—your host."

Marcia Walker glanced down at his outstretched hand, then fixed him with a glare. "Nash? Luke Nash? You're the same man who . . ."

"Yes, Mrs. Walker. Very good. I am the same man who caused some problems for your husband last year."

"You're a . . . a killer . . . a murderer." Her face was flushed with anger. "You're the one who used some kind of death ray to destroy Mojave."

Nash smiled a thin, sardonic smile. "I need better spin control, I suppose. But that aside, I thought you might ask me why you're here."

She nodded and raised her brows in a questioning look.

"Please, come over here and sit down." He indicated a chair facing his desk. She sat with her hands folded in her lap, and stared at him. A negotiation is a negotiation is a negotiation, she thought.

Nash took his own seat and began his pitch. "The situation is this: You have met Ben Bernard. He is the commander of my small but elite military force. It is comprised of a number of Maori 'warriors'—I'm sure you saw them at the Parliament building—plus a corps of very experienced special warfare veterans from various parts of the world. We have men from the Russian Spetznaz, the British Special Air Service, some German Kampf swimmers, the Israeli Sayeret Matkal, a number from the former Yugoslavia, and even a few from Ben's former employer, the U.S. Navy.

"In the name of our Maori friends, we have taken effective control of the government of New Zealand. They have dissolved the white-dominated Parliament and created a new Maori-controlled government. They have even changed the nation's name from New Zealand to Aotearoa."

"You'll never get away with this."

"So far, as you are certainly aware, my forces have gotten away with this very well. Allow me to define 'elite': My force is well-trained and well-armed, and very well led. We have taken over police stations, military installations, government buildings, and broadcast and communications facilities. Our control is complete on North Island and is expanding rapidly on South Island.''

''The United States and other nations won't stand for this. Do you think you can take on the entire rest of the world?''

''That, Mrs. Walker, is where you fit in. Except for perhaps Helen of Troy, you—with your son, David—are the two most valuable hostages in the history of the world. Your husband and other world leaders will do exactly what we tell them to do.''

''Troy was destroyed, Mr. Nash, to get Helen back.''

He glared at her for a moment and then went on: ''At this point, your husband doesn't know where you are or why you have been taken. He will be very cautious in taking any action until he has a better view of the situation. We're going to wait a few days—just to let him worry. And then you and I will have a little telephone conversation with the president. You will help me convince him that his only course of action is to do exactly as I tell him.''

Marcia Walker rose and started toward the door. She had found it best, when losing control of a negotiation, to back off and regroup. But she turned back with one more question.

''What in heaven's name do you hope to achieve by this?''

Nash chuckled as he rose from his chair and approached Mrs. Walker. ''The same thing your husband's been working toward his whole life—and the same thing you want so badly you can't give up your career and especially your husband, despite his crude dalliances right beneath your nose.''

She stared at him and slowly shook her head, as though she could not believe what she was hearing. Then she turned again toward the door.

''And one more thing, Mrs. Walker: You will be treated well while you are my 'guest' here and are cooperative. I would not like anything to happen to you—or to your son. But I don't think I have to tell you that I can be utterly ruthless.''

He paused and then added, "Just ask the people of Mojave. They would tell you—if they could."

As the door closed behind Bernard and Mrs. Walker, David stood close beside Cindy Carson. "I'm scared."

She put her arm around his shoulders and drew him to her. "I'm a little scared, too, David. But I really think we are going to be all right. Whoever has taken us captive obviously wants us alive and well. I think they'll take very good care of us."

The boy was silent. She could feel an involuntary shudder run through his body as he pressed close to her.

A moment later, she heard the key in the lock, and Marcia Walker stepped through the door.

"Mom!" David ran to his mother and threw his arms around her waist.

Cindy stood with a questioning look on her face.

"That bastard!" Marcia Walker put her hand to her lips. "Oh, I'm sorry, David. We don't use words like that, do we?"

She turned to Cindy. "Do you know who that man is? That man I've just been to see? He's the same man who destroyed Mojave last year and would have destroyed the party convention and St. Louis if he hadn't been stopped. The same man!"

Cindy had seen Mrs. Walker in some stressful situations, but she had never seen her as agitated as she was right now.

Later that night, after David had climbed into the upper bunk and quickly dropped off to sleep, the two women turned the lights down and sat close to each other at the table, talking quietly.

"That man Nash worries me very much. He told me he would not want anything to happen to David or me, but almost in the same breath he warned me how ruthless he could be. I know my husband. Chip simply won't sacrifice the country's interests for personal reasons. And, in this case, David and I are the personal reasons."

Cindy put a finger to her lips and then motioned Marcia to

accompany her into the bathroom. Shutting the door quietly, she flushed the toilet and, at the same time, lifted the lid on the water tank to reveal her hidden pistol. She whispered, "It's not much, but it's better than nothing."

"Oh, no, Cindy. You're not going to use that."

Marcia Walker's whisper was so low that Cindy could not tell whether her sentence ended with an exclamation point or a question mark.

"I might have to, ma'am."

"No! Don't even think about it. I still have room to negotiate with this madman. We're not going to resort to violence."

The Secret Service agent's thoughts raced. Why can't some people get it through their minds that, when you are dealing with violent people, violence may be the only answer?

She kept her thoughts to herself. Her lips were set in a tight, thin line as she regarded the First Lady, then nodded. "Yes, ma'am," she lied.

CHAPTER 11

"LOOK AT THESE, CHUCK." PAT COLLINS HELD A SHEAF OF photographic images in her hand as she stepped into Nelson's office, a walled-off area at one end of the barracks.

Nelson looked up from his paperwork. "What have you got, Pat?"

"We're beginning to get some useful intel. We have satellite images along with pictures taken in the first U-2 pass over North Island. And Fort Meade has come through with some very interesting intercepts."

The National Security Agency headquarters at Fort Meade, Maryland, between Washington and Baltimore, served as a giant electronic vacuum cleaner, scooping up radio, telephone, and other kinds of electronic communications throughout the world.

"I think we may have a pretty good idea where they are," she said, going to the map of New Zealand tacked to Nelson's wall. "There's been an unusual amount of radio activity from a point near the west coast of North Island. It seems to be coming from somewhere on the south slope of Mount Egmont."

She pointed to the mountain on the map and then stepped over to Nelson's desk.

"Now look at these satellite images. We don't cover New Zealand routinely. But we have a photo taken just about a year ago, along with one taken last night, our time. Look at the difference.''

Bending over the photos, Nelson quickly recognized the changes that had taken place in the year since the first photo was taken. At the center of the picture were two large buildings, several outlying buildings, and new roads.

Collins pulled out a series of pictures taken by the U-2 spy plane as it had made a pass over the area at 80,000 feet.

''Here.'' she said. ''You can see the new construction better in these photos. You can make out the road entering from the south, and the fence around the area. And you get a pretty good view of the buildings themselves.''

''Do the NSA intercepts indicate that's where the hostages are being held?''

''No, all we've got so far is an indication of an unusual amount of communications traffic. NSA is sorting it out now, but most of what we've seen seems like some sort of business communications, almost like what you would hear from listening in on stockbrokers at work. We'll know a lot more about it in a few hours.''

Nelson flipped through the images and then went to the wall to study the map, holding one of the wide-angle satellite photos in his hand. A plan for getting into the compound—if that turned out to be where the hostages were being held—was already beginning to form in his mind.

''This is good, Pat. But we're going to need a lot more before we can move.'' He paused, studying the map. ''You know what I'd really like? I'd like to get someone into that place.''

She laughed. ''Sure, Chuck. Get someone in there. Just like that . . . you got any ideas?''

''Well, I wonder. The prevailing winds there are from the west. Say we had one of our guys do a HAHO out here over the Tasman Sea.'' He spoke almost to himself, using the acronym for high altitude, high opening. ''If he jumped at 30,000 or 35,000 feet, he could travel a good fifty miles and slip right in there undetected.''

"And then what? Being a good, red-blooded, American SEAL, I suppose he will kill all the bad guys and rescue the fair maiden and her son single-handedly."

Nelson grinned. "Yeah, something like that. What I'm really thinking is that our guy could carry a satcomm system with him. He could poke around there very quietly. And then, hopefully, he could let us know, one, if the hostages are there and, two, what kind of opposition we'll run into when we come in for the rescue."

"I don't know, Chuck. That could work, but . . ."

He scratched his head, still staring at the map. "Yeah, I know, Pat. It's a long shot. But I'd like to know a lot more about the situation before we go in there. If we have to do it without any better intel, we'll have to do it. But I'd sure like to stack the odds a little bit more in our favor."

"Who are you going to send?"

"I want to talk to Jeff about that, but I think Rex Marker might be able to pull it off for us. He's just a youngster but he's bright, and he's our best guy on communications. Remember? He did a fantastic job for us last year when he led our team that scoped out the place in the desert in Uzbekistan. That op was his idea, too. We were all thinking about noisy, big-foot operations like landing C-130s in the sand or sending in the Rangers. He came up with the idea of having four guys just rent a van and drive out there. And it worked."

"When are you going to talk to them?"

"First thing tomorrow. They've been out working on their mountain climbing on Mauna Kea today. Jeff has been bugging me to give them a night in town. He says they're getting like caged animals. I kept them pretty busy in Arizona, and now this. I really don't like the idea of letting them out, but I guess they need to blow off a little steam. What time is it?" He looked at his watch. "They're probably on their way into town now."

"Gee, it's almost eight o'clock. I didn't realize it was so late."

Nelson looked at his desk. "I've still got several hours of paperwork to finish up tonight, and I want to start writing out specs for this op. I can flesh it out as we learn more about what we're getting into.''

"I'm going to spend some time tonight playing with the computer," she said. "We're getting all these bits and pieces from NSA. I want to see if I can pull together anything that makes sense."

Jeff Bonior sat in the right seat of the lead vehicle, staring straight ahead, as the team headed into town. He did not look forward to the evening. The big black SEAL was a born-again Christian and a deacon in his Baptist church back home. He didn't drink and he didn't smoke, and he would never dream of being unfaithful to his wife, Dorothy. Most of these young guys, he knew, would spend the evening getting drunk and, if they got lucky, getting laid. He hoped that some of them would follow his example, but he had long since decided not to try to impose his moral standards on the men. His job tonight would be to try to keep them out of trouble and, especially, out of jail.

The little caravan stopped on a street where the flashing neon signs promised BEER, COCKTAILS and TOPLESS DANCING GIRLS.

The men, except for Bonior, piled out of the vehicles and stood uncertainly on the sidewalk, mapping out their plans for the evening, while the vehicles continued on down the street to a restaurant parking lot.

Bonior and the four drivers found a booth in a back corner of the restaurant. The big chief ordered a T-bone steak, fries, a salad, and iced tea, followed by a chocolate sundae. He ate slowly, trying to stretch out the time. He had a good five or six hours to kill before he would begin rounding up the guys and getting them back to camp.

"Okay, Jer, what are we going to do?" The men clustered around Chief Jeremy Merrifield, the team's explosives expert and leading party animal. He liked to blow things up, and sometimes a night on the town with Merrifield could be almost as explosive as accompanying him on an operation.

"Dancing girls! Nekkid women!" he exclaimed, leading the way toward the bright lights flashing over an establishment in the middle of the strip.

As they stepped inside, they suddenly found themselves groping in the dark. At the far end of the room, a kaleidoscope of flashing lights illuminated a stage on which a young woman was reaching the climax of her act. She was naked except for a tiny G-string and an even tinier luminescent patch covering each nipple. As the hard-pounding music rose in intensity, she moved the upper part of her body rapidly from side to side, causing her ample breasts to gyrate—the left one circling clockwise, the right one counterclockwise. At the same time, her hips snapped back and forth.

Merrifield led the way to a table near the stage. "Oh, man! I want me some of that!" Holding his arms out to the sides, he mimicked the movement of her hips.

One of the SEALs put a hand on his shoulder. "Okay, Jer, take it easy. Let's not get carried away."

Merrifield slipped into a seat and signaled to a waitress. "Give me a bourbon on the rocks with a water chaser. Make it a double."

"What kind of beer you got?" One of the air force special tactics men asked.

"You name it, honey, we've got it," the waitress replied. "Bud, Miller, Heineken, Lowenbrau . . . what'll you have?"

"Oh, hell, give me a Bud."

She returned moments later with her tray laden with beer and Merrifield's double bourbon. He lifted the glass to his lips and took a large swallow.

Another dancer had taken the first girl's place on the stage and begun a slow, suggestive striptease. As each piece of clothing came off, members of the team shouted for more. She winked in their direction and made it clear that she was performing just for them. As she finished her dance, Merrifield stood and moved toward the stage.

"Hey, honey, come on over here and talk to us."

She picked up a shawl with which she had begun the dance and draped it over her shoulders. Rather than covering her, it seemed only to emphasize her nakedness.

She took Merrifield's hand, followed him to the table and then sat on his lap, moving gently to the music. Merrifield ran a hand over her thigh and then up to cup her breast.

"Oooh," she said, "you move fast."

At the bar, four local men had turned to watch.

One of the men, with the broad facial structure and olive complexion of a Polynesian, slipped off his stool and strode across the room. Taking the dancer roughly by the arm, he said, "Come on, Georgia, don't play around with that *haole*."

He pulled on her arm, and she almost fell as she slid off Merrifield's lap.

The SEAL was on his feet. He grabbed the man by the shirtfront and demanded, "Did you call me an a-hole?"

The man was shorter than Merrifield but powerfully built. He leaned into Merrifield's face, the odor of beer heavy on his breath, and shouted: "No. I called you a *haole*—a white son of a bitch."

"You Hawaiian asshole!" Merrifield pushed the man violently. He fell back against a neighboring table and then toppled to the floor in a puddle of spilled drinks.

The woman screamed and retreated back toward the stage, pulling the shawl tightly around her shoulders and across her breasts.

The Hawaiian's friends had remained seated at the bar. But they were watching intensely. Each held a beer bottle by the neck, ready to break it for a ready weapon.

Merrifield strode across the short distance to where the man lay on the floor and kicked him viciously in the side.

The bar's bouncer grabbed Merrifield's arm as the bartender came around the end of the bar to his assistance. "Okay, sailor, that's it. If you don't leave quietly, I'm going to throw your ass out of here and call the cops. It's your choice."

Another SEAL took hold of Merrifield's other arm and began dragging him toward the door. "That's enough, Jer. Let's get out of here."

The Hawaiian had struggled to his feet and followed them toward the door. "You want to fight, I'll fight you. I'll kill you."

Merrifield looked back over his shoulder. "Okay, you son of a bitch. Come on outside."

Most of the bar emptied out, with the patrons following the two men outside and gathering in the corner of a neighboring parking lot.

The Hawaiian danced toward Merrifield and then away, dodging and weaving, jabbing with his left hand while holding his right back against his chest.

Merrifield raised his hands and moved toward his opponent in a boxer's stance.

Two of the Hawaiian's friends started forward, but their way was blocked by others in the crowd amid shouts of "Let 'em fight."

The two men circled each other, throwing a couple of long-distance punches that did no harm. Suddenly, Merrifield grasped the other man's extended left hand, turned, and flipped him over his shoulder into a brick wall. The man lay where he fell. Merrifield leaned over, grasped him by the belt and his shirt collar, and drove his head into the wall, scraping upward so the man's face was torn by the bricks.

Two members of the team stepped forward to haul Merrifield away by both arms.

"Okay, Jer, it's all over. Let him go."

Merrifield shrugged off their hands.

"Gonna kill the son of a bitch." He pulled the man up to face him and then pushed him back against the wall. In rapid succession, he drove his knee deep into the man's groin and struck him hard in the abdomen, just below the diaphragm. The Hawaiian dropped to the pavement, a foul-smelling liquid cascading from his mouth.

As Merrifield bent to lift the man once more, two policemen on patrol rounded the corner of the building and then, blowing their whistles shrilly, pushed their way through the crowd of onlookers.

The first officer, holding his baton in one hand, grabbed Merrifield by the shoulder.

"That's enough, sailor! Drop him!"

Merrifield, still holding his opponent in one hand, whirled so rapidly that the policeman was thrown off balance and fell awkwardly to the pavement. His companion stopped abruptly, drew his pistol, dropped into a crouch and stood facing Merrifield. Even though he held the weapon in the prescribed two-handed grip, the muzzle was visibly trembling.

"Get your hands up! Now!"

Merrifield turned to face him, then let go of the Hawaiian's clothing and slowly raised his hands.

"Shee-it. Look at the little tin cop with his little popgun."

The other officer had regained his feet and had his radio out, calling in a request for assistance. He glanced at the man lying on the ground and added a request for an ambulance. He pulled out his cuffs, stepped behind Merrifield and grasped his upraised right arm. As he did so, Merrifield whirled and glared at him, his nose only inches from the other man's. Slowly, he turned to permit the cop to cuff his hands behind him.

One of the SEALs on the edge of the crowd pulled a cellular phone from a holster on his belt and dialed Jeff Bonior's number.

"Jeff? Hey, man, we got a problem. Jer got in a fight with some Hawaiian, and the cops have him."

"Where are you?"

"We're in a parking lot beside that joint with the dancing girls, right about where you dropped us off. But they're taking him to the car now. I think you'd better figure out where the station is and go there."

Bonior was still in the restaurant, lingering over a cup of coffee, when he received the call. He looked at his watch and sighed. This was what he always feared when the guys were let loose on the town after weeks of hard training. He paid the check for himself and the drivers and asked the cashier for directions to the nearest police station. It was just down the street.

Bonior was sitting in his vehicle across from the station when the police car pulled up and the two officers led Merrifield inside. He got out and motioned the other drivers to join him on the sidewalk.

"I want you to go down where we dropped the men off and pick them up. Bring a couple of them who saw what happened here to me, and then take the rest of them back to the camp."

A few minutes later, one of the vehicles stopped near where Bonior was parked and two men—a SEAL and a Special Tactics man—got out.

"Did you guys see what happened?"

Both began to talk at once, and then the air force man gestured to the SEAL to tell the story.

"Yeah, Chief. We was drinking and watching this girl dance. Just minding our own business. When she finished, Jer, he got her to come over and sit on his lap. Then this big Hawaiian got up from the bar and came over and grabbed her by the arm. Jer hit him. The bouncer made us go outside. So they went out in the parking lot to fight."

"Didn't any of you geniuses try to break it up?"

The two men stood silently, looking at the pavement.

The air force man finally spoke. "We figured they'd just have a little fight—you know, a little entertainment."

"We did try to stop it," the SEAL broke in. "But Jer just pushed us off and turned around and started hammering this guy. You know how Jer gets. And then the cops came."

"Was Merrifield drunk?" Bonior asked.

"I don't think so, Chief," the SEAL replied. "He had maybe a couple of whiskey drinks. The rest of us were having beer, but he was drinking bourbon. He didn't act like he was drunk."

"It was more like he was crazy more than he was drunk," the air force man added. "When we tried to break up the fight, I got up real close to him, and he had this strange look in his eyes. Did you ever see an animal, like a dog, when he's going to attack someone? That's kind of the way he looked. Weird!''

"Yeah,'' the SEAL added. "I saw that, too. When we tried to break it up, I think this other guy was really out of it. I'm not even sure he was still conscious. But Jer was hitting him like he was trying to kill him. And he had this funny—not funny, *funny* . . . he had this *strange* kind of crazy look on his face, like he was getting some kind of weird pleasure out of beating on this guy.''

Nelson looked up as Bonior entered his office. "Have a nice time on the town last night, Jeff?''

"Aw, boss. I hate this stuff.''

"What happened?''

"The guys went to one of those girly shows, and Merrifield got in a fight with a Hawaiian. Jer's in jail.''

"Yeah, so I've been reading.'' Nelson picked up the local newspaper and read an item:

"Navy Chief Petty Officer Jeremy Merrifield was arrested last night and charged with disorderly conduct, police said.

"The twenty-six-year-old Merrifield will be arraigned this morning and then is expected to be released on bail. He is a member of a small military unit that recently began training at a World War Two military camp on the windward shore.''

Nelson put down the paper. "How bad was it?''

"Pretty bad. When I got to the station, they had just brought Jer in, and the cops were pretty steamed up. They were talking about booking him for assault and battery, which would be a felony. He knocked one cop down, and the guy was pissed. He kept saying he should be booked for attempted murder.''

"Murder? Was it that bad?''

"The other guy was taken to the hospital unconscious. From what I've been able to find out, he is in serious condition with severe lacerations of the face and head, several broken ribs, maybe a ruptured spleen—and badly bruised testicles. He really got a working over.''

"What about Merrifield?''

"As far as I know, he doesn't even have a bruise. His big problem is legal. I got with the cops and talked them into booking him for disorderly conduct—a misdemeanor. I think we can get them to drop charges if they're convinced the navy will discipline him."

"You're damned right the navy will take care of him. Has Jeremy been in this kind of trouble before?"

"I pulled his file this morning. He's never been in trouble with the law before, but there's a kind of pattern. He was in a West Coast team after BUD/S, and then he put in some time in DevGru [the SEALs' special hostage rescue unit] before we signed him on. In his evaluations, you keep seeing words like 'aggressive,' 'belligerent,' 'combative.' "

"Yeah, well? After all, he is a SEAL."

"Listen to this. DevGru has some kind of resident shrink. He helps the guys deal with stress and stuff like that. But he also watches them to make sure they don't have some kind of mental problems. Listen to what he wrote about Jer:

" 'In a standardized test and in a subsequent interview by the undersigned, this twenty-four-year-old noncommissioned officer displayed a marked degree of aggressiveness verging on hostility. The tests indicated a latent tendency toward both cruelty and brutality. When questioned about this, the subject became noticeably defensive and belligerent.

" 'It is not uncommon to find high levels of aggressiveness among men in this highly specialized unit where the physical and psychological stresses are so severe. However, this subject appears to harbor a barely suppressed rage that could pose a threat to himself or others and places him near the borderline between acceptable and unacceptable personality traits for assignment to this unit. Unusual care should be taken by responsible officers to monitor the behavior of this individual both on and off duty.' "

"This guy sounds like a time bomb. Where'd you get that thing?"

"It's in his personnel jacket."

"Why haven't we seen it before?"

"I've been trying to figure that out. Remember, when we organized the outfit, we put the guys through a screening—physical, pay records, all that stuff? I think we had them carry their files as they went through the process. It may be that this letter wasn't in there when we looked at it."

"You mean he took it out?"

"Took it out and then put it back. You know it would have raised a lot of red flags if we had seen it. It's not the kind of thing we would just pass over."

"To be honest, Jeff, we relied pretty heavily on what we heard from the teams about the men we were interested in. Merrifield got high marks from everybody on explosives. A real expert. Maybe he looked so good, we just didn't hear anything else." He paused, thinking. "Well, in any event, he's out of the outfit now. Do we have anyone else who can handle the explosives?"

"Yeah, one of the air force men is pretty good—not as good as Jer, but I think he'll be all right. We don't want to try to bring a new man into the team at this point. We'll move the air force guy over to do the explosives work and get along one man short."

Nelson picked up the phone. "I've got another thing I want to talk to you about, Jeff, but let me get Mark in here."

A few minutes later, Lt. Col. Mark Rattner stepped into the room. He took a seat near the wall, draping one long leg over the arm of the chair. "What's doing, Chuck?"

"I've got an idea I want to run by you and Jeff." Nelson went to the map. "We're pretty sure the hostages are being held right about here, in a compound on the south slope of Mount Egmont. What I'd like to do is get a man in there to figure out what's going on and give us a better idea of what we're getting into if we go in for a rescue."

"Yeah, we need all the intel we can get. But how are you going to get someone in there?" Rattner asked.

"That's why I wanted to talk to you. Why can't we have one of our guys do a HAHO from somewhere out here, over the Tasman Sea?" Nelson pointed to the ocean area to the west of New Zealand's North Island. "The prevailing winds are from the west. They could carry a man right in where we want him.''

Rattner and Bonior joined Nelson in front of the map.

"Sure," Rattner said, "I guess you could do it. The tough part would be after he got on the ground. That looks like pretty rugged country up there on the slope of the mountain.''

"Who have you got in mind, sir?" Bonior asked.

"How about Rex Marker? He's our communications expert. How is he on parachuting?''

"He's good. He's been through the high-altitude course at El Centro. Nearly got himself killed out there when he banged into one of the other guys and got knocked out, but he survived all right. Wanted to go back up right after he came to, just to prove himself.''

"That's good. You talk to him, Jeff, and work out a plan.'' Then, turning to Rattner, Nelson added, "Mark, we're going to need a plane. Things are a little touchy with Admiral Bridges. He apparently wants to invade New Zealand. I'd just as soon not have to go through him. Do you think there's any chance of getting Rex on an air force flight?''

"That's a possibility, Chuck. We could set something up through the Strategic Command. We might get him on a B-52 on a routine flight to Diego Garcia. They'd have to swing down pretty far south of their normal course, let him jump, and continue on to the Indian Ocean. Admiral Bridges wouldn't have to know anything about it. It'll probably take a word from Admiral McKay from Washington to make it happen, so why don't I make a few calls and see what we can work out?''

CHAPTER 12

THE SOUND OF THE KEY IN THE DOOR WENT THROUGH THE room like an electric shock. Except for meals brought in at predictable hours, the boy and the two women had been left alone for four days. The three of them stared speechlessly as the door swung open.

One of the guards, dressed in a black jumpsuit and with a pistol at his waist, stepped in, looked quickly around the room, and then focused on Marcia Walker.

He motioned to her. "Please. Come with me." As she listened to his brief command, she tried to puzzle out what kind of an accent he had. The use of his word *please* was similar to the way that Germans use the word *bitte*. But something else about the few words he had spoken made her think that his native tongue was probably some kind of Eastern European language rather than German.

David stepped to his mother's side in a movement that both sought and attempted to give protection.

"Where are you taking me?" Mrs. Walker asked.

"Please, madam. Come with me." The guard stepped forward as though to take her arm.

She leaned down to kiss David on the forehead and then guided him over close to Cindy.

"You stay here with Cindy, David. I'll be back shortly."

She threw back her shoulders and strode past the guard and out the door.

He walked beside her, using hand motions to show the direction. It was the same route she had taken before on the way to Nash's office.

He was sitting behind his desk as she entered the room. The guard closed the door behind her as he stepped outside.

"Ah, Mrs. Walker." Nash rose from his desk and stood waiting as she walked across the large room. "Please have a seat."

"Sir, this outrage has gone on long enough. I demand that my son, Miss Carson, and I be released immediately."

"Please sit down, Mrs. Walker, and let me explain some facts to you."

She glared at him for a moment and then took the chair.

"You are not in a position to make any demands of me, Mrs. Walker. Now . . ." He glanced at his wristwatch. "It is about 7:30 P.M. in Washington. Your husband has had several days to worry about your welfare, and it is late in the day. He will be ready to listen to reason."

"Mr. Nash, you are seriously mistaken if you think that President Walker will put his own personal concerns over the welfare of the United States."

"I am afraid he will have no choice, Mrs. Walker."

"Of course he will have a choice. David and I are very dear to him, but he will not negotiate with you under this kind of personal pressure. I have been married to Maynard Walker for fourteen years, and I know him very well. He will not bend."

"Why don't we find out, Mrs. Walker?" He picked up the phone on his desk, dialed and sat with the receiver at his ear for several seconds as the international circuits routed the call through a landline, up to a satellite 23,000 miles over the Pacific, down to another landline in the United States, and to the phone room of the mansion on Pennsylvania Avenue.

"White House."

"Yes. I have a call for President Walker from Mrs. Walker."

"Just a moment, sir." The operator's voice did not betray the fact that she and her colleagues had been alerted to expect such a call. She signaled to a supervisor, who immediately began the process of tracing the call. Then she rang the number upstairs in the family living quarters where she knew the president was waiting.

"This is President Walker. Who is this speaking?"

"That's not important at this point, Mr. President. I have Mrs. Walker here with me, and I have several requests to make of you and the United States government."

"Let me talk to Marcie."

"No, not yet. First, these are my demands:

"One. The United States will immediately recognize the legitimacy of the new Maori government of Aotearoa—formerly known as New Zealand.

"Two. The United States will assure that no nation, including the United States, positions any military forces within two hundred nautical miles of the coast of Aotearoa.

"Three. I will supply you with a list of defensive weapons. You will make immediate arrangements for their delivery to the government of Aotearoa."

"Let me talk to my wife."

Nash handed the phone to Marcia Walker. "You can tell him you and David are in good health. Nothing else."

She began speaking slowly. "Oh, Chip. David and I are fine . . ." Then she blurted out, "On Mount Egmont. Held by Nash. Mojave, St. Louis . . ."

Nash's finger on the phone switch cut her off.

"That was not very smart, Mrs. Walker. I had hoped that an intelligent word from you would help your husband see the wisdom of meeting my demands."

"You are the one who is not very smart, sir. You cannot dictate terms to the president of the United States. My son and I are of no value to you as bargaining chips. Your best—your only—prudent course of action is to make immediate arrangements for our release." She was a veteran negotiator, but she felt a knot of anger and frustration in the pit of her stomach: She had never been in a position where the stakes were so high and she had so little to negotiate with.

Nash pressed a button on the communications console on his desk. Almost immediately, the door opened, and the guard who had escorted Marcia to the office stepped inside.

"Take her back," Nash commanded brusquely.

As soon as she had left, he picked up the phone that linked him with Bernard.

"She is a stubborn bitch. Pick up Carson."

As soon as Marcia Walker stepped into the room where they were being held, she knew immediately that something was wrong.

David was sitting on the lower bunk, his arms wrapped defensively across his chest. His cheeks were streaked with tears.

Mrs. Walker quickly crossed the room and sat on the edge of the bunk, putting an arm around her son's shoulders.

"Where's Cindy?"

David ran the back of his hand across his mouth and shrugged his shoulders.

"I dunno."

"What happened?"

"That big man—that Bernard—came a couple of minutes ago and took Cindy with him."

"Where did they go?"

The boy shrugged again.

Marcia Walker put both arms around her son and held him close against her breast. Tears came to her own eyes as she realized what was happening: Nash didn't want to harm either of them, didn't want to damage the merchandise. But the Secret Service agent was fair game. He could threaten or even harm her to bring pressure on his two prize hostages.

She sat silently for a few minutes, holding her son. Then she crossed to the table and pulled a handful of tissues from a box.

She patted her eyes and blew her nose softly.

"Here, David." She leaned down and dabbed at his face with a tissue.

He took it from her hand, blew his nose, and looked up at his mother. "I'm okay, Mom. When he came and took Cindy away and left me here alone, I was really scared.''

''I know, David. But we're going to be tough, just as tough as we can be.''

Maynard Walker replaced the phone in its cradle with a sigh.

''Good old Marcie. That Nash fellow is going to find out he is dealing with one tough cookie.'' He looked up at Derek Shepherd, the head of the Secret Service White House detail. ''Did you get it all?''

''Yes, Mr. President, I'm sure we did.'' Since the Watergate disaster, no chief executive had dared to use a system on which all of his conversations were recorded. But the White House had maintained the capability to record individual conversations with a high-fidelity CD-ROM system, far superior to the taping system that had contributed to President Nixon's downfall.

A Secret Service agent knocked at the door and handed Shepherd a CD. He stepped across the room to a CD player. ''Let's find out what we got.''

He pressed the ''play'' button, and Nash's voice could be heard, almost as clearly as if he were in the room. The two men listened intently to Nash and then to the brief explosion of words from Marcia Walker.

''Do you think they were able to trace it, Derek?''

''No, Mr. President. It was very brief and involved a number of circuits, both in this country and overseas. I'm sure he knew how long he could talk before we traced it. In any event, that's really not very important. We know they are on North Island, New Zealand, and now, from what Mrs. Walker was able to tell us, we know they are probably being held somewhere on Mount Egmont. We had already been getting indications from our other intelligence sources that that was where we should look.''

''Nash! That bastard!''

''Yes, we now know, thanks to your wife, that we are dealing with a very dangerous but also very intelligent and resourceful individual. He just barely got away when we raided his compound above Colorado Springs last year. Now he has surfaced again in an entirely different part of the world, and at this point we still have only the vaguest idea of what he is up to.''

"What's our next step, Derek?"

The Secret Service agent gave him a quizzical look. "I'm afraid that is up to you, sir. We are into something far beyond the expertise of the Secret Service."

Walker sighed again. "Yeah, I know that, Derek. I want you to have your experts and people at Fort Meade and the FBI all listen to that recording to see if there is anything there that we overlooked—any hidden clues that might help us."

"Oh, there is one piece of news that I didn't have the opportunity to tell you before, sir. We have analyzed the video image of the hostages as they were loaded into the helicopter. We believe the young woman accompanying Mrs. Walker and David is Cindy Carson, the head of Mrs. Walker's Secret Service detail."

"Yes, I know Cindy. I thought she had been killed."

"That was our assumption, sir, but we are now confident that she is also being held hostage."

"Well, it's a relief to know that she is alive. But why would he take her?"

Shepherd shrugged. "We can only guess, sir. I'd say that he may hope to use her to bring pressure on Mrs. Walker."

The president shook his head. "Get back to me as soon as you come up with anything more."

"Yes, sir." Shepherd stepped toward the door. "Good night, sir. And good luck."

Walker picked up the phone. "Get me Admiral McKay."

McKay felt the silent pulse of the pager at his waist as he worked his way through a reception at the Grand Hyatt hotel in Washington's newly vibrant downtown area, shaking hands with a senator, exchanging a joke with a cabinet secretary, giving a friendly pat on the shoulder to a passing general. He strode quickly to the side of the room where a waiting aide handed him a cellular telephone.

"Mac, can you get over here now? I need some advice."
The president's voice seemed to McKay to carry an extra tone
of urgency.

"Yes, sir. Give me ten minutes."

"This way, sir." The aide guided the admiral into the lobby
and toward the entrance of the hotel. As they walked, he spoke
into a small transmitter, calling the admiral's car. As they
swung through the revolving doors, the black government se-
dan stopped in the drive, and a doorman opened the rear door.

It was only ten blocks to the White House, but the driver
took a slightly longer route so he could swing around onto
Seventeenth Street and enter the White House grounds by way
of the Old Executive Office Building. When he stopped, Mc-
Kay was only a few steps from a side entrance to the West
Wing of the White House. An aide met him at the door. "Sir,
the president is waiting for you in the family quarters. I'll
show you the way."

Maynard Walker set aside his reading glasses, rose from a
wing chair, and strode across the room to take McKay's hand.

"You made good time, Mac. Here, sit down."

The two sat facing each other in chairs near a window looking out over the ellipse and across the Mall to the Jefferson
Memorial.

"There have been a couple of developments. One, the Secret Service has identified that woman seen getting onto the
helicopter along with Marcie and David. They think it's Cindy
Carson, one of their agents. She was the head of Mrs. Walker's
detail."

"That's good news, sir. That means we've got a trained
professional on the inside."

"The other development is more important: He's made contact, Mac."

"Any word of your wife and son?"

"A little. He put Marcie on the phone. She said she and
David were okay, and then she blurted out some information
before he cut her off. Here, we've got it on a CD." The pres-

ident leaned over to press a button, and the two men listened intently to the brief recorded conversation.

"Well." McKay let out a long breath as the recording ended. "Luke Nash. I had hoped we had heard the last of him."

"So had I." The president read from a sheet of paper on the table beside him. "Luke Nash, born Laszlo Nagy in Budapest, 1936. Fled Hungary in 1956 after Soviet invasion. Flew for CIA, moved to the U.S., 1960, worked on Wall Street. Changed his name to Nash. . . .' You know the rest, Mac. Resources, it seems, that are the match of the Soviets, but none of the charm, charity or *bonhomie*. Now, what do you think of his demands?"

"Recognize Ao—whatever they now call New Zealand. Keep military forces two hundred miles away. Supply weapons. The matter of recognition is something for Secretary Trover and his people at State. I'm sure that will take some time. The disposition of military forces and the supply of weapons—those are the two things I can do something about."

"I've been thinking about it since we got the call," the president said. "I think the only urgent matter is the location of our forces. The weapons thing, like the matter of recognition, will take some time—and I think even Nash will understand that. That gives me time to get some more advice before we act."

"We normally don't have much in the way of military forces in those waters. I'll have to check, but we could have a C-130 or two at Christchurch on South Island as part of our support for bases in Antarctica. And of course we have the *Kitty Hawk* and her escort vessels. Last time I checked, they had pulled out of Port Nicholson at Wellington and were standing by off Hawke Bay on the east coast of North Island. For the time being, I can have them pull off two hundred miles—outside territorial waters. That's probably beyond Nash's surveillance capability, but it will still leave all of North Island within range of the *Kitty Hawk's* planes."

"What about the rescue attempt?"

"My Eagle Force has already moved to the Hawaiian Islands and set up shop there. They are making plans and practicing for a rescue."

"What are they going to do? Just getting there is going to be a real problem."

"Commander Nelson, the team's commander—you've met him, sir—Commander Nelson has a preliminary plan. Assuming that Mrs. Walker and David are being held, as we believe, at a compound on the south slope of Mount Egmont—or Mount Taranaki, as it is also called—this is what he has in mind: His men will set up a staging area on Fiji. Then they will parachute into the Coral Sea and rendezvous with the *Kamehameha*, a submarine specially equipped to deliver SEALs across the beach. They will land on the shore near the south slope of the mountain, proceed up to the compound, and effect the rescue."

"It sounds like *Mission Impossible*. You must have an awful lot of faith in these young men, Mac."

"I do, sir. But we really don't have many alternatives. Any large-scale or even medium-scale operation, such as an attempt to land marines or a Ranger battalion, would pose an unacceptable danger to Mrs. Walker and David. And it really isn't necessary. Once the hostages have been removed from Nash's control, we can consider many options, from negotiations to air attack to a landing by marines or Rangers. Our first task is a successful rescue."

"How soon will your team be ready to go?"

"They can move within a few days, sir. I have arranged for the *Kamehameha* to train with them for the next couple of days. Then the sub will sail southwest and take up a position between Fiji and New Zealand. That will take her about a week. Our men will parachute into the ocean and go into the submarine's dry deck shelter during one night. Sometime around midnight the next night, they will go ashore. So we're talking about ten or eleven days from now."

The president sat staring at the Jefferson Memorial and the lights of northern Virginia beyond. At last, he spoke. "It's going to be hard to wait. But I guess we have no choice.

Thanks, Mac. You can get on over to your reception, if you wish.''

"No, I think I have had all the reception I need for one evening, sir. I still have some work to do at the office. I'll talk with Commander Nelson around midnight. He should be up by then. It's important that he know Miss Carson is also a hostage. Good night, sir.''

CHAPTER 13

CLAUDIA BISHOP SMOOTHED THE SKIRT OVER HER HIPS AND took a quick look in the full-length mirror she had had installed on the door of her spacious corner office on the second floor of the Pentagon, between corridors seven and eight—two of the ten corridors that divided the five-sided building into pie-shaped wedges.

Then she strode quickly across the hallway into a room known as "the studio," crowded with reporters, cameramen, and sound technicians. As she entered and took her place on the raised platform before a wall draped in blue, an expectant silence suddenly descended on the room.

"I have a few announcements, and then I'll take your questions," she said, opening her briefing book. "Secretary McKenzie will meet this afternoon with the Israeli defense minister. We may have a briefing afterward—maybe three o'clock. I'll let you know. I think you already have a blue-top on the army's briefing tomorrow on its armor development program. Later this morning, we'll have prepared testimony on the Hill available here as it is delivered."

She turned a couple of pages and then looked up. "Okay, that's it. Any questions?"

Half a dozen reporters raised their hands, calling her by her nickname: "Cookie!" "Cookie!"

She indicated the senior wire service reporter.

"Cookie, what can you tell us about the president's wife and son? It has been five days since they disappeared."

"Fred, as you know, we are monitoring the situation very carefully. But I'm afraid I don't have anything new for you."

"Follow-up, Cookie: We have reports of some unusual ship movements in the Pacific. Our people in Honolulu say crews were called back to their ships in Pearl last night, and they sailed early today. Are preparations being made for a rescue attempt?"

She paused for a moment, gathering her thoughts. "I'm sorry, Fred, but we are not going to discuss ship movements."

"Cookie?" A tall network correspondent caught her eye. He was standing at the back of the room next to his camera so that, when she spoke to him, she would be looking toward his camera. "Has there been any communication from the kidnappers—any demands, any ransom notes?"

"I'm sorry, Bill. That's something you'll have to ask the White House about. We don't deal with that sort of thing here."

"We've been after them, Cookie. They won't tell us the time of day."

"I'm sure, Bill, that if there is anything to announce, they will announce it over there. Bev?" She turned to acknowledge a petite, blond-haired young woman sitting in the front row. Beverly Ruttledge was the Pentagon correspondent for half a dozen trade journals covering a variety of military hardware. The other reporters—most of them men—had learned to value her knowledge of the intricacies of electronics and other technology.

"I understand that, from intercepts picked up by NSA and from overflights, you have been able to pinpoint the location where the hostages are being held. Is that correct?"

"Bev, you know we can't talk about that kind of thing."

A veteran newspaper correspondent in the front row checked his watch. The briefing had been going on for nearly half an hour and had produced little news. "Thank you, Cookie," he said as he closed his notepad and got up to leave. Several reporters moved up to cluster around the press secretary, but she edged her way quickly toward the door.

Her two principal deputies were waiting in her office, where they had listened to the briefing over the system that permitted top officials throughout the Pentagon to hear what went on during the press briefings.

She flung her briefing book onto a sofa.

"Damn it! I hate it when they know more than I do. Why wasn't I told about those ships leaving Pearl? What the hell is going on out there? And where did Bev get that stuff about the NSA intercepts and the overflights? She's got better sources than we have."

The hot line from the secretary's office rang.

"Yes, ma'am." Claudia Bishop cradled the phone on her shoulder as she reached for a pencil and pad of paper.

"Claudia, dear, what was that reporter talking about—ships sailing hurriedly from Pearl Harbor? I haven't received any such reports."

"I haven't either, ma'am. That caught me off base. Shall I check on it?"

"No, don't bother. I think perhaps I'll have a little talk with Admiral Bridges."

When the press secretary hung up, the light on her phone was flashing. She pressed a button and listened as her secretary spoke. "Claudia, there are a couple of the regulars waiting out here. Can you see them?"

It was not unusual for reporters who thought they were onto something to hold their questions until they could speak privately with the press secretary. "Sure, I'll see them. Send them in one at a time."

Moments later, the Pentagon correspondent for the *Los Angeles Times* stepped into the room and closed the door behind him.

He took a seat, balancing his notebook on top of his tape recorder, which was perched on his knee. He smiled. "You sure got through that without telling us anything."

She returned his smile. "We are always just as forthcoming as possible. What's on your mind?"

"I'm not sure, Cookie. Maybe this is just a little police beat story, but I wanted to run it by you. We have a stringer in Honolulu, and he has his own stringers on the other islands. He called in an item about a sailor arrested in Hilo after a fight at a bar."

She shrugged. "So?"

"Well, according to one of the cops he talked to, this sailor belongs to some kind of super-secret commando outfit that suddenly showed up a couple of days ago, set up shop in an abandoned military base, and has been very busy out there. So, question: Does this have anything to do with an attempt to rescue the president's wife and son?"

She leaned forward, making notes as he spoke, avoiding eye contact so he would not see how his words had struck home. After a few moments, she looked up. "Let me check on that for you. I'm sure it's just some sort of routine training exercise, but I'll get back to you."

As he left the room, she instructed her secretary to tell the other reporters she wouldn't be able to see them for a while. She pressed a button to summon Terry Glenn, her military aide, from his office down the internal corridor that connected her office to those of her deputies and aides.

"Yes, ma'am?" Glenn, in his freshly pressed summer whites, made everyone else in the press area—especially the reporters—look shabby.

"Oh, Terry, how many times do I have to tell you? Cut the 'ma'am' shit. Call me Cookie."

"Yes, ma'am . . . er, Cookie. You wanted to see me?"

"Sit down. Do you know anything about some kind of secret commando outfit that might be involved in a rescue attempt?"

"Not specifically, no. But I know there is a unit, made up of SEALs and Air Force Special Operations types, that reports directly to Admiral McKay. It is very hush-hush."

"And he could use these guys for a rescue attempt?"

"I think so. My understanding is that they are trained for very specialized, very secret operations where bigger, more overt units would be inappropriate."

"And if this outfit was getting ready for a rescue, we wouldn't see anything in the message traffic—everything would be handled directly by the admiral?"

"That's right. It would be very close-hold. I can nose around a little, but I'm sure I'm not going to find out anything."

"No, don't do that, at least not right now. If these guys really are preparing for a rescue attempt, we've got one hell of a problem on our hands. The *L.A. Times* is working on a tip they got from a stringer in Hawaii that this mysterious unit is training out there for a rescue. It all started with the arrest of some sailor for getting in a fight in a bar. I don't know how close the *Times* is to going with the story, but there could be headlines tomorrow that would blow the whole operation."

"Wheeoo. All it takes is one guy to screw everything up. I'll keep my ears open, but I won't mention this to anyone."

"Thanks, Terry." As he left the room, she asked her secretary to set up an appointment with Adm. McKay as soon as possible. A few minutes later, her phone rang. "Ms. Bishop, Admiral McKay can see you now if you'd like."

Picking up her notepad, she hurried down the second floor corridor of the E-ring to the chairman's office, located near the River Entrance to the Pentagon. A marine enlisted woman met her at the door and escorted her into McKay's office. He was working at his stand-up desk, the kind known as an admiral's or navigator's desk, which was becoming increasingly popular at the Pentagon.

"Come in, Ms. Bishop. Take a seat." McKay joined her, taking one of two facing chairs near the window. "What's on your mind?"

"Admiral, we may or may not have a problem, but if we do, it's a doozy. I just had a visit from a reporter for the *L.A. Times*. They are working on a story that a secret commando outfit is training in Hawaii for an attempt to rescue Mrs. Walker and David."

McKay raised his eyebrows but said nothing. He was by nature a warm and friendly person. But, like many professional military men, he always felt a little awkward when dealing with anyone from the department's public affairs office. He tended to see officials such as Claudia Bishop as still the reporter she once was—and thus one of that enemy force known as "the press."

"I don't know how close they are to running a story. They got a tip after a sailor was arrested as the result of a barroom fight. He reportedly belongs to this secret outfit." She paused, waiting for a reaction. "So . . . the question is, are they onto something real?"

McKay returned her gaze, making a steeple of his hands with his index fingers pressed against his lips. An expert at body language would have read the gesture as saying: "Hush! Stonewall!"

After a few moments, he stood and faced the window, looking out over the Potomac toward Washington. The silence was broken only by the faint whisper coming from the window. It was part of a security system that created an invisible screen to prevent eavesdroppers from using sophisticated devices to listen in on conversations in his office.

"Can you steer them off this story, Ms. Bishop?"

"You mean mislead them, Admiral? No, I won't do that." She paused, looking up at him. "I gather, Admiral, that we do have a problem?"

He turned to look at her. "Yes, we do have a problem. Yes, we do have a unit training out there. And yes, they are preparing a rescue effort. A breach of secrecy now could ruin our best—perhaps our only—hope of freeing Mrs. Walker and her son. Can you stall them or head them off somehow?"

"I don't know. I could just use the old 'no comment' ploy. But if we don't give them a denial, they're going to take anything we say as confirmation. We could do that and just hope that their information is so thin that they won't print it. The other possibility is to level with them and ask them not to use the story. I could promise them an exclusive interview with the rescuers after the event, or something like that. But as soon as we begin negotiating about holding the story, we not only confirm its truth but widen the circle of people within their organization who know about it."

McKay turned and again stared out the window. Finally, he spoke. "I guess that's the best bet, Claudia. See what you can do. If I can help, let me know."

"At some point, I may ask you to talk directly to their bureau chief here or to their editor back in L.A. Their tendency will be to publish what they know. After all, that's the business they're in. But it will be hard to say no to a direct request from the chairman of the Joint Chiefs—especially if we can promise them some kind of incentive. I'll keep you informed."

He took her arm, escorting her to the door. "Yes, please do. We're going to need a little time to get this operation going, so, if you can make a deal, make sure it will hold for, say, ten days or two weeks."

At the door, she hesitated and then turned to face him.

"Admiral, I'd like to remind you, I'm no longer with the press."

He grinned. "I'm afraid it is still hard to think of you as on our side."

"It would make it so much easier for me—and better for you, too, if you would keep me in the loop. In this case, I was totally blind-sided when I was asked about this commando outfit. Same way with the ship movement out of Pearl. First I heard of it was when a reporter asked me in this morning's briefing."

"I'm sorry about that, Claudia. When we have more time, I'll fill you in on what happened with those ships. And, as far as keeping you in the loop is concerned, no problem—although I think you'll get more than your fill of things by the time this is all over."

CHAPTER 14

MARK RATTNER SLOWED THE BIG PAVE LOW HELICOPTER UN-til his speed was down to only about five knots, and then he descended as slowly as he could, feeling his way toward the ocean somewhere in the darkness below. It would be much easier if he could turn on his bright landing lights, but he wanted to take advantage of this training exercise to make the operation as realistic as if he were hovering just off a hostile coast.

A member of the team stood in the open door of the passenger compartment, leaning out into the wind. When he felt the ocean water being blown back into his face, he knew they were low enough to jump.

He grabbed the arm of the SEAL standing at his shoulder and propelled him toward the door. "Go!"

In rapid succession, he guided the other members of the team out the door and then followed them into the sea.

As he left the door, Rattner pulled up, rapidly putting distance between himself and the ocean's surface and all the perils it held.

The sound of the helicopter, curving off downwind, faded and died. In the water, the men shouted to each other and, one by one, joined up in a circle.

Nelson, who had been the next to last to leave the helo, called off the name of each man, taking roll. When the last man responded, he thought to himself, "All present and accounted for—thank goodness."

In the actual rescue operation, the team planned to parachute from a C-130, but Nelson had decided to have the helicopter drop them because of the time involved in setting up a drop from the plane.

The men conversed softly as they floated, buoyed by their inflatable life jackets. Every minute or so, Nelson tapped his knife against the metal canteen at his waist, making just enough sound to let the crew of the submarine know where they were.

Nelson looked at his watch. They had been in the water for fifteen minutes. The submarine should show up any minute. And then, staring into the darkness, he was aware of a dark shape looming out of the water only a few feet away. He swam to the sub and groped his way along its side to the escape chamber. He lifted a telephone hooked to the side of the chamber and told the sailor standing by inside that they were ready to come aboard.

The men, who had followed Nelson to the side of the submarine, climbed onto the deck. Two men from the submarine crew had already opened the door of the dry deck shelter and guided them inside. As soon as they had all entered, the crewmen dogged down the hatch on the shelter and signaled to the crew to dive. The submarine quickly slipped below the waves. The whole operation, from the moment the sub surfaced until it disappeared again, had taken only seven minutes.

Half an hour later, the *Kamehameha* surfaced three miles off the Hawaii coast. Members of the team quickly took their positions in their two SEAL delivery vehicles and set off toward the beach. A short distance offshore, they anchored the SDVs firmly to the bottom and swam the rest of the way. The landing went smoothly, and they assembled on the beach a short distance from their own barracks.

"That was a good night's work, men," Nelson told them as they gathered around him and began to strip off their masks, unfasten their breathing apparatuses, and peel off their protective wet suits. "Get a little rest, and then we'll hit the mountain again later today."

"Hoo Yah!" shouted one of the SEALs, and the cry was taken up by others. Even the air force men, after some reluctance, had learned to join in the traditional SEAL whoop.

As Nelson approached the barracks where his office was located, the first faint trace of the new day was beginning to lighten the eastern horizon. He was just able to make out the shape of someone standing on the porch.

"Pat? Is that you? What the hell are you doing up at this hour?"

"I don't know what it's about, Chuck, but Admiral McKay's office has been on the line every five minutes. I think they wanted me to swim out and get you. Anyway, he really— really, really, really—wants to talk to you."

"What's it about?"

"They wouldn't tell me anything. They just said the chairman wants Commander Nelson to call him ASAP."

Nelson left his gear on the small porch. He was barefoot, still wearing the lower half of his wet suit. He slid into his chair and picked up the hot line to the chairman's office.

"This is Commander Nelson returning the admiral's call."

"Yes, sir. He has been waiting for you to call back. Hold on a moment, sir."

"Chuck! What the hell is going on out there?"

"Sir?"

"This barroom fight business. What's going on?"

"Barroom fight? Oh, yes, sir. One of the men was involved in a fight the other night, and he was arrested. He has been removed from the team and is awaiting legal action."

"What about the press?"

"The press, sir? Oh, yes, there was a brief item in the local paper—a little police blotter mention of the arrest."

" 'Little police blotter mention'? Do you realize that the *Los Angeles Times* is poking around here asking if we have a commando unit training out there for a rescue effort? This could blow everything."

"The *Los Angeles Times*, sir?" Nelson experienced what William Safire, the *New York Times* columnist and wordsmith, describes as a "klong"—a sudden rush of shit to the heart. "Oh, my God. I never should have let them go to town."

"You're goddamn right you shouldn't have let them go to town. I want that whole operation buttoned down. No liberty. No phone calls home. No nothing. Is that understood? I said, is that understood?"

"Yes, sir. I understand."

"I thought you had better judgment, Chuck. What were they doing in town in the first place?"

"Sir, I agree, I should have known better. But they were liked caged animals, sir. I thought one night out would pay for itself in morale and performance. It was a stupid mistake."

McKay's tone changed abruptly.

"How's the training going?"

"Very good, sir. We just finished an evolution with the submarine. It was not exactly like the op. We used a Pave Low instead of dropping from a Combat Talon, and we only rode the sub for about an hour instead of twenty-four hours, but it was very realistic. The guys did a good job."

"Glad to hear it. Okay, Chuck, you keep on with your training. And keep those guys under lock and key. We'll see what we can do with the press from here. By the way, you got the message about the contact with the president?"

"Yes, sir. It was interesting—although not that surprising—to hear that we're dealing again with our friend, Luke Nash. And I'll bet my old Annapolis classmate, Ben Bernard, is there with him."

"I think that's a safe assumption, they having worked together before. And you heard that Miss Carson was also taken hostage?"

"Yes, sir. She could be helpful if we can find some way to communicate with her."

"Can I talk to you off the record—*really* off the record?" Claudia Bishop held the gaze of the *L.A. Times* reporter.

He returned her look for a few moments. "You know we don't like to do that, Cookie. But, okay, I'll listen. If I get uncomfortable, I'll tell you."

"So we're totally off the record?"

"Yes."

"You asked about whether a commando unit was training in Hawaii for a rescue effort. I've done some checking. The answer is 'yes.' "

He nodded but kept silent.

"If you go with a story on it, that could end our best—perhaps our only realistic—chance to rescue Mrs. Walker and her son."

"Well, you know that's not my decision."

"I realize that. Would it help to talk to your bureau chief?"

"That's the next step. But he doesn't have the last word, either, especially since this tip came to us from Hawaii, through our newsroom in L.A. If we decided to hold the story, we'd have to give some explanation, perhaps even get approval from L.A."

She sighed. "Look, let's call your bureau chief and see if he can come over here and talk to the chairman."

"Admiral McKay?"

"Yes."

"You are taking this pretty seriously, aren't you?"

"Very. Can we call him now?"

"Sure. Let me talk to him."

She dialed, asked for the bureau chief, and then handed the phone to him.

"Doyle? Can you come on over to the Pentagon? We've got something I need your help on, but I don't want to talk about it on the phone. Take a cab to the Mall entrance. You might have to walk up from the guard shack. I'll meet you at the door and get you through the rent-a-cops."

————— ★ —————

Twenty minutes later, Claudia Bishop and the two newsmen walked together down the hall to the chairman's office. He was waiting at the door to his inner office as they arrived.

"Thanks for coming over on such short notice." He showed them to chairs and launched immediately into his plea. "Ms. Bishop tells me that you inquired whether we have a commando unit training in Hawaii to attempt to rescue the Walkers. The answer is 'yes, we do.' But any publicity about this operation would doom any rescue attempt. Frankly, this is our best—and perhaps our only—chance to get them back safely."

"That's what Cookie told me, sir," the reporter responded.

"What do you want us to do?" the bureau chief inquired.

"I don't know how your newspaper works, but what I'd like you to do is to sit on the information you have and give us a chance to pull off this rescue."

"How much time are you talking about, sir?" the bureau chief asked.

"Ten days, two weeks."

"That's a long time to keep something like that under wraps. This is the biggest news story in the world right now. Even if we hold it, someone else is likely to get onto it and use it."

Claudia Bishop cut in. "My guess is, there's a pretty good chance that it will hold if the *Times* doesn't use it. This is the only query we've had, and it's now a couple of days since the incident."

"Well," the bureau chief said, "you just can't be sure. The story could surface any time from any one of a thousand sources."

McKay leaned forward in his chair and held the bureau chief's eyes with his own. "I guess what I'm asking you is to give us a chance. If you can hold this story, we may be able to carry off this operation successfully. If someone else uses it, that's just one of the chances we'll have to take."

The press secretary turned to the two newsmen. "I'll promise that, if I get any hint that the story is going to break, I'll let you know and give you a chance to be first with it."

"And when the operation is over, will we get an exclusive interview with the rescuers?" the bureau chief asked.

McKay looked to the press secretary and then nodded. "Yes, we can promise you that. The fact of the rescue will be announced as soon as it occurs, of course. But we can give you a good interview with members of the team on how it was conducted. The only thing I will ask is that you not use the names of those involved. We may need them again."

"Frankly," the bureau chief said, "we haven't gotten very far in checking out this story. I certainly wouldn't feel comfortable in going with it with what we've been able to develop on our own. But I will have to clear any decision not to pursue the story with L.A. I'll talk directly to the editor. If he okays sitting on the story, I'll just tell the national desk that we haven't come up with anything."

McKay rose and shook hands with the two newsmen. "I'll be very grateful if your editor agrees not to print anything about this now. This is going to be a very difficult operation in any event, and a premature news story would kill it before we could even make the attempt. If your editor has any question about the importance of this matter, you can have him call me directly."

Lucia McKenzie spoke softly, but Adm. Bridges could sense the steel in her voice even over the six thousand miles that separated them.

"Admiral, I just wanted to inquire about the movement of several ships from Pearl Harbor early today. We knew nothing of this movement until we were asked by the press. What is going on out there?"

"Ships? Oh, yes, Madam Secretary, three ships did depart early this morning. Routine training exercises."

"Routine, Admiral? When the crews were called in from shore leave so quickly that some of them were left behind?"

"We have to be sure that our crews are always ready to respond in the event of an emergency. We were caught sleeping once in December 1941. Never again, Madam Secretary."

"Admiral Bridges. We are in the midst of a very tense situation today, with the kidnapping of the president's wife and son. I may have mentioned this before, but let me repeat one last time: *I do not like surprises!* Is that understood, Admiral? *I do not like surprises!*"

"Yes, ma'am. I understand."

Bull Bridges' hand was trembling slightly as hung up the phone.

"Goddamn meddling woman!" An aide stood rigidly nearby, but he understood that the admiral's outburst was clearly rhetorical. "We're trying to deal with the goddamn Chicoms, and she wants to know, 'Where are your ships going, Admiral?'" He did a poor job of mimicking her soft tones.

"Those damned fools in Washington! If anybody is going to get the president's wife and his kid back, it's going to be us. Just leave us alone to do our job."

"Sir, do you really think the Chinese are involved in this?"

"Involved? Who the hell else? They're out mucking around, shooting missiles, in the South China Sea. And then the president's wife and son are kidnapped. Hell, yes, the Chinese are 'involved.' I bet this whole thing is being run from Beijing. I never have trusted those bastards."

Bridges strode across the room to the map of his domain, spread across an entire wall. He thought aloud: "We've got a picket line here between the Chinese and New Zealand. And we've got the marines coming down from Okinawa. Give us a week, and we'll be able to put the marines ashore. We'll get the hostages out and clean up that whole damn mess down there. And if the Chinks want to screw around, we'll give them a bloody nose, too."

CHAPTER 15

SOMETIMES, AS THE EAGLE FORCE SCIENTIFIC ADVISER, DR. James Malcolm felt like a fifth wheel—decorative, but not all that useful. And then there were times when he had the satisfying feeling that his experience and expertise made him just as essential a part of the team as the young guys who jumped out of airplanes and locked out of submarines.

In that sense, today was one of his better days.

"What do you make of these, Jim?" Pat Collins asked. Laid out on her desk were a series of messages emanating from the mysterious compound in New Zealand and captured electronically by the National Security Agency. "I guess it could all be part of some elaborate code, but it really looks like pretty straightforward buy and sell orders of the kind you would expect from a stock brokerage. That fits in with what we know about this Nash guy."

"You're right, Pat. I'm sure that's what they are. But why are we seeing this kind of message traffic from that place?"

"You're the expert. You tell me."

"Well, let's start with the obvious question: What are they buying and selling?"

"If I'm reading it correctly, it looks like metals, stock in mining companies, metals futures—in effect, they are bets on the future prices of metals."

"Metals? What kinds?"

"It looks like most of the trades involve just two metals: nickel and cobalt."

Malcolm stood resting his right elbow on his left arm and his chin on his right fist. "Nickel and cobalt? Strange. They're not some rare and valuable metals, like gold or silver. In fact, they're similar metals, often found together. Why would someone be trading in them—someone bold enough or crazy enough to try to take over an entire country and kidnap the wife and son of the most powerful man in the world? It doesn't make sense."

She shrugged. "No, it doesn't. But it must mean something. It's part of the puzzle."

Malcolm slumped into a chair with his legs stretched out in front of him and sat staring into space, thinking.

"Wait a minute!" he almost shouted as he vaulted out of the chair. "Cobalt and nickel? Buckyballs!"

She stared at him quizzically. "Buckyballs? Come on, Jim!"

"Yes, buckyballs. They are named for Buckminster Fuller. Remember? He was the architect who designed rather spectacular open lattice structures—geodesic domes?

"Back in the mid-'80s, scientists discovered that, if carbon was heated until it became a vapor and then cooled very rapidly, the carbon atoms arranged themselves in a series of linked tetrahedrons that looked very much like Fuller's buildings—hence the name 'buckyballs.' It was almost like magic: the carbon atoms did this all by themselves, arranging themselves into these intricate forms.

"The scientists found that, if nickel or cobalt was added to the carbon as a catalyst, the carbon created long tubes that were incredibly tiny but also incredibly strong.

"The discovery of this effect caused quite a stir several years ago. Then it kind of dropped out of the news. But the possibilities from the exploitation of this technology are mind-boggling."

"But what do you think these people are up to? How does this all fit together?"

"It doesn't, Pat. But maybe we can make it fit together. Give me a few hours, and let's see what I can come up with."

───── ★ ─────

Two hours later, he showed up at her office with a handful of sheets of computer printout.

"We may be onto something, here, Pat. I got on the Internet and began searching around, looking for cobalt, nickel, buckyballs.

"I found that a lot of the pioneering work on buckyballs and the related tubes—they call them 'nanotubes'—was done at Rice University in Houston."

"What are these things good for, Jim?"

"I think the first possibility that occurred to the scientists was that these tubes could be made into wires that would be dramatically lighter than today's electrical transmission lines but would conduct electricity much more efficiently than copper.

"I came across a speech that Dr. R. E. Smalley at Rice made a couple of years ago. He told how Arthur C. Clarke, the science fiction writer, wrote a book back in the 1970s in which he forecast the invention of what he called a 'space elevator.' He didn't foresee this happening until the year 2145, but what he imagined is this: A satellite would be positioned far out in space, where it hovered over the equator. Then, using concentrated heat from the sun, it would create a thin but incredibly strong rope that would be lowered from the satellite to earth to create a space elevator.

"As Dr. Smalley noted, the 'rope' imagined by Clarke is very much like the tubes he has created in the laboratory.

"Personally, I think the uses for a material far stronger than steel, much tougher than diamonds, and much better at conducting electricity than copper are limited only by the human imagination."

"Wait a minute, Jim. Did you say 'Rice'?"

"Yes, Rice University, in Houston."

"That's funny. We received a report from the USS *Kitty Hawk*, which interrogated the Chinese rescued from that submarine that was in a collision with one of our destroyers. Several of those rescued weren't crew members, but scientists. And one of them told the interrogators he had attended Rice.''

''Do you suppose that submarine could have been on its way to deliver those scientists to New Zealand?''

''That would be just a guess. It seems to be kind of a roundabout way of getting them there. They could have just bought a ticket and flown to Auckland.''

''Exactly. So the Chinese scientists may be a piece to the puzzle—hopefully the same puzzle we're working on. Do you think they could be trying to corner the market for those two metals? Buy up so much of the metal itself, or the production facilities, that they control the world supply—and thus the price?''

''Wouldn't that be awfully difficult?''

Malcolm shrugged. ''We're getting in over my head, Pat. I know that, historically, some people have gained control of the market for a particular commodity. But I really don't know whether it would be possible in this case. All we have here is a strong hint that such an effort is under way. They might get away with it, if no one is paying much attention. Nickel and cobalt are not very glamorous metals, so it would not necessarily attract much attention if someone quietly and slowly began buying them up. Most traders in the metals have probably never even heard of buckyballs. But if the buckyball technology catches on, those could be the hottest metals in the world. And whoever controls the metals—and perhaps some of the technology—is in a very powerful position.''

''You know, Jim, there are still a lot of pieces of this puzzle missing. But we may be onto the most important of all: motive. Could you give me a brief memo on the buckyball business? I'll send off a report to Admiral McKay and include that in it. He'll be able to get some people working on it who know a lot more about this business than we do.''

''Sit down, Rex. We want to talk to you about a special mission.''

Rex Marker nodded to Nelson and then glanced at the two other men in the room: Jeff Bonior and Mark Rattner.

"Do you know why we're training here in Hawaii, Rex?"

"No one has told me, sir. But it seems pretty obvious: The president's wife and son have been kidnapped, and someone is going to have to go get them back. That someone, I figure, is us."

Nelson smiled. "So much for secrecy. Yes, that's why we're here. The big gap in our preparations is intel. We have been getting some information from electronic intercepts and satellite and U-2 overflights. But we still know a lot less than I would like to know about what we're getting into."

Marker nodded and waited, uncertain about where the conversation was heading.

"That's where you fit in, Rex," Bonior told him. "We want you to get into that place and let us know what's there and what's going on."

Marker felt a strange sensation in his chest. He wasn't sure whether it was a shudder of fear and apprehension or the thrill of anticipation of a challenging adventure.

"I assume, sir, that we are going to go in by submarine, as we have been training. Is that what you want me to do?"

"No, we want you in there before we land." Nelson turned to Rattner, the air force pilot. "Mark, why don't you fill him in?"

"I've already been in contact with the Strategic Command, Rex. I'm trying to arrange for you to be a passenger on a B-52 making a routine transit to Diego Garcia. But you will go only part of the way. The B-52 will swing south of its normal course, and you will bail out over the Tasman Sea about fifty miles west of the New Zealand coast at an altitude of, say, thirty-five thousand feet. That will permit you to land near your target undetected."

Marker nodded as the pilot spoke, putting the mission together in his imagination. He had been through the SEALs' advanced parachute course at El Centro, California, learning how to jump at extreme altitudes where it was so cold that a man's eyes could freeze shut the moment he left the plane.

He had been involved in many realistic training exercises. But in those exercises, he had always jumped with a squad or even a platoon of SEALs. A thought came unbidden into his mind: They're sending me alone because they don't want to lose more than one guy on this crazy op.

"How will I find this place, sir? I assume I'll jump in the dark."

"We'll try to get a good reading on the winds just before you go out," Nelson told him. "That way, you can calculate your time and distance. And you'll carry a Global Positioning System receiver that will help you find your target in the dark. Our overflights indicated that the compound you will be heading toward is brightly lit at night, probably because there's no one else close by that they need to care about. When you get close, you should have no difficulty picking it out."

"And when I get there?"

"You'll be on your own. You'll be carrying a satellite communications transmitter/receiver. You should at least be able to hide in the woods and give us a report on what you see—fences, traffic in and out, number and positions of guards, that sort of thing. Hopefully, you'll be able to get inside the place. It would be ideal if you could get to the hostages and give us a report on their condition and their location.

"One more thing, Rex: We've just learned that a Secret Service agent—a woman—was taken hostage along with Mrs. Walker and David. If you get inside, you may be able to link up with her. That's probably a long shot, but it's a shot worth taking if the opportunity presents itself."

"Do we know who she is, sir?"

"Her name is Cindy Carson. She was in charge of the First Lady's security detail."

A big grin broke over Marker's face. "Cindy Carson? Frogwoman?"

"You know her?"

"Yeah, she came down to Puerto Rico a year ago last winter and went through some evolutions with us. Some kind of cross-training from the Secret Service. Her brother's in one of the West Coast teams, and she said she'd always wanted to be a SEAL. Since she couldn't be a frogman, she signed up with the Secret Service instead.''

"How did she do?"

"Impressive. She swam, parachuted, qualified with all our weapons, did everything we did. I bet if we let women into the SEALs, she could make it through BUD/S, Hell Week and all. We had a party when we finished up, and the guys gave her a Budweiser. We thought she'd earned it.''

"The SEAL insignia?"

"Yeah. She can't wear it, of course, but she's probably got it framed on her wall at home.''

"An excellent asset, then, but still only a potential one. We should assume that you're going to be on your own. Think you can handle it?"

Marker shook his head slightly, involuntarily. Then he raised his eyes to look at Nelson and said, "I can do that, sir. You can count on me.''

Nelson smiled. "I'm sure we can, Rex. But I want you to understand that this is a very risky mission. You could end up in the ocean. You could end up injured and in snow up to your chin. You could run into guards and be totally outnumbered. So I want to emphasize that this is entirely voluntary. If you don't like the odds, just say so, and you can walk out of here and forget it.''

"Oh, no, sir. Count me in." He paused and then asked, "When do we go?"

Nelson glanced at Rattner for the answer.

"I still have to work things out with Omaha. But let's assume you'll leave tomorrow afternoon. You should be ready to go by noon.''

"Yes, sir. Noon.''

"Rex, I want you to work with Jeff, here, in your planning for this mission. You don't have much time, and we still don't know very much about this place you're going to. But I want you and Jeff to try to think things through as thoroughly as you can and work out a mission plan in as much detail as possible. And, Jeff, I want you to prepare him as much as possible for what to do if things go wrong or he gets in trouble.''

"Will do, sir. Come on, Rex, let's get to work.''

As they rose to leave, Nelson signaled to Rattner to remain seated.

"Mark, I need your advice. I've been trying to figure out some way we can set up a diversion to get those folks looking the wrong direction when we go in. Remember last year, when we went into Iraq, the navy put on a big show, making them think Baghdad was under attack? I wish we could do something like that this time.''

"What have you got in mind?''

"Not much. The guy who is holding the hostages insists that all military forces stay at least two hundred miles away from New Zealand. We're counting on being able to sneak the unit in there by submarine. But there should be some way to create a diversion just before we move in.''

"Hit 'em with some Tomahawks?''

"You mean cruise missiles? Yeah, we could fire them from a submarine. Have them land just before we show up.''

Rattner slowly shook his head. "I don't like it. They're supposed to be plenty accurate. But do we really want to bet the life of the president's wife and kid that one of those things won't hit in the wrong place? I don't think so.''

"Any better ideas?''

The two men sat silently for several minutes.

"Hey, wait a minute, Chuck.'' The air force officer rose and walked to the wall map. "One of the demands this guy made was for some arms. Why don't we give them to him and use that as a cover for a diversion?''

"What do you mean?''

"We tell him, fine, we'll comply with the request, maybe even bargain some more time with it. We load up a C-141 and tell him it will land at Auckland. What we don't tell him is that we'll have a Combat Talon tucked in behind the Starlifter, so there's only one image on the radar. As the C-141 descends toward Auckland, the MC-130 breaks off and heads for Nash's compound right down on the deck, below their radar.''

''And then what?''

''Our guys rig up some dummies with parachutes. As the plane comes over the compound, they dump out the dummies. When we get there, everybody is out looking for them, not us.''

Nelson rose and joined Rattner at the map. ''That just might work even better than you think. We figure Ben Bernard is in charge of security at the compound. And ol' Big Dog is a fanatic on parachutes. He'd use a parachute to get from here to the bathroom if he could, and if he were running this op, that's the way he'd do the insertion. So when they hear the plane or pick it up on the radar and then catch the chutes in their lights, he'll go berserk. He'll convince himself it's the real thing.''

''Do you think we can set it up?''

''I'll check with Admiral McKay about sending in the C-141. He's probably going to be worried about the safety of the crew if they're on the ground at Auckland when we go in.''

''I'm not even sure the C-141 has to land. They can circle Auckland and then make some excuse and fly away. But, just in case they do have to land, let's have some of our guys crew that plane. I'll have Jack Laffer, my deputy, fly the MC-130, and we'll have our guys on that plane, too. We're not going to use all of Eagle Force on the actual operation, and this will have the added advantage of giving them a piece of the action.''

''We're really going to have to do some split-second timing, Mark. I want to hit that place just a few minutes after the chutes come down—just long enough to get them stirred up and looking in the wrong direction. If the diversion happens too early, Nash may harm the hostages. If it happens too late, it's not going to do us any good.''

''Jack has a lot of time in the Combat Talon, and he is a very precise pilot. We can use the satcomm to let him know when we are, say, ten or fifteen minutes from our attack. He'll come in right when we tell him to.''

''I really think this will work, Mark. Why don't you use back channels to talk to some of your air force buddies and start setting things up—very much on the hush-hush? Meanwhile, I'll talk to the admiral.''

As Secretary of State Henry Trover entered the Oval Office, he seemed to carry with him a calming influence: Henry Trover is here, and everything will work out all right. At sixty-six, he had a full head of hair, turning white on top but still dark at the temples. His dark wool suit, from the same Saville Row tailor he had patronized for more than forty years, hung perfectly on his tall, thin figure. His white shirt, accented by his conservative blue-and-red rep necktie, contrasted perfectly with the dark cloth of his suit.

The president shook his hand and guided him to a seat on the sofa. ''Thanks for coming over, Henry. Sorry to pull you away from your duties on such short notice.''

''Not at all, Mr. President.'' Of course, he'd been prepared for this meeting since the kidnapping. Turning to Abdul Rahman, the national security adviser, Trover nodded. ''Good to see you, General Rahman.''

The president took a seat, leaning forward with his elbows on his knees.

''I need your advice, Henry . . . and Abe,'' he said, looking at each of the men in turn.

''Yes, Mr. President,'' the two men murmured, almost in unison.

''I received a phone call from the man who is holding Marcia and David.''

Trover, to whom this was news, leaned forward, listening intently.

''I think we are dealing with the same madman who incinerated Mojave and almost destroyed St. Louis last year. He made three demands: that we keep all military forces—ours and other countries' as well—two hundred miles from New

Zealand; that we recognize the new government of what they now call Aotearoa; and that we supply them with defensive weapons."

"Quite a wish list, Mr. President," Trover said.

"Yes, it certainly is. Now, we've got to figure out how to react. I am not going to do anything that endangers the security of the United States. And I don't want to do anything that appears to be caving in to this kind of personal pressure."

"May I suggest, Mr. President, that an important consideration here is to buy time," Trover said. "I assume you have been thinking about how to rescue Mrs. Walker and David, and that will take time. Perhaps we can go through some motions that appear to be responding to these demands, even though that is not our intention in the long run."

"Such as . . . ?"

"Such as keeping military forces away from New Zealand. Neither we nor any of our allies normally has much military presence in that part of the world. I can talk to our friends in Australia, who would be the most likely to have any ships in New Zealand waters. And, of course, we should check with the French. They do maintain a military presence in the South Pacific in connection with their nuclear test site, although I doubt they would have anything within two hundred miles of New Zealand."

"The *Kitty Hawk* and a couple of her escort vessels are still in that vicinity, sir," Rahman interjected. "We should probably have that battle group move away from New Zealand, at least for the time being. At two hundred miles, she would still be close enough to cover targets in New Zealand, at least on North Island, with her F/A-18s."

"Admiral McKay is taking care of that."

Trover leaned forward. "Now, Mr. President, on the matter of recognition, if and when you are contacted again, you can say that recognition will require the advice and consent of the Senate. That will take time."

"Does it really require involving the Senate?"

Trover smiled. "I think we can safely say that it does because recognition of a new government inevitably involves the matter of treaties—and that is clearly a matter that requires action by the Senate.''

''Okay, Henry. Abe, what about the arms they are requesting?''

''I think it should be possible to buy a good deal of time there, sir, without appearing to be stalling, but without actually shipping any arms, either. At this point, we don't even know what arms they are demanding. When we do get a list, we will have to check on availability. And then we will have to work out the details of how they will be delivered. That could all take several weeks even if we tried to expedite it.''

''Good, that makes sense.'' The president turned to Trover. ''Henry, there is one other matter. This isn't in your field of expertise, but I would like your advice. How do you suggest we deal with this matter in the press? How much do we release, and how much do we hold back?''

''As you know, sir, I have long been an advocate of as much openness in government as possible—even in the conduct of our foreign relations. Some matters must be kept secret, but I am convinced that, in most cases, we are better served by letting the public know and understand what we are doing than we are by trying to keep everything secret—until it leaks out in the press or on Capitol Hill, often to our embarrassment.

''In this case, I think we have to be very cautious. We have to think always of the welfare of Mrs. Walker and your son. Did the kidnapper you talked to say anything about whether or not you should publicize his contact with you, or his demands?''

''No, he didn't get a chance. He spoke briefly and made his demands. Then he gave the phone to Marcie, and she quickly blurted out that they were being held on Mount Egmont by Nash, the same man who destroyed Mojave. He cut her off, and that was the end of the conversation. So I don't know how he would react if we were to reveal the fact that the kidnapper has been in touch and has made demands.''

''I think the prudent thing, at this point, Mr. President, is not to say anything about this contact,'' Trover responded. ''Of course, word will inevitably leak out as we go through the motions of responding to his demands, especially in our contacts with foreign governments. But you may well receive another communication before that happens, especially since the first call was cut short.''

''So we wait and see?''

''That would be my advice, Mr. President. There is, of course, enormous public and press interest in this matter, so we can hardly expect to keep very much secret for very long. But, for now, I would suggest that we simply stick with 'no comment.' ''

CHAPTER 16

BEN BERNARD'S FINGERS BIT INTO CINDY CARSON'S ARM AS he guided her through a hallway. "Please," she said, "you're hurting my arm."

Bernard spun her around so that she faced him, and hit her across the face hard with the back of his hand.

"Now shut up!" Holding her arm even harder, he pushed her on.

When they reached his office, he slapped her again and propelled her inside. Before she could react, he punched her, a sharp blow to her right eye. She could feel blood beginning to flow down her cheek where the skin had been broken.

She tensed at first, preparing to counter his next blow and use his own momentum to send him crashing against the wall. With her training in self-defense, she felt confident that she could hurt him, perhaps even break his wrist. But going toe to toe with him, she decided, wasn't the best opening gambit. So she covered her face with her hands and began to cry. Overcoming the instinct and training that told her to fight back was one of the hardest things she had ever done. But she thought: Just let him think I'm helpless.

Bernard pulled her hands from in front of her face and hit her twice more. A welt appeared under one eye, and the flesh around the other turned purple. Blood dripped from her chin onto her white blouse.

As he pushed her back against the wall and turned away, he was breathing heavily. She could see that he had become sexually aroused.

He took a box of tissues from a shelf and tossed it toward where she stood huddled against the wall. Striding across the room, he opened the door of a small adjoining room. ''Get in there.''

She worked her way across the room, facing him but keeping as far away as possible. As soon as she entered the other room, she heard the key turn in the door.

Marcia Walker had taken to pacing in a tight circle around the room in which the hostages were being held. Finally, completing a circuit, she went to the door and tried the handle. It didn't turn. Then she banged loudly on the wooden door.

Outside, the guard first ignored the pounding. When it persisted, he finally unlocked the door and opened it far enough to look inside.

''What do you want?'' His voice, like that of others they had encountered, carried a heavy eastern European accent.

''I want to see Miss Carson!''

''Ma'am, I am just the guard.''

''Well, get someone here for me to talk to. I want to see her! I want to see her now!''

The guard pulled the door closed and locked it. Then he spoke into his walkie-talkie radio.

''Sir, the lady is demanding to see Miss Carson. She keeps pounding on the door. What should I do?''

''Stand by.'' Ben Bernard picked up the phone on his desk. ''Sir, I think our subject is softening up. She's banging on the door and demanding to see Carson. Shall I take her down again?''

''You've taken care of her?''

''Yes, sir. I didn't break any bones or anything, but I think she knows where we stand.''

''Okay, wait a little while and then take her back. Let Walker get a good look at her. Then you can bring Walker down, and we'll make another call to Washington.''

Cindy Carson hadn't had a chance to look in a mirror, but she knew her face was a mess. Carefully touching it with her fingers, she could feel the cut under her eye and the puffiness where her face had begun to swell.

The gasps she heard from Marcia Walker and David as she was pushed back into their little prison told her as much as a mirror would have.

"Oh, Cindy, what have they done to you?"

Marcia Walker took her in her arms while David held her hand.

Cindy managed a wan smile. "I'm okay, ma'am. Just a few bruises. I think they're using me to send you a message."

"Here, sit down and let me look at your face. David, please let the cold water run on a washcloth and then bring it to me."

She carefully washed Cindy's face, gently wiping away the dried blood. "I wish we had some ice. I'm afraid you're going to have a couple of black eyes."

"It won't be the first time, ma'am. I have two big brothers, and we played pretty rough."

"Cindy, I'm so sorry you're involved in this mess. This whole thing is beginning to get to me."

"I understand, ma'am. But this is all part of a game they're playing. They beat on me; they beat on you."

"I know, Cindy. And, dammit, the strategy is working."

"You just keep your chin up. Remember, they need you and they need David. You are very valuable to them. If they try to make you cooperate, make them pay for it."

Marcia Walker blew her nose softly and wiped her eyes. "You're right, Cindy. They may be wearing me down, but they're a long way from breaking me. They'll find out that Marcia Walker is no pushover."

———— ★ ————

It was more than half an hour before they heard a key in the door. Ben Bernard entered and motioned to Marcia Walker. "Come with me, ma'am."

She stood and looked at him. "You'll have to excuse me." She turned, entered the bathroom, and closed the door. Bernard felt silly, standing there and, a few moments later, listening to the toilet flush.

When the president's wife emerged five minutes later, she had washed her face, applied a thin coat of lipstick, combed her hair, and straightened her clothes. She knew instinctively that personal grooming was one of a hostage's best defenses. Moving purposefully toward the door, she said, "Okay, Mr. Bernard, we can go now. I think I know the way." As he followed her through the door, he had the uncomfortable feeling that she had somehow taken control of the situation away from him.

Walking briskly, she led the way. She didn't stop until she reached Nash's door; then she stepped aside for Bernard to knock once and open the door.

As she entered the room, she saw Nash in his usual position, standing behind his desk. Then she became aware of another man sitting in a chair to Nash's right—a tall, lean man with the broad features and tan skin of a Polynesian. She let her eyes linger on him for a moment and then stood directly in front of the desk.

"You people are savages! Have you seen what they have done to Miss Carson?"

"Miss Carson? No, I have not seen her myself. But I gather from your reaction that you have seen her and that you did not like what you saw. I will have to commend Mr. Bernard. Please sit down, Mrs. Walker—sit down and be thankful that you and your son have not been harmed." His tone added the unspoken word *yet*.

She glared at Nash for a moment, her mouth working in frustration. Then slowly, reluctantly, she sat.

"Mrs. Walker, I would like you to meet Wiremu Kingi."

The man she had noticed upon entering the room rose and nodded his head toward her. He was dressed in slacks, a sports coat, and a necktie, but he held in his right hand a long, intricately carved wooden staff. She assumed it was some kind of symbol of authority.

"I asked Mr. Kingi to come here to help you understand what is happening here in Aotearoa and why your cooperation is important to us."

She looked at him quizzically. "Aotearoa?"

"Yes, that is the name given to their land by the Maori people, the new rulers of what was called New Zealand. Wiremu will correct me if I'm wrong, but I believe it means 'long white cloud' in Maori."

"I don't see what that all has to do with us."

"Perhaps Mr. Kingi can make things clearer. Wiremu, why don't you explain to Mrs. Walker why you have, with our help, seized power?"

Wiremu Kingi moved over closer to Mrs. Walker and stood looking down at her. He began in a deep voice, speaking slowly, ponderously.

"Mrs. Walker, my great-great-grandfather was the last Maori leader to hold out against the depredations of the Europeans—what we call the *pakeha*. He and his people lived—and suffered—in the wilderness on the slopes of Mount Taranaki." He paused. "You may know it as Mount Egmont, but we prefer the Maori word, Taranaki. In fact, his last resistance was staged not far from where we are at this moment.

"The pattern was not unlike what was happening in your own country at about the same time involving the Native Americans. The Europeans tried to force us to sell our land. We resisted because we held our land as a people, not as individuals. The British army sent soldiers to kill us and drive us from our homes. Under this pressure, some of our weaker leaders agreed to sell the people's land. Treaties were negotiated. And then, of course, the treaties were broken, as the European hunger for land continued unabated.

"We were gradually reduced to a subject people, living in poverty, plagued by alcoholism and, more recently, drug abuse. We were a proud people reduced to powerlessness in our own land." His voice rose with indignation as he talked.

"Oh, yes, the *pakeha* talked of how well they treated us, how there was no racial discrimination in what they called

New Zealand. But what does that mean to a man stripped of his dignity, stripped of his manhood?

"Now we have changed all that. We, the original inhabitants of these islands, have taken control. *We* are now the government of Aotearoa. *We* now control our own destiny. We are no longer subjects of an alien race in our own land."

He turned and motioned toward Nash, who was sitting behind his desk. "That has all changed because of the help of our friend, Mr. Nash. He is a true savior of our people. I say to him: *Ka whakapai au ki a koe mo tau atawhai, e hoa.*"

Marcia Walker sat impassively as he made his emotional speech. When he stopped, she stared at him, letting the silence linger. Then she stood.

"Mr. Kingi, do you know who Mr. Nash is? Do you know that this man—this 'savior of our people'—is an international criminal? Do you know that he is a ruthless mass murderer? Do you know that he has the blood of thousands of innocent men, women, and children on his hands? Do you know that he is the man responsible for destroying an entire American city in one of the most ruthless crimes in all history?"

The vehemence of her statement rendered him speechless. He stared at her unblinking and then turned to Nash, a question lingering unspoken in the air.

Nash stood and glared at Marcia Walker. Then he cleared his throat and turned toward Kingi. "Wiremu, Mrs. Walker is under some pressure. I hope you'll overlook her outburst."

"But . . . what she said . . ."

"We'll talk about it later. I'll explain what has made her so emotional." He looked at his watch. "I'm sure you have important business to accomplish." He came around the desk and, taking Kingi by the elbow, moved him toward the door.

As the door closed, he turned. "That was not very smart, Mrs. Walker. I thought it was useful for you to understand the importance of what we have done here, from a human standpoint. And now you have disturbed Wiremu with unpleasant thoughts, with distractions he does not need."

"The truth, Mr. Nash. The truth. I know very little about your relationship with this Mr. Kingi. But it is clear that you have duped him into this dangerous adventure for your own purposes—not because of any great love in your heart for the noble Maori people. You are disgusting!"

"You calm down and listen to me." He stood above her, staring down through his dark glasses. She stood up and returned his stare defiantly.

"It is time for us to make another call to the White House. I will not have any more outbursts of the kind you indulged in during our previous call. That was very imprudent of you."

"I have no intention of cooperating with you in whatever insane game you are trying to play, sir. You can make your call or not. Just leave me out of it."

"Mrs. Walker, you have seen Miss Carson, and you understand why you've seen her. Shall I call Mr. Bernard and ask him to make my message more clear? I don't think you are that stupid. Now, let us make our call. And I'm expecting your cooperation."

She looked at him, smoldering with anger. "What do you want?"

He picked up a sheet of paper from his desk. "Here is a 'script' for you. I want you to read this, exactly as it is written, when I tell you to. I will not tolerate any more outbursts or attempts to communicate more than is written on this sheet of paper. If you say anything other than what is written here, the consequences will be most unpleasant."

She took the piece of paper and glanced through the three paragraphs. Then she nodded.

He picked up the phone and dialed the White House. Moments later, the call went through, and he was quickly connected to the president.

"Mr. President. This is Luke Nash. Our mutual friends are all well and in good health—at this time. I will let you speak briefly to your wife."

He handed the phone to Marcia and nodded toward the sheet of paper.

"Marcie! Marcie! Are you all right?" the president exclaimed.

She didn't respond to his question. Instead, she began reading from the paper in a dull monotone:

"Maynard, [he would know that she never used his formal first name] we are guests here of the people who have liberated the Maori peoples of Aotearoa from their foreign oppressors. We are being treated well, and Cindy and David and I are in good health.

"We are under the control of Mr. Nash. He assures me that nothing will happen to us if you follow his instructions.

"Please, please, Maynard, do exactly as he tells you. If you do, we will be reunited soon."

She handed the phone back to Nash.

"Marcie? Marcie?"

"That's enough for now, Mr. President."

"Let me talk to my son."

"Not now, Mr. President. We will save that pleasure for later. You are aware of what I require of you. Have you carried out my demands?"

"It will take time, sir. I have issued orders that American vessels not come within two hundred miles of New Zealand, as you directed. We are contacting other governments to request that they, too, maintain that distance."

"That's progress. What about my other demands?"

"Both of those will take some time. We are beginning the process for recognition of Aotearoa, but that will take at least several days. It requires approval of the Senate, and that is something I really cannot control."

"You can be very persuasive, Mr. President. I'm sure the Senate can move expeditiously if you explain to the senators how important this action is. Now, what about the weapons?"

"You haven't told us what kinds of weapons or how they are to be delivered. Even after we receive your list, it will take some time to assemble—or even acquire—the weapons and prepare them for delivery."

"I will fax you a list of weapons later today, along with instructions for delivery. You will be hearing from us." He hung up the phone.

"Much better, Mrs. Walker."

He pressed a button, and Bernard entered to escort her back to her cell.

Maynard Walker continued to listen after the phone went dead and then slowly put the receiver back in the cradle.

"That wasn't Marcie, at all. Did you hear how dull and wooden her voice sounded? She was clearly under duress."

Derek Shepherd, of the Secret Service, had been with the president during the phone call. "It sounded to me, sir, as though she was being forced to read from a written script. There was no spontaneity, in either what she said or the way she said it."

"You're right. I think they wanted to send me a message—to worry me—without making overt threats. And they sure as hell succeeded, dammit."

"We'll analyze the tape very carefully to see if it tells us anything. But at least we know for sure that Cindy Carson is a hostage—and still alive."

CHAPTER 17

ABOARD THE USS *KITTY HAWK*, ADM. HARMONY STARED AT the message and scratched his head. He was standing by 200 nautical miles offshore of New Zealand's northeast coast. All of his aircraft remained on the deck, but they were on alert. Two birds stood ready in launching position with pilots strapped in, ready to fly on five minutes' notice.

After the confusion at Wellington, he now had new orders, directly from CINCPAC in Hawaii. He read the new message one more time:

"You are to proceed at flank speed to 14 degrees 30 minutes south, 148 degrees 59 minutes east. There, you will take command of the force designated Strike Force Bravo. Be on alert at all times for Chinese surface, air, and subsurface forces that may attempt to move through your position toward New Zealand. Maintain continuous air surveillance of the seas north and east of the Solomon Islands. You will be prepared to engage such forces if necessary to provide cover for the marine amphibious battalion now en route to your position from Okinawa. Bridges sends."

Harmony shrugged and began giving orders to proceed immediately toward the rendezvous point in the Coral Sea south of Port Moresby, Papua New Guinea. He also sent an urgent message to Hawaii asking that a fleet tanker be ordered to meet him to refuel his ship and his escort vessels. It was at times like this that Harmony fervently wished he had the flexibility of a nuclear-powered carrier, which could sail for years without taking on fuel.

Once the orders were given, Harmony joined the ship's navigator at his desk, on which a large map of the South Pacific was displayed.

Picking up a pair of dividers, Harmony measured off the distance to his destination and then used a handheld calculator to get his estimated time of arrival.

"I figure our ETA at thirteen-forty-five Zulu, sir," the navigator said. Zulu—the time at the meridian running through Greenwich, England—is used by navigators to avoid having to continually change their watches to local time.

"Yeah, that's about what I get. It'll be dark, so I want all our ships to be very alert. This is no time for a collision at sea as we join up."

"What are our orders after we arrive at the rendezvous, sir?"

"We don't have anything specific yet. My understanding is that we are to form some sort of a picket line as the Chinese move down in this direction, following their maneuvers in the South China Sea. And our orders mention a marine unit coming down from Okinawa. I expect we'll get orders soon to prepare for an amphibious landing in New Zealand to rescue the hostages."

"Sounds like a big order, sir."

"Frankly, I'd be a lot happier if I knew more about what ol' Bull Bridges has in mind. The marines do a lot of training in amphibious landings, but they make me nervous. I was just a young lieutenant back in '83 when we invaded Grenada. We were on our way to the Med when we got orders to land marines on the north shore of this little island in the Caribbean."

"Yeah, we studied that in class," the navigator said.

"It worked out in the end, but it almost turned to shit. Fortunately, we had some SEALs along with us. We sent them in while the marines were getting ready to land. They sent back word that boats couldn't land. That meant we had to abandon trying to send the marines in over the beach and instead we had to bring them in by helicopter. If we had run into the kind of resistance some of the other units did down south at St. George's, we would have been in real trouble.''

"There were a lot of communications problems in that op, too, weren't there?''

"Yeah, a lot. We were all on different frequencies. If we're going to go into New Zealand, I'd feel a lot better if we had more time to plan—make sure we're all singing from the same sheet of music and even do a rehearsal. As it is, the marines will arrive on their transport, and we'll probably go right on down and land them. I sure hope it works out all right.''

Harmony remained leaning over the map. "Look at this. It's like a time warp. Up here, where we're going, here's the Solomon Islands and Guadalcanal. Here's the 'slot' where the Japs ran down at night, trying to reinforce their guys on Guadalcanal. This area here, they called it 'Iron Bottom Sound' because so many ships were sunk. There's a lot of history there. A lot of history. And a lot of guys died there.''

The navigator stood studying the map, nodding as Harmony spoke.

Harmony slapped his hand on the map and turned away. "Let's hope we don't make any history. We'll just have a nice, quiet cruise in the Coral Sea.''

"I hope so, sir,'' the navigator said as he turned back to his calculations.

"Thank you for coming by, Admiral McKay.'' As always, Lucia McKenzie was polite and soft-spoken, but she got right to the point. "Please tell me what Admiral Bridges is up to.''

"I have just talked to him, ma'am. As you heard, he has dispatched several ships from Honolulu and is assembling a task force in the South Pacific. It consists of the ships that were involved in monitoring the Chinese exercises in the South China Sea plus the additional ships now on their way. Command will be exercised from the *Kitty Hawk*, which is proceeding north from its position off New Zealand to the rendezvous point.''

"And the marines?"

"Yes, Admiral Bridges has ordered a Marine amphibious brigade to the rendezvous point."

"And what is the purpose of all this, Admiral?"

"Admiral Bridges is very much concerned about the threat from the Chinese, Madam Secretary. He suspects—with some reason, I might add—that the Chinese are somehow involved in what is happening in New Zealand."

"So Admiral Bridges is preparing for a confrontation with the Chinese?"

"As CINCPAC, he has considerable autonomy in positioning the forces under his command, ma'am. He has the responsibility to be prepared for any eventuality."

"And these marines? Is he thinking of invading New Zealand?"

"Again, Madam Secretary, he is making what seem to him to be prudent preparations for any eventuality. If he is asked to attempt a rescue, he will have the forces available."

She sat, tapping on the edge of her desk with a pencil, thinking. After a few moments, she spoke. "I am very concerned about this, Admiral McKay. I think Admiral Bridges tends to be very impulsive, given to taking action and explaining what he has done after the fact. I want to be very sure that he doesn't go off and do something rash while we are in the midst of this very tense and very difficult situation."

"I am watching this very carefully, ma'am. As you know, we are preparing a rescue attempt by a small commando unit under my direct control. I think it is prudent to have a sizeable force available in that area in the event that they are needed. My plan does not require their involvement, but it is better to have them there than to wish later that they were."

"I understand, Admiral. But this Bull Bridges does worry me. To be perfectly frank, I think I might feel much more comfortable if Admiral Bridges were to be replaced by a less impulsive officer."

"Replace Admiral Bridges?"

"From what I hear, his nickname is well deserved. We certainly don't want a bull cavorting around in this particular China shop."

He nodded slowly. "Yes, I share some of your reservations about Admiral Bridges. He enjoys his autonomy, and he does consider the Pacific to be his ocean. But he always, in my experience, has been obedient to direct orders. I will make sure that his orders are such that he doesn't do anything rash."

She sat for a moment looking at him, doubt showing in her face. "Admiral Bridges still worries me."

He stood and walked over toward the window and back again. "Let me share my thinking with you, ma'am. I have known Bull Bridges since we were first classmen at the academy. As you say, he is impulsive. He is very strong-willed. He does things his way. Some would call him arrogant.

"Now, all of these character traits add up to a military man who is poorly suited to life in a peacetime navy. He is not a man who will go along to get along. He is not a man who will tell you whatever you want to hear—not a yes-man, in other words. Those who work with him, or for him, often find him difficult, even abrasive. But I will tell you that, if we ever get into a fighting war, Bull Bridges is the guy I want on my side. He is tough, aggressive, resourceful, imaginative, and one hell of a fighting man."

"Yes, of course, Admiral. But this *is* peacetime and, we would hope, will remain peacetime for many years to come."

"My point, ma'am, is that Bull Bridges is the type of man we want if we ever get into a conflict. And history shows us that, no matter how fervently we work and plan and pray for peace, wars do happen. When that happens, I want a navy that is ready to fight—not only the ships and planes, but the men. Men like Bull Bridges.

"The young men—and women—who will be our future leaders are not stupid. They can read the message we send them by watching who we appoint to lead them. If we choose admirals who advance by sticking up a finger to see which way the wind is blowing before every move, they will see that. But if we choose war-fighters like Bull Bridges, they will see that, too, and understand that tough officers like him can not only survive but prosper in today's navy."

He paused and stood looking down at her, watching for her reaction. Then he held his hands out, palms up, and said, "End of sermon. Conclusion: I very much hope that you will keep Admiral Bridges in his position in the Pacific—not because I am concerned about his future, but because I am concerned about the future of the navy."

She looked down at her desk, making a few notes in her small, meticulous handwriting. When she looked up, she smiled. "That was an impressive lecture. Thank you for helping to clarify my thinking. Bull Bridges stays where he is." She pointed her pencil at him, using it to emphasize her words. "But I want you to ride herd on this bull. Do you understand me, Admiral? I don't want a single teacup in this China shop rattled."

McKay smiled. "I hope you'll pardon the lecture. But it is something I feel very strongly about. And you can count on me. I will talk to Admiral Bridges myself again and make sure that everything remains well under control."

As McKay left the secretary's office and returned down the stairway to his own office one floor below, he thought to himself: Now what have I gotten myself into? I've saved Bull's hide, but now I have to keep him under control. Easier said than done.

McKay believed what he had told the secretary: that it was prudent to mass forces in the South Pacific so that they would be available if they were needed. But he also had to be sure to prevent a confrontation with the Chinese. Perhaps more important, he had to keep Bridges's belligerent moves from interfering with his own very secret plan to rescue the Walkers.

When McKay returned to his office, he found a message waiting on his computer from Claudia Bishop:

Admiral McKay:

The L.A. Times *has agreed not to print anything at this time on your commando unit training in Hawaii. How-*

*ever, there is no assurance that some other news orga-
nization will not get wind of what is going on and run
its own story—perhaps without even checking with us
and thus alerting us that something is about to break.*

*The major news organizations have all become very
nervous about holding stories. Several of them have
been badly burned recently when they delayed publication while doing additional checking only to find themselves scooped by someone who posted his own story on
the Internet.*

*I will watch this very closely up to the moment your
men go into action, but I can offer no guarantees.*

Claudia

McKay shook his head and bit his lower lip as he read the
message. One more thing to worry about.

CHAPTER 18

"SIR, WE'RE JUST ABOUT READY TO GO." JEFF BONIOR ES-
corted Rex Marker into Nelson's office.

"Sit down, Rex, Jeff. Give me a once-over on the mission."

Bonior nodded toward the young SEAL.

"Yes, sir. We're going to meet the B-52 at Hickham. I'll
go out at 30,000 to 35,000 feet about fifty miles west of Mount
Egmont.

"I'll use my GPS to navigate in close to the compound and
then eyeball it from there on in."

Nelson frowned. "Rex, there is often—more often than
not—cloud cover around that mountain. Have you and Jeff
thought about how you're going to find your target if you
come down through the clouds?"

"Yes, sir, we've talked about that. Like I said, our plan is
to navigate in by GPS and then eyeball it. But if I can't eyeball
it, I'll come in through the clouds, land as close as I can and
then orient myself with the GPS. Either way, that should put
me on the ground close to the target."

"I guess that's the best we can do. And then . . . ?"

"As soon as I am in sight of the target, I'll find a hidey-
hole, set up my satcomm antenna and let you guys know I've
arrived. By that time, it'll be getting on toward dawn. I'll stay
in my hide all day, watching. That will give me a good chance
to check the fences, scope out the guard positions and timing,
and monitor any movement in or out of the compound.

"Then, about oh-one-hundred the next morning, I'll move in and try to penetrate the compound."

"Rex, I want you to be very careful about that. Before you move in, be sure that you communicate to us all the intel you have gathered—fences, guards, traffic, everything. And . . . listen to me . . . I want you to use good judgment. If you don't feel entirely confident about your ability to penetrate the compound without being detected, forget it. Stay in your hide. It is more important for us to have you there, in position, than to risk capture."

"I understand, sir."

"The worst thing that could happen would be to have you captured."

"Sir." Bonior's brow was furrowed with concern. "I have supplied Rex with something to . . . something to take . . . if he is captured."

Nelson nodded. One bite of a cyanide capsule, hidden in the mouth, would cause almost instantaneous death, but he didn't like to think about that.

"I doubt it will come to that. If you are captured, the very fact that you are there would be a tip-off that a rescue attempt is underway. But you should not reveal anything about what kind of rescue is contemplated or when it might occur."

He looked Marker in the eyes and held his gaze for a moment. "Do you understand what I'm saying?"

Marker gazed back, unblinking. "Yes sir, I understand."

Nelson held his eyes and then turned his gaze to the window, staring out at the surf and thinking the somber thoughts of a senior military man sending a younger man off to face danger and possibly death. The fact that thousands of commanders had experienced these same thoughts countless times in the past offered no solace. Then he turned his attention back to Marker.

"If you get into the compound, what are your plans?"

"We've been studying the overhead photos, sir, and I think we have a pretty good idea of the layout. One portion of the compound appears to be devoted to laboratories and offices. Here, let me show you." He picked up a folder containing a collection of photographs taken from both satellites and U-2 aircraft.

"This section over here appears to be the laboratory and office area. Then over here, on this side, appear to be some other offices—perhaps the headquarters—and living quarters. We have seen a good deal of apparent movement of men in and out of this section here. We assume that is where the guard force and workers are housed. The thermal images indicate that this region right here is a large room, probably a mess hall or meeting room—perhaps a combination of the two.

"So, if we are right, the hostages are probably being held right about here." He pointed to an area in the office-laboratory building that had been marked in yellow. "My goal will be to penetrate that area and try to make contact with the hostages."

Nelson chuckled. "I imagine it will be quite a pleasant surprise when you show up."

"Yes, I'm sure Mrs. Walker, her son, and the Frogwoman are beginning to think we have forgotten them. Is Miss Carson armed, sir?"

"I doubt it, Rex. Perhaps you can take along a weapon to pass to her if you get inside."

"I'll take care of that, sir." Bonior said.

"Okay. Now, Rex, you are inside and have made contact. What's next?"

"Jeff and I have talked about that, sir. I'll sort of have to play it by ear. But I'll try to communicate with you and let you know the situation. Then I'll try to find a place to hide and wait for you guys to show up."

"That's exactly what I want you to do. Throughout this whole mission, the watchword is caution. If you have any doubt about your ability to penetrate the compound and make contact, remain in your hiding place outside. And remember, your value to us is your ability to communicate. Whatever happens, keep in touch. Let us know what's going on."

"I understand, sir. Jeff has been pounding that into my head."

The three men stood. Nelson gripped Marker's hand with both of his and thought about what to say. Then he said, simply, "Go get 'em, Rex."

Bonior and Marker walked side by side to the helicopter landing pad a short distance away. Rattner and his crew were waiting by the Pave Low.

"We'll be with you in a moment, sir," Bonior said. Then he and Marker checked over the equipment they had left in a little pile at the edge of the landing area. As they checked off each item, they handed it to a crewman to be stowed in the helo.

As they loaded the last piece aboard, Rattner started the engines. The rotor began to turn slowly and then more and more rapidly. Bonior and Marker stuffed plugs into their ears and pulled helmets firmly down over their heads. Even through those buffers, the sound of the engines was still almost painfully audible.

The helicopter rose slowly, moving forward slightly. Then, as soon as he was above the surrounding palm trees, Rattner swung out over the water and set his course for Hickam Field, 185 nautical miles to the west.

Rex Marker squirmed slightly to find a comfortable position on the web seat suspended from the side of the cabin and then sat staring out through the open rear hatch as the ocean appeared to unroll below them like some giant greenish blue carpet.

As they approached Hickam, Rattner requested and received permission to land near the B-52 waiting at one end of the flight line. Marker, leaning forward to look, was surprised how big and ungainly the huge plane appeared, its long wings drooping so low that they had little wheels at the tips to keep them from dragging on the ground.

Rattner followed the directions of a ground crew member who guided him to a parking place behind the plane's left wing. He turned off the engines and waited as the rotor slowly rotated to a stop. Then he pulled off his helmet and stepped back into the cabin.

"Okay, Rex, here we are. Ready to go?"

Marker looked at him quizzically. Rattner tapped the side of his head.

Marker grinned and nodded as he pulled off his helmet and withdrew the plugs from his ears.

"I thought I'd gone deaf, sir."

"You would have if you didn't have all that ear protection. Ready to go?"

"Yes, sir."

A member of the bomber crew was waiting as they clambered out the rear ramp of the helicopter.

He saluted Rattner. "Is this our passenger, sir?"

"Yes, Petty Officer Marker. Rex Marker."

"I've got some stuff in the helo," Marker said.

"No problem." He spoke into a walkie-talkie, and two other members of the bomber crew came over and loaded the equipment onto a small cart.

The crewman guided Marker to a hatch just forward of the wings on the underside of the plane. He helped him up the steps built into the hatch, onto the lower deck of the bomber, and then to the flight deck.

"We'll put you right here behind the pilots," he said. "You can strap yourself in here for takeoff and then feel free to move around. The navigation and communications position is down that hatchway, and the weapons systems officer is back here. We've got some chow aboard. Let me know when you get hungry. It's going to be a pretty long flight, so if you want to sack out, you can just lie down here."

Marker looked around and thought to himself: A pretty fancy taxi for one junior SEAL. He took his seat and buckled himself in as the other crew members climbed aboard and the pilots started the engines.

The plane rumbled slowly down the long runway and then gradually reached flying speed and lifted off. Marker heard the thump as the wheels folded up into place below where he sat. He waited until they had leveled off and then stood up to look out the windscreen between the pilots as they climbed over Waikiki Beach and past Diamond Head before taking up their course to the southwest.

The copilot turned and motioned to Marker to put on a pair of headphones.

"Our flying time will be a little shy of seven hours. I'll give you a firm ETA as we get closer. Feel free to move around. If you have any questions, just ask."

Marker nodded his understanding.

He soon tired of looking out the windscreen at the endless sea below and stretched out on the cot attached to the left side of the plane.

He didn't awake until the crew chief tapped him on the shoulder. He blinked, noting that there was still light in the sky as they flew westward, chasing the setting sun.

The crew chief leaned close and shouted into his ear. "Sorry to wake you. We're moving into position for a refueling. Thought you'd like to watch."

Marker moved up behind the pilots and looked out to the front. The windscreen seemed to be filled with the outline of a KC-10A Extender, a long boom reaching out toward the bomber. Marker could see the boom operator through a window in the tail of the tanker as he extended the end of the boom toward the B-52's refueling receptacle.

The pilot watched the underside of the tanker intently as a string of lights helped him hold his position. Then, with a sudden clunk, the two planes, flying within a few feet of each other five miles above the ocean, were linked together, and the fuel surged through the connection from one to the other.

The boom operator gave the pilot a reading on the quantity of fuel he had transferred and then broke the connection. The B-52 turned smoothly away from the tanker and then steadied on course toward New Zealand.

The pilot turned and winked at Marker.

"You really earned your pay in those few minutes, sir. We were awfully close to that other plane."

The pilot grinned. "Just in a day's work—another dollar and a few more gray hairs."

Marker lay down again but he found he couldn't sleep. So far he had remained calm. But now his mind began to race as he ran through the mission mentally. He finally sat up, fished out a paperback mystery story and tried to read.

The plane slowly dropped behind in its race with the sun, and a spectacular sunset that seemed to cover the entire western sky gradually gave way to a dark, moonless night. Looking out through the windscreen, Marker could see the vast starry display of the southern sky—far more spectacular than the sky as seen from the Northern Hemisphere—laid out before them with the unmistakable brilliance of the Southern Cross hovering above the southern horizon.

The pilot's voice came over the intercom: "We've got about half an hour if you want to start getting ready."

Marker welcomed the chance to do something purposeful. Just sitting in the dark and thinking was beginning to get on his nerves.

The crew had placed his gear in a pile near where he sat. He slipped out of his coveralls and pulled on a lightweight pair of thermal underwear. Over that he drew on a heavy flight suit. Then came thermal boots, laced up over the bottom of the flight suit. Over the suit went a snug-fitting jacket.

He picked up a life vest and held it in his hand for a moment, considering whether it was worth the bulk and added weight. If he fell into the sea, he had no chance of being rescued. He shrugged, slipped the vest over his head, and cinched it around his waist.

After pulling his parachute harness over his shoulders, he had to bend almost double to make enough room to snap the leg straps tightly around his upper thighs before securing the fastening across his chest. With the help of one of the bomber crew members, he strapped a haversack to his leg, out of the way of the parachute on his back. The bag contained a small computer, his satellite communications set, a disassembled H&K MP-5 submachine gun, ammunition for his machine gun and his Sig Sauer P-226 nine-millimeter pistol, water, food, a survival kit, and first aid supplies.

He strapped an altimeter onto his right wrist and then pulled a helmet over his head and plugged his earphones into the plane's intercom system. He tightened a mask over his mouth and nose and plugged into a walk-around bottle. When he was through, he was so heavily laden that he could hardly balance himself without help.

"Rex?" The navigator's voice came over Marker's earphones.

"Yes."

"We're seven minutes and twenty-eight seconds from the drop point. You'll go out at 32,400 feet. We'll have the plane down to about 140 knots but you'll still get a shock. As you go out, you'll have a forty-knot wind from the west. At the surface, our best estimate is that wind speed will be only about seven knots, from the west."

"What about clouds, sir?"

"It is clear at the drop point, but there is a layer of clouds around the mountain. You will probably see the summit sticking through cloud cover, but you will have to descend through the clouds."

"Will I break out of the clouds on the way down?"

"I doubt it. Sorry. That mountain is almost always covered by clouds."

"Okay, thanks."

"Three minutes and thirty seconds and counting."

On the approach to the drop point, the pilot had slowly bled off the cabin pressure so that the hatch through which Marker had entered the plane could be opened. The crewmen had all donned oxygen masks.

A crew member held Marker's elbow as he edged his way toward the hatch and gave him last-minute instructions: "Crouch down facing the front of the plane. Then roll out head first so your feet will be facing to the front. There are some antennas sticking out behind the hatch, but if you roll forward you'll clear the hatch and them. Good luck."

Marker unfastened his intercom connection, switched his oxygen hose from a walk-around bottle to the small oxygen bottle attached to his harness, and leaned down into the wind blowing up through the hatchway. Then, on the word from the navigator, the crewman slapped Marker on the shoulder and shouted, "Go!"

Marker felt as though he had slammed into a brick wall as he rolled out into the fifty-below-zero air. His goggles immediately clouded up, leaving him blind. As he fell away from the plane, he spread his arms and legs to stabilize himself until he had slowed down in the thin air. Then he reached across his chest and pulled his rip cord. He felt a flutter as the small pilot chute popped out and then the jolt as the big, mattress-shaped canopy blossomed above him.

As he hung below the chute, he pulled up his goggles long enough to glance at his altimeter, check the time, and look at the compass on his left wrist.

It was not an unpleasant sensation, swinging gently as he flew to the west while descending. But the canopy above him blocked out most of the sky so that, except for a few stars low on the horizon, he was in total darkness.

Every few minutes, Marker checked his compass and his GPS. So far, he was right on course. He stared downward, trying to see something—anything. And then, far down below, he made out the phosphorescence in the surf line. He felt a thrill of relief: At least he wouldn't fall into the sea. His altimeter indicated that he was still at 9,500 feet. Looking to his left front, Marker thought he could just make out the snow-capped peak of the mountain looming in the darkness. And then he was suddenly into the cloud bank that covered the mountain from just below the peak down to nearly sea level.

Marker kept his legs together and slightly bent. Since his target was on the slope of a mountain, his altimeter gave him only a vague notion of how far he was from the ground. If he didn't break out of the clouds, his first indication that he was about to land would be when he hit something. He hoped it wouldn't be the top of a tree or a rock.

He could feel the moisture on his face as he descended through the darkness. The only sound was the whisper of the chute as the canopy and its shroud lines sliced through the air. Marker kept his hands on his risers, ready to make a last-minute steering correction if he got a glimpse of the ground before he hit.

And then suddenly he felt himself slamming into the top of a tree, falling hard down through the branches, which seemed to reach out to grab him, like the fingers of a giant. They caught at his clothes and scratched his face but didn't stop him. He could feel himself falling helplessly, deeper into the tree. He finally came to a stop, one leg caught awkwardly in the fork of a large branch.

It was eerily quiet. The only sound he heard was the faint whisper of the breeze brushing the trees and the drip of moisture from the leaves.

Marker struggled upward until he was able to pull his leg free and sit on the limb, getting into a position where he could unsnap his parachute fastenings and struggle out of the harness. Then he pulled a flashlight from a holster on his waist and shined it into the darkness below him. The branches and leaves cast shadows downward. Only by moving the light back and forth could he make out what appeared to be the ground, some forty feet below.

He turned the light up over his head. One edge of the canopy had followed him down into the tree, but part of the chute was spread out over the branches. Bracing himself against the stout trunk, he pulled on the shroud lines connected to the lower edge of the canopy. He heard branches snapping above him and the rustle of leaves fluttering down.

Gradually, Marker felt the canopy sliding toward him as he reeled in the shrouds. Then the canopy stuck fast. He put his full weight on the lines, but to no avail. He shined the light up again and saw that most of the canopy had been tucked into the tree, where it would be hidden by the leaves, but a small portion of it remained caught in the uppermost branches.

Marker shook his head and thought: No way I'm going to get that sucker the rest of the way down.

Turning to his other problem—getting out of the tree without hurting himself—he groped down into the equipment bag lashed awkwardly to his right leg and pulled out a coil of thin nylon cord. Carefully tying one end to the branch on which he sat, he tied the other end to his equipment bag and lowered it slowly down through the branches, alternately jiggling and lifting on the line so the weight at the end could work its way through the branches. When it finally came to a stop, caught between two branches, he played out all the slack and then slid down the line to where the bag was caught. Repeating the exercise, he managed to work the bag on down and then followed it to the ground.

Finding a level spot under the tree, Marker pulled the submachine gun out of the bag and assembled it. Next, he found ammunition for both his machine gun and pistol and loaded them. An ammunition belt around his waist was already filled with rounds for his pistol, and his backpack held spare magazines for the machine gun.

Feeling around in the haversack, he found a waterproof map of the area and spread it out on the ground. Taking a reading from his GPS, he marked on the map the point where he had landed. He measured the distance to the compound and found he had about two and a half miles to go. Fortunately, he had landed uphill from his target, so he would be mostly moving with gravity.

He glanced at his watch. It was before midnight, local time. Even if he could make only two miles an hour over rough terrain in the dark, he still had plenty of time to make the hike and get into position before dawn to look over the situation and make his first report back to the team.

Marker hoisted the bag up onto his back and adjusted the straps so it rode firmly against his shoulders and hips. Then, using a long, straight branch as a hiking stick, he began moving downhill to the southeast, groping his way with the aid of the flashlight. He moved slowly, cautiously, over the rough lava rocks. At one point, where wet leaves covered a rock, he slipped and fell on his back, rolling a few yards down the hill. He picked himself up, shook his head to clear it, and, deciding he hadn't hurt himself, continued on down the hill.

As he went, he gradually became aware of a faint sound. Listening carefully, he finally realized that it was the babble of a small stream. Feeling his way carefully toward the sound, he was pleased to find that it was just a little freshet—small enough that he could leap across without getting his feet wet.

After more than two hours, he saw a glow of lights through the trees. Inching forward, he found himself on a rock ledge looking down over a compound ringed by a wire fence. Bright lights on high standards illuminated the fence line and the area between the fence and the buildings.

Marker felt around on his hands and knees, looking for a depression in the earth. He finally found what he was looking for: a hollow in the rock where he could hide himself but still look over most of the compound. He scooped a layer of dirt and leaves out of the hole, pulled his haversack in beside him and then covered the hole with a sheet of camouflage netting. Even in the daytime, a person could pass within a few feet of him without realizing that he was there.

Rolling over on his back, Marker pulled out his canteen and a box of rations and had a meager "dinner." He wasn't sure how long he would have to make his stock of food last, but he was confident he would emerge from this adventure a good deal thinner than when he had started out.

After his meal, he carefully gathered up the remnants and stowed them in his haversack. Like many SEALs, Marker was addicted to chewing tobacco, and, after eating, he longed for a chaw. But he didn't want to use anything that might create a distinctive scent that could attract animals—or, if it came to that, search dogs.

Pulling out his binoculars, Marker lay studying the compound for more than half an hour, trying to memorize the configuration and compare it with the image he had in his mind from studying overhead photography. Even at this hour, he noticed several vehicles going in and out of a narrow passageway that led from a gate through a rock ledge up to a large door into the main building.

He could see guards at the gate, but there were no guards patrolling the fence line. He studied the area between the fence and the buildings for a long time, looking for a pattern of shadows or a depression in the earth that might give him concealment if he decided to cut through the fence and try to get into the compound.

Finally, he put down the binoculars and lay thinking, composing a report to transmit back to Hawaii.

Wriggling around, he opened his backpack to pull out the satellite communications set and its antenna. He erected the antenna on the side of his hole and pulled the camouflage netting over it. Then he groped along the side of the set for the hole to insert the lead from the antenna. As he did so, he sensed what felt like an indentation in the side of the case.

He sat up, put the receiver/transmitter on the ground between his legs and, slipping a red lens onto his flashlight, shined it on the set. What he saw made his heart sink. There was a deep dent in the side of the case.

Shee-it, Marker thought to himself. It must have hit a rock when I fell down.

He flicked off the light, plugged in the antenna lead, and switched on the device.

A small light was supposed to come on.

It didn't.

Marker fiddled with the dials, but he knew it was futile. His fall in the dark had broken something. He had made it all the way to his target, studied the scene, composed his report, and now this! Nothing!

Slowly, hesitantly, Marker folded up the antenna and put it away. Then he pulled a small thermal blanket out of his pack and drew it tight around him. In the morning, he would take a look at the set in the light and see if there was any chance of fixing it. And, if that didn't work, he had to figure out some way to save his risky mission from being a total waste.

With the resilience of youth, he put thoughts of his predicament out of his mind and soon fell into a deep sleep.

CHAPTER 19

"HEY, BOSS, WHAT DO YOU HEAR FROM REX?"

Chuck Nelson was at the ramp of the MC-130 Combat Talon, supervising the loading. He turned and saw Dick Hoffman standing at his elbow.

"What do you mean, Dick?"

"You know . . . have you had any contact with Rex?"

"What do you know about what Rex is doing?"

"Nothing, really. But I've been thinking. Rex is our comm expert. He spends a day huddling with Jeff, and then he disappears. It doesn't take any rocket scientist to figure out he's trying to infiltrate that place where the hostages are held."

Nelson rolled his eyes, wondering if it was ever possible to keep a secret.

"You and Rex are buddies. Did he tell you where he was going?"

"Oh, no. Rex would never talk about things like that. But guys in a little outfit like this just know what's going on."

"I guess you're right, Dick. But I don't want you guys gossiping or speculating about this, even among yourselves. We've already got enough trouble because of Merrifield getting in that fight."

Hoffman waited.

Nelson hesitated, thinking about how to reply. Then he said, simply, "As for Rex, we're waiting for his report. Okay, let's get this bird loaded."

As he watched Hoffman join the other men carrying their gear into the plane, he hoped that the expression on his face or his body language had not betrayed how worried he was. It was now nearly thirty-six hours since Marker had left Hickam Field. If nothing had happened to him, he should have checked in many hours ago.

When the time for Marker's first report had passed, Nelson had waited another hour and then placed a call to Admiral McKay.

"We haven't heard from Marker, sir."

"How long has it been?"

"He should have arrived at the compound—or near it—before noon, our time. He should have reported in by now, even if nothing more than to tell us he's arrived. I'm getting worried, sir."

"Well, let's give him a little more time. He may have landed farther away than he planned, and it's taking him more time to get into position."

"It's frustrating. If he went into the ocean, we'll never know what happened to him."

"There's no sense speculating, Chuck. We just don't know what happened." McKay paused and then continued. "If he went into the ocean or was injured in landing and can't communicate, that's unfortunate. But what really concerns me is the possibility that he was captured upon landing. If that's the case, you guys could be heading right into a trap."

"I know, sir. That's the chance we'll have to take if we don't hear from Rex."

"Well, we're going to have to make a judgment, Chuck. If we have any reason to believe that he has been captured and that your mission is compromised, then we're going to have to scrub this operation. I'm not going to let you walk into an ambush to no purpose."

"I understand, sir. But we'll go in there with a lot of firepower. I feel confident we can get those people out."

"I appreciate your gung-ho attitude, Chuck. But we will monitor this situation up until the moment you go ashore. We also have the possibility that the secrecy of your operation will be blown by the news media because of that stupid incident in the bar. We are going to have to watch both these things up until the last moment, and then I will make the go, no-go decision.''

Chuck Nelson looked down the cargo compartment of the MC-130 at the members of his team, most of them sleeping—or trying to sleep—in various modes of repose. The cavernous interior of the plane seemed designed to make its occupants as uncomfortable as possible: It was too noisy for conversation, too hot or too cold to sleep comfortably, and too dim to read.

At the front end of the cabin, he saw Pat Collins and Jim Malcolm sitting side by side, looking at the screen of a portable computer balanced on her knees. Both were wearing earphones. Nelson donned a set himself, worked his way forward, and sat down beside them.

Malcolm looked up and pressed his intercom switch. ''I think Pat is onto something, Chuck.''

''Look at this, Chuck.'' She pointed at the screen.

He had to crane his neck to get into a position where he could make out what she was pointing at.

''What is it? A spreadsheet?''

''Yes, I put it together to try to track futures trades in nickel and cobalt on the London Metals Exchange and the Comex Market in New York, and trades in stocks in both metals on the New York Stock Exchange and the NASDAQ—the security dealers' exchange that used to be called the over-the-counter market. Now I'm feeding in information from the intercepts of the electronic transmissions from that place in New Zealand. It is beginning to show a very interesting pattern.''

''Doesn't look like much to me.''

''No? I'll show you. See, here I've indicated a transmission from the compound. They seem to go to one of five locations: two in the United States, one in Panama, one in the Cayman Islands and one in Switzerland. We have the National Security

Agency monitoring those five locations. They've given me the identity of each one. I suspect they are tiny, inconspicuous 'fronts' that receive buy-and-sell orders and then pass them on. None of them by itself makes much of a ripple on the markets. But look what happens when you combine their activity."

She clicked on the screen and brought up another spreadsheet. "When you combine them, a pattern emerges. Together, they are buying up significant quantities of those two metals and seem to be seeking controlling interest in the firms that produce the two metals."

Malcolm broke in. "Chuck, we think Nash is sitting down there in his compound in New Zealand and is trying to corner the market on nickel and cobalt—the two elements essential to the production of nanotubes and buckyballs.

"By working through these 'fronts,' he avoids calling attention to what he is doing, especially since he is working on three different markets. The trading appears perfectly normal until you link the activity from these five separate sites and trace it all back to one place. And then it presents this very interesting pattern. He hasn't cornered the market yet, but he is getting close."

"What difference would it make if he did control the markets?"

"At the most basic level—the greed level—he could simply make a lot of money by raising the prices as the demand for these metals grows when the buckyball nanoscale technology comes into widespread use. But I suspect he wants to go beyond that and try to control the technology itself."

"What makes you think that?"

"When we started noticing this pattern, I checked around with some of my friends in the scientific community. I didn't tell them what we were doing but I just kind of gossiped with them. What I picked up was this: A number of young scientists have, over the last six months or so, left their jobs or their universities and dropped out of sight. Several of them told colleagues they were going to move to New Zealand and that they had been offered eye-popping salaries."

"So you think . . ."

"Yes. I suspect that these scientists are now at work at Nash's compound in New Zealand. By assembling this kind of brainpower and providing these young guys with first-rate equipment and unlimited resources, he could very well be in position not only to control the elements involved in the production of buckyballs and nanotubes, but also to make breakthroughs that will enable him to control the essential technology as well."

"How does this stuff in New Zealand—the takeover of the government and the kidnapping—fit into all this?"

Malcolm shrugged. "That's puzzling. The major producers of nickel and cobalt are Canada and Indonesia, not New Zealand. But I have two theories. One, it's a dodge. While we're worrying about the First Lady, he's cornering the twenty-first century. I would bet he abandons New Zealand the second his greed is satisfied.

"Or two—and it works well with one, actually—Nash has a bad case of megalomania. The business last year with the Blackbird—a raw display of power. And then this situation in New Zealand. What more dramatic display of personal power than taking over and controlling an entire country? I suspect he chose New Zealand not because of its mineral resources, but because it is all by itself, surrounded by thousands of miles of ocean. Much easier than taking over Canada or Indonesia or some small country with close neighbors—and much easier to defend, too.

"Can't the government stop Nash from cornering the market on nickel and cobalt?" Collins asked.

"I'm no lawyer, Pat. But I suspect that any such action would require the agreement of a number of governments—Canada and Indonesia, to start with. And while our relationship with Indonesia is okay, I don't think the president will take steps to hurt the economy of our good neighbor to the north—and you can bet Nash figures that, too. In addition, Nash's 'front' companies are located in at least five different countries. And, so far at least, Nash has his own country, which will have to be dealt with in one way or another. Remember the difficulty we had trying to get international support for forcing Saddam Hussein to give up his weapons of mass destruction, even after he had been badly beaten in a war? Some of our friends are probably already preparing to recognize the new country of . . . what does he call it? Aotearoa? Once he's got recognition from a few countries, he'll have smooth sailing. Next thing you know, he'll be demanding New Zealand's place at the United Nations.''

Collins and Nelson nodded, and Nelson responded. ''I see what you mean. Even if we pull off this rescue, there will still be a problem dealing with Nash.''

''A problem, but obviously not the kind of problem we have now, where he is in a position to use the hostages to force action by our government and perhaps others. I think the timing is important. If we—if you—can get the hostages out before he has completed his effort to corner the market on nickel and cobalt, and before he has firm control throughout New Zealand, then his position will be much more precarious. So the outcome right now hinges on whether you guys can pull this off.''

Nelson raised the palms of both hands above his head. ''Nothing like having the weight of the world on your shoulders.''

Nelson's ears popped, and he awoke as the plane descended. He looked out a small window at the forward end of the cabin as they crossed the reef, let down over the calm waters of the lagoon, and settled on the runway of Fiji's international airport at Nadi, on the west coast of Viti Levu, the largest of the nation's many islands.

The plane taxied to a stop on the commercial edge of the airport, away from the main passenger terminal.

''Well, here's our home for the next few days,'' Nelson said as he led the way down off the rear ramp into the sticky tropical heat. Arrangements had been made for them to stay in a barracks once occupied by British troops before Fiji gained its independence.

The men—and Pat Collins—clustered around Nelson.

"Okay, listen up. We're going to stay in this barracks over here. We'll be here for a few days' training. There is a town here—Nandi, spelled N-A-D-I—but you're not going to see it. No one goes anywhere, not even to the terminal over there. Is that understood?"

A grumbled assent came from the group. One of the men laughed. "I've been to Nadi. We're sure as hell not missing much."

Shouldering their gear, the men followed Nelson into the barracks. Two Fijians met them at the door with the island greeting: "Bula!"

"Bula!" Nelson replied, then turned to his men. "You guys find places to bunk and then turn out to get the rest of the gear off the plane."

Nelson found a corner room, commandeered it as an office, and asked Collins, Bonior, and Rattner to join him.

"Pat, I want you to set up shop here. Get as 'comfortable' as you can. You'll be our communications contact and pass on whatever new intelligence you can come across."

"Okay, Chuck. Are you through with me, now? I'd like to see if I can raise Rex."

"Sure, Pat. You can set up your gear next door. Let me know as soon as you hear anything." Nelson turned to the pilot.

"Mark, you'll come with us, along with your crew chief and your Special Tactics guys—your commandos. There is a French-made Alouette helicopter at the compound, from what we can see from the overhead images. When we've located the hostages, you'll fly us out. Can you handle that?"

"Yes, that's a Eurocopter Super Puma. I've flown the military version, the Cougar. That should be no problem. It's big enough to carry us and the hostages."

"Good. Now, Jeff. I think our training is in pretty good shape. We've worked on the mountain, and we've done our ingress and egress exercises on the submarine, plus the landing over the beach. What more do we need to do?"

"I wish we had a full-scale mock-up of that place, boss. There's nothing like making the training as realistic as possible. But we'll do the next-best thing. We've drawn a large-scale schematic of the compound, as accurate as we can make it, and I'll have the guys go over it inch by inch and memorize their positions. But when we get there, we're going to have to adapt to the situation as we find it."

"I guess that does it."

"One more thing. Is there anywhere here we can do some live firing?"

"No, I don't think so. You're going to have to simulate firing as best as you can."

Bonior shrugged. "Okay, we'll simulate. I want the guys to be as sharp as possible on search tactics once we get inside that place."

"How soon do we go in, Chuck?" Rattner asked.

"We have three days until the *Kamehameha* is in position between here and New Zealand. So we'll fly out on the night of the third day, drop into the ocean, and rendezvous with the sub. We'll be aboard the rest of the night and all the next day; then we'll land about midnight the second night."

"Roger, sounds good. I'll have my guys ready."

The three men were about to leave when Collins stepped in from next door.

Nelson looked up. "What's the word, Pat? Is Rex in position?"

She shook her head, a frown furrowing her brow. "No word, Chuck. Nothing at all."

The four of them stood looking at each other. They didn't need to speak. The concern showing in each of their faces said it all.

CHAPTER 20

REX MARKER WOKE JUST AS THE FIRST HINT OF DAWN BEGAN to brighten the eastern horizon.

He crept carefully out from under his net covering and stood up to stretch. He felt stiff and cold from the damp earth.

Taking his canteen and several sheets of toilet paper from his pack, he worked his way back the way he had come the night before. When he had gone about a hundred yards, he stopped, used a stick to hollow out a small hole in the ground, and relieved himself. When he was finished, he covered the hole with dirt and spread leaves over it. He had debated whether to bring along one of the small chemical devices the SEALs use to dispose of their feces, so as not to leave even a trace of their presence, but he had decided it was just too much to carry.

Continuing on, he found the little stream he had crossed on his way, and he leaned down to wash his hands and splash water on his face. He felt his chin and realized he would have a good start on a beard before he had a chance to shave again. He filled his canteen from the stream and then dropped in water-purification tablets. The water looked clean enough, and this was certainly a wilderness area, but he didn't want to take any chances of crippling himself with an intestinal ailment.

Retracing his steps, he settled in under his netting again and resumed his surveillance of the compound. He noted that the lights on the fence switched off automatically at first light. For about ten or fifteen minutes, the area between the fence line and the buildings was only dimly illuminated by the morning light that filtered through a gray, overcast sky.

As he scanned the area with his binoculars, he ate slowly from a packaged meal and sipped from his canteen. When the day had brightened enough so that light was penetrating through the netting and into his hole in the ground, he sat up and began to work on his transmitter. He unscrewed the back of the case but found it jammed in place. Where the case had hit the ground, it had been pressed inward. He carefully pried the back off and looked inside. One of the microchip cards in the transmitter was badly bent.

He tried to pull the card out, but it wouldn't budge. Using the end of a small screwdriver, he worked carefully up and down along the edge of the card where its pins fitted into the receptacle. Little by little, it moved. As he worked slowly, trying not to bend the pins any more than they were already bent, the card gradually came free.

Putting down the screwdriver, he used the thumb and forefinger of each hand to lift the card up out of the case. As he did so, it came apart. He looked down in dismay at half the card in each hand.

Marker brought the two pieces up for a closer look. He held to a faint hope that they could somehow be fastened back together again. But he knew in his mind that there was no way to repair it. Even if he had had a soldering iron, which he didn't, he still wouldn't have been able to restore the tiny connections between the two broken pieces.

He put the pieces to one side and lay back, staring up through the netting, trying to think. He closed his eyes and tried to picture the inside of the instrument. If this were an old vacuum tube radio, perhaps he could have found a way to wire around the damaged part and make it work. But today's electronic devices were far too complex and too miniaturized for such tricks.

Suddenly, he snapped his fingers and sat up. Maybe there was a chance after all. He picked up the instrument and removed the rest of the case. He examined the receptacle from which he had taken the broken chip. It was twisted a little bit but otherwise seemed intact. Very carefully, he bent it back into shape.

Then he turned the set over and looked at the receiver side. His memory was on the mark: The receiver contained a duplicate of the damaged card from the transmitter side. With a growing sense of excitement, he carefully removed the card and slipped it into place in the transmitter receptacle.

He bent the dent out of the case and reassembled the set.

He closed his eyes tightly and, for a few moments, held a thought that was half wish and half prayer. Then he reached down and turned on the set. The power light lit. He slipped on a pair of lightweight earphones and plugged them in. He could hear a faint hum from the set. Smiling with satisfaction, he turned the set off again. He decided to wait until after dark before erecting his antenna beside his hole and attempting a transmission. He knew the team must be anxious to hear from him, but he remembered Nelson's warning to make caution his watchword.

Setting the radio aside, Marker rolled over and resumed his surveillance of the compound, memorizing the timing of the guard rotation and the movement of men and vehicles in and around the area. Gradually, a plan formed in his mind. But he could not carry it out until dawn on the following day. He had a long, uncomfortable day and night ahead of him. Then he thought of the stories some of the old guys told of SEAL operations in 'Nam—how they would go out on ambushes and stay awake and absolutely still for hours. They didn't dare slap at a mosquito or even squirm if a large snake crawled over them in the darkness. Marker settled down, thankful for the absence of bugs, snakes, and alligators. He could put up with a little boredom and a little discomfort.

As darkness settled over the mountainside, Marker moved the netting aside, erected his antenna and connected it to the radio set. Then he plugged the radio into the WEARABLE computer strapped around his waist. During the day, he had keyed into the memory of the tiny computer, designed for use by the SEALs, all the information he had been able to gather, plus a brief description of his own plans. When he pressed the ''send'' button, the message would be sent automatically to a satellite and then back down to the team's receiver.

Marker pressed the button and watched the computer screen. After a few seconds, a message flashed at the bottom: ''Message sent.'' He turned off the set, took down the antenna, and put them both away. His pleasure at getting his report off was shadowed by worry that the set might not have worked properly. The ''message sent'' signal might be misleading. All it told him was that the message had been processed by the computer. It didn't tell him whether the damaged radio had actually transmitted it into the ether. And, having cannibalized the receiver side of the set to repair the transmitter side, he would get no confirming message back. He had thought about moving the card back into the other side of the set but decided against taking a chance of damaging it or the receptacles. It was more important for him to be able to continue transmitting than for him to receive messages. He shrugged: He had done his best; no sense worrying.

After putting the communications equipment away, Marker had another light meal, walked a short distance off into the woods to relieve himself, and settled down to rest as much as he could. He lay in the dark, listening to the faint, mysterious sounds of the forest and running through the plan he intended to put into effect at first light.

The young SEAL slept fitfully, waking a full hour before dawn, then followed the same routine as on his first morning. He carefully rolled up his camouflage net, storing it and the rest of his equipment in his haversack. He made sure his machine gun and pistol were loaded and then strapped the machine gun securely so it would ride on his back next to the pack.

He scattered loose leaves over the impression in the earth that had been his home for a day and two nights and then moved carefully, silently, down toward the fence. He crept to the edge of the woods and lay flat in the grass. As soon as the lights along the fence line went out, he dashed forward and pressed himself against a tall metal light standard. He waited, looking over the entire area. It was so dark that he could hardly see. Good. No one was likely to see him.

Grasping the pole with both arms and pressing his knees against it, he shinned upward. The steel post had been allowed to accumulate a thin layer of rust as a protection against the elements. The rust provided just enough friction to enable him to work his way to a point below the reflector where an insulated power line ran from the pole down to the compound.

Marker hung on the line with his hands and feet, feeling more like a tailless monkey than a man as he slid toward the roof of the building.

He scrambled up over the edge of the building onto the flat roof. Stepping gently so as not to make any noise, he moved as quickly as he could toward an air-conditioning and heating tower in the center of the roof.

As he moved, he suddenly became aware of a loud noise, and then he saw the shape of a large helicopter rise above the far edge of the building and move directly toward him. He flung himself forward and flattened himself on the roof up against the wall of the equipment tower. He lay as still as he could, trying to make himself invisible. He was afraid that the sound of his own heart, louder in his ears than the sound of the helicopter, might give him away.

CHAPTER 21

PAT COLLINS PRESSED THE ''PRINT'' BUTTON ON HER COM-
puter and waited until the printer clicked, hummed, and started
spewing out the text of Marker's message. Then she stepped
next door into Nelson's office.

"Chuck!" She almost shouted in her enthusiasm. "We
heard from Marker. He smashed his transmitter, but he managed to fix it well enough to get a full report out to us."

Nelson was on his feet. "That's great, Pat. Let me see the
report."

"It's still printing out. He's got a lot of detail in it."

Nelson stepped into her cubicle, picked up the first two
pages of the printout, and glanced through them.

"Oh-oh," he said. "Rex is going into the compound. I told
him to be careful. I hope he's not getting in over his head.
Maybe I ought to send him a rocket."

"Nope. You can't. To get his transmitter fixed, Rex had to
use a part from his receiver. He can transmit, but we can't get
back to him."

"Just as well, I guess. He's got a head on his shoulders. He
doesn't need a backseat driver." Nelson picked up each sheet
as it came from the printer and glanced through it.

"As soon as we've got the full transmission, I'll call Admiral McKay. This is a big worry off both our minds.

"It looks like there's a lot of good stuff in here about the
layout and the guard routine. And here, he says he thinks he's

figured out about where the hostages are being held. That's where he's headed.''

"What do you want to do with this report?''

"Let's get Jeff and Mark to go over it, and then we'll work whatever we can into our training and our planning for the op. There are still gaps here, but it's one hell of a lot better than going in blind.''

"What the hell?''

Rex Marker looked up as the helicopter climbed away over the forest. In the dim light, it looked like one of the Pave Low helicopters flown by Air Force Special Operations. His first thought was that plans had changed and the team had decided to make an airborne assault on the compound ahead of schedule. Then he realized the craft was white with blue and red markings, not the olive drab he was used to. He decided those were not friends of his up there.

He waited until the sound of the helicopter faded away to make sure that it would not circle around and spot him. Then he crawled around the corner of the equipment tower and found a solid metal door with a small window near the top. He looked carefully around, then stood up slowly and peered in the window. He could see a metal stairway leading down into the building.

He tried the knob and found that it turned. Slowly opening the door, he slipped inside and then pulled it toward him, holding his hand against the jamb to close the door without a sound.

The stairwell was illuminated by a single light globe in a fixture on the wall. Marker unscrewed it until the light went off. If anyone opened the door, he would have a few moments of warning to hide or react. Then he sat on the top step in the dark and pondered his next move. His plan for getting into the compound had worked perfectly. But from now on, he was going to have to improvise as he went, adapting to whatever he found as he began moving through the compound toward where he thought the hostages were held.

Marker projected a layout of the building in his mind, putting together what he had observed with what he had learned from the overhead photos he had studied back in Hawaii. He had never been so grateful that he had always been good at visualizing things.

He pictured himself sitting in the equipment tower projecting above the roof of the two-story building. At the next landing down, a door opened onto the second floor. Where the staircase reached the ground level, another door opened onto the first floor. The position of the doors was marked by a faint glow in the dark indicating the location of a light switch. In each case, the door gave access to a short corridor running across one end of the rectangular building. Each of those corridors formed part of an interior hallway that circled the building. Doors on each side of the corridor opened into interior and exterior rooms. The interior rooms had small windows facing on an interior courtyard or large light well.

If Marker descended to the ground floor, stepped out into the corridor, and turned left, then rounded the corner into the lengthwise corridor, he should find the door to the room where the hostages were held about halfway down the hallway. He was sure he would also find a guard stationed there.

From where he sat to where the hostages were held could not have been more than fifty feet. But to Marker it seemed to be the longest fifty feet in the world. How could he get to that room, or just make contact, without being detected?

Marker looked at his watch with its illuminated dial. It was an hour and a half since he had left his hiding place.

He was pretty sure that he was correct in identifying an adjoining building as the headquarters and sleeping space for the guard force and others working in the compound. Another large building seemed to be a machine shop. The building he was in, he concluded, contained laboratories, offices, and perhaps some classrooms. That meant this building would probably be bustling with activity during the day—from roughly now until about five o'clock. Then it should be almost deserted during the night, except for the cleaning crew and perhaps some guards or watchmen making their rounds.

Marker reached up, screwed in the light bulb and took a look around the equipment tower. The stairway ran down one side of the shaft. The other side was filled with a large air compressor and other equipment used for heating and cooling the building. Marker found a small access door and peered inside. There was just enough room for him to get inside next to the compressor if he squeezed. He pulled a package of food out of his haversack and then pushed the pack up into a corner where it was hidden behind the machinery. Squirming around to get as comfortable as possible, Marker pulled the little door closed and settled down to wait until after nightfall. He would have a long time to think through his next move.

CHAPTER 22

MARKER THOUGHT A NUMBER OF TIMES DURING THE NIGHT OF the original SEALs in Vietnam, standing long vigils in the dark jungles of the Rung Sat Special Zone. He decided they never could have been as uncomfortable as he felt right now, squeezed in his little space next to the air-conditioning compressor. It was dark and noisy, with not even enough room to stretch a leg or an arm. The best he could do was to wiggle his toes and fingers to maintain circulation.

It was after one o'clock in the morning when he slowly opened the door of the compartment and peeked out. Nothing had changed since he had hidden himself away twenty hours earlier. The same single globe illuminated the stairway. The same doors waited unopened at the first- and second-floor levels.

He reached back behind the air compressor to pull his pack from the crevice in which he had hidden it. He slipped extra ammunition for his pistol and rifle into his pockets and added a couple of stun grenades. He kept his flashlight, but he tucked away his canteen. He pulled a length of nylon cord from the pack and hung it from his belt.

He stood thinking for a moment. Then he took out an extra pair of socks and pulled them on over his boots to muffle the sound of his footsteps. Finally, he pushed the pack far up behind the compressor so it would not be visible if anyone looked inside the compartment. Then he walked carefully down the stairs to the door at the second level.

He slowly opened the door about an inch and peered out into the corridor. He could see to his right up to the corner. Holding the door slightly ajar, he peeked through the crack between the hinges for a partial view to his left. There was no one in view.

He reached instinctively for his pistol and then thought again. If he had to use his weapon, the game would be over. If the sound of firing, even with a silencer, didn't give him away, the discovery of a body certainly would.

At the corner, Marker stood motionless with his back against the wall, listening. His training overcame his natural instinct to hurry and get the job done. He waited for five minutes, listening for the sound of footsteps or voices. Finally, hearing nothing, he moved silently around the corner and started down the hallway that ran on the long side of the building. He counted off the doors as he went. His target was a door about halfway down the corridor. If his calculations were correct, that room would be directly above the one where the hostages were held.

He tried the knob: locked. Pulling a credit card from his wallet, he slipped it between the door jamb and the door and slid it upward, pushing aside the latch. He was thankful that no one had thought it worthwhile to equip internal doors with more secure locks.

Stepping inside, he found himself in a rectangular space that appeared to be a classroom. There was just enough ambient light for Marker to make out rows of student chairs and a blackboard covering most of one wall.

He skirted around the rows of chairs and made his way across the room to the opposite wall. A large jalousie-type window covered its central portion. Marker pressed close against the window and peered out into the rectangular area enclosed by the walls of the building. He could see a faint light coming from the room directly below him, but all the other windows were dark. As far as he could tell, there was nothing there. It apparently served as a large light well, nothing more.

Groping along the edge of the window, Marker located the handle that caused the window, which was hinged at the top, to swing outward. He unlatched a lock at the bottom of the window and then slowly, cautiously, turned the handle until it stopped. Then he pressed harder, trying unsuccessfully to get the window open even another inch or two. He measured the gap with his eye, trying to calculate whether it was large enough to permit him to crawl through. If not, he would have to try to remove the window from its hinges.

A glance at his watch showed him it was nearly 2:30 A.M., a time when even the most alert guard forces tended to nod off.

Unfastening the nylon cord from his belt, he tied one end to the radiator below the window and fed the rest of the line through the window, letting it drop down to the ground. Pulling a chair close to the window, he climbed up and stuck one leg through far enough to get a foothold on the narrow windowsill. Then, careful not to tip the chair, he rolled his body through the opening. The fit was so tight that he feared the window might pop out of the frame and crash to the ground, but it held. He pulled his other leg out, using the nylon line to support himself.

It took only a moment to slide to the ground. As his feet touched down, he found the window of the lower room at eye level. A venetian blind covered the window, its panels tilted so that a dim light from inside the room shone upward. The blinds were at such an angle that Marker could not see inside.

He paused for a moment to catch his breath and consider his next move. No time for caution, he decided. Marker pulled out the knife with the curved blade that he had picked up in Samarkand the year before and tapped on the window three times, very lightly. After thirty seconds, he repeated the signal.

The third time he tapped, David Walker, in his upper bunk, stirred in his sleep and sat up, rubbing his eyes. He listened intently, not even sure he had heard a strange sound. Just as he lay back on his pillow, the sound came again. It was very faint, but it was clear that it was coming from the direction of the bathroom window.

He crawled to the foot of the bed and climbed down to the floor, careful not to shake the bed or make any noise. Feeling his way in the dark, he tiptoed across the room and into the bathroom. As he approached the window, he heard the sound once more. Pulling the shade back, he stuck his head between the shade and the window. There, staring in at him, faintly discernible in the darkness, was a face marked by the beginnings of a beard and streaked with camouflage paint.

David gasped inaudibly and then burst into a big grin. He could see the flash of white teeth as the figure outside returned his grin and pressed an index finger against his lips.

The boy nodded his understanding. Then he pulled up the blind and cranked open the window.

As Marker used his nylon line to get up onto the sill and climb through the window, David went to the other room to get a chair for Marker to use as a step. He could hardly keep from shouting with joy. As soon as Marker was into the room, David slipped back in the other room to waken his mother.

She sat up and was about to speak when she felt her son's fingers across her mouth and saw him cautioning her, with his index finger, to be silent. He took her hand and pulled her toward the bathroom. Slipping on a robe, she followed him.

As she caught sight of Marker, she had to stifle an exclamation. Quickly sizing up the situation, she signaled to David to wind the window closed as she took Marker by the hand and pulled him over close to the shower. Reaching into the booth, she turned on the water. Leaning down close to her son's ear, she whispered, "Go wake Cindy. Tell her to stay there and be quiet."

She turned to Marker, pointing to her ears and then to the ceiling, hoping he understood that there were probably listening devices in the room. He nodded his understanding and whispered, "Ma'am, I'm Rex Marker. I'm a SEAL. We're going to get you out of here."

"What do you want us to do?"

"Nothing. I'll come back here tomorrow night about this time. The rescue team knows where you are. They'll come for us, and we'll get you out."

"Are you sure they're coming? Our kidnapper made me call the president and warn him not to attempt a rescue. This man, this Nash, said he would kill David and me if anyone tried to rescue us."

Marker nodded. "What did the president say?"

"He didn't have time to respond. I don't know whether or not the president called off a rescue. But I know he is not the kind of man to succumb to threats."

"I'm sure they'll come. And we'll get you out of here." Marker tried to put more conviction into his voice than he felt. After all, it had been more than three days since he had left Hawaii.

He glanced into the other room but could see nothing in the darkness.

"You sent David to waken Miss Carson, the Secret Service agent?"

"Yes, Cindy is here."

"Well, it's good that you're together. That will make it easier when the team comes to get you out. If they try to split you up, do whatever you can to try to stay here together."

"We don't have much control over that. But we'll do our best."

"Is this room guarded, ma'am?"

"Yes, the door is kept locked, and there is an armed guard outside the door. The guards are changed every two hours, on the hour."

"How are they armed?"

"I don't know about guns. But they have a pistol in a holster and a rifle of some sort. What do they call it, an AK something?"

"AK-47."

"Yes, I think that's it."

"Is there much foot traffic in this hallway?"

"It seems to come and go. My guess is that most of the rooms in this building are classrooms or meeting rooms. I hear people walking and talking, and then it will be quiet for forty-five minutes or an hour, then more walking and talking."

Marker glanced at his watch. "I'd better be getting back."

"You're not going to stay here?"

"No, I don't think that would be safe. I have a hiding place that I think is pretty secure. So I'll be getting back there."

As he turned toward the window, Marcia Walker caught him by the arm, pulled him toward her, and gave him a kiss on the cheek. The stubble felt prickly on her lips. "Thanks for coming to get us, Rex."

In a room in another part of the building, a security officer stifled a yawn, shifted the earphones on his head, and made a note on his log sheet.

"Damn," he said to himself, "why are those crazy Americans taking a shower in the middle of the night?"

CHAPTER 23

REAR ADMIRAL LI ZEMIN TRIED UNSUCCESSFULLY TO IGNORE the thrill of excitement that he felt as he stood on the bridge of his new diesel-powered destroyer while it sailed southeast out of the South China Sea, passing south of the Philippines and into the Celebes Sea. From his flagship, he commanded the largest and most powerful task force the Chinese had ever sent beyond their coastal waters and out into the open ocean.

The excitement he felt was heightened by the most recent intelligence reports. Even though they were fragmentary, they told of a gathering of American vessels just to the east of the Torres Strait off Port Moresby. It will be interesting, he thought, to see how the Yankees react when they see us approaching. For half a century—far too long, he thought—the Americans had been able to think of the entire Pacific as their own ocean. He still rankled at the memory of the humiliation he had felt when a U.S. battle group put itself between the Chinese mainland and Taiwan in 1996.

This time, he thought, it will be the Americans who will be humiliated.

Li was too realistic, however, to delude himself into believing that his force would be any match for the Americans if this confrontation at sea turned into actual combat. He was acutely aware that, as he sailed out of the South China Sea, he had left behind the protection of the Chinese aircraft based in southern China. From here on, the Yankees owned the air.

Even during the maneuvers near the Spratly Islands, U.S. carrier aircraft and planes flying from Vietnam had been constantly overhead, in obvious control of the air, and there was nothing he could do about it.

At his headquarters in Hawaii, Bull Bridges studied the large map on the wall of his office and nodded in satisfaction.

Black ship symbols indicated the disposition of his forces. Arrayed across the narrow passage from the Arafura Sea into the Coral Sea—with Papua New Guinea to the north and the northeastern corner of Australia to the south—was a line of cruisers, destroyers, and frigates. Two submarines waited quietly to the north of the line of surface ships. Back behind the line stood the USS *Kitty Hawk* with her surveillance and strike aircraft.

To the northwest, red symbols indicated the approaching column of Chinese vessels.

"Good! Good!" Bridges murmured to himself. "We're going to cross his goddamn 'T'."

It was every combat sailor's favorite dream to be the crossbar; his worst nightmare to be the post. As the column of vessels approached, all of the American ships would be able to bring their guns to bear, while only the lead Chinese ship could return the fire.

To Bridges, contemplating the map, it seemed an almost perfect copy of the conditions during the battle of Surigao Strait on October 25, 1944. In that battle, Japanese Rear Adm. Shoji Nishimura, with his ships in line, sailed through the Surigao Strait toward the Leyte Gulf. At the entrance to the gulf, American Rear Adm. Jesse Oldendorf was waiting to cross his *T* with thirty-nine torpedo boats, twenty-one destroyers, eight cruisers, and six battleships.

In this case, advancements in technology had changed the odds somewhat. Instead of waiting until they came to the head of the column to fire, the trailing ships in the Chinese formation could launch missiles from their positions back in line.

Still, the odds strongly favored the side that successfully crossed the other's *T*.

Bridges was also just as conscious as Admiral Li of his control of the air. Even without the advantage of his dominance of the tactical situation, his aircraft could hammer the Chinese, sending them to the bottom or forcing them into a panicky retreat back toward home waters.

Bridges turned to an aide. "Send our guys a reminder. I want our aircraft out there booming those Chinese day and night. I don't want them to forget for a minute that we have mastery of the air."

"Yes, sir. Sir? Do you think this is going to turn into a . . . into a real confrontation?"

Bridges turned and looked intently at his aide. The light from the window behind him shone on his closely cropped gray hair.

"No, I don't think so. I don't know what the Chicoms are up to. But if they want to get involved in that situation down in New Zealand, they've got another think coming. They'll get the message. And then they'll turn around and go home like good little Chinks."

"And if they don't, sir?"

"They'll turn around. One way or the other, they'll turn around."

Adm. McKay and Claudia Bishop sat across from each other at the small, round conference table in the chairman's office. The public affairs officer had her spiral notepad on the table before her.

"Admiral, we're getting an awful lot of queries from the press about ship movements in the Pacific. It started the other day with those ships leaving Pearl early in the morning, apparently in a hurry. The press wants to know what's going on."

McKay sighed. "Let's think this through, Ms. Bishop." He rose and went to a large wall map of the world. "The Chinese have completed their maneuvers in the South China Sea. But instead of heading back to port, as we expected, they have a task force headed in this direction." He passed a hand over the map, indicating a movement past the southern tip of the Philippines through the Indonesian archipelago and down past northern Australia, into the Coral Sea.

"We have the *Kitty Hawk* and her escort vessels here." He indicated the passage from the Arafura Sea into the Coral Sea. "Admiral Bridges, in his wisdom, has dispatched some additional vessels to beef up his force down there. In addition, a marine brigade is headed south from Okinawa and should arrive in the Coral Sea tomorrow."

Claudia Bishop leaned forward, taking notes as the admiral spoke.

He looked down at her notepad.

She glanced up and saw the worried expression on his face. She put down her pen and smiled. "Still thinking of me as one of the enemy, Admiral?"

He responded with a rueful smile of his own. "Old habits are hard to break."

"I can do my job only if you trust me. You go ahead and give me the facts, and then we'll decide what to do with them."

"Fair enough. Actually, that's about the way things stand right now. The Chinese are sailing southeast. We don't know whether they are heading for New Zealand. If they do intend to go there, we don't know why. Are they somehow involved in this business with the president's wife? We just don't know."

"What's going to happen when the Chinese approach our ships? What are Admiral Bridges's orders?"

"Right now, we're in a wait-and-see posture. We don't know what the Chinese are up to, so we're positioning our forces for any eventuality. At this point, Admiral Bridges has no further orders."

Claudia Bishop could not help framing what she had heard in terms of a news story.

"So, as I understand it, Admiral, the U.S. and Chinese navies are moving toward a confrontation in the Coral Sea."

"I wouldn't put it that bluntly. But, yes, there is the possibility of a confrontation."

"What kind of a confrontation? You mean actually shooting at each other?"

"I certainly don't think it will go that far. But, yes, that is within the extreme range of possibilities."

The press secretary made a few more notes and then looked up. "That's pretty explosive, Admiral. You can imagine what the press would do with this information."

"Yes, that's what worries me. How much do you have to tell them?"

"We don't *have* to tell them anything. But several of the correspondents have pretty good sources in the navy. It's quite possible that someone can put together enough bits and pieces to make a pretty good guess about what's going on. The press also has a lot better sources of information than it used to. They can buy satellite images that are as good as the ones you get. Some of the networks can afford to hire planes to fly out over that area and see what's going on for themselves."

"So you think we have to tell them something?"

"I have never believed in stonewalling. Every time government officials try that, they get bitten in the rear end. We should put out accurate information, and as much of it as we can. And, at the same time, we can put our own interpretation on that information."

"What do you suggest?"

"Well, first, we're not going to put out a press release. Instead, we'll draw up what we call a 'response to queries'— even though the queries haven't yet been made. Then, as we do get questions, the people in our press room can provide appropriate responses. I think we will say that, yes, we do have a number of ships in the South Pacific and that they were sent there as part of routine maneuvers. If we are asked whether additional ships have been sent to that area, we will say that this is a routine rotation, replacing ships that have been at sea for a long time. Can we honestly say that?"

"Yes, that's true. The result, of course, will be an augmentation of the forces in that area until the ships on scene are actually rotated back out."

"We don't have to say that. If the reporters figure it out—which they will—we'll let them say it on their own."

"What are you going to say about the Chinese?"

"Nothing. If anyone asks, we'll tell them to ask the Chinese."

"Well, I guess that's about the best we can do."

"It's only a stopgap, of course. If an actual confrontation with the Chinese occurs, that will be a whole new ball game. How soon could that happen?"

"Let's say twenty-four hours, give or take a few hours."

"Please keep me informed, Admiral. We're going to have to be right on top of this as it develops. There can't be any secrets between us."

"Yes, I understand that. I will keep you personally informed of every development."

She closed her notebook and stood to leave.

"By the way, Ms. Bishop, have you gotten any more queries about our rescue attempt?"

"No, nothing more. Of course, the press is in a frenzy over this whole kidnapping business, and they could stumble across something. But so far the *L.A. Times* is continuing to hold the story, and no one else has asked about it."

"Let me know immediately if you suspect that there may be a break. That will influence my go, no-go decision up to the last minute."

"I'll let you know if there's even a hint of anything breaking."

———— ★ ————

Dr. Jim Malcolm stepped into the small, makeshift office where Pat Collins had set up her intelligence collection and analysis operation. He straddled a chair and sat with his arms resting on its back.

"This is the part I hate—waiting, not knowing and not able to do anything," he said.

She laid aside a computer printout and nodded. "I know what you mean, Jim. The guys are just about loaded up and ready to go. They're burning off adrenaline as fast as they generate it, and all we can do is sit here and stew.''

He studied her face for a few moments, debating what to say next. Then he smiled and said, ''I hope this is not too personal, Pat, but it's hard not to notice you and Chuck. I think you two are becoming an 'item'.''

She blushed. ''Is it that obvious, Jim?''

''Yeah, it's pretty plain that you two like each other a lot. Is it all right to ask if you're going to get married?''

''It's all right to ask. But I'm not sure I can give you an answer. I would like a man around the house, and my kids could certainly use a dad. But I think I'm still a little gun-shy. When Jim died, I thought my world had come to an end. I swore to myself that, if I ever did get married again or even allowed myself to feel close to another man, it would not be a SEAL. I think I love Chuck . . . no, I know I love Chuck. I really do. But thinking about what might happen to him just tears me up. Like last year. On that operation in Iraq, he took a bullet in the shoulder and came very close to dying before they got him out to the carrier and a doctor. And now there's this rescue attempt in New Zealand. This could be even more dangerous than anything else he's done. And then what comes next? Do I wait and wonder every time he goes out the door until, someday, they come and tell me I'm a widow again?''

He nodded understandingly as she spoke. When she stopped, he said, ''Can I give you some fatherly advice, Pat?''

With his white hair and piercing blue eyes, she realized he even looked a little like her father. She smiled. ''As long as it's free . . . Dad.''

''It's a decision only you can make, Pat. But if you ask my advice—which you didn't—I'd advise you not to let Chuck get away. He'll give you a lot of worries. But he'll also give you a lot of happiness, too. Life doesn't come with any guarantees. You've got to take it as it comes.''

''I know that, Jim. Chuck and I have talked a little about getting married, and I'm really leaning in that direction. But I guess I'm still scared. We'll just see how it works out.''

Malcolm sat for a moment watching her and then changed the subject: ''I've been doing some more research and studying up on how a person goes about cornering the market. This buckyball business is really beginning to make sense.''

''How so?''

''We probably still don't have a line on all the 'front' companies Nash is using to buy up nickel and cobalt assets—the metals themselves, interests in companies that produce them, and futures on the two metals. But I think we have enough now to see a clear pattern.''

She nodded. ''For one thing, the prices of both metals have begun to rise in response to his purchases. Do you know how much he has to buy up before he corners the market?''

''I don't think anyone really knows. The figure is obviously well below one hundred percent. And a lot of it is psychological. If people who need a commodity like one of these metals start to think that the price is going to go up, they begin buying, and that makes the price go up even more.

''I've been looking for some precedent for this kind of thing, to see how it works. I couldn't find any record of people trying to corner the nickel or cobalt markets, but there have been several instances involving silver. Back in the 1970s, a couple of flamboyant Texas brothers, Herbert and Nelson Bunker Hunt, bought up more than a billion dollars' worth of silver and silver futures contracts. Whether they were actually trying to corner the market or whether they just thought that the price of silver was going to skyrocket was never clear. The fact is that they came so close to controlling the market that the government took action against them. Unfortunately for them, the price of silver collapsed, and they were forced to mortgage everything they owned to keep from going bankrupt.

''In a more recent case, Warren Buffett, one of the nation's most successful investors, secretly amassed the world's largest cache of silver—again, about a billion dollars' worth. He later publicly announced his purchases—and, in his case, the purchases seem to have been a straightforward investment rather than an attempt to corner the market. But the result was a twenty-five percent increase in the price of silver.''

Pat Collins leaned forward, trying to absorb Malcolm's explanation. ''So, what you're telling me is that it is at least theoretically possible for a person like Nash, operating in secret, to corner the market?''

''Right—especially if the person manages to use a series of 'fronts' to conceal who is behind the scenes. At this point, we may be the only people who know—or at least think we know—what Nash is up to. Once other people in the market catch on to what is happening, that could cause the price of these two metals to skyrocket. Companies that need the metals will bid up the price to protect themselves, and speculators will jump in to try to get their share of the action. And Nash will see the value of his holdings soar.''

''Isn't he also taking a risk?''

''Oh, sure, a big risk. If the companies that use these metals in their products decide there is not going to be a shortage, or if the speculators drop out of the market and turn their attention elsewhere, the prices can drop sharply. Nash could lose millions, even billions. An increase in the supply could have the same effect. Most of the world's nickel is now produced in Canada and Indonesia. If new deposits were to be discovered in those countries, or somewhere else, that could increase the supply and push the price down. Nash is playing a risky game. But, from what I can see at this point, it could be an enormously profitable one.''

''And if the buckyball technology catches hold?''

''Of course. If demand increases and Nash controls a large stock of these metals, then the price goes up again and he gets even richer.''

''This is really scary, Jim. If something happens and the team can't pull off this rescue, it not only leaves the hostages in Nash's hands but it leaves Nash free to gather all this power to himself.''

CHAPTER 24

TUCKED AWAY IN HIS TINY HIDING PLACE WITH THE HUM OF the air conditioner drowning out all other sounds, Marker was unaware as the big Eurocopter Super Puma helicopter—the one he had at first confused with a Pave Low—swung out over the forest and settled on a course that would take it around the mountain to the west and then north to the town of New Plymouth.

The crew chief sat behind the pilot, idly peering out at the tops of the trees streaming by below. Suddenly, something unusual caught his eye. He tapped the pilot on the shoulder and made a circling motion with his finger.

The pilot circled to the left as he asked, "What's up?"

"I saw something back there, like a big piece of cloth."

As the chopper came around, the pilot exclaimed, "I see what you mean." He circled and descended. "I'll be damned. Looks like a parachute."

He picked up his microphone, radioed a brief report back to the compound, and then returned for a landing.

Ben Bernard was waiting at the helipad as the machine settled to the ground and the pilot cut the engines back to idle. He was up the steps while the rotor still circled overhead.

"What did you see?"

The pilot and crew chief both began talking at once. "Looked like a parachute, sir."

"Let me see it." Bernard pulled the door closed and stood behind the pilot as the machine took to the air.

"Get down as close as you can."

The helicopter circled tightly over the point where the edge of the parachute was visible, caught in the branches at the top of a tall tree.

"Looks like a ram air chute to me. Goddamn! We've got company. Okay, let's get back to the pad."

The machine had barely touched down when Bernard flung open the door and jumped to the ground, barking orders into a walkie-talkie. "I want a full sweep of the area north and west of the compound. Get every man out. There's someone out there, and I want him alive! He is probably armed, but I want him alive!"

Bernard turned to the pilot. "Can you land some men out there near the parachute?"

"We can try, sir, but I didn't see any clearings nearby. We don't have a winch aboard, so we can't lower anyone through the trees."

Bernard thought for a moment. "Okay. You get back in the air with a couple more observers and do a search of the whole area between the parachute and the compound. I'll ride with you and control the search from the air. The guy we're looking for couldn't have gone very far. He must still be there. We'll form a search line and move out toward the parachute. You watch for any movement in front of the search line. When we get close, he'll probably get antsy and make a break."

As soon as two more observers had joined them, Bernard climbed into the helicopter, and it took off in the direction of the parachute. Scores of men dressed in black jumpsuits were already visible working their way uphill through the forest toward the parachute.

"Mr. Bernard!" Nash's stern voice startled Bernard. In the excitement, he had forgotten all about his boss.

"Yes, sir."

"What the hell is going on out there?" When Nash became excited, his voice tended to lapse into the Hungarian accent he had almost lost since escaping from his native country during the Russian takeover in 1956.

"Sir, I was about to call you. The pilot spotted a parachute hung up on the top of a tree about forty-five hundred yards northwest of the compound. We have begun a search, and I am in the helicopter heading out toward the chute."

"I do not like surprises, Mr. Bernard. Keep me informed!" He paused and then asked, in a more conversational tone, "What does this mean?"

"I think it means we have a visitor, sir. It looks to me like a chute—what they call a 'flying mattress'—of the type used by my old friends in the SEALs."

"One man?"

"I don't know, sir. If there is more than one, the others might have been able to hide their chutes. Whatever is out there—whether it's a one-man scouting effort or a full-scale rescue attempt—we'll find them."

"Rescue attempt?"

"Yes, sir. But I doubt that's what this is. If that's what's happening, we should have seen some activity already. My guess is a one-man penetration, trying to gather intel. I think we'll find one guy hidden out there in the woods, keeping an eye on us."

"Very good, Mr. Bernard. You have given orders to capture this person alive?"

"Yes, sir. Very clear orders."

"Good. I would like very much to have a little talk with him."

Bernard shuddered involuntarily. He had been in some nasty situations in his career as a SEAL and after he had been thrown out of the navy in a case of sexual harassment. But he knew that what Nash meant by "a little talk" could be very unpleasant indeed.

Luke Nash was on his feet and crossing the floor toward him as Ben Bernard stepped into his office.

"Did you get him?"

"No, sir. Not yet. But it's only a matter of time."

"Time? Your people have been out there crawling around in the woods for five hours now. Why haven't you found something?"

"The man we are looking for—I am now convinced it is one man—is a highly skilled professional. It would be a mistake to underestimate the degree of his training and his resourcefulness. He is obviously making himself very hard to find. But we will find him!"

"I don't like this, Bernard. I don't like it one bit. We don't know how long this man has been here or what he has seen. I want him caught!"

The pager at Bernard's waist vibrated with a silent signal. He looked down, checking the number of the caller.

"Excuse me, sir." He brought his walkie-talkie to his lips and spoke into the microphone. "Bernard here."

He listened for a moment and then returned the radio to its holster.

"They've found where he was hiding. There's a depression in the earth, covered with leaves, but they can see the imprint made by his body. They've also found two spots near the stream where he relieved himself."

Nash was almost screaming. "You've been searching for five hours and all you can find is a little hole in the ground and a couple of little piles of shit? Well . . . shit! That is just not good enough!"

"We'll get him, sir."

"You let your men handle that. I want you to bring me the kid. Then have the First Lady brought in. I want to give her a taste of separation anxiety. Then I'm going to make sure this rescue attempt, or whatever it is, stops right now!"

Bernard was happy with any pretext to get away from Nash's anger. He murmured, "Yes, sir," and slipped out the door.

The armed escort had barely motioned for Marcia Walker to enter Nash's office before she flung open the door and strode purposefully across the room. Bernard, holding David by the arm, watched as she gave her son a look that told him everything was about to be set right and then bore down on Nash. Nash, who had been pacing in front of his desk, turned to confront her. Bernard noted that he had the same look in his eye as the First Lady did.

She stopped with her face no more than twelve inches from Nash's and fixed her gaze on his dark glasses, trying to see the eyes hidden behind them. When he took a step backward, she moved forward, maintaining the distance between them, deliberately invading his ''space.''

''Sir!'' She used the word with the same impersonal tone as a highway patrolman about to hand a motorist a ticket. ''This charade has gone on long enough. Whatever grandiose scheme is going through your mind is bound to fail. The sooner you realize that and release us, the better it will be for you and all of your people here.''

Nash leaned down until his nose was only inches from hers and snarled: ''Bitch! You tell your husband to back off. And you let him know you mean it.'' He turned toward Bernard. ''Bring the kid over here.''

Nash walked around his desk, leaned over, and withdrew a .38-caliber pistol from a bottom drawer. He met Bernard as he crossed the room and grabbed David roughly by the arm, jamming the muzzle of the pistol into his cheek.

The boy gave out a squeal of pain and struggled to get free. Nash twisted his arm and held the pistol firmly against his cheek.

''Pick up the phone. You know the number. You tell that husband of yours to back off—keep away from this island. You hear me? You tell him he's going to have a dead kid.''

Bernard, alarmed at the tone of his boss's voice, took a step forward and then stopped. He couldn't be sure whether Nash was really out of control or whether he was putting on an impressive display of feigned fury for Mrs. Walker. He had the feeling that things were going badly wrong, but he didn't know what to do about it.

Marcia Walker stared at Nash. Her initial display of defiance seemed to have served only to infuriate Nash rather than to intimidate him, as she had hoped.

He waved the gun at her and then jabbed David again in the cheek, eliciting another yelp of pain. "Go ahead. Call! You warn him!"

She returned his glare for a moment, then picked up the phone and dialed. She listened to a series of clicks and buzzes as the circuits closed, and then she heard the familiar voice of a White House phone operator.

"June, this is Mrs. Walker. May I speak with the president, please?"

The operator's voice betrayed no emotion as she replied, "Yes, Mrs. Walker. Just a moment, ma'am."

"Marcie! Are you all right?" The anxiety in the president's voice was obvious. A shudder of concern and sympathy swept over her. In a fleeting thought, she felt sorry for her husband and recognized that it was strange to feel sorry for him while she and David were the ones being threatened.

"Listen to me, Chip. Mr. Nash thinks you may be trying to rescue us. He wants me to tell you to 'back off.' Please, Chip, do as he says."

"Is David there with you? Is he all right? Let me talk to him."

She turned to Nash and held out the phone.

"David's father wants to talk to his son."

Nash looked at the phone and then down at David.

"Talk to your father, David!" He twisted the boy's arm viciously, eliciting a loud scream.

"Go ahead, Mrs. Walker. Talk to your husband. Tell him you and the boy are still alive. But tell him you will be killed at the first indication of a rescue attempt. The rescuers will find you in pieces—if they even survive that long."

Marcia brought the receiver back to her ear.

"Chip. He is hurting David. Please do as he says!"

Nash pushed David back across the room to where Bernard stood, then reached over and pressed the switch to disconnect the call.

"Get 'em out of here," Nash ordered Bernard.

"Do you want the boy in with his mother?"

"I don't give a shit."

Maynard Walker stood for a moment, holding the phone to his ear, after the line went dead. Then he slowly placed the handset back in the cradle.

Abe Rahman had been in the Oval Office when the call came through. Listening to one end of the conversation and watching the president's face, he understood the grave nature of the situation. Even from where he was standing, on the other side of the president's desk, he could hear David's piercing scream. Rahman's instinctive reaction was to step behind the desk and wrap an arm around the president to comfort him. But he restrained his instinct and just stood there, thinking sadly about how much a president is sealed off from normal human contact.

The president sighed and stood with his head bowed. Rahman couldn't tell whether he was thinking or praying or both. Finally, he looked up.

"Where does the rescue attempt stand, Abe?"

"They're ready to go, sir. The *Kamehameha* will be in position tonight."

"What about that SEAL who parachuted in?"

"He landed safely, but his radio was broken at some point during or after the landing. He was able to repair it, but he is able only to send, not receive, messages. He transmitted one detailed message describing the situation there and said he was going to attempt to enter the compound. That's the last we heard."

"Mm-hmm. That accounts for this call. My guess is that they are somehow aware our man is in the area but have not been able to find him. That means they don't know he is inside the compound—if he did manage to get in. Did he say anything about how he was going to get in?"

"No, sir. He just said he was going to try. And, of course, we can't get back to him to ask any questions."

The president picked up the phone. "Would you please ask Admiral McKay to come over here as soon as he can? Thanks."

It took McKay's driver less than fifteen minutes to whisk him across Arlington Memorial Bridge to the White House. When he arrived, the admiral was surprised to be ushered immediately into the Oval Office. Even when there was urgent business to conduct, he assumed he would have a wait of fifteen or twenty minutes or more before being shoehorned into the president's schedule.

"Mac." The president met him at the door. "I've just had another call. We've got problems." Walker related the details of the call: the scream, the threat, the men on the ground. "So I don't think they've caught the man you sent in, but they must certainly be alert and prepared for a rescue attempt."

"Sir, have you seen the transmission from the man we parachuted in there?"

"No, but Abe told me about it."

"From his description of the scene in and around the compound and his estimate of the strength of the guard force, I think a rescue attempt still has a good chance of success. The fact that they are alert probably won't make a great deal of difference. We assumed they would be on high alert anyway."

"What if they capture your man?"

"That is a problem, sir. He does not know the details of our plans for the rescue. But he certainly knows enough about the size and composition of our Eagle Force and about the training they have been going through in the last few days to give them some valuable information."

"Yes, I was afraid of that."

"But we have good reason to believe that, even if they attempt to torture him, he will not provide them with any useful information."

Walker turned and looked at McKay, a quizzical look on his face. Then he just nodded. He didn't want to ask if the young SEAL was prepared to commit suicide before revealing any information.

McKay returned his gaze and nodded almost imperceptibly.

"Let's say we decide this rescue business is too dangerous, too risky. What's our alternative?"

McKay shrugged. "There really aren't any alternatives, sir. I'm sure Bull Bridges would be delighted to invade New Zealand, and I'm sure the marines could land successfully. But then what? Nash still has the hostages. There is no chance that a big, overt military operation could succeed in rescuing them before they were killed. And that's without even considering the diplomatic repercussions with the rest of the world."

"Can we negotiate with him?"

"You're getting out of my field now, sir. Perhaps Secretary Trover at State or some of his experts can advise you on that. Maybe even the FBI. They have some highly trained hostage negotiators. But my guess is that there is very little room for negotiation. Nash can use the hostages until you have acceded to his demands, and then he can just discard them. I'm sorry, sir, but I'm afraid that's the box we're in."

"Is there any point in stalling for time, hoping something will turn up?"

"We could always try that, sir. But the situation could become even worse. Nash is shrewd and crafty, but he is certainly not entirely stable. We know the terrible things he has done in the past. We don't know what he might do in the future, especially if he comes to feel that we are stringing him along."

"So you think we ought to go ahead with the rescue attempt?"

"I do, sir. But I also intend to monitor the situation right up to the moment our men go ashore. We can back off at any time before they are actually on the beach."

Maynard Walker stood for a long time looking out at the Rose Garden. His voice had a note of resignation in it as he spoke without turning around. "Okay, Mac. And God go with them."

CHAPTER 25

EVER SINCE HIS FIRST SEA DUTY AS A NEW ENSIGN, BEN BERnard had made it a habit to check the log kept by the watch officer at least once a day. Here on the slopes of Taranaki, where there was very little to record, he had often thought this was one habit he could do without. Still, he couldn't quite bring himself to give it up.

As his eyes followed his index finger down the page, he noted with satisfaction that the search for the intruder had been properly entered. His satisfaction was limited by the fact that, after finding evidence of the man's hiding place, the trail had gone cold. It was as though he had disappeared into the air.

Bernard's finger slid to the bottom of the last page. He flipped the log book closed and turned to go. Suddenly he stopped, turned and opened the book. There it was, at the bottom of the page:

"0322: sound of shower."

"0343: sound of shower stops."

Bernard scratched his head and stood staring at the entry. Who was taking a twenty-minute shower? At three o'clock in the morning?

He flipped back through the log book, checking entries for each day of the hostages' captivity. Sounds of the shower were recorded at various times, mostly in the evening, but not in the middle of the night.

"I wonder . . . " Bernard murmured. Then, spinning on his heel, he strode into the next room where several members of the guard force were sitting at a card table, playing poker. They looked up as the door swung open so hard that it banged against the wall, and Bernard entered. "You guys . . . come with me!"

The four men almost had to run to keep up as Bernard hurried down the corridor, out the door, across a small courtyard, and into the building where the three hostages were being held.

"Open up!" Bernard commanded. The guard unlocked the door and swung it open as the little parade led by Bernard arrived. The guard caught the eye of one of the men following their leader and gave him a quizzical look. The other man shrugged, his hands spread open at his sides, and followed Bernard into the room.

Marcia Walker rose from the table and turned to face him. "Where is he?"

The president's wife stared back at him with a cold, hard glare.

"Where is who?"

"Has he been here?"

"Has who been here? What is this all about, sir?"

Bernard brushed past her into the bathroom. A moment later, he stepped back into the main room. The men who had accompanied him stood uncertainly in the doorway.

"Search this place!"

The men remained standing. One finally summoned the courage to ask: "What are we looking for, sir?"

"For that son of a bitch we've been looking for, goddammit. Find him! Find any evidence he's been here."

The four men looked around the room. There was obviously no place where a person could hide. One man walked to the bunk bed and the cot, lifting the mattresses, one after another. Then he bent down and looked under the beds.

Another man went into the bathroom, looked behind the shower curtain, and then opened the medicine cabinet. He felt silly, but at least he was in a different room than Bernard.

He returned to the main room, looked at the other men, and then turned to Bernard. "There's no one else here, sir."

Bernard looked around the room and then up toward the ceiling. "Check up there," he commanded. One of the men climbed onto the table in the center of the room and lifted out one of the large panels that rested on metal latticework suspended from the concrete floor of the room above. Standing on tiptoe, he stuck his head up into the space above the panels.

"Nobody up here, sir. Couldn't be. There's no room."

Bernard stood in the center of the room, his hands on his hips, staring at each hostage in turn. The two adults returned his stare. David, who had been napping on his top bunk, lay with his head propped up with one hand, sleepily looking around the room.

Bernard stepped over to the bunk and grabbed the boy by the arm, pulling him so that he had to jump to avoid falling to the floor. "Come on, kid."

Marcia Walker stepped between the burly ex-SEAL and the door.

"Leave my son alone!"

"Bitch!" Bernard pushed roughly past her and went out the door, pulling the boy behind him. His four men exchanged glances and then followed him out the door. Marcia Walker tried to follow them, but the guard blocked her way, then closed and locked the door.

She turned and opened her mouth to speak, but before she spoke, Cindy Carson pointed at the ceiling and held a finger in front of her lips. The president's wife nodded and then said, "What was that all about?"

"I don't know, ma'am. Were they looking for someone?"

"They apparently think someone was here. Oh, I just wish it were true."

Bernard pushed David into a small room adjoining his office and locked the door. He pressed a button on his desk, summoning an aide from an outer office.

"I want this place searched. We've got an intruder here, and I want him found."

The aide looked at his watch. It was almost midnight. He was about to ask Bernard if he really wanted to conduct a search at this late hour but thought better of it and responded, "Yes, sir."

An alarm bell summoned the guard force to their assembly room. They straggled in sleepily, some still in the process of dressing.

Bernard took his place at the front of the room and waited impatiently for the men to line up by squads.

"We have an intruder in the compound. We are going to conduct a search from top to bottom. I want every room, every broom closet, every place a man could hide, searched—thoroughly searched. Is that clear?"

The men nodded. A few murmured, "Yes, sir."

Bernard gave crisp orders, assigning each squad to a section of the complex, and then ordered them to report back to him as soon as they had finished their search.

"This man we are looking for is a professional. He is armed, and he will not hesitate to kill. You have to be just as professional. Don't let him get the drop on you. But I do not want him harmed. Do you understand me? I want him alive and unharmed. It is vital that I be able to question him and that he be alert, so he can give me the answers I need."

"Any questions?" He looked around the room. "Okay, get to work."

———— ★ ————

Rex Marker wiggled his toes, trying to bring some feeling back into his feet and legs. He looked at the illuminated dial on his watch. It was almost 12:30 in the morning—the quiet hour.

Cautiously, he opened the panel on the air-conditioning unit and peered outside. Nothing had changed. He stepped out onto the landing and stretched. His fingers and toes tingled as the blood rushed back into them. Reaching up behind the air-conditioning unit, he pulled out his pack, took out his computer, and typed a brief message reporting that he was inside the compound, had made contact with the hostages, and found them in good condition. He didn't know that, since he had visited them, David had been separated from his mother. His report described the interior of the building and told where the hostages were being held.

Marker saved the message and then, taking his pack with him, stepped out the door into the darkness on the roof of the building. Huddling in the shadow next to the wall of the equipment tower, he pulled out his satcomm radio, erected his antenna, and transmitted the message in a three-second electronic burst. Then he quickly folded up the antenna and tucked it back into his pack along with the radio and computer.

Hefting the pack up onto one shoulder, he worked his way back around to the door and cautiously opened it just a crack.

''Holy shit!'' In a fleeting glimpse, he had seen two armed men standing on the landing just below the door. They had opened the panel on the air-conditioning unit and were using a flashlight to look inside. Marker quietly let the door settle back against the jamb and flattened himself against the wall.

He could feel his heart beating heavily against his rib cage. His mind raced. He pulled his pistol from its holster, slipped the silencer onto the muzzle, and held the weapon at the ready as he inched away from the door and around a corner of the equipment tower.

Had he left behind anything that would betray his presence? He couldn't think of anything. He'd taken his pack, so the only evidence of his presence would be several plastic bags he had used to relieve himself. But he had thrown them back behind the air conditioner. And with the strong flow of air through the unit, he was sure no one would notice the odor.

Marker checked his watch. He would allow the searchers fifteen minutes to complete their work. That should be ample time. If they decided to come out onto the roof, he would have to shoot them. But if that happened, the game was up. It would be only a matter of minutes before their absence was noted and the entire search focused on this area. He looked around the roof. There was no place to hide.

Inside the tower, one of the searchers closed the panel on the equipment chamber and attached a yellow sticker to indicate that it had been searched.

The other searcher shone his light on the door Marker had gone through onto the roof.

"What about the roof?"

"No, he couldn't be hiding up there. Anyway, they'll make a pass over the whole place with the chopper. If he's up there, they'll spot him."

As he spoke, the searcher climbed the stairway to the door, put a strip of duct tape across the crack between the door and the wall, and initialed it.

Then the two men descended the stairs and left the area.

Marker waited in the dark, listening for any sound that would indicate the men coming out onto the roof. Suddenly, his ears were assaulted by the sound of the helicopter as it rose between the building on which he stood and the one next door, its searchlight sweeping across the rooftops. Marker shrank back against the wall, trying to make himself invisible as the light crossed the roof and then settled on the building next door.

He slipped back around the corner and pulled at the door. It didn't open.

"The bastards locked it," Marker thought to himself. Looking back over his shoulder, he saw the helicopter beginning its turn toward the roof where he stood, the searchlight cutting a bright slice out of the darkness. He put his pistol back in its holster, grasped the knob with both hands, and gave it a strong tug. At first the door resisted, and then it pulled open. As it did so, he could hear the duct tape tearing loose.

Marker paused and peeked through the doorway. He heard the helicopter hovering overhead. Looking over his shoulder, he saw the searchlight make one pass across the roof a few feet from where he stood and then begin a new sweep directly toward him. He gave a hard pull, ducked inside, and slammed the door closed behind him as the light flashed past. For a moment, he stood with his back against the door, breathing heavily. He hadn't even had time to pull his pistol.

The searchers were gone. The only signs that they had been there were a yellow sticker on the panel on the equipment cabinet and the duct tape on the door. Marker checked the tape and carefully pressed it back into place, trying to smooth out the area where it had stretched, but not torn. He stepped back and looked at it. Even from a short distance, it did not appear to have been disturbed.

He checked his watch and sighed. It was not yet 2 A.M. He had another twenty-four hours to wait and hide—if the team was still coming, and if it was on the original schedule. If only he hadn't had to cannibalize his radio to fix the transmitter, he would know when to expect the team to arrive. That would make his job a lot easier. For now, all he could do was hunker down again and hope he wasn't discovered.

He opened the panel, pushed his pack up into a corner, climbed in and pulled the panel closed. He was thankful the searchers had not put duct tape across the panel. If they had, there was no way he could put it back in place once he had closed the panel from inside.

CHAPTER 26

LT. SAM SIMMONS TOOK THE Q STREET EXIT FROM THE DU-pont Circle metro station in downtown Washington. He liked the way the long, steep escalator emerged from the darkness of the station, seeming to rise toward a big circle of blue sky. The morning sun was warm on his back as he circled back above Dupont Circle, enjoying the riot of color in springtime Washington, to the coffeehouse/bookstore on the eastern side of Connecticut Avenue.

Picking up a cup of coffee, a sweet roll, and a *Washington Post*, he threaded his way across the room to a corner table. He was wearing chinos, a blue button-down shirt, and a light tan jacket. His navy uniform would have seemed distinctly out of place in this shop, with its wide selection of books that many of his military colleagues would have considered dangerously left-wing.

Simmons had been waiting only a few minutes when Wang Dongfang slipped into the seat across from him.

"Hi, Sam, what's doing?"

The American answered in Chinese.

"Aw, c'mon, Sam. Let me practice my English."

Simmons took a bite of his sweet roll and grinned. "Why don't you get yourself a cup of coffee, and we'll talk?"

Wang went to the counter and returned with a cup of tea and a butter croissant.

He settled into his place and looked across the table at Simmons. "So?"

"So . . . we may have a little problem on our hands."

"I thought we had that incident at sea all taken care of."

"Yeah, we did. Now we've got a new one."

"Like what?"

"You know, your guys finished up their exercises in the South China Sea, and now they're heading down into the Coral Sea. Admiral Bridges, out in Hawaii, has a task force deployed in the channel south of Port Moresby. A few hours from now, they're going to meet."

"So what's the problem?"

"Bridges—and some of our people here—think this is somehow related to what's happening in New Zealand and the kidnapping of the president's wife and son. Specifically, they think your task force is on its way to New Zealand. Bridges wants to prevent that."

"Showdown at the OK Coral?"

Simmons laughed. "Yeah, something like that. I don't know how much you know about Admiral Bridges, but he is one independent son of a bitch."

"Yeah, I know a lot about Bull Bridges. That's my job." He paused to butter his croissant. "So what do you want me to do about it?"

"We—the people I work for—need some fast answers. If we go through routine channels, we'll get fuzzy diplomatic answers sometime next week, or next month. We need straight answers this afternoon."

"What are the questions?"

"The main question is what the hell is the Chinese navy doing so far out in blue water? Are they headed for New Zealand? Does what they are doing have anything to do with the fact that the president's wife and son are being held hostage? And we hear that Beijing is about to recognize Aotearoa. What's the rush?"

Wang pushed his cup and plate aside. "If I can get some answers for you, will they believe me? After all, we're pretty low on the totem pole, rankwise."

"Yeah, if you get the answers, they'll believe what you tell me."

"Where can I reach you this afternoon?"

"I'll be in my office. If I don't answer, leave word and I'll get right back to you."

Admiral Li could not help cringing as the three F/A-18s swooped across the sea at mast height, then kicked in their afterburners as they passed over his ship, hammering it with a triple sonic boom. The Hornet was a notoriously loud airplane under the best of circumstances. But when three of them deliberately broke the sonic barrier, the sharp crack of sound seemed to tear a hole in the atmosphere and suck in a man's very soul.

As the planes streaked skyward in a vertical climb, their path marked by white contrails streaming from their wingtips, Li Zemin watched them with a mixture of anger and envy.

Satellite images transmitted from Beijing gave him a rough picture of the size and disposition of the American force lying in wait just to the south of the Torres Strait. But without aircraft of his own, he still felt more than half blind. And the American commander, with total control of the air, had a perfect picture of every ship in his entire formation.

What were the Americans up to? From what he could see of the disposition of their forces, they were in a perfect position to try to prevent him from proceeding down into the Coral Sea—if they wanted to. But why would they want to?

Li was worried. And when he was worried, he took action. As soon as the sound of the American planes had faded, he sent a flash message to all of the ships in his formation, ordering them to battle stations.

Adm. Harmony sat in his cushioned swivel chair on the bridge of the *Kitty Hawk*, watching the planes being moved about on the deck and catapulted off the bow of the ship down below.

"Sir?" An aide caught his attention. "Sir, we have just received this intercept."

Harmony took the flimsy sheet of paper and scanned it. Sliding down off his chair, he stretched and went to a large map board on which the disposition of the American and Chinese vessels had been marked. Picking up a pair of dividers, Harmony marked off the distance between the lead Chinese vessel and the line of destroyers and frigates he had positioned across the mouth of the strait.

Pulling a pad toward him, he stood for a moment, thinking, and then wrote a message for Adm. Bridges:

> *Chinese vessels have gone to battle stations. Approaching at 25 knots. Expect them to exit Torres Strait at approximately 1700Z. Request instructions.*

Harmony handed the message to an aide: "Get this off to Admiral Bridges ASAP." He looked at his watch. It was 1:50 A.M., local time. If his calculations were correct, the first Chinese vessels would emerge from the strait a few minutes after 5 A.M., just as the sun was rising behind the American fleet—right in the eyes of the Chinese. He decided to let his crews rest rather than to bring them to battle stations.

In Hawaii, it was the middle of the previous day, and Adm. Bridges was in the midst of a vigorous game of tennis with an officer half his age. Bridges glared across the net. It was set point, his advantage, and it was his serve.

He tossed the ball high in the air and sent it across the net so fast it almost smoked, into the corner of the service court to his adversary's backhand. Bridges hesitated, not sure his opponent would be able to get his racket on the ball. He was a moment late in moving to the net as the young officer sent the ball back to Bridges's left with a strong, two-handed backhand. The admiral turned, lunged for the ball, and tipped it as it flashed past him.

"Good shot," he acknowledged through clenched teeth as he pulled a ball from his pocket and prepared to serve again, this time at deuce. As he reached the service line and turned, he noticed a yeoman standing near the net with a piece of paper in his hand, looking expectantly toward him.

"Excuse me a second," Bridges told his opponent as he went to the sidelines. He glanced through the message and then dictated a reply.

"Message Admiral Harmony: 'Hold your position. Prepare for action but await instructions.' "

Bull Bridges realized, as he dictated the message, that if he were on the receiving end of such wishy-washy instructions, he would be pissed. But this was a case where he wanted to keep his options open. Caution overrode his normally aggressive nature.

"Take another message." The yeoman waited with pencil poised above a spiral notebook. "Message to secdef: Chinese approaching our force in direction of New Zealand. Expect exit from Torres Strait at 1700 Zulu. Chinese have gone to battle stations. Recommend resistance to movement of Chinese into Coral Sea. Await instructions."

Bridges picked up a towel draped over the end of the net and wiped his face and head. Then he stepped back onto the court.

"Service!" he shouted as he slammed the ball across the net, this time into the right-hand corner of the service court. He prided himself not only on the power of his serves but on his unerring accuracy.

The young officer on the other side of the net was good. He caught the ball with a strong forehand, but the ball went directly at Bridges, who had followed his serve with a rush to the net. He met the ball with a hard overhand shot that sent it into the far left corner of the court, beyond his opponent's reach.

Bridges brushed the sweat from his eyes with the double terry cloth cuff on his left wrist as he took position for his next serve. Again, it was set point, his advantage.

The ball went straight to the left corner of the service court. Bridges's opponent lunged for the ball but missed.

He rushed to the net with outstretched hand. "Congratulations, Admiral. Man! You have a killer serve."

Bridges was grinning with pleasure. "Not bad for an old fart, huh?"

The younger man laughed. "Not exactly the way I would put it, sir."

The admiral looked at his watch as the two men walked side by side to the locker room, talking over the high points of the match. It would still be a couple of hours before the Chinese ships reached the waiting American force. He'd have to make a decision soon. Knowing Washington, they would leave him dangling until the last minute.

It was late afternoon in Washington, and the windows of the Pentagon were blazing with light when Admiral McKay arrived at Lucia McKenzie's office. She was glad for her stamina at times like these, for being able to look fresh as though she had not been slogging through paperwork for nearly ten hours. She'd learned that any sign of weakness in times of crisis, no matter how understandable, could easily destroy one's credibility and authority, even among those she felt she could trust.

"Please, sit here," she said as McKay entered, indicating the couch set perpendicular to the window. She took a chair across a low coffee table from him. "We're very close to a decision point in the South Pacific, aren't we, Admiral?"

"Yes, we are, ma'am. We've both seen Admiral Bridges's latest message. We're going to have to give instructions to our forces out there. Do they try to stop the Chinese, or do they let them steam past—possibly heading down toward New Zealand?"

"I've been in constant touch with Secretary Trover at State," she responded. "They are trying to find out the intentions of the Chinese. But I get the impression that the Chinese military may not be talking to their diplomats. We're not getting any straight answers. If their intentions were innocent, why wouldn't they just tell us?''

"We're dealing with a Byzantine bureaucracy," McKay sighed. "Even if the diplomats know what the military is doing, it's part of the game to keep us guessing."

"How much time do we have?"

"We're almost out of time. The Chinese have already gone to battle stations, and they'll reach our first line in about an hour. We should give Admiral Bridges definite instructions within, say, the next twenty minutes."

"What about your back-channel approach to the Chinese?"

"Lieutenant Simmons met with his Chinese counterpart earlier today. He's a military man and may be able to cut through the fog bank we're running into with the diplomats. Simmons is standing by in his office, but he hasn't had a response yet."

"Let's hope it comes soon, Admiral. This whole thing threatens to get out of control."

"I agree, ma'am. My thought now is that, unless we get definite word on China's intentions within the next few minutes, we have to assume that their plan is to interfere in the situation in New Zealand. We should not let that happen, and the best place to stop them is as they emerge from the Torres Strait."

"And how will we stop them?"

"We can try to contact their commander. We believe that is Admiral Li aboard their lead destroyer. If we cannot reach him by radio, we will use a blinker message as soon as their lead ships come into view of ours. We will order them to turn around and sail back north."

"And if they don't?"

"Let's hope it doesn't come to that. Admiral Li is very aware of our control of the air. Admiral Bridges has been quite aggressive in that regard. I think if it comes to a confrontation, the Chinese will turn around and sail for home."

The secretary of defense held McKay's eyes with hers. "And if they don't, Admiral?"

"If they don't, we will have no choice but to take offensive action. We will quickly sink one of their smaller vessels as a warning. We won't attack their flagship because we want someone in control.''

"What about American casualties?"

"I can't rule that out, Madam Secretary." McKay had unconsciously adopted a more formal manner of speaking as the conversation had taken on this more serious aspect. "We have the preponderance of power and will certainly prevail. But the Chinese ships are equipped with a variety of missiles, and those are very difficult to defend against. Even a single hit on one of our ships could cause a number of casualties. We have to be prepared for that."

Lucia McKenzie rose and moved back toward her desk. "Why don't you have your Lieutenant Simmons take the initiative again? We haven't the time to wait."

McKay moved toward the door. "I'll call him from your outer office, ma'am, and I'll let you know as soon as I hear anything."

CHAPTER 27

YEOMAN NANCY POLLOCK'S MOOD ALTERNATED BETWEEN pride and deep boredom as she sat staring at a computer screen in a small, windowless office in the corner of the Pentagon devoted to public affairs.

Claudia Bishop herself frequently looked in for a few minutes to ask how she was getting along and to emphasize the importance of what she was doing. But surfing through the Internet, over and over, hour after hour, had quickly become a drag.

Until recently, it had been possible to keep pretty good track of what was going on in the world by monitoring the wire service machines, looking at a few daily newspapers, and checking the televised news programs. Much of this work was done on a daily basis by the staff of the Current News, which clipped news articles and even transcribed radio and television programs and distributed them throughout the Pentagon. Officials seldom missed an item of interest, even if it was an article in a specialized publication with a circulation of a few thousand.

That orderly system had broken down with the increasing popularity of the Internet. Now, anyone, anywhere in the world, could post ''news'' or opinion or the most off-the-wall rumor on the Web and give it wide circulation in a matter of seconds.

For a while, the established news organizations and government officials were able to ignore this new phenomenon. But they quickly learned that they could do so only at their peril when Matt Drudge startled the world with a report that *Newsweek* magazine was working on a story about an affair involving the president and a young former White House intern. Never mind that the magazine was not comfortable enough with its reporting to print the story. Drudge got wind of *Newsweek*'s work and put it on his Web site, spreading the story around the globe in moments.

It was just such an unpredictable action that worried Claudia Bishop most. If someone like Drudge somehow got word of the attempt to rescue the president's wife and son, secrecy would be lost, and the operation would have to be called off.

To help in her search, Nancy Pollock set up a program that automatically monitored the major news organizations' Web sites for any mention of certain key words, such as *New Zealand, hostages, kidnap,* and *rescue.*

With that system in place, she then spent her time working her way through the Internet, checking sites such as that maintained by Drudge and then following links from those sites to other sites. She also used several search engines—electronic systems for searching the Internet for key words—in a kind of broad-net fishing expedition to see if she could come up with anything.

On the third day after the kidnapping, she had come across a new Web site, called *nzsnatch*, that specialized in news and rumors about the kidnaping. She had not yet been able to determine who was operating the site, but whoever it was was doing something very similar to what she was doing—plus circulating every rumor and tidbit of fact and gossip he or she could find. Nancy Pollock made it a habit to come back to this site at least every fifteen minutes and to follow up any new links to other sites.

It was late in the evening on the fourteenth day since the kidnaping when she switched to *nzsnatch* and was startled to see an alarming new item. She picked up the phone, dialed Claudia Bishop's office, and was immediately put through.

"This is Yeoman Pollock, ma'am. I think I have something here. Listen to this: 'Surfer alert: Watch *nzsnatch* for a big break in the kidnap story. A real bombshell coming up!' "

"Good work, Nancy. That's all? No hint of what they have coming up?"

"No, that's it, ma'am. Nothing more."

"Okay, I'll pull it up on my computer, but you keep monitoring it, too."

The press secretary didn't hang up the phone. She simply switched to another line and pressed the button for the hot line that connected her to Admiral McKay.

"Admiral, we just picked up an item on the *nzsnatch* Web site promising a big break in the kidnapping story."

"Yes, I know, Claudia. My people have been monitoring the Net, too. You don't have any idea what it is, do you?"

"Only a wild guess. The people who operate these freelance Net sites rarely do any of their own reporting. It's possible that they've picked up a leak from a newsroom of one of the newspapers or networks. I wonder if it could be that story about the rescue attempt that the *L.A. Times* agreed to hold."

There was a pause on the line as he thought for a moment. "Well, if that's it, that shouldn't cause us any big problem. They didn't really know very much."

"They didn't know very much when we talked with them. But the fact that they didn't print the story then doesn't mean they haven't been working on it, trying to develop it in case they decide to use it. If that's the source of this 'bombshell,' it could cause us real problems."

"Yes, I see what you mean."

"What's the time situation, Admiral? When is the rescue going to begin?"

"We still have a couple of days to go. Claudia, is there any possibility we can talk to these people who run this Web sit and get them to hold it or to tell us what they have?"

"We're not even sure who operates this site. And, even we did know, I'd be afraid to try to deal with them. T would take whatever we said as confirmation and just go a with it. By trying to talk to them, we'd just make matters worse.''

''I was afraid you'd say that. . . . Well, let's just monitor it and see what happens. If necessary, I can call off the operation right up to the last minute. But if we have to do that, our chances of rescuing Mrs. Walker and David drop very close to zero.''

Adm. McKay glanced at the wall of his office, where a series of clocks told the time at various locations throughout the world. He had only a few minutes left to decide whether to confront the Chinese fleet as it emerged from the Torres Strait or to permit it to sail on in the direction of New Zealand. And now here was this new problem to worry about.

Admiral Harmony had tried unsuccessfully to nap during the long night. Now it was nearly 4:30 in the morning. He stepped off the bridge into the head—like the bridge, it was illuminated only by a dim red light—and stood for more than a minute at the urinal, getting rid of some of the coffee he had drunk during the night. He couldn't help being nervous about the possibility of action within the next hour, but his anxiety was mingled, deep down, with anger at his superiors back in Hawaii and Washington for leaving him out here at the point of the spear without definite orders.

In half an hour, the Chinese fleet would come steaming down out of the Torres Strait. And then what should he do? If he let the Chinese through, who knew what kind of mischief they could be involved in down in New Zealand? But if he stopped them . . . who knew whether the confrontation would ⸱top short of a nuclear exchange? Harmony zipped up his trou-⸱⸱s and returned to the bridge to carry out the next movement ⸱ is dangerous minuet.

⸱der battle stations!''

⸱en flashed orders to the other ships in the formation ⸱nd of alarm signals rose from the bowels of the

⸱ony thought to himself, here we go!

He turned to an aide. "Have you been able to establish radio contact with the Chinese?"

"No, sir. I don't know whether it's the language problem or something else, but we haven't been able to raise them. We are getting good intercepts of their own radio transmissions, and we have aircraft monitoring their movements. They are proceeding toward us at about twenty-five knots. As you know, they went to battle stations some time ago."

"Come in, Henry, come in." The president grasped the elbow of his secretary of state and guided him to a chair. "You've read that report on this buckyball business?"

Secretary of State Trover nodded a greeting to General Rahman and then turned his attention to the president.

"Yes, Mr. President, I've read it very carefully. It appears to me to pose a very serious threat to our national security—in the long term."

"That's the way it looks to me, Henry. If this fellow Nash succeeds in controlling both the raw materials for this process and the technology involved, this would put him in a very powerful position."

"Very powerful, indeed, sir. Since receiving this report, I've done some research on my own. This technology could have just as dramatic an effect on the global economy and on the life of the people of our nation in the next century as the development of computer technology has had in the last few decades. For a man like Nash to gain control over this technology would be an unmitigated disaster."

"That's why I asked you here, Henry. I know science and technology are not subjects with which the State Department normally deals. But you've been around this government a long time. What I need is the best advice you can give me based on your long experience. What can we do about this threat?"

Trover sat silently for so long that both the president and his national security adviser had begun to stir restlessly before he finally spoke. When he did speak, it was in slow, measured tones, almost as though he were dictating a statement that he would not have an opportunity to edit later.

"First, Mr. President, I would say that this matter is inextricably linked to the fact that your wife and son are being held hostage. Whatever you may do about this matter could affect whether and when they are released.

"Two, notwithstanding the fact that action on your part might increase the danger to the hostages, I think it is essential, in the interest of our national security, that Nash's attempt to seize control of this new technology be stopped as soon as possible—at once! If he succeeds in achieving control, it will be very, very difficult to wrest it away from him."

"Actually, Henry, Abe and I have been exploring our options to try to stop Nash from continuing to attempt to corner the market in nickel and cobalt. Under the present circumstances, we've pretty well ruled out any large-scale military action. And that has left us with a blank screen."

"If you'll permit me, Mr. President: When you asked me to consider this matter, I did a little research. Back when I was a neophyte in Washington, right after World War II, I was involved for a while in our strategic reserve program. You may recall that, during the Cold War, we stockpiled a number of metals, as well as a large petroleum reserve, that we might need in the event of a major war."

"Yes, Mr. Secretary, but, except for the petroleum, that program has pretty well been phased out, hasn't it?" Rahman asked.

"Yes, you're right, General. But as I said, I did a little research. We do, in fact, still have a significant supply of these two metals—cobalt and nickel—left in what you might call our forgotten reserve."

The president leaned forward. "Go on, Henry."

"We can dump those metals onto the market. This will have two immediate results. First, it will increase the supply of the two metals, making it much more difficult—perhaps impossible—for Nash to corner the market. And, two, it will depress the price of the metals, dramatically decreasing the value of Nash's holdings. He has been spending very heavily in his covert scheme to control the market. Conceivably, by flooding the market we could ruin him financially.''

Rahman glanced at the president for a reaction and then spoke. "The drop in price would also hurt a lot of other people who happen to be in the market, wouldn't it?"

"Unfortunately, yes. But I would say there would be a mixed effect. While the increase in supply and the drop in price will hurt those who have bought the metals recently, it will be a boon for those industries that use the metals in their business."

Trover again focused his attention on the president. "If you will permit me to go on to consider one issue of primary importance, sir: If we release these metals onto the market, will that pose an added danger to Mrs. Walker and David?"

The president, who had seemed lost in his own thoughts, raised his head and looked at Trover expectantly.

"My answer to that question, Mr. President, is that such an action might actually have the effect of protecting, rather than increasing the danger to, the hostages. 'How so?' you may ask. In those circumstances, the hostages would become much more valuable to Nash as a bargaining chip. They would represent his only remaining hope to recoup his fortunes and solidify his control over New Zealand. Without them, he would be vulnerable not only to financial ruin but to capture, trial, and a long prison sentence."

The president sat for nearly a minute, silently regarding his secretary of state. "I don't know, Henry. Aren't we taking an awful chance? He might be so angered that he would lash out at the nearest target—the hostages."

"You are right, of course, Mr. President. He might. But all of our experience with him leads us to believe that, while he may be deranged, he is shrewd and calculating, capable of acting in his own self-interest. My conclusion is that, whatever surge of anger he may feel, he will recognize the value of the hostages and act to protect them."

The president sat for a moment, thinking, and then abruptly stood up. Trover and Rahman quickly rose.

Putting an arm around Trover's shoulder, the president said, "Good old Henry. I knew you'd come up with something." Then, turning to Rahman, he added, "Let's do it, Abe. Let's bury the SOB in a nickel and cobalt coffin."

————— ★ —————

David Walker felt tears welling up in his eyes as Bernard pushed him into a small room adjoining his office and locked the door. He sat down in a chair next to a large desk, pulled out his handkerchief, dabbed at his eyes, and blew his nose. He felt desperately alone and frightened.

But his mind was active. Encouraged by his parents, he had begun reading at an early age, a practice that had given his vivid imagination a wealth of material to work on. What was that book he had read several months ago? About a man kept prisoner—*The Count of Monte Cristo*?

He began replaying the story in his mind, recalling how Edmond Dantès had escaped from a dungeon on the Château d'If after being imprisoned for fourteen years. If Dantès could escape, then maybe he could, too.

But he was not going to wait fourteen years, and he certainly wasn't going to let anyone tie a cannonball to his feet and throw him into the sea, as had happened to the prisoner in Alexandre Dumas's story.

The brief flash of hope he had felt quickly evaporated as he looked around the room. There was only the one door, and that certainly didn't lead to freedom, even if he could get through it. High on the wall above the desk was a small window. From where he stood, David could not tell whether it opened to the outside or into a light well—and, anyway, it seemed impossibly high.

He put an ear to the door and listened. He could hear someone talking, his words punctuated with exclamation points, as though he were giving orders. David couldn't tell whether it was Bernard or someone else. But it sounded as though the person, whoever it was, was going to be busy for awhile.

Standing back against one wall, David tried to measure the distance to the window. It was a good ten feet from the floor, maybe seven feet from the top of the desk. Pushing a pile of papers aside, David put the chair on the desk and then climbed up on it. Even when he stood on tiptoe, his grasp fell several inches below the window ledge.

He climbed back down to the floor and looked around. Under the desk was a wastebasket. He emptied it on the floor and placed it upside down on the chair. Then he climbed back up on the table, stepped up on the chair, and balanced himself on the inverted basket. Stretching upward, he curled his fingers over the window ledge and pulled himself up.

He could see through the window to the outside, which was brightly lighted. If he could somehow get in a position to open the window, he could slip through it and drop to the ground.

As he lowered himself, he groped with the toe of his shoe for the wastebasket. He touched it with one foot and let his weight down, feeling for the basket with the other foot.

Suddenly, the basket tipped and rolled out from under him, falling to the floor with a clatter. His fingers slipped from the windowsill, and he fell with a crash onto the chair and then to the desktop.

He shook his head and tried to sit up.

As he did so, the door swung open, and the bulk of Ben Bernard filled the doorway.

"What are you doing, you little shit?"

Bernard glanced around the room, and it was immediately apparent to him what the boy had been trying to do.

David sat up and then slid off the table to the floor. He had a knot on his head and a sore elbow, but he was sure he wasn't badly hurt. He looked up at Bernard, thinking, this is not the way Edmond Dantès would have handled things. Suddenly he felt like a vulnerable little boy again.

Bernard grabbed him by the arm and dragged him into the other room.

"I was just about to come get you anyway. Sit here." He pushed him roughly into a straight-backed wooden chair without arms.

David sat, crossing his legs at the ankle and folding his hands in his lap in a defensive gesture.

Bernard made two quick phone calls and then turned his attention to David.

"Well, Dave—that's what people call you, isn't it?"

The boy sat silently.

"Why don't we have a little talk, just you and me?"

David had seen enough detective stories on television to sense what Bernard was up to, now playing his own version of the "good cop," as contrasted with his "bad cop" behavior a short time before.

"I just need a little help here, Dave. If you can just help me out by answering a few questions, we'll get along just fine. We can be real buddies."

David continued to observe him silently. It was obvious to both of them that Bernard's lame effort at communicating with a nine-year-old left a good deal to be desired.

Bernard twisted his chair around and leaned down so that his face was only a dozen inches from the boy's face. The man's breath had a sour, unpleasant smell that made David wrinkle his nose and turn away.

"Now, all I want you to do is tell me a few things. Did someone come visit your room last night?"

"What are you talking about?"

"Well, that's better. The cat didn't steal your tongue after all. What I'm talking about is this: an intruder—you know what that word means?"

David nodded.

". . . an intruder is inside our complex here. He got into your room somehow last night. I want to know where he is."

There was no response.

"Did you see this man? Did you talk to him?"

Still no response.

"Who took a shower in the middle of the night?"

David blinked and gulped. Bernard sensed that he had hit a sensitive topic.

"I don't know. Maybe my mom. Maybe Cindy."

"In the middle of the night?"

All Bernard got in response was a shrug.

Bernard turned back toward his desk and sat so that he was not looking directly at David. He picked up a scabbard holding a knife with a seven-inch blade, withdrew it from the case, and began whetting the edge of the blade on a small stone.

David's eyes opened wider. He couldn't take them off the knife as it slid back and forth across the stone, the sharp edge of the blade glinting in the light from a desk lamp.

The sharpening went on for several minutes. Neither the man nor the boy spoke. Finally, Bernard ran the blade lightly against the skin of his thumb, laid the knife down on his desk pad, and turned to face the boy.

"All I need from you, son, is a little cooperation. And I don't have an awful lot of time. Do you understand me?" He turned, picked up the knife, and sat examining the blade.

"I don't know anything, sir."

"Oh, I think you do, David. I think you know a lot." He tested the blade against his thumb again. "And I think you are going to tell me what you know. One way or the other . . ."

David shrank back in his chair, getting as far away from this big hulk of a man as he could. But he tried to make his voice as defiant as possible. "I'm not going to tell you anything . . . because I don't know anything."

Bernard swung around in his chair and leaned forward. The knife rested in the palm of his right hand. With his left hand, he reached out and picked up the boy's right hand and held it with the fingers engulfed by his huge fist.

"Do you play a musical instrument, David? Piano? Violin?"

David tried to pull his hand away, but Bernard held onto it—not hard enough to hurt him, but firmly.

"Do you take lessons? What instrument do you play? A horn, maybe?"

David stared at him and then murmured, almost inaudibly, "Trumpet."

"A trumpet? Good. Let's see, how many valves does a trumpet have? Three?"

The boy nodded, his gaze focused on the knife in the man's hand.

Bernard laid the knife on the desk.

"Let's see . . . first valve . . ." He grasped the boy's index finger between his thumb and first finger. "Second valve . . ." He touched his middle finger. "And third valve . . ." He picked up his third finger. Bernard shook his head. "It would be pretty hard to make much music on the trumpet without all your fingers, wouldn't it, David?"

The boy tried unsuccessfully to jerk his hand free. "You leave me alone, you . . . you . . . *bastard.*" The word sounded weak and ineffectual in his ear, but it was the best he could do.

"All I want you to do is give me a little information. Where is the man who came to visit you? Is that too much?"

Holding the boy's arm by the wrist, he placed his hand on the edge of the desk, fingers extended.

"Why don't you just tell me what I need to know?" He squeezed the wrist. "Tell me now!"

Lt. Sam Simmons had tried to keep busy, but he couldn't really concentrate on anything. All he could think about was the telephone. He felt like a lovesick youngster, waiting for a ring that never came. A couple of times he had lifted the receiver to make sure he had a dial tone. Even after Adm. McKay himself had urged him to call Wang Dongfang, he had resisted. Wang knew the situation, knew the danger of a confrontation at sea, knew how urgent it was to get answers to what his navy was up to. Better to wait until the last minute, he had argued, and the admiral had reluctantly agreed.

This, however, Simmons told himself, this really *was* the last minute. He straightened the papers on his desk one last time and then reached for the phone. As he did so, it rang. He was so startled that he instinctively pulled his hand away from the receiver but then quickly picked it up.

"Lieutenant Simmons, sir. This is not a secure phone."

He heard a brief chuckle and then the voice of his friend. "Okay, Sam, I've got it. This is just some muscle-flexing by our navy. Admiral Li's orders are to sail down into the northern portion of the Coral Sea, swing around the Solomon Islands, and then head northwest back toward the mainland. Long-planned. Nothing to do with the situation in New Zealand."

"Okay, friend, I owe you another lunch."

Simmons switched to another line and dialed the chairman's office.

"Sir, my source says the Chinese fleet is sailing under long-standing orders to enter the Coral Sea and circle back home east of the Solomons. He assures me this has nothing to do with the situation in New Zealand."

"You're confident this is solid information?"

"Yes, sir, I am. He's a straight shooter."

"Thank you, Lieutenant. You better be right."

The line went dead.

CHAPTER 28

THE *KITTY HAWK* MADE A SWEEPING TURN, LEAVING A CURVING wake glowing dimly in the predawn night.

Adm. Harmony stood on the bridge, peering into the distance with his glasses. The ship had made a long run to the northeast, into the wind, as it launched one flight of aircraft and recovered another. Now she was swinging around again toward the northwest, speeding downwind toward the approaching Chinese fleet.

At this distance, and with all the ships in both fleets blacked out, Harmony knew he was unlikely to see anything. Still, he couldn't resist trying. The leading Chinese vessels were already within the radar fans emanating from the forward American ships, confirming the information about the disposition of the Chinese fleet provided by the *Kitty Hawk*'s aircraft.

Harmony glanced at the clock on the wall. It was 4:47 local time—less than a minute since he had last checked the time. In thirteen minutes, the Chinese would begin to emerge from the strait. If he was going to stop them, that would be the time.

In Hawaii, Bull Bridges stood staring at the message in his hand, murmuring a string of oaths under his breath.

"I'll be goddamned! Back down? To the goddamn Chicoms?"

Finally, he turned to an aide, who stepped back involuntarily to take himself out of range of the admiral's wrath.

"Message Admiral Harmony: 'Stand down. Permit the Chinese vessels to proceed unimpeded. Make no hostile moves.' "

"Sir, our forward destroyer reports he is being painted by target acquisition radar." The voice of the yeoman on the bridge of the *Kitty Hawk* was as calm as if he were giving a routine weather report.

"What source?"

"A tin can just astern of the lead Chinese, sir."

"Any other threat radar?"

"No other reports, sir."

"Message: 'You are cleared to fire Harpoon at threat source.' "

Aboard the American destroyer, target acquisition radar had pinpointed the Chinese ship, and the hatch on the capsule for the Harpoon antiship missile, with its 500-pound warhead, was already open.

"Sir, the Chinese has turned off his radar."

The captain of the destroyer hesitated, uncertain whether or not to fire. If the Chinese fired first, it could mean the loss of his ship.

Aboard the Chinese flagship, Admiral Li was furious. In a rapid-fire string of orders, he commanded the destroyer captain to turn off his target acquisition radar—and not turn it on again unless he received a direct order.

When he received word that the American destroyer had also turned off his acquisition radar, he breathed a long sigh of relief. One careless or overeager destroyer captain had come within a hair's breadth of starting a war.

Moments after he had been informed that both the Chinese and American ships had turned off their threat radar, Harmony was handed Bridges's message. It was eight minutes before the hour. He strode across the bridge, barking orders.

"Signal all ships: 'Stand down from battle stations. Turn away from approaching vessels. Turn on all running and deck lights'."

Aboard his flagship, Admiral Li had been mirroring Harmony's actions, pacing the bridge, watching the clock, and staring into the darkness with his glasses.

And then, suddenly, the lights of one American vessel after another came on. As he scanned the area in front of his bow, he could see the American ships turning away, giving him free passage from the strait out into the Coral Sea.

Two F/A-18s flew slowly past his ship at mast height, one on each side, rocking their wings. Their landing lights were on and their gear down—a clear signal that they had no hostile intent.

Far off on the horizon, he could make out the shape of the *Kitty Hawk* with all its deck lights on. A blinker flashed a coded signal. An English-speaking sailor at Li's elbow wrote down the letters as they were flashed and then handed him the message:

"To Admiral Li. Happy sailing. Jerry Harmony sends."

Admiral Li studied the message, slowly translating it into Chinese. Then he laughed, tucked it into his pocket, and dictated a message of his own:

"To Admiral Harmony. We live in interesting times. Li Zemin sends."

Lucia McKenzie had asked Adm. McKay and Claudia Bishop to join her in the secretary's office as they waited for word from the South Pacific that the Chinese ships had passed the American fleet without incident.

When the message from Adm. Harmony arrived, McKay rose from his chair and solemnly shook hands with the defense secretary.

"Very well done, Admiral," Lucia McKenzie said. "That was a complication that we certainly didn't need."

As they congratulated each other, Claudia Bishop was busy making notes on her pad.

McKay looked down at her. "Taking notes? Playing reporter again?"

She rose to her feet and stood facing the two officials. "As a matter of fact I am, Admiral. I think we can use this to our advantage."

He gave her a quizzical look. "What do you have in mind?"

"If you approve, I'm going to leak this story to the *L.A. Times* tonight."

"Leak it?" The two voices sounded almost as one. McKay stared at her sternly. "Are you crazy?"

"No, let me explain. We're worried about that so-called 'bombshell' on the Internet. We still don't know what that's all about. But we can use this to set off a bombshell of our own—something to focus the world's attention, to focus it away from New Zealand while the commandos do their work."

McKay exchanged a glance with the secretary as they both processed the idea. "How much are you going to tell them?"

"Everything . . . well, not really everything. But I want to give them enough to write a very dramatic, attention-grabbing story—how war at sea was narrowly averted . . . something everybody will be talking about tomorrow."

"Why the *L.A. Times*?"

"Two reasons. One, we owe them one for holding that other story. If I called some other reporter cold with a story like this, he or she would be suspicious, wondering what my motive was. With the *Times*, it will seem natural. The other reason has to do with the time. With the lag between here and the West Coast, the *Times* still has time to do a thorough, detailed story for its late editions. It's so late now that, if we gave it to the *Washington Post* or the *New York Times*, they might be able to squeeze only a fragmentary version of the story into the paper.

"As soon as the *L.A. Times* goes with the story, they will make it available to the Associated Press, which will spread it around the world. The story will be sure to dominate the morning television programs.''

Lucia McKenzie had listened intently. ''That makes sense to me, Cookie. Do you agree, Mac?''

The admiral had a dubious look on his face, but he finally nodded his assent.

''Good,'' the secretary continued. ''I assume Claudia would like you to appear on one, or perhaps all, of the morning news programs—if you can be available. Isn't that right, dear?''

''Yes, ma'am. I'm glad you brought it up. I think that would help to achieve our goal—which is to swing attention away from what is happening in New Zealand and keep it focused elsewhere long enough for the rescue effort to succeed.''

McKay had the uncomfortable feeling that these two women had seized control of the bridge and were steering in a direction he was not sure he wanted to go—at least, not this fast.

''How much do you want me to tell?''

''Well, we certainly don't want to talk about the back-channel communication through the young naval officers. If there is any question about how we communicated with the Chinese, you can simply say that's something you can't talk about or say it's something the State Department handles, and that's not your field,'' the press secretary said. ''And, ma'am, I think it would be well for you to give a heads-up to Secretary Trover at State. I'll do the same for my counterpart over there.''

''Then it's agreed?'' Secretary McKenzie asked. McKay nodded. ''Okay, Cookie, you'd better get to work.''

———— ★ ————

Chuck Nelson blinked his eyes and looked around as he felt the hand of the aircraft crewman on his shoulder. He fumbled for the intercom button.

''Time to go?''

''Yes, sir. The navigator says we have about twenty minutes.''

Nelson looked at his watch, then stood and stretched before working his way back through the cabin of the MC-130 Combat Talon, alerting the members of Eagle Force to be prepared to jump.

The men stood on either side of the cradle holding their rubber boat and began the careful process of checking each other's equipment, with special attention to their parachute harnesses. Each man double-checked to see that his buddy was properly attached to the static line that would trigger his parachute just moments after he had stepped off the rear platform formed by the lowered cargo door.

Nelson took his position at the head of the line near the door, so he would be the first one out and the first into the ocean.

As the cargo door descended, Nelson unhooked the intercom connection from his helmet and turned his attention to the airman who had taken up a position to one side. He was attached to the plane by a long tether. He held up his hand with two fingers extended, indicating that they were two minutes from the drop point.

At the one-minute mark, he released the lock holding the boat in place and stepped aside.

The nose of the plane rose sharply. The boat began to move and then gained speed as it slid down the deck toward the open door. And then it was gone, in what the SEALs like to call "a rubber duck insertion."

Nelson stepped off the platform and almost immediately felt the jerk as his canopy opened above him. A red light attached to his helmet gave the men following him a beacon to follow.

When they went out of the door, they were only five hundred feet above the water's surface. They had often practiced such low-altitude jumps as a way of minimizing the danger of being hit by gunfire from the ground on the way down. In this case, there were no hostile guns waiting below. But by jumping so low, they should all land within a few yards of each other—and of the boat.

As Nelson felt his feet touch the water, he twisted the Koch fitting on his chest and tapped it with the side of his hand to release his parachute. He was a moment too late. Instead of blowing clear, the canopy settled down over him.

Rolling over onto his back, he pulled the tab to inflate his life vest. Then he groped for a seam of the parachute and began pulling it forward over his head, making sure to push aside the parachute cords as he worked his way out from under the canopy.

As he emerged, he looked around for other members of the Eagle Force and their boat. All he saw was water. Even the moderate two-foot sea was enough to block the vision of a man whose eyes were only a couple of inches from the surface.

"Hey! Anybody here?"

"Yeah, skipper. Right here."

"Keep talking." Nelson swam toward the sound of the man's voice. He heard other members of the team calling out their positions.

"I've got the boat." Nelson recognized Jeff Bonior's deep voice.

"Okay, Jeff, keep talking. We'll come to you."

As the men gathered around the boat, Nelson ordered: "Sound off."

In alphabetical order, each man called out his name.

Nelson and Bonior both listened carefully, checking off the names against a mental roster.

"Hoffman?" Silence. "Hoffman!"

"Yeah, I'm coming." Dick Hoffman's voice seemed to come from a distance, but, within a couple of minutes, the young SEAL joined his teammates as they climbed up into the boat.

Nelson settled himself against the side of the boat and pulled off his helmet. Then he took his canteen out of its case, leaned over the side, held the canteen under the water, and tapped it with his knife. Nelson couldn't hear the slight metallic sound, but he knew it was loud enough to be picked up by crewmen on the submarine.

This part of a rendezvous at sea always made him nervous. Up until this point, he felt as though he were in control. But now all he could do was hope that the air force crew had dropped them at precisely the right place in the ocean and that

the submarine crew knew exactly where they were and would
be able to find them. If not, they would be left all alone in a
tiny boat, hundreds of miles from the nearest land. If that
happened, they could always radio for help and hope that rescuers would find them. But a call for help would mean that
they had failed in their mission—and this was one mission
where that was not an option.

Every fifteen minutes, Nelson leaned over the side of the
boat and repeated his signal for the submarine. After each
attempt, the men scanned their limited horizon for a periscope
or a conning tower emerging from the deep.

After the third attempt, Nelson checked his watch.

"We're still okay, Jeff. They're not really supposed to be
here for another twelve minutes. We don't have to start worrying yet."

"Okay, boss," Bonior replied. "You tell us when to start
worrying."

"David. Listen to me. I don't want to hurt you. I really
don't. But you have to talk to me. You have to tell me what
I want to know. . . . You're going to tell me what I want to
know. The only question is whether you cooperate or whether
I have to make you talk. Do you understand?"

David blinked. He didn't want this man to see tears, to
know how afraid he was. He pulled against Bernard's grasp,
trying to free his hand.

A knock at the door startled them both.

"Yes, what is it?"

The door opened, and one of Bernard's guard force stepped
inside.

"Sir, the boss wants to see you."

Bernard let go of David's hand and pushed the knife under
some papers.

"I'm busy."

"Yes, sir. But he said he wanted to see you right now."

Bernard stood with his back to the door and slipped the
knife into the wide upper drawer of the desk.

"What do you want done with the boy, sir?"

Bernard stood, looming over David.

"Lock him in there." Bernard motioned with his head toward the room where the boy had been imprisoned.

"I have to go to the bathroom."

"Oh, shit. All right. Take him to the bathroom and then take him back to his mommy. I'll talk to him later."

———— ★ ————

"You have still not found the intruder?"

"No, sir. We have made a very thorough search of the entire complex."

"The hostages told you nothing?"

"I was in the process of interrogating the boy when you called. If he knows anything, I think he would break down and tell me."

"What means of interrogation were you using?"

Bernard hesitated. He had killed men without a second thought. But the idea of mutilating a nine-year-old made him feel squeamish and, even if he couldn't admit it to himself, a little ashamed.

"I wanted him to think I might cut off some of his fingers."

Nash's lips spread into a thin smile. "Excellent. The threat of disfigurement. That should certainly loosen his tongue."

"Yes, sir."

"However, I don't think it would be wise to carry this threat to the point of actually cutting him. We are dealing with the president's son. And there may be negotiations after this current situation is resolved. If his son were physically harmed, I'm not sure we could count on the president to continue to act rationally. Do I make myself understood?"

"Yes, sir. I understand." Bernard felt a wave of relief pass over him. He would not have to carry out his threat against the boy. Even more important, Nash had called at the right moment. With the frustration he felt, he might well have cut the boy had he not been interrupted.

"Good. Take the boy back to his mother. Let him tell her what you were planning to do. Let her think on that a while.

Now, you're sure your people have searched this complex as thoroughly as possible?''

''Yes, sir. And they've come up with nothing, nothing at all. The only evidence we have that our security has been penetrated is the sound of the shower from the hostages' room at an unusual time in the middle of the night. Maybe I jumped to a faulty conclusion. I'm beginning to think I was wrong. Maybe he is not inside here after all.''

''Which means he's somewhere out there?''

''Yes. But all our activity has certainly driven him away from the complex, so he can't be watching and reporting on our activities. If he's out there someplace, he's not doing us any harm.''

''I don't like this, Mr. Bernard. But . . . ,'' Nash shrugged. ''Let's look ahead a little. If our intruder is part of a planned rescue attempt, how do you think the rescuers will come?''

''Well, as far as we know, the Americans have been staying away from the islands, and so has everyone else. I don't think we face a full-scale military attack—an amphibious assault, for example. You have warned the president that any such attempt would result in the deaths of his wife and son. I think he believes you. So, if there is a rescue attempt, it will be a small-scale, surreptitious operation.''

''Your SEALs?''

''Yes, SEALs or special operations forces of some sort.''

''What do you think they would do?''

''Well, if it was me running this op, I'd have some guys come in by parachute. They could jump at high altitude out over the ocean, ride the prevailing winds for thirty, forty, fifty miles and drop down on us in the dark. That's the way I would do it.''

''Can we see them coming by radar?''

''Probably not. They don't make much of an image on a radar screen. Actually, I think we have taken about as much in the way of precautions as we can. I have my people on high alert, and we can illuminate the entire complex at any time. There is no way they can drop down on us without us seeing them.''

"That will be all." Nash, who had been standing behind his desk, sat and turned his attention to his computer. He then said over his shoulder, as an afterthought, "While you shouldn't harm the boy, perhaps it's time we exercise Ms. Carson's full value to us—and take poor Mrs. Walker's mind off her son." He then took hold of his mouse.

Bernard, still uncomfortable with Nash's abrupt way of dismissing him, hesitated for a moment and then left the room.

Moving his mouse with practiced speed, Nash double-clicked on the icon for his financial management software. A moment later, his investment portfolio spread itself across the screen.

Nash had set his goals for achieving control of the market for nickel and cobalt in a special budget account that permitted him to compare his actual purchases with the amounts needed to corner the market.

As he scanned the screen, Nash nodded in satisfaction. He had achieved 95 percent of his goal for nickel and 92 percent for cobalt. A few more days, a few more millions of dollars, and he would control the market for both metals. Then, with the work of the scientists he had gathered at his compound, he would soon be in total command of the most important technology of the twenty-first century.

Hiding the financial management software, Nash clicked on the icon that would launch him onto the Internet. Instead of connecting his computer in New Zealand directly to the Web, however, he had set up the system so his computer was linked to a machine in Los Angeles that logged into the Net for him, making it impossible for anyone to trace back through the Web to his location.

The Los Angeles computer had been set to open with a program that automatically scanned the financial news services, using key words, and then collected and saved news of interest.

Nash scanned down through the news items collected since his last visit to this site. He had trained himself to be a speed reader, so fast that he could digest the contents of a screen as it scrolled past. Suddenly, he stopped the scrolling and sat forward to focus on a brief Bloomberg News Service item with a Washington dateline:

''The Administration announced today that it will begin an immediate sale of nickel and cobalt from the national reserves. A spokesman said the metals were in adequate supply on the open market, permitting a reduction in the amounts stockpiled in the event of an emergency. Prices of both metals dropped in early morning trading.''

Nash reached deep into his reservoir of Russian for a stream of profanities.

Quickly switching to another address on the Internet, he checked the latest quotations for nickel and cobalt. Both had dropped precipitously in the twenty-four hours since he had last looked at them. Nash pulled up a calculator on the screen and made a quick estimate of the millions he had lost as a result of the government's decision to dump its reserve metals on the market. Without even looking, he knew this action had put him much farther—perhaps impossibly far—from reaching his goal of cornering the nickel and cobalt markets. And, just as bad, it had left him with metals for which the price was now much lower than what he had paid.

Nash remained staring at the computer screen, stunned. He had always prided himself on being at least one step, and usually many steps, ahead of any adversary. But he had been so confident that his operations in the metals market were well hidden that he had never dreamed President Walker might spring this kind of bold financial ambush on him.

As he recovered from his shock, he made some quick mental calculations. If the prices of the two metals stabilized soon, his losses would be large but not catastrophic. But then he realized that he had been looking only at the metals he actually owned. He called up his financial management software again and checked his futures contracts—the agreements he had made to buy nickel and cobalt at specific prices at future dates. He didn't even have to use the calculator to realize that if the prices dropped even a little more, he faced financial ruin.

CHAPTER 29

DICK HOFFMAN SWITCHED HIS M-16 ONTO AUTOMATIC AND fired a short burst at the boat floating alongside the submarine. It shuddered and then slowly slipped from sight, the point where it had sunk marked by a brief explosion of bubbles.

The young SEAL swung the rifle back behind his right shoulder and stepped through the opening into the large dry deck shelter that took up much of the aft portion of the submarine deck. As soon as a crewman had closed and dogged the latches on the hatch, the members of Eagle Force felt the down-elevator sensation of the craft submerging.

As the boat leveled off, the hatch into the interior of the submarine opened, and the skipper climbed up into the DDS.

"Welcome aboard, men. Are you all comfortable?"

His greeting was met with a sardonic laugh from the men, still occupied in moving equipment around and trying to find space to sit or lie down.

The captain shook Nelson's hand.

"Everything okay, Chuck?"

"Perfect. It always amazes me when you guys pop up out of the ocean right on time and right where you're supposed to be. Nice work."

"Thanks. Actually, our inertial navigation system does ninety-nine percent of the work for us. We update it whenever we have a chance, but it does a remarkable job." He looked around the compartment. "Is there anything you guys need?"

"Knowing my men, I'd say that we're all pretty hungry."

"Right. Our galley is getting something together for you right now. One thing we do on this boat is eat good. We've also got a big film library, so you can watch some movies to pass the time."

"Good. I think we're all set, then."

The captain reached into his pocket and pulled out a folded sheet of paper. "I almost forgot this. We received this message for you earlier today." He patted Nelson on the shoulder and climbed back down through the hatch.

Nelson unfolded the paper and held it under a light.

After a moment, he called over Bonior, the team's top enlisted man, and Rattner, the air force pilot who served as Nelson's second in command.

"Marker came through," he told them. "He actually got inside and is hiding there now. He's given us a good description of the compound, especially the building the hostages are in, and he's pinpointed where they are."

Rattner stood with his chin cupped in his right hand, his elbow resting on his left fist. "So they're all in there together? That should make our job easier."

"At least at the time he sent this. Let's see . . . this is about five hours old. At least at that time they were all together. But we can't be sure until we get there. Nash could move them or separate them. If he's done that, he could really complicate our lives. I've been figuring all along that if we hit them in the early morning hours, the hostages would probably have been locked away for the night."

"Our best bet will be to make contact with Rex," Bonior volunteered. "He's been inside that place for several days now. If any of the hostages have been moved, he might have an idea of where we should look."

"That would be nice, but we don't have any way to communicate with Rex, and we don't know where he's hiding. We're just going to have to rely on him to make contact with us." Nelson handed Bonior the sheet of paper. "Jeff, you take this information Rex has given us on the layout of the compound and update what we already know. And then go over it with the guys so that everyone has a clear idea of where things are. Make sure everyone understands any changes in our plans that we'll have to make because of this new information.''

Bonior took Marker's message. "Will do, boss.'' He moved off under another light and carefully went through the message again, highlighting points with a yellow marker.

''Oh, David!'' Marcia Walker swept her son up in her arms as he was pushed through the doorway. She hugged him tightly and then held him out at arm's length. ''Are you all right?''

David felt the sudden release of tension after his ordeal, and tears gathered in the corners of his eyes. But he bit his lip, brushed his eyes with the back of his hand, and produced a wan smile.

''I'm okay, Mom.'' His smile turned to a grimace. ''I don't like that Mr. Bernard.''

''No, David, none of us like him. He and that Mr. Nash are evil men.''

''He threatened to cut off my fingers.''

She shuddered involuntarily as she took her son's hands in hers, looking at them anxiously.

''Did he hurt you?''

''No, but I think he was going to. A man knocked at the door and told him the boss wanted to see him. He hid the knife and told the man to bring me back here.''

''You're safe now, David,'' Cindy said, putting a comforting hand on his shoulder.

He looked up at her. ''I don't know, Cindy. He said he would talk to me later.'' He turned to his mother. ''Mom, I'm scared.''

''Why did he threaten you, David?'' Cindy asked.

''He said there was a man inside the compound—an intruder. He wanted to know if I had seen him.''

Cindy put a finger to her lips and pointed at the ceiling.

David nodded. "I told him I didn't know what he was talking about."

"A man? An intruder?" his mother asked. "He still thinks someone is inside the compound?"

"Yeah, that's what he wanted to know."

"Well, I just wish it were true."

David looked up at his mother. "Mom, you won't let them hurt me, will you?"

His mother took him in her arms again. "No, David, I won't let anyone hurt you." She almost choked on her words, conscious of how little power she had to protect her son or herself. "Why don't you hop up in your bunk and get some sleep? It's very late. And don't forget to say your prayers."

Marcia Walker stood on the edge of the lower bunk to reach up and tuck her son in and give him a good-night kiss. Then she signaled to Cindy to join her in the bathroom.

"Mom?" The boy's voice sounded sleepy even though he had just lain down. "C'mere."

He motioned to her to bring her ear close to his lips, and he whispered, "Mr. Bernard wanted to know who was taking a shower in the middle of the night."

Marcia Walker patted her son on the arm, joined Cindy in the bathroom, and turned on the shower.

"David says Bernard asked who was showering in the middle of the night. I suspect he thinks we're using the shower to cover the sound of our voices."

"I don't think it makes any difference what he suspects," Cindy Carson replied. "If the sound of the shower worries him, we'll just let him worry."

"I'm terrified that they may try to pressure my son into talking."

"Yes, I've been thinking about that," Cindy replied. "There's no way we can protect David if they want to take him away and interrogate him. In fact, there's no way we can protect any of us. I have a weapon hidden, but using it at this point would be futile." She paused and thought for a moment. "You know, I think we can just tell David to tell the truth—tell them everything he knows. He was very brave to resist.

But all he knows is what they already suspect, and they have certainly already searched this place as well as they know how.''

''I think you're right, Cindy,'' Mrs. Walker replied. ''Under intense questioning, David might tell them *more* than he knows. They'll end up not sure whether they're hearing the truth or the imaginings of a nine-year-old. That goes for all of us. They could try to question any one of us. We can just tell them the truth. A man did come in here. There will be a rescue attempt. But we don't even know who the man is, and we certainly don't know where he is right now.''

''They may ask how he got in here. That would be a problem if he is going to try to contact us again,'' Cindy said. ''But it doesn't take a rocket scientist to figure that, if he didn't come in through the guarded door, he must have come in the window. I'll bet they already have a guard out in the courtyard, watching the window. So we don't really lose anything by telling what we know.''

''Mom!'' The boy's shrill voice cut through the sound of the shower.

Seconds later, the door to the bathroom burst open, and Bernard stood in the doorway. ''What's going on here?''

The two women stood silently, watching him.

''Turn off the goddamn water!''

No one moved.

Bernard pointed at Carson. ''I said, 'Turn off the goddamn water.' Don't you understand English?''

She pushed aside the shower curtain and leaned down to turn off the faucet.

Bernard brushed past them to the window. He pulled up the shade and tested the window to make sure it was closed.

''So!'' He turned to glare at the women. ''You think you can talk without us hearing? We'll see about that.''

Bernard stepped back out into the main room and barked orders to the men who were standing idly, waiting for instructions.

''I want one man inside this room at all times, and I want another man outside the window. I don't want anyone coming in or out of this room that we don't know about. And I don't want these people whispering among themselves.''

Bernard glared around the room, then abruptly issued an order to one of the guards: ''That one there.'' He pointed at Cindy Carson. ''I think it's time for some real discipline.''

The guard, his AK-47 hanging on a strap behind his right shoulder, stepped toward her, smiling.

She backed into the farthest corner of the room and cowered against the wall, her arms across her breasts. The guard was not a big man, but he was lean and obviously in top physical condition. As he advanced toward Carson, she began to cry softly.

''Just like a woman,'' Bernard said, leaving.

The guard, meanwhile, grabbed her roughly by the arm and hauled her toward the door.

Marcia Walker moved between them and the exit.

''You leave her alone. Can't you see she's suffered enough?''

''Get out of the way, lady. I have my orders.'' He brushed past her. ''Do you want to be next?''

As they progressed down the hallway, Carson let her steps lag so that he almost had to push her to keep her moving.

''Please,'' she said. ''Where are you taking me?'' She had played scared at first, hoping to get a chance at the upper hand as she had earlier with Bernard, but now she was discovering that she *was* scared. She sensed something worse than a beating was in store for her.

The guard simply pushed harder on her arm, propelling her forward.

They went across a courtyard and into the neighoring building. The guard guided her into a small room a few doors down from the one where Bernard had beaten her.

He locked the door on the inside. She again backed toward the wall, getting as far from him as possible. The guard leaned his rifle against the wall in an opposite corner and turned toward her, one hand on his crotch.

———— ★ ————

"Look at this, boss." Jeff Bonior spread out a sheet of paper with a diagram of the Taranaki compound. "This is the layout we put together from the satellite and U-2 images. The red lines indicate the changes we've made based on Rex's message."

"Not much change, is there?"

"No. But look here. Rex has pinpointed where the hostages are being held. They're over on the right side of this big main building here. It looks as though it contains labs and classrooms, and they're in either a classroom or some kind of office space."

"How do we get there?"

"The most direct approach would be to get into this interior corridor here. That leads directly to the room where they are."

"Any other ways to get there?"

"Not really. This side of the building is rectangular, built around a big light well or central courtyard. I suppose we could get into the courtyard and then try to penetrate their room through the window, but that gets pretty complicated. I think the best way is right down this corridor."

Nelson traced the path Bonior had recommended with his index finger.

"Yeah, Jeff, that looks like the best way . . . the only practical way. And then, once we get them, where do we go?"

"What we want to do is get to the helicopter pad. It's over here, to the right. To get there, we have to go down this corridor we were in originally, cross this little courtyard, and go through this neighboring building and out the side door to the pad."

"What's in the neighboring building?"

"Rex didn't get inside there. But the best guess is that it probably contains Nash's office, other offices, and a mess and recreation area on the first floor with sleeping rooms on the second deck."

"We might run into a few unhappy folks trying to get through that building. Is there any other way to the helipad?"

"Not really, boss. We'd have to get outside and go around the whole building. I think our best bet is to go through there fast and dirty. Anyway, by the time we get there, we should have them pretty well confused.''

''Let's hope so. With our arrival, plus the diversion, they'll have a lot to think about.'' Nelson turned to beckon his second in command. ''Mark?''

The air force pilot joined the two SEALs.

''Here's what we think the place looks like, based on the message we got from Rex. We've got to get through this building, cross a courtyard here, and then move through this neighboring building to the helipad. Once we get there, how long will it take you to get the helo going and get us out of there?''

''That depends, Chuck. Usually, in a place like that, the pilots would leave the key in the ignition. If it's there, we can get the engines going in a matter of seconds. If the key is not there, we're going to have to hot-wire it, and that could easily take a couple of minutes.''

''Okay, once you get the engines going, how long until we lift off?''

''It'll probably take me another couple of minutes to run through the preflight checks and start moving.''

''You can't speed that up?''

''Not without taking a risk. I have to make sure the engine is operating properly and test all the controls to be sure they're responding and are not locked up. If we take off without making those minimal checks, we could come right back down again. We don't want to do that.''

''Is it going to take you any time to familiarize yourself with the controls?''

''No, I've flown this type of bird, and I studied a cockpit layout while we were back in Hawaii. My takeoff will probably be sloppy, but once we get a little altitude we'll be fine.''

''What about the weight?''

''The Super Puma carries twenty passengers—plenty of room for Eagle Force plus the hostages. The altitude at the compound is only about 1,150 feet. We shouldn't have any problem at all.''

Bonior, picturing the situation as they hustled the hostages onto the helicopter and then sat there for a minute or more under fire from Nash's men, regarded the pilot with a skeptical gaze. "Right, sir. No problem at all."

———————— ★ ————————

"Yes, Ms. Bishop is available. . . . Well, I'll just hold until Admiral McKay comes on the line." Cynthia Bishop's secretary was an old hand at the telephone warfare that goes on constantly behind the scenes in Washington. The trick was never to keep your boss waiting on the line for someone else to pick up the phone.

She checked her watch and was not surprised to note that it was a full three minutes before she heard the voice of the chairman of the Joint Chiefs.

"Yes, Admiral, Ms. Bishop is here. If you'll hold for a moment, I'll put her on the line."

A light on the console on her desk indicated that the press secretary was still occupied with her last call. The secretary pressed the intercom button to let her boss know she had an urgent call. The other light went out.

"I'll put you through now, Admiral."

"Hi, Admiral. Why didn't you use the hot line?"

"Oh, it's not an emergency, Cynthia. I'm just getting a little antsy. Have you heard anything more about that Internet business?"

"No, they still keep promising their big news, but they haven't posted anything new for hours. I'm beginning to suspect they don't really have anything."

"But we can't be sure?"

"No, that's the problem. If we were dealing with a mainstream news organization, I might be able to find something out. But with these people, who knows? I wouldn't dare try to query them."

"Meanwhile, we certainly got a lot of attention from that business with the Chinese navy. Along with it, we're getting some flak up on the Hill—and from some of our 'friends' in other countries—for our brinkmanship."

"That's the price we pay for being the world's only superpower, Admiral. Everybody knows better than we do what we should do, but no one wants to do it themselves. And even when they know we're right, they still carp.''

"Well, you were right. That story certainly focused the attention of the world away from where we don't want it right now. But I'm not sure how much good that will do us where it means the most—down in New Zealand. I've still got a few hours before I give the go or no-go signal for the operation. We have to assume that Nash and his people suspect there will be a rescue attempt. But if I'm convinced we've lost the element of surprise entirely because of some news leak, then I'm going to have to call it off.''

"Are you going to consult with the president on the decision, Admiral?''

"No. I'll inform him of what I decide to do and try to keep him informed as the operation proceeds—if it proceeds. But this is the kind of decision I get paid to make.''

CHAPTER 30

NELSON, BONIOR AND RATTNER SAT AT THE BACK OF THE DRY deck shelter talking quietly among themselves.

"This worries me," Nelson said. "Why hasn't Admiral McKay given us the 'go' signal? Is something wrong that we don't know about?"

"Maybe it's communications," Bonior suggested. "We've been running submerged. Maybe he's been trying to reach us."

"Naw, I thought of that. I checked with the skipper, and he says they've had no communications problems. They've been sending and receiving messages all along."

"What are your orders, Chuck?" Rattner asked. "What if you don't hear from Washington, one way or the other?"

"The orders are very clear. Unless we get a firm 'go' signal before we leave the submarine, we don't go. We assumed all along that, once we leave the sub, we might have difficulty communicating. So we can't go without the signal. But once we shove off, we're on our own. We can communicate if we feel the need for it, but the admiral does not really expect to hear from us—or for us to hear from him—until the operation is wrapped up and the hostages are safely out of there."

"Well, at least that doesn't leave the decision up to you," Rattner said. "It would be worse if you had to decide whether or not to go without some clear-cut orders from Washington."

"I still don't like it," Nelson said. "If we're going to stay on schedule, we're going to have to be in our SDVs within the hour. We've only got so many hours of darkness, and our attack has to be coordinated with the airdrop. If they futz around in Washington past the time we should move out and then give us a delayed 'go' signal, we're going to be in trouble."

"At some point, you would be justified in saying it was too late. Tell them, 'hell no, I won't go.' " Rattner said.

Nelson laughed. "Yeah, right! I tell the chairman of the Joint Chiefs that we've decided not to go rescue the president's wife and son. 'Sorry, boss, you called too late!' "

"No, I guess that's not the world's best idea," Rattner responded.

Nelson stood and turned toward the other members of Eagle Force. Several of them were asleep. Others talked quietly among themselves or read paperback books. Four men played a lackluster game of poker.

"Okay, men. Let's get the show on the road. Make sure all your equipment is loaded in the SDVs, and be sure to double-check your Draegers."

The men stood, stretched, and began moving around their cramped quarters. They paired up in buddy teams to check over their equipment and then began squirming into their wet suits.

Nelson turned to Bonior and Rattner. "We'll go through all the motions, up to the moment when we leave the deck, hoping the message comes. If we don't get the signal, we'll go into standby mode—and just wait. . . ."

———— ★ ————

Rex Marker turned the latch on the equipment door and stepped out onto the landing. As he stood up, a wave of dizziness swept over him. He grabbed a railing and held on, waiting for his head to clear. Gradually, the room stopped spinning, and he was able to stand erect without holding on.

Shit! he thought. I was afraid of that. I've been sitting in that cramped position for hours. And I haven't had enough to eat or drink for a couple of days.

Standing close to the rail in case he had to grab it again, he stretched his arms over his head and bent his body at the waist, forward and back and from side to side. Each time his head moved away from the vertical, he felt another sensation of dizziness, but nothing like the attack when he had first stepped out of his hiding place.

Before he left Hawaii, Nelson had given him a need-to-know briefing—everything he needed to know to carry out his mission, but nothing he didn't absolutely need to know in case he were captured and tortured. Among the many things he didn't know was the timing of the assault or how the attack would be made. But, of course, he had been a SEAL long enough to figure some things out for himself. The attack would certainly come in the middle of the night, when the guard force would be least alert and would be hampered by the darkness. He also assumed that, as soon as Nash's guard force became aware they were under attack, there would be a lot of noise.

The noise was what Marker was counting on as a signal to go into action. As soon as he sensed that the attack had begun, he would hurry to join the hostages and do what he could to protect them until the rescuers arrived.

Marker rummaged in his knapsack. All he could find was a small package of crackers—some kind of hardtack—and a chocolate bar. He bit into the bar and hungrily chewed a chunk of chocolate, ignoring the waxy taste of whatever had been mixed with the chocolate to keep it from melting.

He shook his canteen and heard only a slight sound. He had filled it during his visit to the hostages, but the water was almost gone now. He unscrewed the cap, took a tiny sip and sloshed it around his mouth to moisten a bite of the cracker.

Well, he thought to himself, so much for breakfast . . . or is it dinner . . . or lunch?

———— ★ ————

Admiral McKay had told his secretary not to disturb him as he tackled a mountain of paperwork. He admitted to himself that immersing himself in work was his way of easing some of the tension he felt whenever he had a difficult decision to make—a decision he had to make without as much information as he needed.

How much did Nash and his people know about the rescue attempt?

Had they captured Marker and tortured him?

Would someone irresponsibly post something on the Internet that would endanger the whole enterprise?

Most worrisome of all: Were the hostages injured or ill so that they could not cooperate with their rescuers, or were they already dead, making the whole rescue effort an exercise in futility?

McKay sighed, looked at the row of clocks on his wall and then pressed a button to summon an aide.

A young naval lieutenant appeared at the door almost immediately.

"Sir?"

"Send the 'go' message."

"Yes, sir. Right away, sir."

The submarine lay on the surface, rocking gently. Nelson took one last look over the two SDVs. His men were all strapped in. Their masks dangled at the sides of their faces, ready to be pushed into position so they could begin breathing from the delivery vehicles' oxygen supply systems.

"Sir, you have a message." A crewman approached Nelson with a paper in his hand.

Nelson stepped inside the shelter and held the sheet of paper under a dim red light. It was difficult to make out the words, but he knew what he was looking for: "Proceed with mission. McKay sends."

"Okay, let's go." Nelson spoke both to his men and to the submarine crew members standing ready to launch the two craft into the ocean. He quickly strapped himself in beside Bonior and waved his hand over his head to indicate that he was ready to go.

They parked the SDVs on the bottom a short distance offshore and then swam the rest of the way. The landing on the rocky shore went smoothly, almost as though they were back in Hawaii, running through one more drill.

Nelson quickly dispatched SEAL Dick Hoffman and air force Master Chief Tim Hutchins into the neighboring town of Opunake. Less than half an hour later, driving two stolen vehicles, they came rolling down the highway, deserted in the midnight darkness.

The two drivers slowed to a crawl as members of the Eagle Force fitted themselves and their equipment into the vehicles and then set out on the route they had memorized that would take them up the side of Mount Egmont, toward Nash's compound.

As the guard moved toward Cindy, she turned around protectively and pressed her face against the wall. She held her hands low across her body. "Please, no," she muttered.

"C'mon, baby," the guard said. "It doesn't have to be like that." He let the words stretch out as he reached out toward her hips with both hands.

Just before he touched her, though, she spun and cracked him across the eyes with the butt of the pistol she'd pulled from her slacks when her body was blocking his view.

He staggered back across the room, stunned. As his eyes came into focus, he saw that the small pistol now grasped in her two hands, was aimed at his abdomen.

"Okay, lover boy. Hold your right hand over your head. With your left hand, undo the belt. Let the gun and radio drop to the floor gently."

He hesitated a moment, sizing up the situation, trying to decide whether he could grab the gun before she shot him.

She gestured with the pistol. He had the sinking feeling that he was facing a professional like himself, who would not hesitate to kill. He fumbled with the belt buckle and then lowered it, with the pistol and radio, to the floor.

"Now! Hands against the wall. Legs apart. Move!"

He followed her orders, leaning against the wall with his arms outstretched.

She stepped up behind him and hooked a foot inside his left

ankle, ready to topple him if he moved. Holding the pistol against his back, she ran her free hand over his body. She found a long, thin knife in a scabbard built into one boot. She pulled it out and tossed it across the room.

"All right, you can stand up now and turn toward me." She backed across the room, keeping the pistol pointed at his midriff. "I want you to get undressed. Sit in the chair, there. Use your left hand to unlace your boots and pull them off. Keep your right hand up over your head."

He hesitated for only a moment before he sat down and followed her orders.

"Now stand up. Keep your right hand up there. With your left hand, pull down the zipper on your jumpsuit and take it off."

He began to pull the zipper and then turned away from her.

"No, no! Face me. I want to see both your hands."

He turned toward her, extricated his arms from the jumpsuit and let it fall at his ankles.

"The T-shirt, too." She watched as he pulled it over his head. "Good. Now back over there against the wall, and resume the position with your hands against the wall. Move!"

She kicked off her shoes, dropped her slacks and slipped into the jumpsuit, keeping her pistol pointed at his back the whole time.

The suit was several sizes too big, but that didn't worry her. She rolled the sleeves inward so they hung just to her wrists and pushed the tops of the legs into the boots so that they would appear to blouse properly below the knee. Retrieving his belt, she strapped it around her waist. Even in the last notch, it hung at an angle across her hips. She thought she probably looked something like an old-fashioned Wild West gunslinger.

She cinched up the adjustment on the inside of his helmet and tried it on. Her hair was already short enough, she figured, so she didn't have to try to hide it under the helmet.

"Now," she asked, "what shall we do about you?"

He looked over his shoulder at her.

"Never mind. That was a rhetorical question." She looked around the room for something to tie him with. Her eye fell on the telephone.

Picking up his knife from where she had thrown it, she cut the long telephone extension cord and ordered him to hold his hands behind his back. She tied his hands tightly together with one end of the cord and then backed away.

"Lie down on the floor. Face down. Bend your legs at the knees."

She bound his ankles together and then looped the other end of the cord around his neck. It wasn't tight enough to choke him, but if he struggled to get loose, it would cut off his air supply.

"One more thing, and then we're done." She put down her pistol and twisted his T-shirt as though she were trying to ring it out, then used it to fashion a gag across his mouth and around his neck.

She stepped back and surveyed her handiwork. Slinging his AK-47 over her shoulder, she started toward the door, then stopped, turned, bent down, and gave him a sharp pinch on the buttock. "There, that ought to hold you for a little while, lover boy."

Opening the door a crack, she looked up and down the hall. No one was visible. She closed the door softly behind herself, slipped the key into the pocket of her jumpsuit, and then leaned back against the door. For the last forty-five minutes or so, she had been running on pure adrenaline. Now, with the guard locked up, she felt both relieved and very tired.

She also realized that she had been focused so intently on how to disarm the guard and free herself that she had not thought beyond this moment. Where was she going to go now? How was she going to get herself and the First Lady and David out of this mess? She took a deep breath and tried to think ahead. One thing was perfectly obvious: She couldn't risk standing in the hall more than a moment or two; she had to move.

Suddenly, she heard the sounds of footsteps on the gravel walkway in the courtyard between the two buildings. Fumbling for the key to the door she had just locked, she slipped back inside the room and flicked off the lights.

Holding the door open just a crack, she saw Mrs. Walker and David pass by, followed by Bernard and the guard who had been stationed at the door to their cell.

As the footsteps receded down the hall, she pulled the door open far enough to see that there was no one else in the hallway. Then she stepped out into the corridor, locked the door once more, and moved quickly to the courtyard and across into the other building.

Nash was standing in the middle of the room as the First Lady and her son entered, hands on his hips.

"Mrs. Walker. Your husband has done something very stupid."

She stopped and stood in front of him, returning his stare.

"I want you to talk to him. Tell him that he must reverse his order releasing nickel and cobalt from the stockpile. It must be done immediately."

"What are you talking about? Nickel? Cobalt? I don't understand."

"You don't have to understand. Just tell him what I said." She shrugged her shoulders.

There was a brief knock at the door, and a young man entered with a sheet of paper in his hand. "Sir, this fax just came in. I assumed you would want to see it."

Nash took the paper, returned to his desk, put on his glasses, and read the message at a glance.

"Well, yes. This is much better." He turned to Bernard. "The White House confirms that a C-141 carrying the arms we requested is en route to Auckland. It is due early in the morning.

"Now, Mrs. Walker, we will call your husband. I will talk to him first and give him my instructions. Then I will put you on the phone. You will tell him that he has two hours to follow my directions. You can tell him what happened to Miss Carson. You may surmise the worst—and you would be correct. You may also surmise correctly that that was intended as a warning of much worse to come if my orders are not followed to the letter. Tell your husband that as well.''

Nash pushed a button to activate his speakerphone and then dialed the White House. As soon as he identified himself, he was put through to the president's office.

''Maynard Walker here.''

''Mr. President, you know who this is. Your wife and son are here with me. I am going to give you one last chance—but only one.''

''Let me speak to my wife.''

''Certainly. Mrs. Walker, you may speak to your husband.''

''Chip! I don't know what is going on, but Mr. Nash is very agitated. He keeps talking about about nickel and cobalt. He wants me to tell you to stop whatever you are doing.''

''Are you and David all right, Marcie?''

''Yes. He hasn't harmed us. But one of his men beat up Cindy Carson. She has a couple of black eyes and a cut on her face. Then they took her away. I don't know what they've done to her now. They may have killed her.''

''What does he want me to do?''

Nash broke in. ''This is what I want, Mr. President. First, I understand that an aircraft carrying the arms we requested is inbound to Auckland. That, at least, is some progress. Now, I want you to reverse the order releasing nickel and cobalt from the strategic stockpile and issue a statement saying the order was a mistake. I want that done immediately.''

''That will take some time, sir.''

''You can make things happen when you want to. I will give you two hours. We will also examine the cargo of the plane arriving in Auckland to be sure that my orders have been followed. If your order regarding the strategic metals is not rescinded, or if the arms cargo is not satisfactory, the game is over. And, I emphasize again: There must be no rescue attempt. If there is the slightest hint of such an effort, the game will be over for your wife and your son. Do I make myself clear?''

''Chip! Please do as he says.''

''Marcie, you and David hang in there. Mr. Nash, you will find the arms cargo just as you specified. I will rescind the stockpile order, but please give me time to do it. It will gain you nothing to harm your hostages.''

''Two hours, Mr. President. Two hours.'' Nash pressed the button to cut the connection.

Maynard Walker hung up the phone and leaned back in his chair, one hand over his eyes. He remained motionless for nearly a minute as Abdul Rahman stood expectantly near his desk. He finally uncovered his eyes and sat forward.

''This game is getting awfully damned dicey, Abe. But I think he's taken the bait. We've given him plenty to think about for the next couple of hours. That move on the strategic stockpile really got his attention. If our calculations are right, he is looking at some catastrophic losses unless we reverse that order. That's the stick. The C-141 with the arms is a kind of carrot to make him think we're going along with his demands.''

''Are you going to rescind the order, sir?''

''Oh, sure. We can always slam him again as soon as the hostages are free. . . . You take care of that. It'll just take a couple of phone calls. But make sure the news doesn't come out on the wire service tickers until about fifteen minutes before his deadline. I want to keep him worried as long as possible while we get everything in place. How do we stand on the rescue?''

''I checked with Admiral McKay a short time ago. Everything is on schedule.''

The president, lost in thought, nodded but didn't respond.

CHAPTER 31

MAJOR JACK LAFFER HELD A TIGHT FORMATION OFF THE RIGHT wingtip of the bigger C-141 as it passed the North Cape of New Zealand's North Island and flew south along the island's west coast.

As the pilot of the other craft turned over Matakawau and began his descent toward Auckland International from the southwest, Laffer eased back slightly on his throttles and went into a steep, diving bank toward the ocean. At a hundred feet above the surface, he leveled off and set his course to the south-southwest, toward the city of New Plymouth.

Behind him, the navigator monitored the radio for a signal from Nelson.

When the message came, the transmission lasted less than a second, giving the time for the drop to begin.

"Navigator to pilot: We have a little time to kill. Let me give you a new heading. We'll pass to the north of New Plymouth and Mount Egmont and then swing around to come in over the south slope of the mountain from the west."

"Ah, roger. Let's stay out over the ocean as long as we can. Less chance of anybody hearing or spotting us."

"Sir, there are two little towns near the coast—Rahotu and Oaonui—on the west side of the mountain. Otherwise, it looks as though the area is very sparsely populated. I'll bring you in midway between the towns. It will only be about two minutes from where we cross the coast to the drop point."

"You have our egress plotted?"

"Yes, sir. As we briefed, we'll come in low, pop up to five hundred feet for the drop, and then buzz the compound. We want them to know we're there. Then just put her on 180 degrees until we're out over the water. That'll only take a couple of minutes. Then I'll vector us in to the tanker."

The sliver of the new moon gave just enough light so that Laffer could make out the surface of the ocean two hundred feet below the plane and the faint line of the horizon, far in front. Off to the left, he could see the bulk of the mountain, its cap of snow faintly luminescent.

Laffer felt comfortable dividing his attention between the instruments and the view out the windscreen. But for the dash to the target at treetop level, he would rely on his night vision goggles to pierce the darkness.

Cindy Carson had gone only a few steps into the neighoring building when she heard the order: "Freeze!"

Raising her hands, she turned slowly toward the man standing a few feet behind her, a small machine gun aimed at her midriff.

"Frogwoman! Thank God, I damn near killed you."

"Rex? Is that you? Oh, I'm so glad to see you." She threw her arms around him in a fierce hug.

He returned her gesture with a one-armed squeeze and then broke free from her embrace.

"We've got to move, Cindy. This place is crawling with people."

"You're right. Follow me."

She led the way down the hall to the room where she and the Walkers had been locked up. The door had been left ajar.

She leaned close to his ear and whispered: "In here. They've taken Mrs. Walker and David over into the other building. We can hide in the closet. They won't think of looking for us here."

He followed her into the closet. They sat side by side in the darkness, leaning against the wall. She spoke in a low voice, barely louder than a whisper.

"I'm sure the room is bugged, but we can talk quietly in here with the door closed."

Marker laid his weapon down carefully on the floor beside him. "So what's your game plan now, Frogwoman?"

"I'm making it up as I go along. When I ran into you, my plan was to come here and wait until the Walkers came back and then figure out what to do next. What are you doing here, and what's your plan?"

"I'm making it up as I go along, too. They almost caught me when I got out of my hiding place to send off a message to Eagle Force, so I figured I'd better give them a moving target. You don't have anything to eat here, do you?"

"No, I don't think so."

"Well, okay. I'm really getting hungry, but I'll just have to wait."

"Do you know when they're coming?"

"Not really. They didn't tell me a hell of a lot before I came on this mission. What I didn't know, I couldn't tell if I got caught. But my guess is that the rescue should come soon, early tomorrow morning. They're sure as hell not going to come in broad daylight. So if I'm wrong, we're going to have to hang in there for at least another twenty-four hours."

She put a hand on his arm. "I'm not sure we can hold out that long. They're really beginning to put the pressure on us. There's a man named Bernard who is in charge of the guard force. He beat me up. He didn't really hurt me too bad, but he messed up my face—a cut and a couple of black eyes. I think he wanted to send a message to Mrs. Walker."

"Ben Bernard? Big Dog? Yeah, I know the son of a bitch. He's bad news. Say, how come you're wandering around here dressed like one of them?"

"A guard came and took me away about an hour ago. I managed to hide a little pistol when we were seized, so I got the drop on him. He's tied up in a room in the other building. He's not going anywhere soon, but it probably won't be too long until they find him. And then the shit will hit the fan."

"As far as I can tell, the shit has already hit the fan. I think there's a big search already going on for me. My parachute canopy hung up in a tree, and I couldn't get it all the way down. They probably spotted it and started looking for me. I don't know whether they know, or just suspect, that I'm inside the compound. But as soon as they discover you escaped, they'll really start going over this place."

"What do you think we ought to do?"

"I'll pass on that bid. What do you think?"

"Well, I think we're probably about as safe here as we could be anywhere. I doubt they would think we would try to hide in our little cell. I suggest we wait until they bring the Walkers back, find out what they know, and then try to decide what to do next."

"Sounds good to me."

"Okay, take them back. . . ." Nash paused. "No, take *her* to the room. You keep the kid."

Bernard opened the door and spoke to a guard standing outside. "You take Mrs. Walker to her room and remain at the door until you're relieved. I'll take care of the boy."

The guard grasped the First Lady's arm and guided her down the hallway. She looked over her shoulder and tried to turn back as she heard her son's voice: "Mom . . . Ow! You're hurting my arm."

Bernard waited until the guard and Mrs. Walker had stepped through the door into the courtyard and then took David to his office and locked him in the room where he had been held before.

When the guard and Mrs. Walker arrived back at the hostage cell, they found the door partially open, just as it had been left. The guard held the door as the First Lady stepped inside. He closed the door but did not lock it because he didn't have the key.

Marcia Walker stood uncertainly, just inside the door, collecting her thoughts, and then walked across the room toward the bathroom. As she passed the closet door, she heard a faint sound, a *pssst.*

She stopped and turned toward the sound, restraining her impulse to speak. Inside the closet, she saw Cindy Carson, a finger to her lips. The First Lady nodded her understanding. Carson beckoned her into the closet and then closed the door so that only a sliver of light shone through.

"Thank God. You're okay, Cindy. Nash hinted at the worst," she whispered.

"I'm fine. The guard isn't. Mrs. Walker, Rex Marker is here, too."

The First Lady blinked to adjust her eyes to the darkness and was able to make out the form of a man sitting behind Carson. She reached out to take his extended hand in both of hers.

"We can whisper in here, ma'am."

"What about the rescue? Are they coming soon?

"We're not sure, ma'am. My radio is broken. I have been able to transmit several reports, but I can't receive. But I think—I hope—they will be coming for us early tomorrow morning, just a little while from now."

"How are they going to get us out of here?"

"I really don't know the details, ma'am. I was kept in the dark on purpose, in case I was captured. But, from what I was able to figure out from our training, Eagle Force—that's our outfit—will storm through the compound, try to find us, and then we'll steal these folks' helicopter and fly away."

"How soon do you think they will come?"

"Like I said, maybe only a couple more hours. I figure it doesn't make sense to try something like this in the daylight. So we're talking about sometime after midnight but well before first light."

The First Lady thought for a moment. "And so, I gather that if they don't come tonight, we're going to have to wait at least another twenty-four hours?"

"Yes, ma'am. That's the way I figure it."

"I don't think we have twenty-four hours to spare, Rex."

"How so, ma'am?"

"I just came back from Nash's office. He gave the president a two-hour deadline. And that must be half an hour ago now."

"What kind of deadline, ma'am?"

"He just said, 'The game will be over.' It was clearly a threat to harm—or kill—David and me and Cindy. As you can see, they have already hurt Cindy."

"Yes, I saw her face."

"How long do you think we can hold out here, Rex?" Cindy asked.

"As soon as they find that guy you tied up, this joint is going to be crawling with searchers. But this is probably as good a hiding place as any. The last place they are likely to come looking for us is right where you people have been locked up."

Carson tapped the walkie-talkie radio she had taken from the guard. "We also may be able to keep track of their search. I'll see if I can set the radio to monitor their communications."

The First Lady laughed under her breath. "Yes, Cindy. I'm sure that will make for some interesting listening. But that still leaves us with the problem: What do we do if that two hours runs out and our rescuers have not arrived?"

"Mrs. Walker, do you know where David is?"

"No, I don't, really. I assume he's being held somewhere in that other building, but I don't know where. Whatever we do, we've got to find him."

Cindy patted her arm reassuringly. "Don't worry. We'll find him."

"All right. This is our game plan." Marker had assumed command. "Cindy and I will hide here in the closet and monitor the radio. We'll hear some weapons fire when Eagle Force arrives, and we'll just wait here until they come for us. If the two hours runs out before they arrive, we're going to have to move."

Marker could not see the faces of the two women, and neither of them spoke. But he could hear the unasked question hanging in the air: Move where?

Finally, Mrs. Walker spoke. "Cindy, you said you were a pilot. Can you fly a helicopter?"

"I've had a few hours at the controls of a helicopter, but most of my time has been in light, single-engine aircraft."

"But could you fly one if you have to to get us out of here?"

Her reply, when it came, started hesitantly but finished strong. "Well, if it comes to that, I guess I could fly a lawn mower out of here."

Ben Bernard knew he should be getting some rest. But he couldn't resist pacing the perimeter of the compound, frequently casting an anxious eye toward the sky.

The radio at his waist buzzed. Bernard brought it to his ear and pressed the button to activate it.

"Sir, radar reports a contact. A four-engine aircraft is approaching from the west at low altitude."

"That's it! Alert the antiaircraft crews."

Threading his way across the mountainside with his night vision goggles, Jack Laffer held the Combat Talon just above the treetops. In the rear compartment, four members of the aircrew stood at the open cargo door. They hung on as Laffer pulled back on the stick and climbed sharply to five hundred feet. As he leveled off, they quickly pushed the dummies, with their parachutes attached to toggle lines, out the door.

Bright searchlights flashed on, sweeping the sky in the direction from which the plane had come.

At first, the machine gunners saw nothing. Then one of them spotted a parachute and opened fire. Another parachute was illuminated and came under fire.

The gunners swore in frustration. It seemed as if their tracers were hitting the chutes and even the figures dangling below them. But the chutes continued to descend on course and undeterred.

It took only a few seconds for the parachutes to disappear into the treetops. The firing stopped, the searchlights switched off, and an eerie silence descended over the compound.

As soon as the last "body" disappeared into the darkness, Laffer dove back down closer to the ground, descending the mountain to the south. The antiaircraft gunners loosed a few futile shots, but Laffer flashed by so low and so fast that they couldn't get him in their sights.

Bernard hurried back to his office, calling Nash as he went to warn him of the attack.

The shouting woke David Walker in the next room. Bernard had removed both the chair and the wastebasket David had used to try to reach the window the last time he was imprisoned in the small room. Bored and exhausted, the boy had stretched out on the desk and gone to sleep.

Now, rubbing his eyes, he slid off the desk and placed his ear to the door to Bernard's office.

He could hear voices but not loudly enough to tell what they were saying. And then he heard and felt the *crumpf, crumpf, crumpf* of an antiaircraft gun.

Crouched in the closet, Marker, too, heard the sounds of the guns.

"Oh, the rescuers are coming!" Mrs. Walker whispered excitedly.

"No, I don't think so, ma'am, not quite yet. Those are antiaircraft and heavy machine guns. My guess is that this is some kind of diversion. Let's hang in here just a little while longer."

Bernard, receiving blow-by-blow accounts from the searchlight and gun positions, mapped out his strategy.

On a chart of the compound and its surroundings, he drew a circle around the area where the parachutes were seen to land. Then he drew two lines from that side of the compound forming a *V* shape.

He barked orders, sending half his guard force out to take up positions along the two arms of the *V*. The other half, he held in reserve.

This isn't so bad, he thought. When they try to move in on us, they'll walk right into an ambush. So much for the rescue attempt.

As his driver pulled to the side of the road and stopped, Nelson heard the sounds of the antiaircraft guns and the crackle of machine gun fire.

Good, he thought. Right on schedule.

Moments later, he almost ducked as the dark shape of the Combat Talon roared over their position, just above the treetops.

He signaled to Bonior to move out. Three minutes later, Bonior radioed that the guard post was clear. The two vehicles rolled silently past the guard shack and a short distance up the road before the drivers pulled to the side and stopped again. Bonior and his men started up the left side of the road, Nelson and his men on the right. They walked carefully, keeping several yards between each man.

As they came in sight of the gate set into the towering wall of lava between them and the compound, the two squads moved off into the forest on each side of the road.

They heard sporadic bursts of gunfire and a few confused shouts, most of them seeming to come from the northwestern side of the compound, some distance from where they were.

One man in each squad unwrapped a long rope from his body and threw a grappling hook high onto the wall. Within a minute, both squads were atop the barrier and working their way over the concertina wire lying along the top of the wall.

As he lay on the ground and watched to make sure that all of his squad had surmounted the wire obstacle, Bonior radioed to Nelson that he and his men were inside the compound.

Dividing his force at this point, until he knew what they would run into once they were atop the wall, had made sense to Nelson during his planning for the operation. But now that they were atop the wall and inside the wire barrier, he wished he had kept the entire force together and struck on only one side of the road.

Well, he thought, no sense worrying about that now.

"Jeff," he spoke softly into the radio. "Can you get your guys over on this side of the road?"

"Yeah, we'll patrol down there and sneak across."

Marker looked at his watch. It had been almost ten minutes since the sound of the guns had stopped. If the rescuers didn't show up soon, they were going to have to move out.

"Are you getting anything on that radio, Cindy?"

"Just a second." She turned the gain switch to clear the static, and then a voice came through: "She's not here, sir!"

"She's not there? Where the hell is she?"

"I don't know, sir. Marco is all tied up, and he's nearly naked."

"Naked? How many men do you have?"

"There are three of us, sir."

"Okay, I can't give you any more right now. You start searching for her."

Carson turned down the volume.

"Well, we expected that."

Marker looked at his watch again. "I don't think we can wait any longer. We're going to have to move before they come to get you, Mrs. Walker." He rose and helped the First Lady to her feet.

"Please come with me, ma'am."

He led her to the door to the room and whispered, "Call to the guard. Get him to open the door and step inside." Marker stepped back so he would be hidden as the door opened. He fitted a silencer onto his pistol and held it ready in his right hand.

Mrs. Walker tapped on the door and spoke in a loud, commanding voice. "Guard! I need you!"

The door opened and the man stepped inside.

"What's the problem?"

Mrs. Walker took a few steps back, and he followed her. As he did so, he caught sight of Marker out of the corner of his eye. He whirled, bringing his AK-47 into firing position.

A single shot from Marker's pistol caught him between the eyes.

"Oh . . . oh . . . oh . . ." The First Lady backed away from the corpse, the back of her hand over her mouth.

Marker grabbed her by a wrist. "Okay, ma'am, let's hang in there. We're going to have to get out of here." He leaned down, grabbed the fallen guard by the web gear, dragged the body into the bathroom, and took the man's rifle and pistol.

"Cindy, can you handle an AK-47?"

"No, I brought along that guard's rifle, but I was never checked out in foreign weapons."

"What about this submachine gun?"

"Yes, I'm an expert with the MP-5."

"Here, you take mine. And here's some ammo. I'll carry both the AKs. We may need them."

Marker looked at Mrs. Walker's empty hands. "How about you, ma'am? Can you handle a pistol?"

She looked with repugnance at the pistol in his hand and then slowly nodded. "Yes, I think so."

He handed her the pistol taken from the guard. "Here—it's all loaded, and the safety is off. If you have to use it, hold it firmly with both hands, point it where you want to shoot, and pull the trigger. It has a kick, so hold tight!"

Marker opened the door and looked up and down the corridor. "Okay, let's move."

"What about my son?"

"We'll find him for you, ma'am." Marker knew it would be foolish to say he didn't have the vaguest idea how to find a nine-year-old hidden somewhere in a complex under siege.

★

Bonior's men crept over to a ledge about eight feet above the road. Working in twos, they lowered themselves into the roadway, dashed across and then helped each other up the other side. But as the last man climbed the wall, a chunk of lava broke loose and tumbled down onto the roadway. The men waited, hugging the ground and trying to make themselves invisible. And then, just as they were preparing to join the other squad, lights along the top of the building flashed on, and a loud siren sounded. The doors to the building swung open, and a guard force platoon emerged, holding their weapons at the ready.

Even though they were still separated by about thirty feet, Bonior and Nelson shouted the same word at the same moment:

"Lights!" There was a brief crackle of gunfire and then silence. All the lights had been shot out. The Eagle Force members pulled their night vision goggles down over their eyes and moved cautiously to the ledge. They could see about twenty members of the guard force down below, without night vision goggles, milling about in the dark. They shouted in consternation as they were picked off, one after the other. The survivors scrambled back inside the building, several of them pulling wounded comrades by the clothing.

Nelson turned to SEAL Chief Jack Berryman and ordered him to fire at a large tank next to the building. Nelson knew, from studying satellite photos, that the tank contained natural gas that ran the generator supplying electrical power for the compound.

Berryman took aim and fired a single steel-tipped shell into the tank with his .50-caliber sniper rifle. Moments later, he fired at the same spot with an incendiary round.

The tank erupted in flames, and then all the lights in the compound went out.

———————— ★ ————————

David Walker sat on the edge of the desk, listening to the muffled sounds of gunfire outside.

He had not heard anything from the adjoining office for a long time. He felt very much alone and frightened, but his spirits were buoyed by the thought that the shooting must mean someone was trying to rescue him.

Any minute, he thought, they'll come for me, and we'll get out of this place.

Then a new thought came into his mind: They don't know where I am. Maybe they'll go away and leave me here.

He decided to try the door. He knew it wasn't going to open, though—and it didn't.

He looked toward the window, high on the wall. There was just enough light outside for him to make out the vague outlines of the opening. But, without the chair and wastebasket, the window was hopelessly beyond reach.

David sat on the floor, leaning against the wall, and stared at the window, trying to think of some other way to get to it. Then it dawned on him that, even if he couldn't get to the window himself, somehow he could use it to send a message.

He recalled noticing some kind of paperweight on the desk. Feeling around, he located a rough chunk of lava. He hefted it in his hand. The porous lava was not very heavy. But it just might be heavy enough to break the window if he could throw it hard enough.

He stood back against the wall opposite the window and threw the stone as hard as he could. It hit the wall below the window and clattered back down onto the desk and then to the floor. Following the sound, he groped around on the floor until he found it. Taking a deep breath, he threw once more. Again, the missile fell short.

Sitting down again against the wall, he stared up at the window. There must be some way to break the glass—but maybe he just wasn't strong enough.

Then another thought came to him. Maybe he could make a sling.

He pulled off his shirt and tied the sleeves together, forming a pocket at the neck. He stood in the middle of the room, twirled the weighted shirt in a circle, and let fly. The rock slipped loose and slammed into the side of the desk.

Wrapping the piece of lava more carefully, he again took up his position, twirled his homemade sling, and let go. The lava chunk hit square in the middle of the glass, shattering it with a satisfying crash. David could just make out the shape of his white shirt, draped through the broken glass.

He sat down again, wrapping his arms across his chest in a futile effort to keep warm. Well, he thought, maybe they'll see my signal and come and get me. That's the best I can do.

Ben Bernard was standing near the fence on the northwestern side of the compound waiting for the expected assault by the parachutists when he heard the sound of gunfire around the other side, near the main entrance to the compound. As he turned in that direction, puzzled, the gas tank exploded and the lights went out.

Bernard ran to the building and into the wide central corridor that led to the entranceway. As he arrived at the doorway, the remnants of his guard force came streaming back into the shelter of the building, trying to escape the deadly fire pouring down on them from the elevation beside the roadway.

Several men dragged wounded comrades. As soon as they were safely inside the building, they knelt, struggling to hold flashlights in their teeth while providing first aid. Many of the men stood bewildered, in shock. Some swore violently while others simply stared vacantly.

Bernard grabbed one of the men by the arm, shone a flashlight on his face, and demanded, "What happened?"

The man was clutching his left shoulder. Blood seeped between his fingers.

"The sons of bitches ambushed us, sir. They're up on the ledge, shooting down at us. We couldn't even see them."

"How many of them are there?"

"From the amount of firepower they've got, I'd say there's a hundred of them up there."

Bernard mentally discounted the estimate. He knew that soldiers—from generals to privates—always tended to overestimate the enemy's strength. From his experience as a

SEAL, he calculated that he might face a force of about platoon size—fifteen to twenty men. If he was right, he also knew that the rescue force would rapidly lose its combat effectiveness: It would have to start rationing its bullets or take the risk of running out of ammunition. As a SEAL, he had often taken comfort in the knowledge that an eight-man SEAL squad had the firepower of an infantry company of as many as 150 men—but only for a brief fight.

Now, the situation was reversed, and he would soon have the edge in firepower—if the force up on the ledge was all he faced.

He brought his radio to his lips. "Any contact out there?"

The leader of the team that had set the ambush for the parachutists responded. "No, sir. All quiet out here."

"Shit!" Bernard swore under his breath as he tried to size up the situation. If the rescue operation involved a big outfit like the army's Delta Force or the navy's DevGru, there could still be parachutists hiding out there in the woods, and perhaps other units ready to hit from unexpected directions. He might face as many as a hundred highly trained commandos.

He made a quick decision.

"Okay, hold your position. Buzz me immediately if you have any contact."

He raised his voice to shout over the din of the men clustered in the hallway.

"I want every able-bodied man to fall in. On the double!"

"Sir," one of the men responded. "I can't stop the bleeding. If I leave him, he's going to die."

"Fall in! Everybody! I mean everybody!"

The man who had been attempting to staunch the blood flowing from his buddy's chest rose reluctantly, patted the shoulder of the wounded man, and joined the others forming up around Bernard.

One of the wounded men shouted, "Water! For God's sake, water!"

Several men looked in his direction and then moved away to gather around Bernard just as his walkie-talkie crackled.

"Sir!" Bernard could sense his man's urgency even through the tinny sound of the little walkie-talkie speaker. "I can't raise Guard Post Two."

"When did he last check in?"

"On the quarter hour, sir. About twenty minutes ago."

Bernard was puzzled. What was going on? The force that had engaged his people in a firefight hadn't had time to get to the hostages and eliminate the guards. Was there a force already inside the building that he didn't know about?

"You and you!" Bernard picked two men at random. "You know where the hostages are? Get over there and see what the hell is going on. Contact me as soon as you get there."

The two men took off in a dead sprint before Bernard stopped speaking. Neither wanted to face Bernard's considerable wrath by seeming to shrink his duty—not when that wrath was already so worked up.

CHAPTER 32

MARKER WAS NOT SURPRISED WHEN THE LIGHTS WENT OUT; SEALs like the dark almost as much as they like the water. That's why he'd brought his night vision goggles. "Let's form a chain, holding hands," Marker said. "I'll lead the way."

"Where are we going, Rex?"

"Perhaps you can help me, ma'am. I want to get to the helicopter pad. It's over on the other side of this neighboring building. That's where the team will meet us. Have you been in this part of the complex?"

"Let's see . . . yes, I remember. I was taken to Nash's office twice. We went down this corridor we're in. Then we crossed a little courtyard and went into the next building. I wish I could see."

"It's better if we don't use a flashlight. We might have the edge if we run into anyone." Marker paused, causing the others to bump into each other. "Wait a minute—let me scope this out."

He moved forward, stepping out the doorway into the courtyard. No one was visible.

He moved back inside and took Marcia Walker's hand. "Okay, ma'am, let's get across this courtyard as quick as we can."

As soon as the guard force retreated inside the building, Eagle Force broke through a large window into what looked like a laboratory and went through a door to the right, into a long corridor.

"This is it." Nelson spoke softly, more to himself than to the team. As the team members emerged into the corridor, they took positions along the wall, weapons held upright, at the ready.

The hall seemed deserted, but the team moved cautiously, uncertain what lay ahead.

Then, as they moved around a corner, two men holding flashlights entered the corridor at its opposite end. Nelson and Bonior, who were acting as point men, one on each side of the corridor, fired at the same moment. The two men dropped.

The two leaders hastened their pace. When they reached the door to the room where Marker had told them the hostages were held, Nelson cautiously turned the doorknob. He nodded to Bonior, who kicked open the door and went right on in, sweeping the right side of the room. The man behind him covered the left side, finger on the trigger of his automatic rifle.

The two men quickly checked the room.

Bonior turned to Nelson. "There's no one here, boss."

One of the men dropped to a knee on the other side of the room from the beds.

"Look at this, Chief." He pushed up his night vision goggles and shined the beam of a flashlight on the floor. Bonior and Nelson joined him, looking down over his shoulder.

On the floor was a large, reddish brown stain.

Nelson reached down, touched the stain with an index finger, and then brought the finger up into the light of his flashlight.

"Blood. And it's still wet."

One of the team members carefully pushed open the bathroom door.

"This is where the blood came from, boss." He pointed at the body of the guard.

Nelson joined him at the door. "Whew. That's a relief. I thought they might have hurt our people. It looks like our people did the hurting."

"That looks to me like Rex's work, sir." Bonior had joined him at the door.

"Yeah, it sure does. Neat head shot." He stood staring at the body for a moment, thinking. "Question now: Where the hell have they gone?"

"I'll bet Rex is trying to get them to the chopper," Rattner suggested. "We're probably only a few minutes behind them."

Marcia Walker grasped Marker's arm.

"We've got to find my son! I'm not leaving this place without him."

"I understand, ma'am. Let's try to get to the helicopter and link up with the team, and then we'll find him."

She loosened her grip on his arm.

"Promise me. Promise me we'll find David."

"Yes, ma'am. I promise." He made the promise sincerely. But he had no idea whether or how he would be able to keep it.

The two women clustered behind him in the doorway to the courtyard.

"Okay," Marker said, "there's just enough light out there to see what we're doing. I'll lead the way, and I want you to follow me—fast!"

"Ready? Let's go." Marker stepped out the door and dashed down a set of steps and into the courtyard. Marcia Walker and Cindy Carson followed closely behind.

Halfway across, Marcia Walker stopped. "Look! Up there!"

Marker turned, irritated. "Move it, ma'am. Goddammit, move it!"

She remained in the middle of the courtyard. "Look. That's David's shirt hanging out that window."

Marker glanced upward. "Okay, I've got it. Now let's move it. Get out of the courtyard."

Ben Bernard did not like this at all. He was both literally and figuratively in the dark.

He waited five minutes for a report from the two men he had sent to check out the hostages. When they failed to respond, he called repeatedly, as though shouting into the microphone would bring an answer.

Shining his light over his assembled men, he noted that the wounded were still lying untended, several of them pleading for water. One called over and over for his mother.

"Follow me!" Bernard moved off at a trot down the wide corridor. His plan was to get between the force that had cut down his men and the helicopter. If there were other units that he didn't know about—either inside the compound or somewhere outside—he would just have to deal with them when he ran into them.

When he reached the doorway into the courtyard, he paused. There was no sign of the intruders. He felt a resurgence of his normal confidence.

I've got the sons of bitches now, he thought. They have to pass through here to get to the helipad.

Moving quickly, he positioned his men along a low wall that bordered a path crossing through the courtyard. A fountain rising to the left afforded additional shelter. Within moments, the courtyard lay in silence, faintly illuminated by the moon.

Nelson pushed aside the dinner plates on the table and looked through several sheets of paper he found lying there.

If Rex had had time, he would have left us a message, he thought.

All he found were doodles and meaningless phrases.

Taking one last look around the room, he said, "Okay, men, we're going to move out toward the helipad. But we're not going to rush. We're going to take it slow and easy, feel our way along. These guys we ran into in the corridor probably came to find out what was going on over here. That means they'll either be looking for us or trying to ambush us." He glanced once more around the room and then gave the order: "Move out."

Spacing themselves out and hugging the walls, the team moved down the corridor and turned the corner toward the courtyard. Nelson leaned down and retrieved a walkie-talkie from the body of one of the men they had killed.

As they approached the doorway, Nelson motioned for a stop. Then, wearing his night vision goggles, he carefully scanned the area between them and the building on the other side of the courtyard.

Bonior joined him in the doorway.

"See anything, Jeff?"

"Looks clean, boss."

Nelson stepped out the door.

He seemed to see the flash of fire from the muzzle of an AK-47 at the same moment a stream of bullets cut into the wall just above and behind his head.

Nelson dropped to the floor as the firing stopped.

"Son of a bitch! I told you to hold your fire!"

Nelson recognized the angry voice. It was "Big Dog" Bernard.

Bonior flipped his M-16 onto full automatic, leaned out the doorway, and raked the top of the rock wall. He knew he was unlikely to hit anyone, but his firing kept heads down on the other side long enough for Nelson to crawl back inside.

"Is there any other way around to the helipad, Jeff?"

"I don't think so, boss. From all the intel we have, this looks like the only way—unless you want to go clear outside and around the building."

Nelson ordered two of his men to take up positions inside the doorway so they could see if anyone moved toward them from the courtyard but far enough back so those outside could not see them.

The radio Nelson had taken from the dead man crackled.

"Rick. Any contact out there?"

"No, sir."

"Okay, we've got these guys pinned down in the corridor leading from building two into the courtyard. We're in the courtyard between building two and building one. Bring your men into building two behind them."

"Wilco."

"Well, this is getting interesting." Nelson held the radio as though he expected it to tell him something more.

Picking four men, he posted them at the opposite end of the corridor in position to confront anyone coming from that direction.

"Let's give them something to think about." Nelson moved up close to the door and reached in a pouch pocket for a grenade. Pulling the pin, he counted, "One thousand one . . . one thousand two," and then threw it through the doorway in the direction of the rock wall. It exploded in the air. One of Bernard's men screamed.

Every man along the wall opened up, hammering the doorway with bullets, but Nelson was already well back inside.

Nelson turned to Bonior. "How much time do you figure we've got, Jeff?"

"My guess is that the people Big Dog was calling are outside the fence, looking for our decoy parachutists. It'll take them a good ten minutes to come around the fence and get in here behind us."

"You've got some wire, don't you?"

"Yes, sir. Like piano wire. A roll of it."

"Take two men and go back down the corridor we came through. Rig a booby trap on the door. And then put a couple in the corridor—a wire across the hallway, low down. That'll slow 'em down—at least a little bit."

Bonior took two men and hurried down the corridor.

A plan formed in Nelson's mind. He didn't like it, but it was the best he could think of.

Jeff Bonior was slightly out of breath as he arrived back.

"All set, boss. We've got some nice little surprises for them. It should slow them down."

"Yeah, but not much. From all we were able to find out, these guys Bernard has working for him are real pros. I don't think they'll spot the traps, but they'll keep coming anyway."

Nelson called together all his men, including those he had posted at the end of the corridor.

"Here's the plan," he said. "As soon as we hear the booby traps go off, we'll go out the door as fast as we can, shoot our way across the courtyard, and make a dash for the helicopter. I'm betting Marker and the hostages will meet us there."

As he spoke, Nelson tried to sound as confident as he could, but he didn't like the odds. He had to admit to himself that they would almost certainly take some casualties trying to cross the courtyard and that, caught between the enemy in front and the enemy behind, they might not make it at all.

The men checked their weapons and then sat down along the hallway, backs against the wall. Several of them quietly chewed tobacco.

"Follow me, ma'am. Let's hold hands again."

Marker moved slowly down the corridor, scanning the area ahead through his night vision goggles. He strained, trying to form a picture in his mind of the building's interior. His first goal was to figure out the location of the room where they had seen David's shirt in the window.

Silently, they turned a corner and moved down an adjoining corridor. As Cindy Carson, bringing up the rear, passed the corner, a door up ahead opened and a figure holding a flashlight stepped out.

"Who's there?" The light waved back and forth and came to rest on Marker's chest. "Halt! Get your hands up!"

The glare of the flashlight blinded Marker. He pushed his goggles up onto his forehead and slowly raised his hands.

"Drop your weapons!"

Cindy Carson, standing behind Marker, lowered her machine gun and leaned to place it on the floor. As she did so, she pulled the pistol from the holster at her waist and fired just to the right of the flashlight.

There was a thud as the man's body hit the floor. The light fell so that it shone on the figure sprawled in the doorway.

"Let's move!" Marker took Marcia Walker's hand again and stepped cautiously toward the body.

Holding his pistol aimed at the figure on the floor, Marker picked up the flashlight and shone it on the man's face.

"Why, that's Mr. Nash!" Marcia Walker exclaimed. ". . . Is he dead?"

Marker had already noticed the steady rise and fall of Nash's chest. Blood seeped through his clothing from a wound in his right chest.

"No, he's not dead." Marker pointed his pistol at the man's forehead.

"Oh, no! Don't kill him!" The president's wife reached for Marker's wrist.

"I'm sorry, ma'am, but we can't leave him here behind us. It's not safe." His trigger finger tightened.

"No. I won't allow it. We can't just kill a defenseless man." She moved around between him and Nash so that she could look him in the eye in the reflected glare of the flashlight. "That's a . . . that's an order, Petty Officer Marker."

Marker stared at her for a moment and then shrugged and lowered his weapon.

"Okay, ma'am. If you say so. I hope we don't regret it."

Clicking off the flashlight, Marker pulled his goggles over his eyes and led the way on down the corridor, counting the doors.

He signaled a stop and then cautiously opened a door on the left side of the corridor. There was no one inside. Marker scanned the room and noted a door in the opposite wall.

Moving toward it, he said, "Let's try this door. I'll bet we'll find David there."

The door was locked. Marker knocked and called, "David! David! Are you in there?"

"Oh, boy. I knew you'd come. Open the door."

"Stand back from the door. It's locked, so I'm going to have to try to break it open."

"Okay. Hurry up."

Marker stepped back and then hurled himself against the solid wooden door. He thought he heard a faint cracking sound and hoped it was the door and not his shoulder. He tried once more and just bounced off.

"David? You can hear me okay?"

"Yes."

Turning to the boy's mother, Marker asked, "Is he left- or right-handed?"

"Right."

"All right, David. Face the door. Now, I want you to move as far as you can to the right and crouch down in the corner. Do you know which direction is right? Your right hand is the hand you eat with."

"I know my right hand from my left."

"Yes, I'm sure you do, but I just wanted to be sure. Now, I want you to crouch down, face into the corner, and cover your head with your arms. Are you doing that?"

"Yes." His voice was muffled.

Marker drew his pistol, fired at the lock, and pushed the door open.

"David!" His mother wrapped her arms around him. "Oh, I was so worried."

Marker took her by the arm. "We're going to have to get moving, ma'am."

Nelson and Bonior huddled near the doorway into the court-yard, trying to see what was happening outside. There seemed to be no movement.

"They're just waiting for us, boss. They know the other guys are coming, and then we'll have to do something."

"You're right, Jeff. We've got ourselves in a real box. If we could somehow get out of this corridor and get some elbow room, we'd at least be able to bring our firepower to bear. But they've got us trapped right here." In naval terms, Bernard had crossed Nelson's *T*.

"I think there are rooms facing onto the courtyard. Maybe we could get in there and fire from the windows."

"Yeah, I thought about that. But at some point we're going to have to get across the courtyard, and we're all going to have to be together when we do it. So I don't want to spread us out."

"Do you have a better plan?"

"This is what I figure: We'll hammer them as much as we can—maybe inflict some casualties, at least make them keep their heads down. When those other guys arrive, we'll try to pin them down. Then we'll try to get across the courtyard by twos. We'll move two men out on the little porch to provide suppressive fire. Two men will dash for the building across the way. We'll repeat that until we're all across."

"Yeah . . . might work." Nelson could tell from the tone of Bonior's voice that at least this one veteran warrior didn't think they had a snowball's chance in hell of getting across the courtyard unscathed.

A loud explosion seemed to fill the corridor with sound.

"Here they come. That's the welcome mat you left for them, Jeff."

Dick Hoffman and Tim Hutchins took up positions halfway down the corridor, lying flat on the floor and facing in the direction the sound had come from.

At Nelson's signal, two men stepped to the doorway, hurled grenades and quickly ducked back inside. As soon as the grenades went off, the two men stepped through the door and raked the top of the rock wall with automatic rifle fire.

A second explosion reverberated through the corridor.

Hoffman looked across to Hutchins. "Any minute now."

"Right. Hold your fire."

The two men lay motionless, staring intently through their night vision goggles at the end of the corridor.

Slowly, a partial shape appeared at the corner, and then a man emerged, flattening himself against the wall with his rifle at the ready. After a moment, he motioned with his right hand,

and three more men moved into the corridor and began feeling their way in the dark.

"Now!" Hoffman spoke just loudly enough for Hutchins to hear his voice. The two men opened fire simultaneously, cutting down the four men at the other end of the corridor.

As the party led by Marker stepped into the corridor from the area where David had been held, they heard the sound of an explosion coming from the direction of the building across the courtyard. It was followed a short time later by another explosion.

Marker stopped to listen. As he did so, he heard an intense exchange of gunfire coming from the direction of the courtyard.

"Follow me." He moved at a trot toward the sounds.

He halted just inside the entrance to the courtyard and looked out. It took him only a moment to size up the situation. Eagle Force was bottled up where the corridor in the opposite building opened into the courtyard. Marker could make out at least a dozen men sheltered behind the low wall running across the courtyard, firing at the doorway.

Gathering the former hostages around him, Marker gave them quick instructions.

"Cindy, I'd like you to crawl outside the door and lie on the landing. At my signal, I want you to begin firing. Put your weapon on semiautomatic. That means you have to pull the trigger each time you want to shoot. Fire short bursts, three to five at a time. It doesn't really make much difference where you aim as long as you put a lot of bullets out there.

"Mrs. Walker and David, you stay back away from the entrance."

"Rex, I can shoot, too," Marcia Walker said.

"Oh, no, ma'am. It's too dangerous."

"Nonsense. You can use all the firepower you can get."

Marker studied her for a moment.

"Yes, I guess you're right, ma'am. We've got to win this little battle, or we're all in real trouble. You lie down next to

Cindy and look for movement. She is going to kind of spray the area. But, with your pistol, I want you to look for movement and try to make your shots count. . . . David, you stay back there and root for us.''

''This is not working, boss.'' Bonior leaned close to Nelson's ear to make himself heard. Every time a member of Eagle Force tried to get into firing position near the door, the area was struck by a fusillade of bullets. Behind them, the corridor was quiet, but they knew it would be only minutes before the attack from that direction was resumed.

''What we need now is a miracle, Jeff.'' Nelson remembered how Bonior had asked him to kneel and pray with him when his daughter had been struck in a drive-by shooting.

''I've been praying, boss. The Lord always answers my prayers—but not always in the way I expect.''

A momentary silence had descended over the little battlefield. Suddenly, the stillness was shattered by an eruption of gunfire from the other side of the courtyard. Cries of surprise, anger, and pain rose along the rock wall as Bernard's men—at least, those who had not been hit—turned to face this unexpected challenge.

''Let's go!'' Nelson shouted. He grasped two men by the shoulders and moved them into position at the door to put down suppressive fire along the wall. He grasped two others and urged them toward the open doorway. They hesitated a moment and then dashed for the opposite doorway, firing as they ran. Two more quickly followed.

Marker set aside the first AK-47 and reached for the other one with its full magazine. He found himself keeping up a steady chatter, like a baseball outfielder.

''That's the way, Cindy. Keep their heads down.''

He paused for a quick glance at Mrs. Walker.

''You got him! Good shooting, ma'am! Keep picking 'em off!''

Marcia Walker lay flat on the concrete landing between Marker and Carson, holding the pistol in both hands. She closed her left eye and squinted down the sights with her right, aiming at one man after another, trying to remember to squeeze rather than jerk the trigger.

Her pulse pounded in her ears and her breath came in short gasps, but she felt strangely calm and clearheaded, focusing her entire attention on this simple, deadly action: aim, squeeze . . . aim, squeeze. Somehow, her mind screened out consciousness of the bullets whizzing past her head and any sense of danger. She felt a sensation almost of exhilaration, unlike anything she had ever felt before.

It barely subsided during the few seconds it took Marker to reload her gun, then reload again a few moments later.

"Oh, shit. Here they come!" Hoffman opened fire as three men dashed around the corner into the corridor he and Hutchins were guarding. Two of the men dropped, but the other continued to fire.

Hutchins lobbed a grenade that hit the floor, bounced, and then went off. The firing ceased for a moment, but three more men emerged, firing as they came.

"That's it!" Nelson exclaimed as the last two men safely made their way across the courtyard.

He and Bonior took up positions on each side of the hallway behind Hoffman and Hutchins and put down a barrage of suppressive fire as the two rear guards rose and dashed for the door.

As soon as they passed him, Nelson shouted, "Okay, Jeff. Move it!"

As Bonior made one last sweep of the corridor with bullets and then turned and scampered for the exit, Nelson reached into his pocket for two grenades. He pulled the pin and threw the first grenade underhand, so that it skittered down the corridor. As it went off, he sent the other grenade bouncing after the first, then turned and, running in a crouch, dashed for the door.

Nelson fired from the hip as he crossed the courtyard, but

he suddenly became aware that no one seemed to be shooting at him. Bernard and what was left of his force had turned their entire attention to the murderous assault from their rear.

As the first members of Eagle Force reached the opposite doorway, they instinctively positioned themselves to add their firepower to that of Marker's small unit. As soon as they were in position, Marker signaled to Mrs. Walker and Cindy Carson to move back into the interior of the building and join David. He continued to fire.

As the second two men made it across the courtyard, Marker moved back.

As he gathered his little group around him, Mark Rattner, the pilot, joined them.

"You guys sure moved in at the right time, Rex. We were in deep kimchi over there."

"Yes, sir. The U.S. Cavalry to the rescue. Let's get moving, sir. I think we can go right through this building to the helipad."

"You're in command, Petty Officer Marker. Lead on." Rattner recognized that, in a situation like this, a SEAL petty officer was better equipped to lead them to safety than an air force lieutenant colonel.

Behind them, the sounds of gunfire subsided and then increased in volume once more. Marker read the sounds: Eagle Force had made it across the courtyard, but now the enemy's reinforcements had arrived on the scene and were making an assault across the open space.

With Marker leading the way, Rattner and the former hostages dashed as quickly as they could down the dark corridor. As they went, Marker noted that Nash no longer lay where he had left him a short time before.

A momentary thought crossed his mind: I should have killed the son of a bitch. But he did not dwell on a decision he couldn't change. There was too much more to worry about.

"There she is, sir." Marker was first out the door and leading the way toward the helicopter. "You get her started, sir. Mrs. Walker and David, you get into the helicopter and lie flat on the floor. Cindy, you take cover here. Watch those windows and the roofline. If you see any movement, shoot."

Satisfied that he had done all he could until the rest of the force arrived, Marker set up the satellite communications he had managed to carry with him and sent off a message appealing for help. He had no idea whether anyone was close enough to do them any good, but he figured it wouldn't hurt to try.

"Let's fix up a little welcome for these guys, Jeff." Nelson knew their respite would last only a few minutes, until Bernard pulled together the remnants of his force and resumed the attack.

Bonior called two men; both carried two-and-a-half-pound canvas "socks" of C-4 plastic explosive.

Bonior moved his men down the corridor and set to work rigging their explosives. They shaped the plastic around two grenades and fastened them to the walls on each side of the corridor next to supporting columns. Then they attached a long cord to the ring on each grenade and ran the cords down the corridor. Moving on back away from the door, on the other side of a hallway at right angles to the one in which they were working, they repeated the grenade-explosive setup.

Stepping back to look over their handiwork, Bonior thought: I sure hope this works. Darn it, I wish Jerry Merrifield hadn't been so stupid. This is where we need a really good explosives man.

Bernard's men gathered around him in the darkness of the courtyard. They were afraid to use flashlights for fear of marking themselves as targets. They could hear Bernard's anger and frustration expressed in a torrent of profanity.

Angry as he was at the losses he had suffered from Marker's strike from behind, Bernard still thought with the perfect clarity of a professional warrior. He would have given a million dollars if he had had the foresight to equip his men with night vision goggles, but that couldn't be helped now. They'd just have to do the best they could in the dark.

"Okay, listen up. They've got the advantage in that corridor now. We're going to have to go through there, but we're going to try to go around them, too. You guys"—he pointed to one squad leader—"I want you to go in through these windows and try to work your way up to the roof. Get on the other side of the building so you can shoot down at the helo. Get moving."

He turned to another squad leader. "Give them five minutes. Then we're going in through the doorway. Use lots of firepower. Make them shoot. They may already be low on ammo. But watch for traps like the ones you guys ran into back there."

Bernard checked his watch. Five minutes had elapsed.

One squad of half a dozen men remained with Bernard as a reserve in the courtyard as the other squad began its assault.

Two men dashed for the door as their comrades raked it with fire. As soon as they reached the door, two more moved forward. The first two crept through the door on their bellies, trying to see into the darkness. To their surprise, they were not fired upon.

The leader of the squad spoke into his microphone. "Sir, we're not receiving any fire. We don't see anyone."

"Move forward cautiously. Look out for booby traps."

Crouching against the wall of a cross-corridor, Nelson listened in on the exchange on the radio he had taken from the dead enemy.

That's fine, Big Dog, he thought. Just keep on coming.

Bernard's anger and frustration were turning to worry. He didn't like this being in the dark, trying to figure out where the other side was and what they were doing. He was especially concerned about the ominous silence. Why weren't they shooting?

He remained in the courtyard, listening. But he heard nothing—nothing on the radio, no gunfire. Finally, the urge to be in motion overcame his caution.

"Let's go." His reserve squad gathered around him and moved cautiously through the doorway into the black interior of the building.

Nelson leaned around the corner and peered down the corridor, watching Bernard's first squad move slowly toward him.

"Ready, Jeff? On my signal. . . . Pull!"

The leader of the squad heard the simultaneous clicks as the pins were pulled from the two grenades and the arming levers popped up. He stopped, feeling the same sudden dread experienced by a man who hears a snake's rattle but doesn't know where the strike will come from.

"Drop!" he shouted. "Grenade!"

His men dropped to the floor before the explosion came, but the blast, augmented by the plastic explosive, caused far more damage than the grenades would have caused alone. The walls on both sides of the squad buckled, and the ceiling caved, crushing them.

On the second floor, two of the men who had gone in the windows were above the point where the explosion occurred. Both fell into the hole, seriously injured.

Bernard coughed deeply, choking on the mixture of smoke and plaster dust. As he cleared his throat, he began to swear.

"Son of a bitch. I knew they'd do something like that. Son of a bitch."

He clicked the button on his radio. "Squad one. What is your situation?"

The man on the second floor began to speak and then was overcome with a fit of coughing. He finally managed to talk. "I've got two men down the hole, sir. We're trying to work around it, but I haven't figured out how to do it yet."

Nelson listened to the transmission.

Oh, oh, he thought, he's got somebody up above us.

"Jeff. Big Dog has some of his guys trying to work their way through the building above us."

"Want me to go after them, boss?"

"No, I don't want us divided up. It's going to be hard enough getting us out of here as it is. Instead, leave me a couple of guys. You take the rest and set up a perimeter around the helicopter. Watch the windows and the roofline. Don't let anyone get in position to shoot down on the bird."

"Will do. Here's the cords to the other two grenades." Bonior passed over the ends of the two cords.

Bernard pulled out his flashlight and shone it down the corridor, assuming he was safe behind the debris left by the explosion. What he saw made his heart sink. A huge pile of rubble blocked the corridor.

Moving toward the barrier, he swung his flashlight back and forth, looking for a possible opening, or at least a place where they might claw their way through.

"Up there . . . on the right side . . ." he commanded. "Start digging."

"We don't have any shovels."

"Use your hands, goddammit. Use your helmets. Don't screw around. We've got to get through there."

Bernard stood for a moment, watching as his men attacked the pile. Then he turned, dashed back out into the courtyard, climbed in a window, and set out to work his way across the building above the area of destruction.

Nelson waited until four men had emerged from the pile of rubble and begun to come cautiously down the corridor toward him. Then he moved back around the corner, pulled on the two cords, and covered his ears. Three seconds later, the building shook with another tremendous explosion.

The sound was still echoing through the corridor when Nelson signaled to the two men who had remained with him and dashed down the corridor toward the doorway to the helipad.

As they emerged, they saw the blades circling and the machine straining to become airborne. Members of the force lay in a semicircle, forming a perimeter around the helo and scanning the upper floors of the building.

Nelson sent the two men with him on to the helicopter and then took up a position in the center of the perimeter. With hand motions, he withdrew the men, two at a time, and sent them to board the machine.

Holding his left hand tightly over the wound in his right chest, Luke Nash worked his way along behind the roof's parapet. His breath came in short, rasping gasps. He felt dizzy and nauseous, but the anger that boiled inside of him would not let him give up or even stop to rest.

Moving up close to the roof's edge, he carefully pushed his AK-47 up onto the parapet and then raised himself high enough to see the helicopter down below.

He blinked and drew the back of his hand across his eyes, trying to make them focus on the tail rotor of the helicopter, its spinning blades faintly visible in the dim light. Placing the rifle on full automatic and holding it as firmly as he could with his right hand, he pressed the trigger.

The first bullet passed just above the rotor, and then the muzzle of the rifle swung up and to the right, almost pulling the weapon out of Nash's grasp.

Every man on the perimeter aimed for the point on the parapet where they had seen the muzzle flash of Nash's weapon. Bullets struck the wall at the edge of the roof, creating a shower of sparks.

Holding his weapon close to his chest, Nelson rolled across the helipad until he was next to Bonior.

"Looks like one guy up there," he shouted.

"Yeah, so far. I think we really slowed them down with that C-4."

"There!" Bonior shouted. He fired a short burst.

"Did you get him?"

"I don't know. At least I can't see the weapon anymore."

"Let's get out of here." Nelson signaled to the two other members of Eagle Force remaining on the perimeter, waving them back to the helicopter.

"You next, boss. I'll keep their heads down."

Nelson patted his longtime swim buddy on the shoulder and then ran for the helicopter door. At the door, he and Rex Marker stood scanning the roof. They could see shapes along the parapet as men moved into firing position.

"Move it, Jeff!" Nelson shouted. The sound of his voice was swallowed by the roar of the engine, but Bonior seemed to hear him anyway. He rose, turned, and then dropped to the tarmac.

"Oh, shit. Jeff is hit." Nelson scanned the roofline. He saw three men—then four—outlined against the dark sky.

"I'll get him," Marker said.

"No. We've got to get the hostages out of here. Stay in the helo."

"We can't leave Jeff. SEALs have never left a man behind."

"Get in the chopper. That's an order."

Nelson fired a long burst along the roofline, then turned and dove onto the floor of the helicopter. Scrambling to his feet, he worked his way to the cockpit, leaned over Rattner's shoulder, and shouted, "Take off!"

As the machine rose, Marker stepped down onto the skid and was about to jump to the ground when another SEAL grabbed his webbing and held tight.

"We can't just leave Jeff!"

Standing in the cockpit, Nelson leaned down and shouted in the pilot's ear. The machine came to a hover slightly higher than the rooftop and then moved sideways toward the roof.

The men in the rear compartment, suddenly realizing what was happening, cheered as they poured a withering fire along the roofline.

Moments later, Rattner dropped the machine back onto the pad. Two men leaped out to grab Bonior and pull him aboard, and then they were airborne again, swinging out to the south, down the slope of Mount Egmont and toward the sea.

CHAPTER 33

JEFF BONIOR SAT IN THE SUNSHINE ON THE FRONT LAWN OF HIS home in Little Creek, watching his daughter playing on the swings. For several weeks the previous year, as she recovered from having been shot while she was on those same swings, she had been afraid to go near the apparatus. But, with the resilience of a child, she had quickly overcome her fear. Bonior's wife, Dorothy, emerged from the kitchen door with a tray bearing a glass of lemonade and a plate of cookies.

"How are you feeling, Jeff?"

He turned to smile at his wife. "Better every day, Dottie."

She set the tray down and touched his leg next to the scar that marked a white line on his dark skin. "Has it stopped hurting?"

"Yeah, pretty much. The thing that bothers me is the numbness around the wound. The doctor says the nerves are kind of disconnected. He says it might take a couple of years to get all the feeling back. But I can live with that. The important thing is that I can walk and run. I'm going to start going in to the team a few hours a day next week, and in a couple of weeks, I'll be up to par."

His wife gazed at him wistfully. "Yes, I knew you'd feel that way, Jeff. I was kind of hoping that you'd decide you'd had enough and call it quits. But I knew you wouldn't be happy. And the only thing worse than wondering where your

SEAL is and whether he'll come home in one piece is having an old grouch around the house.''

He took her hand and held it against his cheek, looking up at her. ''I love you, Dottie. I don't know how you put up with me, but I'm glad you do.''

Maynard and Marcia Walker walked hand in hand along a familiar path at Camp David. Towering oak trees still provided shade from the autumn sun; their leaves had turned to gold and then to brown but had not yet fallen to the ground.

''You know, Marcie, this whole episode has had at least one bright side to it. I don't think I ever realized how much I love and rely on you until I was afraid I might lose you. I know I haven't been a very good husband, but from now on, I'm going to the best husband you ever had.''

She laughed. ''Best . . . and only.''

''Yes, and only . . .''

She stopped and took both his hands in hers. ''Chip, there was a time last year when I really, seriously considered moving out on you. I was very unhappy with your behavior . . . very, very, unhappy. I was just not going to put up with your relationships with other women, no matter how fleeting and ephemeral they might be. But I think . . . I hope . . . we're over that rocky spot in our marriage now.''

He drew her toward him. ''I promise, Marcie. . . .''

''Dad! Dad!'' David ran down the path carrying two base-ball mitts and a ball. ''Let's play catch, Dad. I've got to build up my throwing arm.''

His father put an arm around the boy's shoulder. ''From what I hear, you already have a pretty good throwing arm.''

''I couldn't throw that rock as high as the window until I made a sling. I've got to work on my throwing arm.''

''Okay, David, let's get out on the lawn and get warmed up. Please excuse us, Marcie.''

Chuck Nelson couldn't ever remember feeling so relaxed.

He and Pat Collins lay submerged to their chins in a tub filled with the hot mineral water that bubbled from deep under the ground in the volcanically active Rotorua area of New Zealand.

"It's nice that it's 'New Zealand' once more," he said.

"Oh, I kind of like 'Aotearoa,'" she replied. "It has a nice sound."

"Yeah, I know. If anything good came out of this whole mess, it's that the Maori are getting the attention they deserve. As soon as the marines came in and restored the elected government, they began listening more carefully to the native people."

"Those poor people—even old Wiremu Kingi—they were all taken advantage of by Nash. That man is pure evil."

"I hope we've heard the last of him, but you never can tell. When the marines got to his compound, he and Ben Bernard were gone. From what I hear, Nash was pretty well wiped out financially when he failed to corner the nickel and cobalt market, but he could have a lot of assets no one knows anything about."

Pat stretched a foot out and rubbed her toes against Nelson's.

He wiggled his toes. "You want to play footsie?"

"Oh, I don't know. There are better things than footsie." She turned and pushed with her feet so that she glided across the tub until she lay against him. Then she grasped the side of the tub on each side of his head and leaned down to kiss him.

ORR KELLY, a veteran Washington newsman, has covered the Pentagon, the Justice Department and the nation's intelligence agencies for the *Washington Star* and *U.S. News & World Report* magazine. He has written extensively on military history, with books on the Army's M-1 Abrams main battle tank, the Navy's F/A-18 strike fighter, the Navy SEALs and Air Force Special Operations. *SEALs Eagle Force: Eagle Strike* is his second work of fiction. It follows the first book in the series for Avon, *SEALs Eagle Force: Desert Thunder.* He lives in Washington, D.C., with his wife, Mary, with whom he co-authored *Dream's End: Two Iowa Brothers in the Civil War.*

SEALS

THE WARRIOR BREED

by H. Jay Riker

The face of war is rapidly changing, calling
America's soldiers into hellish regions where
conventional warriors dare not go.
This is the world of the SEALs.

SILVER STAR
76967-0/$6.99 US/$8.99 Can

PURPLE HEART
76969-7/$6.50 US/$8.99 Can

BRONZE STAR
76970-0/$6.50 US/$8.99 Can

NAVY CROSS
78555-2/$5.99 US/$7.99 Can

MEDAL OF HONOR
78556-0/$5.99 US/$7.99 Can

MARKS OF VALOR
78557-9/$5.99 US/$7.99 Can

Buy these books at your local bookstore or use this coupon for ordering:

Mail to: Avon Books, Dept BP, Box 767, Rte 2, Dresden, TN 38225   G
Please send me the book(s) I have checked above.
❏ My check or money order—no cash or CODs please—for $_____is enclosed (please
add $1.50 per order to cover postage and handling—Canadian residents add 7% GST). U.S.
residents make checks payable to Avon Books; Canada residents make checks payable to
Hearst Book Group of Canada.
❏ Charge my VISA/MC Acct#_____Exp Date_____
Minimum credit card order is two books or $7.50 (please add postage and handling
charge of $1.50 per order—Canadian residents add 7% GST). For faster service, call
1-800-762-0779. Prices and numbers are subject to change without notice. Please allow six to
eight weeks for delivery.
Name_____
Address_____
City_____State/Zip_____
Telephone No._____

SEA 0699

SEALS
THE
WARRIOR BREED

Do you have what it takes to be a
NAVY SEAL?

Test your knowledge and your readiness at
www.avonbooks.com/seals

- Learn more about the history and the traditions of the elite force.

- Sign up for e-mail notification of the next Avon SEALS book.

- Browse through our list of SEALS books.

NAV 0499